YVES BO

C000041414

The

Nuremberg Enigma

A novel

Lark & Frogmouth Books

Published in 2016 by Lark and Frogmouth Books
© Yves Bonavero 2016

First Edition

The author has asserted their moral right under the
Copyright, Designs and Patents Act, 1988, to be identified
as the author of this work.

All Rights reserved. No part of this publication may be reproduced,
copied, stored in a retrieval system, or transmitted, in any form or by any
means, without the prior written consent of the copyright holder, nor be
otherwise circulated in any form of binding or cover other than that in
which it is published and without a similar condition being imposed on
the subsequent purchaser.

A CIP catalogue record for this title is available from the British Library.

By the same author
Something in the Sea (Bloomsbury, 2006)

"I was gripped and enthralled..."
William Boyd, winner, Whitbread Award and the Somerset Maugham Prize, nominated for 2002 Booker Prize

"... an astounding tale... an astonishing and gripping story..."
Guardian

"The plot is tight and exciting, and the writing has great authority... it gives a sort of 'Conrad' feel... admirable stuff... I was so gripped by the story that there was no way I was going to stop... the framing device of the story is absolutely wonderful... simultaneously original and traditional... I enjoyed reading it enormously."
Sara Maitland, winner, Somerset Maugham Award, Scottish Writer of the Year

"...grips the reader's attention... difficult to put down... the ending is as surprising as it is shocking."
Yorkshire Gazette & Herald

"Something of an ancient mariner saga... curiously hypnotic."
Literary Review

"A chilling psychological thriller by a debut writer of whom we will certainly hear more."
Daily Mail

"...it kept me turning the pages through two solid chunks of reading... The description of the storm, for example... is terrific... I like the premise too. I like the use of the Little Mermaid fairytale

and I think that the device of the story within a story is very effective... I enjoyed it a lot."
Patrick Neate, Whitbread Novel Award winner

"...will keep you mesmerised until you have to separate the smokescreen from the final punchline."
Time Out

"...remarkable... a genuinely compelling, almost hypnotic story. The spiritual stuff is great, magical and tender... The opening storm, the nautical veracity and the details are terrific. Gripping. Kurt's story is intoxicating, mesmeric. And it makes me want to shout '*Carpe Diem*'. It made me very glad of my own family. It made me sad. It's a great read... I'm full of admiration."
*Richard Holmes, film producer and scriptwriter (*Shooting Fish, Waking Ned Devine*)*

"...before I knew it, it was 2:30 in the morning and all hopes of a romantic evening with my wife had long since evaporated... far more subtle than a straight thriller... the storytelling is strong enough to keep you enthralled... with its copious thought-provoking sub-plots. Just don't start it if you need a good night's sleep."
Motor Boat & Yachting

"...a tremendous plot. The menacing atmosphere of a storm at sea and a strange port at night is good, and the action... is gripping... a brilliant plot, interesting characters..."
David Reynolds, short-listed for the J.R. Ackerley Award, 2002

"...a damn good read... ends with a brilliantly written stream of consciousness, leaving you itching to know more."
Oxford Times

"Bonavero's debut is impressive: a tight plot, characters one cares about, an eye for detail and the nuances of the jet-set life acutely observed. This is much better than a beach read. But for peace of mind, don't take it on the water."
The First Post

"The book is an excellent, if properly unsettling read... The tale's twist leaves one shocked... it would make a wonderful tension-building movie, of a noir genre rarely achieved today... The success of the writer is that we feel sympathy for the characters... the good and bad, the strong and weak, but above all the innocent."
The Yacht Report

"As a piece of storytelling this is close to perfection. As a first novel it is a triumph... By sunrise, each person is changed forever. That the entire novel takes place over just a few hours is no bone for contention in this absorbing tale, such is the engrossing quality of content. The ending is disturbing, compelling and breathtaking. Unforgettable."
The Book Pl@ce

"A remarkably taut and chilling thriller that kept me reading well past my bedtime... Bonavero's tight and claustrophobic plot had me riveted to my chair... I came away from this novel feeling energised and entertained... A minor masterpiece."
Therapsheet

"Boats have provided some of the best comedy in literature, as well as some of the most engaging thrillers, from Erskine Childers' *The Riddle of the Sands* to last year's disturbing mystery thriller *Something in the Sea* by Yves Bonavero."
Financial Times

For Anne

Chapters

'What's a story? A discovery or a lie?'
Malcolm Bradbury, "To the Hermitage",
first published 2000 by Picador

'There is no solid evidence of Hitler's death.'
Marshal Zhukov to General Eisenhower,
Frankfurt on the Main, 9 June 1945

'Hitler is alive.'
Stalin to President Truman, Secretary of State
James Byrne and Admiral Leahy,
during the Postdam Conference, Berlin, July 1945

'No one has to date recovered or reproduced
a single one of [Hitler's] dental X-ray films.'
"The Odontological identification of Adolf Hitler",
Reidar F. Sognnaes & Ferdinand Strom
Acta Odont. Scand. 31, 43-69, 1973

Prologue in Hell

WHAT ARE BIRTHDAYS, if not woeful harbingers of our death? Yet, today, Adolf Hitler is supposed to be celebrating. As though orchestrated by Goebbels' Ministry of Propaganda, the weather has changed overnight. After weeks of cold and wet misery, it is going to be a fine spring day. By mid-morning, the sun is already pleasantly warm.

The Führer is not in the mood. The whole thing is an unwelcome embarrassment. Yet, frustratingly, it seems unstoppable. Reichsleiter Martin Bormann, on the other hand, is looking forward to the day. Hitler's fifty-sixth birthday. Friday 20th April 1945.

As THEY WATCH him shuffling, stooped and unstable, the whole of his left side trembling, many of his courtiers feel Hitler is disintegrating fast.

Though the Führer's birthday has been a national holiday since 1933, neither the Red Army, relentlessly pounding Berlin's suburbs with heavy artillery, nor the starving Berliners huddled in the shelters and cellars of their crumbling tenement blocks, seem intent on putting the flags out. In fact, only those who manage to get the latest copy of the rag which passes for a newspaper are reminded of Hitler's birthday as they read the speech Goebbels has made for the occasion, replete with mentions of 'golden fields of grain' and 'peoples at peace'. For the first time, most of them discreetly snigger; a minority rail against defeatist traitors and vehemently assure their neighbours that there is nothing to worry about, since their Führer knows exactly what he's doing. None of them knows that, since the afternoon of 16th January, as palls of acrid smoke hung low over the eviscerated city – the aftermath of the thousand-bomber raid performed by the US Eighth Air Force that morning – Hitler has joined their troglodytic lifestyle.

His new quarters are significantly better than any shelter available to his compatriots; predictably, the *Führerbunker* is the safest in Berlin. The complex is some eighteen metres below ground level, its exterior walls built of concrete two metres thick, the roof protected by a concrete layer three metres deep. Luxurious it is not: low ceilings, rooms the size of monastic cells, bare bulbs providing only bleak lighting. Where Speer's slave labourers had time to finish plastering, the walls are painted either battleship grey or rusty brown; where they haven't, the rough structure drips a toxic moisture.

THE FÜHRER SIGHS. What with his Thousand-Year Reich noisily crumbling on top of him and his capital under constant bombardment, there is damn little to celebrate. His panic attacks, insomnia and manic-depressive episodes, amplified by the twenty-eight pills a day and the injections of glucose, amphetamines and barbiturates prescribed by his personal physician, leave him confused and exhausted.

Tradition demands that, on the stroke of midnight, Hitler's personal staff line up to proffer their congratulations. On 19th April, however, the Führer tells his valet Linge that he wants no such celebration. Naturally, his order is ignored. At the appointed time, a queue builds up outside Hitler's rooms. Here they all are: his senior SS adjutant, SS Sturmbannführer Otto Günsche; Himmler's liaison man, SS Gruppenführer Hermann Fegelein; General Wilhelm Burgdorf; Ribbentrop's liaison man Ambassador Walter Hewel and several others. But Hitler is in such low spirits that again he orders Linge to turn away the visitors.

In June 1944, in one of the show weddings that Hitler and Goebbels liked to arrange, Fegelein had married Gretl Braun, sister of Hitler's mistress Eva. Fegelein now asks his sister-in-law to intercede. Eva obliges. Touched, the Führer wearily trudges down the lined-up sycophants, receiving their mumbled wishes with a vacant stare and limp handshake. Then, he must go through the same charade again as the top brass join him for the first military briefing of the day. Oh, how different it is from the heady, decisive sessions of 1940, when German Panzer divisions conquered whole countries at the stroke of the Führer's pen! Though no clear picture emerges, it is now obvious that the Russians are closing in fast from all directions. Their encirclement of Berlin will be complete within days.

It is a dejected Führer who, at the end of the meeting, invites Eva Braun into his study for a cup of herbal tea. In the week since she's arrived in the bunker, making it known that she intends to remain till the end, Hitler and his mistress have been living in separate quarters and not keeping the same time.

She pours the tea, brings him a cup and sits down on the narrow sofa next to him.

'How is it going?' she asks hesitantly.

Oblivious to her question, he stares straight ahead through dirty reading glasses. On his lap lies the already well-thumbed copy of Thomas Carlyle's 1858 biography of Frederick the Great that Goebbels gave him a few weeks ago, on National Hero Day.

'Poor darling,' Eva says, patting his shaking left hand. 'You must be so tired. I really don't know how you manage. The thing is: you worry too much. I may be only your loyal *Tschipperl* – but I know one thing: you will win. You always do. Am I right?'

'The darkest hour is nearest the dawn,' he mumbles, quoting Carlyle. As he turns to her, touching her knee, she wonders whether she sees tears in his swollen, rheumy eyes.

'My pet, could you please ask Morell to come?' he asks, as though reading her mind. 'I haven't had my eye drops yet. Nor my injection.'

As she rises to ask Linge to fetch Doktor Morell, he's again staring at the grey wall.

Theodor Morell arrives a few minutes later, carrying a black leather bag. His swarthy complexion makes him look anything but Aryan, and he specialises in venereal diseases, but Hitler's trust in him is boundless. The doctors who warned him that the allegedly harmless charcoal tablets prescribed by Morell for intestinal gas in fact contain both strychnine and atropine have done so at the peril of their lives. Theodor Morell is a protégé of Martin Bormann's.

The physician prepares several syringes and glass phials.

'What can I do, my Führer?' he asks.

'He needs his eye drops,' Eva answers. 'And he absolutely must sleep.'

Though the ten percent cocaine solution is the only one Morell hasn't prescribed personally (it is the reputable Berlin doctor, Erwin Giesing, who has initially ordered one daily administration to treat permanent sinusitis), Hitler now requests these eye drops some ten times a day. Morell is happy to oblige. Eva stands next to him, wiping the surplus liquid from the drooping black sacks under her lover's eyes with a perfumed handkerchief. Some drops escape down the deep creases than run down the sides of his large pulpy nose; inured to his terrible breath, she catches them with a kiss on both corners of his mouth. Then she rolls up the left sleeves of his pearl grey tunic and green shirt.

'Other side,' says Morell. 'He's shaking too much.'

'But he's got no veins left,' she protests.

'The other side,' he repeats.

Shaking her blonde head, she complies. From elbow to wrist, Hitler's inner arm is a mess: a mushy, purple-blue haematoma, a dozen recent needle pricks clearly visible between yellowish streaks. Blood is oozing through soaked plasters. Morell fills a syringe with morphine, laces a tourniquet on Hitler's arm, lays a towel across his lap, waits a short while and then lightly taps the damaged vessels, looking for a few millimetres of clean vein. As the needle goes in, Eva turns away. She dislikes the sight of blood.

Hitler remains impassive, his eyes closed.

'Will that be all, my Führer?' Morell asks, packing his bag. 'If you feel tired in the morning, I've just received a unique booster, made by my own laboratory. A mixture of pulverised bulls' testicles and hormones from healthy Bulgarian stock. Just let me know.' Never before has Morell disclosed the ingredients of his mysterious concoctions to his patient.

Oddly unfocussed, Hitler's pale eyes, more grey than blue, glazed and empty, the whites heavily bloodshot, are now wide open and fixed on his physician. All of a sudden, as though hit by lightning, he starts screaming.

'You traitor!' he points at Morell with trembling fingers. 'Filthy treacherous quack! I should have listened to

Doktor Brandt. Look what you've made of me! Treason! This is treason! But it's not too late – oh, no. I'll pulverise your testicles – if you have any. No – I'll have you hung from a meat hook – like the others!'

He's shaking all over, moustache a-twitter, yellowish foam dribbling down his chin.

'Thank you, Doktor Morell,' Eva ushers the fat man towards the door. Taking a couple of steps back towards Hitler, who's still panting, she has to step round a puddle where Morell had been standing.

It is already nine o'clock on the morning of 20th April when Adolf Hitler finally goes to bed, only to be woken an hour later and told by General Burgdorf of the Soviet breakthrough near Cottbus. Before going back to bed, Hitler, trembling in his nightshirt, orders Linge to wake him up an hour later than usual, at 2 p.m.

Cocooned in his lair, the Reich Chancellor as usual slumbers through the morning. Meanwhile, American and British bomber forces, too, are keen to mark the occasion appropriately. Squadron after squadron of USAAF Flying Fortresses and Liberators, fifteen hundred four-engined bombers in total, relentlessly drop their birthday presents of explosives and incendiary bombs on and around the *Führerbunker*.

Linge wakes his master at the appointed time and immediately administers a dose of cocaine drops. After breakfasting and playing with his Alsatian puppies – Blondi has littered in March – Hitler totters up the four flights of steps into the Reich Chancellery garden.

Holding his right hand behind his back with the left one, he walks slowly past the delegations of the Courland Army, the SS Berlin division and two dozen boys from the Hitler Youth who've distinguished themselves in fighting the advancing Soviet tanks. Nearly choking with pride, those he pats on the cheek, all war orphans from Breslau or Dresden, feel chosen for a higher destiny by a new and all-powerful father.

'Children. His life now depends on a few children!' Traudl Junge blurts out to Eva, who's standing in the afternoon sun with Hitler's personal secretaries, watching from a distance.

'The whole German nation is defending him – down to the last child,' Eva takes Traudl's hand. 'What else could he want?'

But Traudl, trying to conceal her tears, looks away. She's Hitler's youngest secretary. Her husband, a sergeant in Hitler's honour bodyguard, the *Führerbegleitkommando* or FBK, has died on the Russian front in 1944.

'Come on, girls!' Eva calls. 'Spring's here. Can't you smell it?'

It is true: despite the smoke and the terrible smell of war, now and then, when the wind drops, the incongruous aroma of lilac wafts into the destroyed Chancellery garden. Between the shell and bomb craters, small clumps of daffodils defiantly exhibit their vibrant yellows among blue and mauve crocuses that seem made of delicately coloured Meissen porcelain. Although the Bunker's inhabitants have hardly been aware of it, above the dust and grime and toxic fog there is still a sky, and above that sky a sun. Through the shattered glass of the greenhouse comes the distinctive perfume of jasmine and hyacinth. Eva runs to it and comes back with a dozen red and yellow tulips.

'There!' she offers them to Traudl. 'Aren't they just beautiful?'

EARLIER THAT MORNING, Hermann Göring has woken up in his estate at Karinhall, north of Berlin, to the sound of Marshal Rokossovski's artillery. Göring, whose looted treasures have already been loaded onto a convoy of Luftwaffe lorries, had his palatial mansion wired up with explosives. He pulls the plunger and, without looking back at the fuming ruins of his collapsed monument, makes his way to Berlin in order to congratulate the Führer on his birthday.

Like Göring, many Nazi dignitaries are travelling on hazardous roads or trying to fly into the capital in order to attend the Führer's birthday reception. Together with scores of lesser officials, Generals Keitel, Krebs and Jodl, as well as Grand Admiral Dönitz, Himmler, SS Gruppenführer Kaltenbrunner, the minister in charge of war production Albert Speer and Foreign Minister Ribbentrop congregate in the half-wrecked, ghostly Reich Chancellery. As the Führer slowly, almost reluctantly, walks in, they all extend their right arms: '*Heil Hitler!*' In the empty, marble-clad great hall, whose ceiling-high windows are now open to all winds and to the constant rumble of Soviet artillery, Hitler reiterates to them his conviction that the Russians are about to suffer their bloodiest defeat at the gates of Berlin. His audience desperately wants to believe him; yet, somehow, his old powers of oratory seem to have lost their magic. The battle for succession, which has been simmering for years between Göring, Goebbels and Bormann, is entering its decisive phase.

Given the imminent Soviet assault on Berlin, the immediate preoccupation of most of Hitler's paladins is how to escape before the few remaining access roads are closed. Dönitz is despatched to take supreme command in the North and continue the struggle in case the Reich should be cut in half. Göring asks Hitler for a private word, and tells him he needs to leave Berlin that very night to take command of the Luftwaffe in Bavaria. As such defeatism would be considered treasonable, he does not inform Hitler that he's already sent his wife and daughter there. Hitler absent-mindedly waves him away. Himmler, Kaltenbrunner and Ribbentrop soon depart, followed by Speer. Bormann, of course, stays. He senses his hour has come.

The concept of personal loyalty has always been key to Adolf Hitler's interaction with his entourage, as well as essential to his exercise of absolute power; accordingly, there is in his mind no worse crime than betraying the Führer's sacred person. So far, he's refused to believe that any of his companions, marshals and ministers could be cowards; it is, therefore, with surprised sadness more than anger that, with the most perfunctory of valedictions, he watches the knights of the Third Reich hastily scatter in all directions like mice before a cat. As for himself, and to the surprise of all present at the evening military briefing, Hitler announces that he will stay in Berlin until the last minute and only then fly south to lead the German resistance from the so-called Alpine Redoubt.

Later that evening, in the now-quiet bunker, Adolf and Eva invite their dwindling retinue for a drink in his study. Hitler's secretaries, his remaining adjutants, his young Austrian cook Constanze Manzialy, all vie for space and air in the small, poorly ventilated cubicle. The red and yellow tulips Traudl Junge has brought back from the garden are on display on the small table. Of the war there is no talk.

Once Adolf has retired through the rear door to his bedroom, unusually early for him, Eva drains her glass of champagne and says: 'The night is still young. Why don't we have a ball in the Chancellery? I want to dance. I need to dance!'

She looks surprised when Bormann immediately agrees, but soon recovers her composure and runs past him to the door, calling: 'Come on girls! Let's get changed!'

Stocky, bull-necked Bormann had been posted to the Reich Chancellery in 1938 as representative of Rudolf Hess, then Secretary and Deputy to the Führer. Hess's hope that his fall from grace was to be reversed through Bormann's good offices was misplaced. No sooner had

Bormann arrived at Hitler's court than he commenced undermining Hess's residual influence in the more compelling cause of his own vast ambition.

Because of Hitler's lackadaisical and largely nocturnal work habits, his office, until Bormann's arrival, had been a shambles. In particular, anybody could go to Hitler and, if they caught him in a good mood, obtain whatever decree, favour or promotion they fancied. Bormann soon put paid to this amiable chaos. He placed his desk in the ante-room to the Führer's office, thus taking control of all non-military traffic, correspondence and access to Hitler. Except for half a dozen ministers and the military top brass, nobody had direct access to the Führer any more. In one fell swoop, Martin Bormann had become one of the Third Reich's most powerful bosses, controlling not only the Party's finances, but Hitler's personal purse as well. Eva particularly resented having to ask Bormann for money whenever she wanted new French dresses, shoes or perfume.

In his efforts to ingratiate himself with Hitler, Reichsleiter Martin Bormann pretended to be a non-drinker, a non-smoker and a vegetarian. But when Eva, who feared him less than the other residents of the Bunker, had dared tell Hitler that Bormann in fact kept a stock of salami in his room and behaved like a predatory, over-sexed toad, she'd got nowhere. 'I know he's a brute,' her lover had replied. 'But he's loyal.'

However, in the confined environment of the *Führerbunker*, Bormann finds it difficult to maintain his grip on Hitler's communications. Much to his chagrin, six officials in addition to himself can still get through directly to Hitler. In order of official precedence, they are Göring, Goebbels, Himmler, Speer, Dönitz and Keitel. This has to change.

As all return to their quarters to freshen up, Bormann makes his move. He walks swiftly down the corridor to the room shared by the guards on duty and the switchboard. Designed by Siemens to suit wartime divisional headquarters, this switchboard isn't big; it has a plug-in panel with room for only one operator. Sergeant Rochus Misch isn't a professional, but he's learnt to use similar equipment at Berchtesgaden. As he becomes aware of Bormann's silent hulk behind his back, he turns around, looks up and takes off his headphones. Bormann waves the FBK guards out of the room. Misch's standing orders are always to put calls from the half-dozen top-ranking officials straight through to the Führer; he's therefore confused when Bormann, in a low voice, insists that all calls henceforth be routed through him.

'All calls, Herr Reichsleiter?' he repeats.

'You heard.' Bormann is already halfway to the door.

'But... what about Doktor Goebbels, Herr Reichsleiter?'

'What about him?'

'What am I to tell him?'

'Tell him the procedure has changed.'

Sergeant Misch has been officiating at the centre of Hitler's reduced communications network for a long time, and he isn't stupid. He knows that Bormann is out to slit Goebbels's throat by cutting his line to the Führer, and has no desire to end up sacrificed in the inevitable cross fire.

'And if Doktor Goebbels asks on whose authority...?'

Bormann turns around and towers above Misch.

'Are you trying to be smart, fuck-face?' he hisses. 'Anybody asks, you tell them it's a *Führerbefehl*. A Führer's order. Clear?'

'*Jawohl*, Herr Reichsleiter.'

'Good. Another thing, Sergeant Misch. I'll have your ass if you ever tell anybody different. Understand?'

'*Jawohl*, Herr Reichsleiter!'

SINCE IT IS one of her main activities, which she practises up to half a dozen times a day, Eva Braun is good at changing clothes. Leading a party of noisy revellers out of the Bunker's entrails through the long tunnel to the Reich Chancellery and up the stairs to the living room of Hitler's old apartments, her lithe body looks stunning in yet another sequined evening dress. More than her immaculately-curled fair hair, plucked eyebrows, perfectly-applied red lipstick or deep cleavage, more than her French perfume, it is the sparkle in her eyes and her glowing cheekbones that immediately draw the attention of the courtiers.

Like the others, she has already drunk too much champagne, and isn't about to stop; yet she differs from most of her companions that evening in that her happiness is neither induced nor magnified by alcohol, but simply liberated by it. Her bliss is as genuine as it is complete: even though her lover is inexorably entombed in his cave – or perhaps because of it – she is nearer to him than ever before, and senses that her position will soon be impregnable. After all these years, for a couple of weeks already, Adolf has stopped humiliating her in public. 'The greater the man, the more insignificant should be the woman,' he'd publicly declared in front of her and some officials, back in 1934 – the stinging words still ring in her ears. Thank God both her suicide attempts have failed! Eleven years later, she's about to prove all of them wrong. As the faithful desert Adolf Hitler in droves, she will be his rock.

With wistful, dreamy smiles, all the women who still reside in the Bunker, a dozen of them in total, watch Eva as she starts whirling and twirling with abandon. Most of them cannot help liking the young, uncomplicated Bavarian girl; even those who are in love with Hitler (perhaps the majority) can't find it in their hearts to hate her. Soon they all join in as, with a stiff bow, men in SS uniforms unsullied by the dirt of battle, some from the Bunker, others from the units stationed in the Reich Chancellery barracks, yet more from Ribbentrop's nearby Foreign Ministry and Goebbels's Propaganda Ministry, all oblivious to the fact the German people have long since stopped associating the red of blood with roses, invite them to dance to the tune of the only record they could find: *Blutrote Rosen erzählen Dir vom Glück.*

In the centre of the bare room is a massive round table designed by Speer. The quantity of food and drink on it seems sufficient to feed all Berliners, on their current ration, for a whole day. Standing next to it with his protégé, Doktor Theodor Morell, Martin Bormann is trying to ascertain Hitler's current health. What with the music, the general din and hysterical laughter, the background rumble of artillery and the fact that Morell's mouth is constantly crammed with food, Bormann is making slow progress.

Now and then, much to Bormann's irritation, unstable dancers lightly brush against them and distract the physician. When Else Krüger, Bormann's tall and elegant secretary, a glass of champagne in her hand, dizzily bumps into Morell, the Reichsleiter swiftly grabs her with one hand and slips the other under her skirt. As he clutches her crotch and squeezes hard, she turns apoplectic with a mixture of pain and fear, too terrified to scream. She drops her glass. Morell starts to laugh, exhaling a peculiar mixture of pickled herring and foie gras.

'All right, sweetheart. I'll see you later,' Bormann pushes Elsa back with a final twist and turn. Doubled up, the girl stumbles backwards before running away in tears.

'I must salute you as an eminent colleague, Herr Reichsleiter,' Morell chuckles. 'Did you know I originally trained as a gynaecologist?'

'Yes,' Bormann replies matter-of-factly. 'Munich, August 1910. After you came back from Grenoble and Paris. It has even occurred to me that, given the Führer's lamentable condition after eight years of your ministrations, perhaps you should go back to obstetrics.'

The grin vanishes from Morell's rubicund face. He wipes his mouth.

'I am doing my best. My very best... day and night. But – evidently – the problem is the constant stress... It's too much for any man.'

'Are you suggesting that the Führer is an ordinary man, Herr Doktor Morell?'

'Herr Reichsleiter! Nothing of the kind, you know it. How could anybody who's had the privilege of meeting our Führer, even for one minute, fail to see that he is no ordinary man? But he's carrying Germany on his shoulders. Surely that's enough to wear down any giant. That's where the insignificant Doktor Theodor Morell comes in – to keep his superhuman strength up.'

With jerky little stabs of his folded napkin, Morell wipes the perspiration from his neck and forehead. He jumps when Bormann put his hand on his shoulder and comes closer.

'A lot depends on you, my dear insignificant Theodor. Do not disappoint me. Do not betray our Führer. You know what happens to those who betray the Führer, don't you?' Morell manages only a slight nod. 'Good. Remember: he has to be fighting fit, and ready to travel at any time,' Bormann continues, his mouth now against Morell's ear. 'No more messing about. And... easy with the morphine, Theodor. Just play it safe. Just...'

Bormann's hand is still resting on Morell's shoulder

when a huge explosion deafens them. The gramophone falls to the ground as fragments of glass, bottles and food are hurled at the walls, injuring several guests. Among the shrieks, those who have been standing near the huge windows, perhaps a dozen couples, are trying to get back on their feet. The air is thick with dust.

'Hermann! For God's sake – what on earth was that?' Eva breathlessly asks Fegelein, with whom she's just been dancing.

'Quick. Cover your mouth,' he pants through his handkerchief. 'Far too early for English bombers – not yet midnight – and we haven't heard any sirens. Perhaps the fucking Ivans are so close they can shell the bloody Chancellery. Anyway – back to the Bunker. Better not to say anything to Adolf.'

Just as he finishes speaking, the huge crystal chandelier that has survived years of saturation bombing and, though unlit, provides the only remaining note of luxury in the stark, stripped-out venue, crashes onto the table. Stunned by the ear-splitting racket, for a couple of seconds most of the drunken revellers assume that another bomb or shell has struck the building. The flickering glow of the many fires raging outside is now blanked out by yet more thick dust, rendering the room almost completely dark. Invisible bits of ceiling continue to rain down at random, prompting screams of terror.

As Eva leads a procession of whitish ghosts back to their cave, only the couples busy making love at the time of the blast stay behind, pretending, or perhaps hoping, to be dead. In the staircases, corridors and recesses, surprised by the premature end of the main party, dozens of intertwined shadows are hastily disentangling themselves and fumbling with their uniforms.

Others, too drunk or simply past caring, drape their greatcoats, a rug or a remnant of curtain around themselves and wait under cover of darkness for the commotion to subside. Already, some are snoring. Halfway along the ground floor corridor, Bormann suddenly stops Morell in front of a window sill on which a woman is sitting astride a man in the uniform of a SS Sturmbannführer. Silhouetted against the orange backlight, magnificently oblivious to the stampede, they're kissing, an empty bottle of Camus cognac at their feet. Thanks to his ever-alert predatory instinct, Bormann somehow recognises the youngest of the four *Blitzmädel*, or German Army Signal Corps women, who work in the Bunker; a fair, graceful and demure girl from Bremen, hardly twenty, who'd soon caught his eye.

'What do you say, esteemed colleague?' Bormann shakes his head. 'Hardly surprising our best fighting units are decimated by syphilis, is it?'

Morell is struggling to hold his ground against the tide of people scurrying towards the various tunnels leading to the upper Bunker of the Old Reich Chancellery and nearby Ministries. He eventually manages to get closer to the window and bends down to get a better view.

'You're right, Herr Reichsleiter,' he confirms. 'Saboteurs everywhere.'

Bormann grabs the girl's hair and yanks it. With a shrill yelp, she falls over backwards onto the hard marble floor and, too shocked even to think about covering herself, turns around in a blind panic. She tries to focus. Bormann bows deeply and releases a handful of blonde hair on top of her.

'*Es tut mir wirklich leid, Gnädige Frau.* I am so terribly sorry to interrupt', he says in his most formal accent. 'But work has to come first. Please be so kind as to report to my office in fifteen minutes.'

ADOLF HITLER AWAKES to the news that the centre of Berlin is under artillery fire. He wants to believe that long-range batteries near the river Oder are responsible; much to his dismay, confirmation soon reaches him that the shelling originates from Russian guns located in Marzahn, a suburb barely eight miles away. In a frenzy of contradictory orders, he orders the Panzer Corps of SS Obergruppenführer Steiner to launch a counter-attack. When warned by Karl Koller, Luftwaffe chief of staff, of the inadequacies of the untrained, lightly-armed naval and Air Force troops supposed to support Steiner's offensive, Hitler resorts to his latest mantra: 'You will see, Koller. We're going to lick them! The Russians are just about to suffer the bloodiest defeat in their history before the gates of Berlin.'

Soon his euphoria gives way to depression, and he calls for Morell. Mindful of Bormann's exhortations, the physician is preparing a glucose injection when Hitler suddenly flies at him again.

'What the devil is this? You son of a Jewish bitch! Do you really think I am stupid? I know what you are trying to do!'

'But... this is only gluc... gluc... glucose, my Führer,' Morell stammers. 'It will make you...'

'Shut up!' Hitler's face is contorted by rage and nervous tics. 'I know everything! I know you've been instructed to drug me with morphine, so that my disloyal generals can ship me to Berchtesgaden. Or deliver me in a cage to Stalin! Well, if you take me for a madman, you have another thing coming. I'll have you shot!'

Syringe in hand, the quivering Morell stands silent as Hitler struggles for breath and, in a broken voice, finally summons his valet. Linge, who's been discreetly standing in the doorframe, steps forward.

'Linge,' the Führer whispers, wiping his mouth with shaking hands, 'get rid of this scumbag. And wake me up in an hour.'

NEXT DAY, 22nd April, all hell breaks loose. Hitler arrives at the midday briefing looking haggard and agitated, only to be told that Steiner's attack, on which he's pinned all his hopes, has never taken place. In fact, a whole Soviet Army Group is fast closing in on Steiner's battered force of some ten thousand men, and half of his remaining fifty tanks have run out of petrol. The Russians have overcome Berlin's inner defence cordon and are now advancing toward the centre.

Adolf first turns chalk white, then his face takes on a bluish hue. There will be no last throw of the dice. There are no more dice to throw. Trembling, slumped in his chair, he remains silent for several minutes, then orders everybody to leave the room, except his four most senior generals – Keitel, Jodl, Burgdorf and Krebs – and Martin Bormann. All are wondering whether the Führer is suffering a heart attack, a stroke, or finally losing his mind.

For a full hour, Hitler rants and rails against the long-standing treachery of the Army and now of the SS, the cowardice of the troops and the unworthiness of the German people. Eventually, drained and weeping, he collapses back in his chair. Then, for the first time ever, Adolf Hitler, Führer of the Thousand-Year Reich, admits that the war is lost.

Although the five men in the conference room, and all those eavesdropping against the thin plywood partition, have known it for months if not years, it comes as a devastating shock. There will, after all, be no miracle. The magician's box of tricks is as empty as it looked.

Bormann is the first to regain his composure. He urges Hitler immediately to leave Berlin and fly to Berchtesgaden to continue the fight. Without looking at him, still pale as death, Adolf grabs the table with both hands, gets to his feet and shuffles back to his small sitting-room, where Eva is waiting. Having rested a while, he calls his remaining secretaries, Traudl Junge and Gerta Christian, his cook Constanze Manzialy and Bormann's secretary, Else Krüger.

'*Es ist alles verloren, hoffnungslos verloren,*' he tells them. 'Everything is lost, hopelessly lost. You must all prepare to leave. A plane will fly you out this afternoon.'

'What about you?' Eva asks.

'For the time being, I must stay in Berlin.'

Eva walks across the small room, puts her hand on his shoulder and smiles. 'Don't you know I am never going to leave you?' she asks. 'I am staying. Wherever you go, whenever you go, I go with you.'

Adolf, sitting on his small sofa, suddenly pulls Eva's head down to him and, to the amazement of the other women, kisses her full on the lips. It's the first time his entourage has seen a sign of physical intimacy between them. Confused and embarrassed, the other girls find themselves protesting that they, too, will remain at Hitler's side.

He gets up and goes over to their weepy little group. Misty-eyed, tweaking ears and patting cheeks like a benevolent uncle, he sighs: 'Thank you, ladies. Thank you. Ah, if my generals had only been half as brave as you...' All of a sudden the pang of jealousy the women have just felt dissolves into elation. With a radiant smile, Eva hugs each one of them.

One of Hitler's valets, Corporal Schwiebel, then pours tea. Eva passes the waffles. Once more, the Führer holds forth about the loyalty of dogs and women, the treason of Prussian generals and the good old days at the Berghof.

Bormann, in the meantime, is busy organising *Operation Seraglio*, the wholesale evacuation to Berchtesgaden of the Bunker's papers and inhabitants. He summons Lieutenant General Hans Baur, Hitler's personal pilot, who's in charge of providing the necessary transport. At the outbreak of war, Baur's total resources amounted to two pilots and six transport planes. By 1944 they'd swollen to twelve pilots and forty planes. Since the first week of April 1945, he's been instructed to prepare for an evacuation with his remaining ten medium-range transport planes, some of which he has already been forced to re-position from Tempelhof to Gatow airfield.

'It's for tonight,' Bormann says as soon as Baur arrives from his quarters in the new Reich Chancellery. 'Forty people altogether. Can you do it?'

'Yes,' Baur replies. 'The sooner the better. Gatow's already under sporadic fire.'

'Can we get fighter cover?'

'Possibly. Our main fighter base at Rechlin is still operational. But its runways are damaged by so many bomb craters that taking off is very difficult by day and impossible by night. All in all, it is probably safer to forget about fighter cover and fly out under cover of darkness.'

'Two more things, General Baur,' says Bormann. 'First, the Führer will only be flying out in a few days. As you know, he'll need long-range transport.'

'I still have three long-distance transport planes in Rechlin, Herr Reichsleiter. Junker 390s.'

'Good. Protect them well. Where can they fly?'

'Anywhere the Führer wants to go. That's my job. They all have charts and flight plans for Scandinavia, Greenland, Africa, Madagascar. Even Manchukuo.'

'Fuel?'

'More than enough.'

'Good. Another thing, General. Several tons of top secret personal papers and files are on their way to the airfield. I want you to separate the freight from the passengers. No mixed cargo. Do you understand?'

'No problem.'

Bormann points to three boxes of documents piled on his desk. Even from a distance, Baur can read the label on the top one: 'TOP SECRET – A.H. DENTAL RECORDS, 1923- .'

'I want you to ensure that these boxes are loaded into the baggage plane,' Bormann says. Baur nods.

'One detail: unlike the others, this freight plane must never arrive in Munich.'

Baur gapes at Bormann.

'Where should it fly to, Herr Reichsleiter?'

'Up to you, General. Preferably into heavy flak. Alternatively into a mountain.'

'What... what the hell... Are you insane?' Baur explodes. 'Are you suggesting I should destroy one of the few planes we have left, together with one of the Führer's personal pilots?'

'*Führerbefehl*, General. I am sure that you understand that in exceptional times exceptional measures are needed.'

'But – why don't you just get rid of the stuff here?' Baur asks, involuntarily clicking his heels.

'You'll see. Just too much of it. Tons. And we left it too late. Paper in such volume does not burn. All it would take is a shell to explode nearby and it would be scattered to the winds. Besides, how do you stop people from reading, copying or stealing some of it? Too risky. It's got to disappear into thin air.'

As Hans Baur, still shaking his head, leaves Bormann's room, the Bunker's corridors are crowded with several dozen members of Hitler's entourage and their personal possessions. On his way out, Baur has to negotiate his way round Doktor Morell who, having somehow managed to append himself to the group, is obstructing the top landing, sitting on a vast trunk.

Between 9 p.m. and midnight on the evening of Sunday 22nd April, under Russian fire, nine of Baur's ten planes successfully take off for Munich and Salzburg. The tenth one, piloted by the experienced Major Friedrich Gundlfinger, seems jinxed. First, it is delayed in Berlin by engine trouble. By the time it's fixed, a critical couple of hours have been lost, which means that the aircraft will only reach its destination in broad daylight, when the skies of southern Germany will be swarming with American fighters. Second, it runs into heavy German flak over Nuremberg, presumably because Baur has neglected to announce the delayed flight plan.

When Baur wakes up the next morning, Major Gundlfinger's aircraft is already reported missing. With it, ten crates full of the original stenographic transcripts of Hitler's *Table Talks*, the repetitive rantings he's inflicted on his lunch and dinner guests during the years 1943 to 1945, have disappeared. Several other trunks full of documents personally selected by Bormann have also vanished without trace, among them Hitler's dental records.

That afternoon, Bormann summons Doktor Hugo Blaschke, Hitler's dentist since 1934, whose loyal services have been rewarded by the title of Professor and the rank of Brigadier General, Waffen-SS. Since the middle of January, he's been operating from the dental station in the Voss-strasse shelter of the Reich Chancellery. An hour later, Else Krüger nervously reports that the dentist is nowhere to be found. Rumours circulate that, having personally delivered his patients' file cards and X-ray pictures to the Bunker, as requested by Bormann, he's attached himself to *Operation Seraglio* and flown overnight to Salzburg, in the belief that his services would be needed in Berchtesgaden. The chances of getting Blaschke back to Berlin are negligible. This is a massive blow to Bormann's crucial project.

'Fraülein Krüger,' he asks, 'would you be so kind as to ask SS Standartenführer Rattenhuber to come and see me immediately?'

Johann Rattenhuber, chief of the Sicherheitsdienst, the much feared SD, lives in the upper Bunker together with a dozen of his detectives, all in SS uniform. Being responsible for Hitler's safety, back in January he'd strongly advocated that the Führer move underground to the Bunker, winning the day against Goebbels who viewed such a retreat as humiliating. Within minutes he's standing in front of Bormann.

'What concerns you, Herr Reichsleiter?'

'Blaschke has deserted.'

'The dentist? How? Where to?'

'It seems he managed to fly out with the *Seraglio* group yesterday. Without authority.'

'I see. What do you want me to do?'

'You know the penalty for desertion. Find him. Have him dealt with.'

'If he's down in Bavaria, it won't take me long, Herr Reichsleiter. I'll be on the phone to our Obersalzberg and Berchtesgaden detachments immediately. Is the Führer aware of the situation? Don't forget that Professor Blaschke is a high-ranking SS officer. He might be entitled to a court-martial.'

'Of course the Führer knows,' Bormann lies. 'As it happens, he needs his personal dentist today more than ever before. He's very upset. Keep me informed, will you?'

'*Heil Hitler!*' Rattenhuber barks before turning round.

After the departure of so many, the Bunker is peculiarly quiet that Monday afternoon. All know that the final countdown has begun. The old Prussian discipline begins to fray as the remaining FBK bodyguards and SD security men raid the drinks cupboards. Many soldiers aren't saluting any more.

Hitler himself seems remarkably relaxed, possibly

thanks to the stock of pills that Morell has left behind. When Albert Speer, guilt-ridden and in need of absolution – he's disobeyed the Führer's scorched-earth policy, and failed to annihilate all of Germany's infrastructure in front of the advancing Allies – appears out of the blue, a listless Führer receives him almost absent-mindedly, apparently unimpressed that his old architect, minister and friend has risked his life to make amends.

At 8 p.m. that evening, the Bunker's superficial calm is shattered. A telegram sent by Göring from Berchtesgaden arrives. It is addressed to Hitler. The Reichsmarschall wants to know whether, in line with the 1941 succession law, he should take over from Hitler, in case Hitler were 'hindered in his freedom of action or decided to stay in Fortress Berlin'.

Given the desperate military situation, this is a legitimate and constitutional request. However, Bormann has no intention of letting Göring succeed Hitler, now or ever. Despite his sonorous but hollow title of Reichsleiter, Bormann's power stems from, and entirely depends upon, his position as Hitler's secretary. He also knows that one of Göring's first acts, were he ever to become Führer and Chancellor, would be to have him shot.

For years, Martin Bormann has been lying in wait. Now he moves in for the kill. Waving Göring's telegram, he storms into Hitler's office, accusing the Reichsmarschall of treason and of planning a *coup d'état*. He recommends that Göring be shot immediately.

Initially, the Führer seems to take no great interest

in the incident. But Bormann knows which buttons to press. A masterful invocation of betrayal of the Führer's 'Sacred Person' soon whips up Hitler's fury – yet he won't have his old comrade, one of his first followers and still a popular Nazi figure, executed. He orders that Göring instantly be stripped of all rank and office, and made to resign 'for health reasons'. Within the hour, Göring sends another telegram confirming his compliance. Although Bormann would have preferred him dead, he's nevertheless eliminated the regime's number two.

Satisfied, he returns to his office and resumes his search for a dentist. It is getting urgent. The thought crosses his mind that, having lost his practitioner, he should at least secure the patient. He orders Heinrich Müller, the Gestapo chief, to haul in Gustav Weber and detain him in the Gestapo cellar in the nearby Dreifaltigkeit chapel.

On his way to bed around 3 a.m., Bormann meets Speer, who's leaving the Bunker. Both nod without stopping, each aware of the other's loathing.

SS OBERSTURMBANNFÜHRER Doktor Ludwig Stumpfegger, an orthopaedic surgeon by training, has just been appointed to succeed the departed Doktor Morell. A good friend of Martin Bormann – indeed, judging from the amount of time they spend drinking together, perhaps Bormann's best friend – he solves the Reichsleiter's problem over breakfast the next morning, 24th April.

'So, old Blaschke's bolted, eh?' Stumpfegger muses,

pouring himself some coffee. 'Who would have thought – after all these years?'

'Traitors everywhere, Ludwig. The Führer is surrounded by traitors. His survival – final victory – both now depend on the loyalty of a handful of men.'

'You know you can count me in, Martin.'

'I know.' Bormann pauses and lowers his voice. 'Right now the Führer needs a replacement dentist.'

'Have you asked Kunz?'

'Who?'

'SS Major Helmut Kunz. Friend of mine. Definitely one of us,' Stumpfegger explains. 'He's still running a dental lab in the New Reich Chancellery. He's agreed to help Goebbels kill his children, should it come to that.'

'Has he? Ludwig, get him to come and see me immediately, would you?'

'I'll try and find him for you. What's the emergency? The Führer never mentioned any toothache to me.'

'Better safe than sorry, Ludwig.'

Stumpfegger can see that Bormann's putting on his official mask.

'Sure,' he says. 'In the same vein, would you like one of those?'

He takes out of his pocket one of the ampoules of potassium cyanide that he's started distributing to the Bunker's residents and delicately places it on Bormann's plate. All Hitler's personal staff, secretaries and adjutants have already received one. Bormann stares at the brass-ringed blue glass capsule for a couple of seconds, picks it up carefully, and gives it back to Stumpfegger with a thin smile.

'I don't think so,' he says. 'Thanks all the same.'

Stumpfegger looks up, opens his mouth as if to ask a question, then thinks better of it. With a shrug, he puts the phial back in his pocket.

THE STRANGE LIFE that for many years has been Gustav Weber's has suddenly taken a distinct turn for the worse. Indeed, he's often pondered whether the life he is living is indeed his, or somebody else's; lately, he's come to the not unreasonable conclusion that it is no life at all. Weber is a middle-aged man of average height and build, remarkable only because of his greying moustache and blue eyes, whose irises have recently grown much paler. This is thanks to the dye perfected by Doktor Joseph Mengele on inmates of the Auschwitz concentration camp, most of whom have been blinded in the process. Out of the four body doubles Goebbels recruited in 1933 to impersonate the Führer, Weber is the undoubted star; he can fool anybody. Various experiments have confirmed that, from a short distance or in less than perfect light, he can unfailingly deceive even Hitler's valets and adjutants.

Initially, all four doubles received voice and movement instruction together in Berlin, mostly studying newsreels, but occasionally also discreetly attending political meetings and rallies. Imitating Hitler's distinctive walk and mannerisms presented no particular difficulty. Mastering his voice and conversational style, however, proved difficult for some. But Weber had a good ear. Within twelve months he could recite passages from Hitler's *Table Talks* in a soft Austrian accent that satisfied his voice coach, an actress who had been specially selected by, and regularly slept with, Goebbels.

For two years, Weber led a reasonably good life: he was paid much more than in his previous job as a lorry driver, his family was looked after in Bavaria, and the work wasn't particularly demanding. Furthermore, as a fully paid-up member of the Nazi Party since 1931, he took pride in his achievements and in his contribution to the safety of the Führer.

In 1937, Weber was removed to one of the Gestapo's safe houses in Berlin, where he was detained for the following eight years – for his own safety, it was explained to him. Although he was allowed out for one hour a day, disguised as Gustav Weber and escorted always by two SD secret policemen, no telephone calls or letters were allowed. He never saw the other three *Doppelgänger*, or his family, again. He found solace in increasing quantities of Bavarian beer which his guards were only too happy to supply and share.

Worse was to come. As the ageing process diluted the resemblance between his features and those of his teetotal model, corrective action had to be taken. His nose in particular seemed to be growing larger, possibly because of his alcohol consumption, which also caused arterial spiders to appear on his cheeks and forehead. Weber underwent several operations at the biggest cosmetic surgery clinic in Berlin, owned and operated by the Zeitfeld dynasty of plastic surgeons. For years, this institution had been patronised by the Nazi establishment, who frequently relied on its expert use of advanced silicates to straighten crooked noses or build weak chins up to the official canon of Aryan male beauty. Nevertheless, Bormann, fastidious as ever with regard to administrative detail, had seen to it that the father and son who ran the clinic were liquidated at the beginning of March 1945; the building, complete with all its files and records, was burnt to the ground. Allied bombs were officially blamed for these regrettable developments.

Though Weber always received medical attention worthy of the Reich Chancellor himself, repeated operations and general anaesthetics, combined with an unhealthy lifestyle, had left him tired and confused. Moreover, before the last surgery at the end of 1944, he'd been ordered to dry out, and deprived of alcohol since. For the last few months, drenched by cold sweat and beset by acute anxiety, he had spent his time trying to steal the odd Münchener beer from his SD jailers, staring into space or crying.

When the RAF bombers arrived on their nightly round, the SD men had to carry him down to the shelter beneath the safe house; in the few hours' lull between the all-clear and the start of the USAAF daylight bombardment, they sometimes brought him back upstairs and dumped him on his bed, where he lay prostrate and shivering. On the rare occasions when he spoke, he begged his guards to let him see his family.

As it happened, Gustav Weber's mental state by April 1945 wasn't much better than that of his alter ego, Adolf Hitler, so that their uncanny similarity extended to their haggard look, bloodshot eyes, hunched posture and slow movements. Deep-seated depression had robbed both men of their vitality; both seemed to be shrinking into themselves, and subject to erratic mood swings. Altogether, the physical and psychological resemblance between Hitler and his *Doppelgänger* had grown more astonishing than ever; yet Bormann knew that henceforth it would be foolhardy to rely on an award-winning performance from Weber, who was clearly falling to pieces.

Only in one respect are Hitler and Weber clearly distinguishable: their teeth. When, early in March 1945, Bormann realised this, he immediately mentioned it to Hitler as evidence of Goebbels' incompetence at best and, at worst, his treachery. The Führer instantly grasped the significance of this glitch and ordered his secretary to iron it out. As Bormann took control of it, Weber's life was about to plumb new depths.

Throughout his life Gustav Weber has been blessed with healthy teeth, with infrequent visits to the dentist whenever a rare cavity demanded filling. Most of his teeth are still natural. For this privilege, he's about to pay dearly.

The Führer's mouth, conversely, is a warzone. Since childhood, he's been bedevilled by rotting teeth and recurrent toothache. As a result, by early 1945, only five teeth, namely the first right premolar and the four incisor teeth in his lower jaw, remain without partial or prosthetic replacement. Over many years, some of the teeth which are missing altogether have been replaced by bridges, while those which have kept their roots were capped with various crowns, some with and some without a post in the root canal.

In addition, because of the Reich Chancellor's absolute refusal to accept any removable replacements, his jaws have been equipped with the most unorthodox prostheses. On the right side of his upper jaw, a bridge extends from the three-quarter gold crown on the canine all the way to a full gold crown on the second premolar, ending in a cantilevered replacement for the first molar. On the left, a bridge extends from the canine to the third molar, both covered with full gold crowns.

Initially, Professor Blaschke was less than keen to take responsibility for the vast treatment programme demanded by Bormann for Weber. Not only did it involve destroying two dozen perfectly healthy teeth, but months, if not years, would be needed. The present state of the Führer's jaws, after all, was the result of several decades of more or less inspired efforts by many specialists. With his inimitable persuasive skills, Bormann however left the dentist in no doubt that he had no choice in the matter, and a maximum of six weeks to deliver the goods.

Given the magnitude and the urgency of the task, Blaschke was faced with several challenges. Assuming the dental labs could supply all prostheses without delay, the work could only be completed by means of almost daily sessions, leaving insufficient time for any healing. Working on so many teeth at the same time, and in particular drilling into many perfectly healthy and live teeth would produce almost intolerable pain before the nerves died. Where healthy teeth had to be pulled out, several weeks would be required for the gum and jaw to heal.

Minutes after his meeting with Bormann, shaking his head and mumbling to himself, SS Brigadier General Professor Hugo Blaschke D.D.S. started working on a plan.

FIRST, HE WOULD HAVE to take out all of Weber's redundant teeth, in order to allow maximum time for healing. On the lower jaw alone, half a dozen teeth had to go. Only five teeth would remain intact; the balance must be adapted to receive two bridges, one on each side. These pontics worried Blaschke; he did not know exactly what should lie underneath them, since the originals had been made for Hitler before 1934 by another dentist. Besides, the bridge on the lower right side was unusual insofar as it terminated in a cantilevered suspension, that is, a non-supported, freely-suspended substitute tooth, replacing the first molar on the right side. It is never good practice to use the cantilevered bridge extension unless absolutely necessary, but the Führer had always demanded them in order to avoid removable replacements.

Blaschke's main challenge, however, was the nine-unit bridge in Hitler's upper jaw. It rested on four remaining natural teeth only. Of the five replacement teeth, only one, the upper right lateral incisor, was correctly supported on both sides. At each end of the bridge were not one, but two freely-suspended teeth, replacements for, respectively, the first and second premolars on the right side, and the canine and first premolar on the left side.

Doktor Hugo Blaschke had his work cut out. That afternoon, a bedraggled Gustav Weber was delivered to his surgery in the New Reich Chancellery cellar by two uniformed SD men who, at the dentist's request, remained in the room. He explained to his patient that it was time for a thorough check-up, and that he would take there and then any corrective or preventative measures necessary.

Nodding meekly, Weber timidly mentioned that he wasn't aware of any particular problem, and certainly wasn't in any pain. Blaschke and his assistant exchanged glances; then the dentist injected liberal quantities of Novocain into Weber's gums. Though Weber would soon have grounds to be thankful for this potent local anaesthetic, the injections themselves were painful and he became agitated. Guessing that his patient was likely to grow more upset as he realised that his teeth were being extracted one after the other, Blaschke injected him with a small dose of morphine – he certainly didn't want the man to fall asleep. While waiting for the analgesics and sedatives to take effect, he started work on the initial mouldings the lab would need to manufacture the prostheses.

It did not take long for the SD men to flinch. Hardened though they were – torture was new to neither of them – they had looked after Weber for years, shared many a Münchener with him, and knew him to be a harmless, decent fellow. Moreover, they've often witnessed the awesome transmogrification of Gustav Weber into their beloved Führer, and had each time been transfixed, their dreams and nightmares changed forever by this experience. Soon, hand over mouth, both men stumbled out of the dental station.

At the end of the first, long session, though Blaschke had changed into a fresh gown halfway through, dentist, patient and assistant were all covered in blood. Weber's lower jaw was a bloody, pulpy mess. All the healthy teeth he had just lost were neatly lined up on a steel tray, complete with flesh and bone fragments still stuck to their roots. In the knowledge that Weber would be in terrible pain as soon as the Novocain wore off, Blaschke provided him with ample supplies of painkillers. His main concerns, however, were infection and nourishment.

Over the following weeks, during which Blaschke operated every couple of days on a dazed and drugged patient, Doktor Morell not only injected Weber daily with glucose and vitamins to supplement his liquid diet, but also ensured that he remained full of morphine. Soon Weber's inner arms were turning black and blue, just like Hitler's. Nevertheless, at the beginning of the fourth week, Weber had lost so much weight that Bormann became worried the *Doppelgänger* was melting away. Accordingly, Morell arranged for Weber to be force-fed through a tube.

By early April, Blaschke began to believe that, barring any complications, he might be able to meet his six weeks' deadline. His massive use of iodoform had, so far, succeeded in keeping infections at bay, and only the monstrous nine-unit bridge remained to be tackled. Then, one night, during the confusion caused by a particularly cataclysmic series of RAF bombing runs, Weber disappeared.

Of the two SD men who left the shelter to look for him, one was killed by falling masonry, and the other soon returned with severe burns. Only next morning, after Heinrich Müller had unleashed the full might of his Gestapo, was a moustacheless Weber retrieved, wearing slippers, a coat over his nightgown, from the silent procession of thousands of homeless Berliners and refugees from the East trekking westward on foot, horses, carts, bicycles, wagons or cows.

AT THE CRUCIAL TIME, the fruits of so many years of effort by Goebbels and Bormann almost eluded them. They immediately blamed each other. Goebbels pointed to Bormann's ineptitude, and asked Hitler to put him back in charge of the doubles' programme. Bormann, having eavesdropped on Goebbels' conversation, immediately counter-attacked and reassured Hitler that he had the situation under control.

The grievously burnt SD guard was hauled out of the emergency casualty station under the New Reich Chancellery and summarily shot. The task of looking after Hitler's increasingly precious *Doppelgänger* was entrusted to a new detachment of four experienced and reliable Gestapo agents.

Bormann isn't prepared to let the disappearance of Professor Blaschke destroy his masterplan. His natural paranoia exacerbated by the practitioner's defection, he decides to have Weber incarcerated in the nearby Gestapo cell until a replacement dentist can be found: better safe than sorry.

Ever suspicious, Bormann has rifled through the boxes containing Hitler's dental records as soon as he's received them from Blaschke. You never know what you might find in such files; perhaps they will mistakenly contain another patient's notes, or be glaringly incomplete, suggesting foul play. Or you might find some long-forgotten personal notes, handwritten scraps of paper, the record of a loose telephone call, unguarded remarks about the Führer exchanged between colleagues – many a seemingly upright Nazi has been exposed by such details.

In the event, no such titbits attract Bormann's practised eye. He does, however, take two items out of the boxes. The first is the nine-unit bridge manufactured for Weber's top jaw. The other is a detailed chart showing in diagrammatic form the exact dental status of Adolf

Hitler as of 16th February 1945, the date of his last routine check-up at Blaschke's dental station in the Reich Chancellery. Rather than entrust anybody with this crucial document, only one copy of which exists, Bormann tears off all references to the patient's identity, folds it in four and places it in his breast pocket, with the intention of personally burning it as soon as he has an opportunity to leave the Bunker.

As Doktor Kunz stands in front of him, Bormann gives him both items and explains the situation.

'Let me recapitulate, Major. As far as I understood from Blaschke, his work is nearly complete. Your task is two-fold. First, check the patient's dental status against this chart and confirm to me that there are no discrepancies other than this missing bridge. Second, install the bridge within the next forty-eight hours. Any questions?'

Kunz looks at the unorthodox contraption in his hand and hesitates. It is obvious that such a device can only be put into a specially prepared mouth, and he's never seen the patient.

'No questions, Herr Reichsleiter.'

'Good. One last thing. Your work must remain secret. Do not discuss any aspect of it with anybody but me. You are to return this dental chart to me personally tomorrow. Do not make, or permit to be made, any copy of it.'

'Understood, Herr Reichsleiter.'

'Excellent. Remember we live in treacherous times. No room for mistakes.'

ON WEDNESDAY April 25th, the Soviet Army captures Tempelhof airport and closes in on Berlin's inner ring, the Zitadelle. Russian artillery and planes are now pounding the Chancellery area incessantly, unnerving the *Führerbunker*'s residents. On Friday April 27th, General Kasakov's guns, located some two miles away in the Tiergarten, unleash the sort of ferocious artillery barrage that the Wehrmacht used to inflict on unfortunate cities such as Leningrad and Stalingrad. Fierce street-fighting is now raging a few blocks away, around the Potsdamer Platz and the Reichstag.

Only at night does the fighting abate. Sometimes it stops completely for a few hours. Taking advantage of such a lull, just before midnight on Friday Kunz asks for Weber to be brought to his emergency dental station for what he hopes will be the final session. Since his deadline has expired, Bormann has been relentlessly breathing down the dentist's neck. It is plain that German resistance to the Red Army onslaught can only be sustained for a few more days, if that. Yet, the patient's condition is so appalling that Kunz has encountered the greatest difficulties in finishing the job. Weber is so terrified that every time he is brought to the surgery he screams his head off and flails about, rolling wild eyes and wetting himself. He has to be strapped to the chair, restrained by two orderlies, his mouth prised open. Since they make him almost comatose, increased morphine doses have proved counterproductive. On a couple of occasions he attempts to bite the dentist's fingers, so that Kunz has to resort to reprisals. Only after he starts drilling into a live tooth without local anaesthetic does a convulsed Weber, shaking, twisting and contorting like a live eel in a frying pan, indicate his capitulation.

As Kunz makes his way to the dental station on that Friday night, he encounters obstacles of a novel kind. In the last few days, as the Russian dragnet closes inexorably in, two or three thousand Germans – fighting men, wounded soldiers, government officials and Nazi bureaucrats – have crowded into the Reich Chancellery area. Many Berlin women have been brought in by their boyfriends in the FBK or the remaining SS units; many more, terrified by harrowing tales of rape by the Red Army soldiers, have flocked to the Chancellery on their own, looking for shelter; scores of prostitutes have simply stayed there, at their usual place of work. In the apocalyptic atmosphere, the conjunction of free-flowing alcohol, distraught women in search of protectors and young men about to die is proving a potent aphrodisiac. In the two neighbouring barracks buildings in the Hermann-Göring-Strasse, as well as in the Reich Chancellery, a permanent orgy has been building up as many of the women who, red-eyed and wild with panic, have fled their Berlin apartments in terror of rape by the Russians, quickly lose their inhibitions and throw themselves into the arms of the first German soldier they can grab. Initially, those interested in group sex would seek dark corners; now they don't bother.

Walking through the emergency casualty station where

his colleague, Professor Schenck, up to his elbows in entrails, arteries and gore, has been operating non-stop for almost a week, Kunz is surprised to see SS Colonel Doktor Stumpfegger chasing a half-naked woman between and over the cots in which soldiers are lying unconscious and dying by the dozen. As the pervasive smoke, rubble dust and cordite combine with putrefying flesh and excrement, the stench is unbearable. Though a surgeon by training, Stumpfegger has been far too busy partying to lend a hand at the blood-soaked operating table where Schenk, an internist and nutrition expert, groggy with exhaustion, managed, on a mixture of coffee and tranquillisers, to carry out some four hundred operations in seven days.

The door of the dental station is ajar and, to Kunz's surprise, its feeble lights are on. From the doorway, through the ubiquitous acrid smog, he can just make out that the dentist's chair is fully reclined, and occupied by an unclothed girl. She's strapped in with the ties normally used to restrain Weber, and overcome by fits of hysterical laughter as a fully-clad, bull-necked fellow, sitting across her knees with his back to the door, is trying to insert Kunz's dental mirror into her. This accords neither with Kunz's sense of order nor with his understanding of hygiene.

'Put this back immediately!' he barks, striding across the room.

They take no notice of him.

Leaning over the man's back, Kunz wrenches the

speculum out of his hand and throws it across the room towards the sink, which he misses.

'Get the fuck out – now!' Kunz growls. As he starts un-strapping the woman, he can't help noticing she is in her late teens, unusually beautiful and in an advanced state of inebriation. She's also vaguely familiar. No sooner has her hand been freed than she catches his and, giggling wildly, tries to place it on her breast.

'Will you please behave? I've got work to do here,' Kunz says in a softer voice.

The man slowly sits up and turns around. It is Reichs-leiter Martin Bormann. Drunk.

In a flash Kunz remembers where he's seen the girl. She is, of course, the new, demure Blitzmädel from the Army Signal Corps that Bormann has been stalking since her arrival.

'What the hell are you doing here?' Bormann asks. 'Do you know who I am?'

'Yes, Herr Reichsleiter,' Kunz answers.

'And who the fuck might you be, Herr... Herr Kunz?' Bormann is now tottering on his feet.

'Your dentist, Herr Reichsleiter. You gave me work to do.'

Bormann lets out a triumphant laugh.

'Liar! My teeth have never been better. Why are you lying to me? You think I'm a fool, don't you?' He turns to the girl. 'Fräulein, be so kind as to call Heinrich Müller, would you? Tell him we have a traitor here.'

The girl has stopped giggling. She looks confused.

Covering her breasts with one hand, she's feeling the floor with the other, looking for her clothes, but her legs are still strapped to the chair. Kunz picks up her blouse and knickers and throws them at her. Then he takes the nine-unit bridge from the shelf and waves it at Bormann.

'Remember this, Herr Reichsleiter? You gave it to me. Secret project. Very important. I must finish it tonight.'

Bormann steadies himself against the X-ray machine and tries hard to focus on the prosthesis.

'You're late! I remember clearly: you've missed your deadline. Traitor! You'll be shot. That's all there is to it.' All of a sudden he straightens his back, grabs the dentist's lapel and starts bellowing at the top of his voice: 'Guards! Guards!'

Assailed by Bormann's alcoholic breath, Kunz is at his wits' end. He wonders whether to try and fetch Doktor Stumpfegger, Bormann's friend, but remembers he too is engaged in satyric pursuits. When Bormann eventually stops, gasping for breath, only the vague and spasmodic rumble of war can be heard; nothing massive, isolated rifle shots, the hiss of flares, sporadic mortar shells. Then, the shuffle of heavy boots in the corridor. A group of Gestapo men burst into the room. In their midst, supported by two of them, a dishevelled, unshaven Weber is panting noisily.

'Here's your patient, Major,' their leader salutes Kunz. 'Sorry to be late. We had to take cover on the way from the cell. Random artillery fire.'

Kunz bends over the dental chair and frees the girl's

legs. She gets up, immediately falls down and starts sobbing. The dentist gestures towards the chair. Leering at the crying creature, the Gestapo agents carry Weber to it and tie him down. Bormann looks at the proceedings with a frown of intense concentration.

'Well, Major, you've got work to do, haven't you?' he mumbles. 'Better get on with it, then.' He turns to the girl who's still sitting on the floor, arms around her knees, and brutally pulls her up. 'Come on, darling little cunt,' he purrs. In tears, clutching her knickers and blouse in one hand, she obediently takes his arm with the other and follows him, leaving the rest of her clothes scattered across the room.

THREE DAYS LATER, on Saturday 28th April, Adolf Hitler decides to marry his mistress, Eva Braun. In his capacity as Gauleiter of Berlin, Goebbels has to provide a registrar. Just before midnight, one mystified Walter Wagner, a middle-aged municipal employee fighting deep in the vaults of a wine cellar on Unter den Linden, is whisked to the Bunker in an armoured car. For the last two weeks, he's fought – a lot – and slept – very little – in his soiled brown Nazi Party uniform, and his Volksturm armband is no more than a half-burnt rag. Dirty, greyish stubble covers his shallow cheeks.

Wagner is ushered down to the lower Bunker, where the happy couple is waiting in the small conference room. For the first time in his life, he's in the presence of the mythical Führer. There is space only for the two witnesses, Martin Bormann and Joseph Goebbels, who glower at each other.

Shaking like a leaf, in a quivering, high-pitched voice, Wagner asks the Führer, as prescribed by the law, whether he's a third-generation Aryan and free from hereditary diseases. Hitler, whose hearing never recovered from the 1944 bomb explosion that nearly cost him his life, first makes him repeat, then answers in the affirmative, as does the bride. Wagner quickly mumbles his way through the short formalities of a war wedding.

Eva is wearing Adolf's favourite dress, a short-skirted black taffeta frock with two gold clasps at the shoulders, which reveals her shapely calves. Beaming a radiant smile at Wagner, she takes a step forward and starts writing her maiden name at the bottom of the certificate; then, realising her mistake, she corrects the entry to 'Eva Hitler, née Braun'. Her new husband follows. Bormann and Goebbels sign as witnesses; they both notice that Hitler's hand has been shaking so much that his signature is an illegible scribble.

With a sigh of relief, Wagner looks at this watch. As it is just past midnight, he picks up the pen and punctiliously changes the date on the certificate to Sunday, 29 April 1945. Then, with a proud smile and a deep bow, he shakes hands with the bride and groom, offering them his sincere congratulations and best wishes for a long and happy life. He's treated to two glasses of champagne and a liverwurst sandwich, chats happily with the beautiful

Frau Hitler for a quarter of an hour, and then is escorted out of the bunker, feeling utterly optimistic about the war and deeply guilty about having ever doubted the Führer. This time, no armoured car is waiting for him.

Five minutes later, on his way back to his foxhole, he's shot dead on the Wilhelmstrasse. Down in the Bunker, the wedding reception is in full swing. In Hitler's small study, Joseph and Magda Goebbels, Generals Krebs and Burgdorf, Ambassador Walter Hewel, Traudl Junge and Else Krüger are drinking champagne and reminiscing about pre-war days; another half dozen people keep wandering in and out.

'Come here, Else!' Eva calls loudly, grabbing the secretary's hand. 'I need your help, darling. Don't you agree there is nothing in the world like the colour of the autumn light in Munich – you know, that special ochre? And the lakes of Bavaria – just think of the Chiemsee, the mountains behind it, the old convent on Fraueninsel – isn't it just sublime?' With her sparkling eyes and pink cheeks, she's very much the life and soul of the party.

'Maybe,' Else smiles. 'But, if water is what you like, what about the Rhine waterfall at Schaffhausen? Surely that is unique.'

'Ladies, ladies,' Adolf Hitler interjects with a benevolent smile. 'Is this worth arguing about? Remember that from Berchtesgaden, up in the clouds, we can see neither.'

'That's true,' both women say simultaneously.

'Perhaps that was the problem?' Traudl Junge muses aloud.

'What do you mean, Fraülein Junge?' Goebbels turns to her. He's at his most dangerous when he talks in that soft tone.

'I... I don't know,' she retreats quickly. 'Perhaps we were too high above the clouds at the Berghof, too cut off...'

'Cut off from what, Fraülein Junge?'

Recognising the danger, Eva steps in. She knows that Goebbels has always resented her and how humiliated and angry he's feeling. The sort of clandestine marriage ceremony he's just been ordered to arrange at short notice has nothing in common with the kind of Hollywood nuptials that, left to his own devices, the Reich Minister of Propaganda would have staged so spectacularly, preferably with a more suitable bride; as for Walter Wagner – well, there certainly was nothing Wagnerian about him, and the miserable little clerk has just added insult to injury. Nothing could have been further from the proper Valhalla ceremonial than this rushed underground war wedding; nothing could have been more different from confident, uplifting Valhalla music than the constant drone of the diesel engine that powers the inadequate lighting and ventilation systems. But Eva is now the Führer's wife.

'Why don't you leave poor Traudl alone?' she asks sharply. 'This is my wedding, and I will not have my friends harassed.'

Goebbels bows and moves away.

'All right, Fraülein Junge,' Adolf says. 'Don't drink too much, child: we have work to do.'

As he retires to his private quarters, Traudl Junge in tow, it is nearly 2 a.m. Leaning on the table, Hitler begins dictating his last will and testament. He starts with his private will, in which he leaves all his possessions to the Nazi Party. Martin Bormann, his 'most faithful Party comrade', is named executor of the will and charged to ensure that any private mementoes of value are remitted to Hitler's mother-in-law.

Then he turns to his political testament whose main practical point, apart from blaming the Jews for the war, is to organise his succession. First, Himmler and Göring are expelled from the Party and discharged from all their functions for having dared negotiate with the enemy behind Hitler's back and for the heinous crime of disloyalty to his sacred person. Goebbels is appointed Chancellor of a Reich the size of a football pitch, and Martin Bormann leader of the National-Socialist Party. Grand Admiral Dönitz becomes head of state and of the armed forces – but not Führer.

His obsessive fear of the Jews reappears in his conclusion: 'I do not wish to fall into the hands of enemies who, for the amusement of hysterical masses, will feel the need for a show organised by Jews.'

As his speech becomes ever faster and less coherent, Traudl Junge can only keep pace because she's heard it all many times. After fierce haggling between Goebbels and Bormann, a dozen names were then added to the list of new ministers.

At 4 a.m., Bormann, Goebbels, Burgdorf and Krebs

affix their signature to the political testament, and Hitler's adjutant his to the private will. However, as Hitler retires to rest, no such respite is afforded the exhausted Traudl Junge. Pale as death, his hysterical state betrayed by streams of tears, Goebbels suddenly appears in front of her, demanding that she type his last testament too. Despite a thumping headache, she works bleary-eyed for another two hours as the new Chancellor pours forth declarations of undying loyalty to his predecessor.

'In the delirium of treachery which surrounds the Führer in these crucial days,' he pants, 'there must be a handful who stay loyal to him unto death.'

Clickety-click goes the typewriter, as Traudl's fingers take over from her brain.

However, when he dictates that his wife and six young children are 'in full and informed agreement with that policy', Traudl Junge's fingers seize up. She loves the five girls, particularly Helga, twelve, the eldest and brightest, and sweet little Regine, the youngest, not yet five, to whom she had just given her best silk scarf, as the child is suffering from tonsillitis. Like all the other childless women in the Bunker, Traudl is also very fond of ten-year old Helmut, the only boy. As tears well up in her eyes, her typing is reduced to a slow, erratic accumulation of mistakes that she makes no attempt to correct. She knows, perhaps better than Goebbels himself, why these children have been brought to the *Führerbunker* instead of being flown to safety in Bavaria. Their mother, madly in love with Hitler for years, is going to outdo the banal girl who, having just become Frau Hitler, is preparing to die with him. Magda Goebbels' sacrifice will be of an altogether different class: on the concrete altar of Hitler's tomb, in addition to her own, she will offer the corpses of her six children.

EXACTLY A WEEK before, Hitler had given command of the government area – the *Zitadelle*, in which the *Führerbunker* was located – to thirty-four-year-old Major General Wilhelm Mohnke, a tall, lean SS officer with the sort of chiselled face and front-line combat experience that Hitler prized. Both men had known each other since 1933 when Mohnke was a young lieutenant in the Führer's bodyguard, the FBK.

'General Mohnke, you're a professional soldier, one of my most trustworthy generals,' Hitler had said, shaking all over. 'As I give you command of the *Zitadelle*, my life is your hands.' He'd gestured to Mohnke to come closer and, fixing him at point-blank range with his hypnotic blue stare, had lowered his voice. 'Now listen carefully. I have a request. Under no circumstances can I risk being captured alive. Whenever you feel that the military situation is such that you cannot hold out for more than twenty-four hours, you must immediately report it to me. This is a personal request – and also an order. Do you understand?'

A man of few words, Mohnke had saluted and gone back to his command post.

On MONDAY 30th APRIL at 6 a.m., after only a few hours' sleep, Wilhelm Mohnke is woken by a call from Sergeant Rochus Misch: Hitler wants to see him.

Mohnke knows that the time has come to give the Führer the twenty-four-hour notice he's requested. Though his troops are still clinging to their positions on the Potsdamer Platz and around the Reichstag, he realises that one last assault will bring the Soviets victory. Like everybody else, Mohnke expects this final push to take place imminently, so that Marshal Zhukov may present Berlin on a plate to Stalin, well in time for the May Day parade in Moscow.

Unusually, Adolf Hitler receives Mohnke in his bedroom. Sitting in slippers on the edge of his bed, he's wearing a dark dressing gown over his blue pyjamas. The general begins with a situation report. Russian troops have encircled German positions on the Potsdamer Platz, only three hundred metres from the Bunker. They are in the area of the Adlon Hotel, four blocks away. Subway tubes under the Voss-strasse have been infiltrated.

Hitler asks no question, offers no comment, issues no order. To break the awkward silence, Mohnke resumes:

'My Führer, my troops have been decimated, they are running out of ammunition, and those left fighting are exhausted. I cannot guarantee that they can hold out for more than one day. Tomorrow is May 1st – you know what this means to the Russians. If they launch a frontal tank assault…'

'Thank you, General Mohnke,' Hitler interrupts. 'You

have fought bravely, and so have your soldiers. Now, on your way out, please stop by Bormann and give him an update, would you? And – good luck.'

Taken aback by Hitler's composure – the Führer seems curiously detached, and even appears to have got rid of all the tremors that had shaken him during their previous encounter – Mohnke salutes and turns around. He finds Bormann badly hung-over; however, the news has a remarkable effect on the Reichsleiter who sobers up almost instantly, aided by several cups made from the last real coffee beans in Germany. Their aroma goes straight to Mohnke's head; he suddenly feels weak at the knees, and possessed by an irresistible craving for a last cup. Bormann doesn't offer it. Instead, he asks to be put through to Hans Baur, Hitler's pilot. Their conversation is brief.

'Tonight,' Bormann says before hanging up.

Then he turns to his friend SS Doktor Ludwig Stumpfegger, sitting at the same table.

'Ludwig, I think you'd better get ready.'

Stumpfegger nods, drains his cup, gets up and leaves the room.

General Mohnke makes his way back to street level just as the guns of the 69th Elite Storm troops of the Russian Third Assault Army, in preparation for the infantry attack on the Reichstag, launch a titanic artillery barrage. Deafened by the continuous explosions, he notices that his own forces are wisely holding their fire, waiting for the tanks' onslaught. Corpses and stray limbs litter both pavements. The stench of death is overpowering. Wondering whether it will be his last, he lights up a cigarette and greedily fills his lungs with an acrid mixture of tobacco, sulphur and cordite smoke.

EVA HITLER hasn't turned up for lunch. Traudl Junge goes to her room. She finds Eva sitting at her dresser, sorting out her valuables and preparing the gifts she wants to leave to her friends and family. Eva jumps up, runs to Traudl and kisses her on both cheeks.

'Traudl, my darling! How are you?'

'I am well enough – thank you. What about you? You missed lunch.'

'Did I? It really doesn't matter, does it?'

Never before has Eva alluded openly to her impending suicide. Traudl, wide-eyed with embarrassment, keeps silent. Not yet twenty-five, she certainly has no intention of dying in this rat-hole.

'Look!' Eva points at the silver-fox fur coat on her bed. 'It's for you.'

'But, Eva…'

'Oh, come on. I know you've always liked it, and it'll suit you admirably. You'll need it next winter, believe me. Will you remember me when you put it on? If you do, then give my best to my native Bavaria. *Das schöne Bayern!* I miss it so much!'

As Traudl embraces the radiant Eva, their tears mix; yet only Traudl's are truly sorrowful.

Shortly after 3 p.m., Adolf and Eva Hitler come to the

main corridor of the lower Bunker, where all the members of their entourage except Hans Baur, who's otherwise engaged, and Magda Goebbels, are waiting to say their farewells. The Führer is wearing his usual grey-green tunic and black trousers, his wife a dark dress with a pink floral motif. The newly-wed couple slowly walk down the funereal line, awkwardly shaking hands and exchanging mumbled banalities with the mourners. Mercifully, this leave-taking ceremony lasts only a few minutes, after which Hitler's valet, Linge, opens the door leading to his master's private quarters. Adolf gallantly gestures to Eva to go first. Then, moving slowly but steadily, without shuffling his feet, he follows her, and closes the door behind him. As ordered, Major Otto Günsche, Hitler's twenty-seven-year old senior SS adjutant, stands guard outside the door, pistol in hand; yet he can't stop a crazed Magda Goebbels, suddenly appearing like one of the Furies, from storming into the Führer's room.

'Please, my Führer!' she begs on her knees. 'Don't leave me! Have mercy on me! Come with me to Berchtesgaden, and lead us to victory!'

Stony-faced, Eva looks away.

It takes Adolf a couple of minutes to disentangle himself from the convulsed creature at his feet; then Günsche has to drag her back to the corridor that reverberates with her shrill wailing. Eva puts her hands over her ears until the sound-, gas- and fire-proof heavy steel door is firmly shut. Silence again reigns in her tomb.

Only then does Eva notice that Angelika Raubal is staring at her from the dresser. Smiling, in all the freshness of her everlasting youth. Mocking. Eva is nonplussed. Has she not succeeded, over the years, in destroying all the pictures of her erstwhile rival? Where does this one come from, and who dared put it on her dresser now, at the hour of her death? Never mind. She's about to wipe the smile off the little slut's face, once and for all.

Eva knows only too well why Angelika – or rather Geli, as her uncle Adolf used to call her – committed suicide at the tender age of twenty-three. The girl had found out that Uncle Alf was two-timing her with the younger Eva Braun, and selfishly attempted to secure her place as Hitler's only true love for eternity. To think that the vulgar strumpet nearly succeeded! But the hour of reckoning is nigh. She's going to be put back in her place in no uncertain fashion. Only one woman has been chosen to partake in the Führer's death. His one and only wife: Eva Hitler, née Braun.

Defiantly, she turns Geli's photograph round to face the wall.

Panting, Adolf sits down at one corner of the narrow, blue and white sofa on which Eva is seated. Neither speaks. She looks at him, sighs contentedly, snugly pulls up her feet under her body and re-arranges the folds of her chiffon dress, hoping he might touch her legs. Hitler puts the small Walther 6.35 pistol, which he's been carrying for many years in a concealed holster under his tunic, on the table in front of the sofa, next to the vase in which the wilting tulips are shedding their last red and yellow petals. Then he takes two cyanide capsules out of his pocket and places them on the table. Eva puts a similar glass phial next to her own Walther 6.35 pistol and another in her mouth.

Eva's absolute nightmare is to survive Adolf's suicide, and somehow find herself looking at his corpse. She's therefore gone to Doktor Stumpfegger for advice. 'We both want to go together,' she told him. 'What method will guarantee that?' 'Simply bite into your capsule the second you hear a shot,' Stumpfegger replied. For weeks, Eva had mentally rehearsed her own suicide, trying to develop a Pavlovian reflex linking the sound of explosions to a biting reaction.

With a perfectly steady hand, Adolf Hitler picks up from the table the heavier Walther 7.65 pistol that his adjutant has loaded. Holding his wife of forty hours in his pale grey-blue gaze, he slowly lifts the gun to the right side of his head, which Eva can't see, since she's sitting on his left, and fires a bullet into the concrete ceiling.

Like a mechanical doll, Eva clenches her teeth. Only in her wildest dreams has she imagined she might be granted the privilege of a *tête-à-tête* death with her love; the smile that floats on her serene face, as it slumps forward, reflects only unalloyed, thankful happiness. A poor substitute for incense, the acrid smell of bitter almonds combines with that of cordite in a peculiar aroma.

Adolf Hitler drops his pistol on the floor in front of the sofa. Dust is falling on his hair from the impact site on the ceiling. For a while he looks silently at his wife's corpse. Then he turns around Geli Raubal's picture frame, kneels down in front of her image and wails '*Ach Gott!* Geli, Geli, my darling! How could you do this to Uncle Alf – yet again? Geli, Geli, you ungrateful, silly girl…'

A FEW MINUTES LATER, Doktor Stumpfegger and a group of four stretcher-bearers walk into the primitive operating theatre deep in the cellar of the New Reich Chancellery. The body on the stretcher is hidden by a blanket. Professor Schenck, staggering with exhaustion, is in the process of amputating the legs of a sixteen-year-old Hitler Youth who's single-handedly attacked and nearly destroyed a Russian T-34 tank with a Panzerfaust, before being crushed under its steel caterpillars. For the first time, Stumpfegger is wearing an operating gown, whose immaculate whiteness contrasts sharply with the universal bedlam, gore and blood. Since the emergency casualty station has opened, Schenck has been operating with only a basic set of surgical tools, and he's now running out of most essential supplies, morphine, plasma, iodine and even bandages. His nurses have to rip bloody rags, splints and casts from the corpses piling up in the corridors. The stench is lethal; there is neither space nor time to bury the dead or the amputated limbs: they can only be dumped on the Voss-strasse during rare nocturnal lulls in the bombardment.

'Professor Schenck, I need to borrow your operating table,' Stumpfegger announces. '*Führerbefehl.*'

Frowning, Schenck stops sawing, slowly turns around and looks up in a daze.

'Ah – Stumpfegger, it's you. At last! Where the hell have you been? Anyway – better late than never. All yours.' Knowing no explanations are needed, since (unlike himself) Stumpfegger is a qualified orthopaedic surgeon, he hands his colleague the saw, throws up his hands in the direction of the patient, steps back, sits down against the far wall and immediately falls asleep.

Stumpfegger waves at his stretcher bearers, two of whom lift the unconscious boy from the table and drop him unceremoniously on the filthy floor where, his half severed leg sticking out at a ninety-degree angle, he's left to bleed. Both nurses gape as the other two men discard the blanket covering their own patient and lift him onto the blood-smeared table. Either anaesthetised or unconscious, he's a middle-aged man in a grey-green tunic on which the Iron Cross First Class is clearly visible. As the Red Cross nurse, Sister Erda, suddenly recognises her Führer, she falls on her knees, clasps her hands and intones:

'Oh God in heaven, please save our Führer, and lead him to victory! Almighty God, please do not take our beloved Führer in our hour of need!'

Next to her, Sister Gudrune is sobbing. Stumpfegger looks at them, and two of his men escort the nurses away. He then opens his black leather pouch and meticulously selects several shiny, brand new instruments that he lays out on a stool. He puts on thin rubber gloves, adjusts each finger carefully and picks up a scalpel. Flattening the patient's right hand against the table, he starts work, first cleaning and disinfecting it, then applying a tourniquet to the wrist before methodically chopping off, one after the other, starting with the thumb, the last phalanx of each finger. He then walks around the table, nearly bumping into the still-twitching body of the Hitler Youth.

With exquisite precision, the blade always unerringly finding the joint, he severs the fingers of left hand, while behind him his assistants are painstakingly suturing the wounds. All amputated segments, complete with nails and fingerprints, are counted, recounted and collected in a paper bag.

PART ONE

'By 1933 Germans had won more Nobel prizes
than anyone else, and more than the British
and Americans put together.'
*Peter Watson, "The German Genius", first published
by Simon & Schuster UK Ltd, 2010*

1

T for Target

A QUICK LOOK at my watch as my armoured car finally jerked forward: it was 10:30 on the morning of Friday 30th March 1945, and we were already two and a half hours behind schedule. Not our fault. Both B and D companies of 1st Bucks Battalion had been ready since 07:00. At long last, amidst the roar of diesel engines, screeching clutches and clouds of noxious black smoke, our convoy started moving.

It had rained all night. The girls in flimsy, flowery dresses who'd thronged the streets of Brussels when the sun was shining earlier in the week were nowhere to be seen. Actually, that's not quite true: one of them, hiding under a shapeless dark raincoat, veiled like a Catholic nun, had made her way to St Jean barracks to see Max off. Ignoring our catcalls and jeers, he managed to steal a kiss from her.

Silly old Max. Women will be the death of him. But he won't listen.

UNLIKE ME, after several months on garrison duty in Brussels, most of our men had mixed feelings about leaving the fleshpots of the Belgian capital. Though it'd been only two weeks since I joined D Company in charge of No 15 Platoon, I couldn't wait. I hadn't volunteered for service to work as a jailor in a military prison full of drunken, murderous soldiers, or to spend my time in Belgian brothels.

I turned seventeen on 26 May 1942. On my birthday, without telling my father, I cycled from Rugby to the recruiting office in Coventry, swore an oath of allegiance to His Majesty King George VI and took the King's Shilling. I was looking for action. Doing my bit. Fighting.

But they didn't call me up until November 1943. Then I had to undergo five months' training at York as a rifleman. Only on 1st November 1944 was I commissioned as 2nd Lieutenant the Rifle Brigade.

A year before joining the Army, I took the Oxford scholarship examination with distinction, and received a guarantee of a place to read French and German. The fact that I speak both languages – German like a native, French passably – obviously helped. I suspect it also proved decisive in my posting to 1st Bucks Battalion, which had just been allocated to the newly-formed T Force. Thankfully, no-one asked why my German was so perfect. Many of my school friends joined the forces out of what sounded to me like romantic misconceptions, jingoism, a thirst for revenge or simply an excess of testosterone. Some had enrolled out of patriotism, or because it was expected of them; girls looked askance at any young man who wasn't in uniform. Others wanted to go after the Hun. Like them, I was looking forward to fighting; but only as a pretty distasteful means to a noble end. I didn't wish the extinction or humiliation of the German people. I wasn't not interested in plundering their wasted country, or violating their womenfolk. I only wanted to liberate Europe and Germany from the National-Socialist tyranny that had enslaved them, brought untold destruction and suffering and – worst of all – eradicated their spirit. I wanted to be able to read Goethe's *Faust* and listen to Beethoven's *Battle Symphony Op. 91* without being called unpatriotic – if only because he wrote it to commemorate Wellington's victory over Joseph Bonaparte at the battle of Vitoria, and dedicated it to our king George IV. Who cares about these things today?

When you join the Army, dreaming of action and glory, you've no idea how vast, amorphous and shambolic it is; nor do you suspect that henceforth your days will be spent waiting. The worst kind of waiting: enforced idleness, never quite sure what you're waiting for, nor how long it may take. That's why this day was a minor miracle.

I, 2nd Lieutenant Peter Birkett, commissioned in the Rifle Brigade, posted to 1st Bucks, was driving towards Holland with the 5th King's. That fact alone is testimony to the mysterious workings of the Army. In fact, it all stemmed from the recent creation of T Force.

T for Target.

I have to be careful what I say here, because we're not supposed to talk about T Force. So, let me begin with S Force. The need for a special force to seize intelligence targets before the enemy could destroy them first came to light during the Italian campaign and resulted in the creation of S Force. S Force entered Naples and Rome with the vanguard to secure sites where it was hoped to find scientific, military or technical secrets. Obviously, I have no idea about what they discovered – and if I did, I would keep it to myself. All I know is that, soon after the Normandy landings last year, the brass decided to create a similar force to retrieve valuable intelligence from the clutches of the retreating German armies, from Belgium to Holland, and from Scandinavia to Germany itself.

Apparently, Hitler was now pinning his final hopes on the ability of his scientists to produce new miracle weapons – a slightly unnerving prospect, given their undoubted technological prowess. Just consider the V-1 flying bombs and V-2 rockets raining down on southern England. Could their accuracy be about to improve, their lethal payload increase massively? Was there any truth in the rumours that some kind of German nuclear bomb of unimaginable power was almost ready? Could a single bomb really destroy a whole city? And what about gas? It seemed odd that the Germans hadn't used it yet. Was it true that they were developing a new generation of war gases, waiting till we crossed the Rhine to unleash its horrible power against us? And what about these super-fast submarines, capable of staying under water for weeks on end, relying on some new power source: did they really exist, and if so, could they threaten vital shipping lanes?

Nobody seemed to have a clue. Which is why T Force was created. Our job was to secure and investigate the sites where such research or manufacturing was believed to be taking place before the retreating Germans destroyed them. That meant we had to move in the immediate wake of the assaulting forces, which should be fun. I suspected, though it isn't politic to say so, that our government from Churchill downwards was also quite unhappy about the wholesale looting of German research and industry by the Red Army. Whatever we get, Stalin won't get his bloody paws on.

As soon as I heard about the creation of T Force, I volunteered for service in the new unit. His Honour Judge Norman Birkett, my father, obligingly made the War Office aware of the fact that his son spoke German. Eventually, a couple of weeks ago, I was posted to the 1st Battalion of the Oxfordshire & Buckinghamshire Light Infantry Regiment, just allocated to T Force. Yet my elation was short-lived as it turned out that we would be missing the action. Just as Montgomery's 21st Army Group was preparing to launch its spring offensive, 1st Bucks was well and truly mired in garrison duty in Brussels.

The day after I reported for duty, we were called to assist the Military Police in checking for deserters in the city. This was an eye-opener. We hauled back more than four hundred absentees, some running thriving black market empires, many in a drunken stupor or ethylic coma, most from the beds of girlfriends or prostitutes whose pimps they had become. Then four of the thugs in the military jail we guarded managed to escape, assisted by one of the privates on warder duty whom they had presumably bribed. It fell to me to find them. All five of them were re-arrested within three days.

Twenty-four hours later, I nearly got killed. Three criminals in the detention block attempted a break-out. When I arrived on the scene, they were holding up the guard commander, who nevertheless refused to give them the keys. Another guard, Rifleman Richardson, heard the commotion and rushed downstairs with his Sten sub-machine-gun. Suddenly, the ring-leader fired a burst of his own Sten gun that missed me by a whisker. Before I had time to draw my revolver, Richardson fired back and wounded the ring-leader and one of his accomplices in the stomach. Unfortunately, he also put a couple of bullets though the head of the captive guard commander. The third prisoner put his hands up.

In my letters to my father, I made no mention of these incidents. I was in shock, and they made no sense to me. What the hell was I to make of the fact that the bullets that nearly killed me in my second week of active service – before my twentieth birthday – had been fired by a compatriot, a fellow soldier, somebody on my side? And that my survival had been entirely fortuitous? Nothing in my officer's training had come into play. I was only alive because of a combination of brute chance and the reflex actions of Rifleman Richardson. How does one thank a man who's just saved one's life? At first, I was standing dumbstruck, taking in the carnage, heart pounding painfully. I couldn't even utter the simple, manly words that were obviously called for – something like: 'Good show, Richardson. Much obliged.' In fact, we were both trembling like leaves. Later, I wanted to shake his hand, but the moment had passed.

That evening, after I'd finished writing my reports and stamping endless forms, I sat at my desk wondering about the families of the three dead men, thoroughly tempted to light the cigarette I was fidgeting with. Then Max Harrison's cheerful bass broke into my thoughts.

'Don't do, it old boy.'

'Don't do what?'

'Light that cig.'

'Why not?'

'Because you don't smoke – remember? I'm the smoker here. You always say that to send the currency value of cigarettes up in smoke is stupid – don't you?' He laughed, before adding: 'Heard you had a busy day. You all right?'

'I suppose so. What about you?'

'Bloody paperwork. We'd be better off working in some bank or insurance company and getting properly paid.'

The all-too-plausible vision of Max-the-bank-manager made me smile. Like me, Max is about twenty, and trained in the Rifle Brigade, before being posted to T Force as a platoon commander. In every other respect we are chalk and cheese, which probably explains why we get along so well. In particular, he's as short and rotund as I'm tall and lean. He has blue eyes in a round friendly face, and blond hair which he wears too long. He normally emanates an aura of untidiness, perhaps because no uniform could possibly suit him, or due to the cigarette ash on his lapels and trousers. Unlike me, he's a chain smoker and a heavy drinker; yet his most compulsive addiction is to women.

'How long do you think it will be before we get relieved?' I asked.

'My dear fellow – that sort of question is best left unasked when in the Armed Forces. There should be a regulation prohibiting soldiers from ever asking questions beginning with "How long?" or "When?" Come to think of it, there most likely is such a regulation lurking in the small print, and you're liable to be court-martialled for having contravened it. No point in asking: "How long will the war last? When will we go on leave? When are we going to move out of this giant bordello of a town and go chase the Germans out of Holland?" Believe me – nobody has the foggiest.'

'Being a soldier is a bit like being a child again, isn't it? Except we can't ask the "why" questions. And we can kill people.'

Max smiled. 'Is it? It seems to me you've just made a very mature statement. After all, it takes an adult to know what a child is.'

'Too deep for me. I hope the new offensive starts soon,

and that we run with it. So, you heard what happened at the jail today?'

'Yes – but not from the horse's mouth. Let's go for a drink and you can tell me all about it.'

'All right. Where?'

'Have you been to 72 Rue Royale? Apparently they have the loveliest girls in town. Actresses, models, dancers. Nobility, even. Very up-market.'

'Really? Sounds splendid. Not sure I'm up for it, though. It's been a long day. Besides, it's nearly nine-thirty: curfew starts in an hour and a half.'

Among many things I had no intention of publicising to my comrades was the fact I was still a virgin and, for some odd reason, quite valued that status.

'Shall we try the Hotel Plaza, then?' Max suggested. I understand they have vast stocks of captured German Army gin, which they are selling for three francs. Unbeatable.'

In front of every single bar and café we passed on our way to the Plaza, girls accosted us, offering sex in exchange for soap or a bar of chocolate. Seedy-looking civilians emerged from dark alleys and unlit corners, waving pornographic postcards and trying to entice us into sex shows. Despite the official prohibition, hundreds of starry-eyed British and Canadian soldiers, many with girls, were drifting in and out of squalid basements in unsteady shoals, happily lost in the Belgian Babylon and far too drunk to salute officers. Only when a Military Police patrol appeared did they attempt to help the most intoxicated among their comrades to walk in a reasonably straight line until the danger had passed.

The bar of the hotel Plaza was so densely packed that we had trouble making our way through the heaving bodies. I surveyed the scene from my six-foot height, looking for a suitable spot. An officer waved at me from a corner table: Major David Hunt, the Battalion Second in Command. We fought our way to his table and saluted sharply. Well, I did – Max's limp rendition of a salute, a vague wave utterly devoid of martial intent, far from highlighting his military status, tends to obscure it quite effectively.

'Care to join me?' Hunt asked. 'You don't have to – but it might be your best bet.'

'Delighted – thank you, sir.'

I ordered a Belgian beer, while Max went for a double German gin and some local sausages.

'To the victors the spoils!' Max raised his glass.

'Indeed,' the Major replied, with a twinkle in his eye. 'In more ways than one, as no doubt you have noticed. So, how do you gentlemen find war?'

David Hunt is one of the few officers who've served with the Battalion since the D-Day landings. Broad-shouldered, of medium build, he has a reputation for fairness and unflappability. His drooping dark eyes, sandwiched between jet black eyebrows and the thin black line of his trimmed moustache, unceasingly darted left and right.

'Not much of a war for us, I'm afraid, sir,' I replied. 'I'm beginning to wonder whether we haven't left it a bit late.'

Hunt took a sip of green-tinged Moselle and carefully wiped his moustache.

'I shouldn't worry about that. The Germans aren't defeated yet. Far from it. They had plenty of time to re-group during the winter. By golly! Have you chaps for-gotten how they came out of the Ardennes forest and savaged the Yanks?'

'No, sir,' Max replied. 'Do you think they are busy springing more traps for us?'

'You can bet your bottom franc that their High Com-mand is planning more counter-attacks. They're good at it. It will make our job at T Force difficult.'

'I had a look at the list of priority intelligence targets in Holland, sir,' I said. 'Dozens of them. Assuming we can find and secure most of them, we'll be thin on the ground. I reckon most targets won't even get allocated a full platoon. Some of these facilities are huge, Acres and acres. Not much we can do if and when the Germans decide to pay us return visits.'

'You may well be right, Birkett,' Hunt fixed his gaze on me for a moment. 'Nevertheless, our mission is clear, gentlemen: we are to secure the targets intact, and pre-serve them from destruction and counter-attack.'

'I can't wait,' Max said. 'Sounds much more fun than this dreadful garrison business – though Peter had a bit of excitement today, for a change.'

'So I hear,' Major Hunt replied. 'Baptism of fire, eh?'

'In a manner of speaking, sir. Bad business, really.'

'Exactly what happened?'

After I finished recounting the incident, Major Hunt repeated: 'Bad business indeed. Fortunately, we'll soon be moving on.'

'If I may ask, sir,' I ventured, 'is there any news?'

'As a matter of fact, yes. The bad news is that 1st Bucks isn't going to be relieved from garrison duty for a few weeks, and so will miss the offensive. The good news is that half of us are temporarily going to be put under command of 5th King's, who are ready to move out on T Force duties with the 2nd British Army.'

Max and I looked at each other and self-consciously took a sip from our respective glasses at precisely the same instant.

'Thank you, sir,' I said. 'Good news indeed – for those who are going. May we ask…?'

'No final decision yet. I'll be taking with me two companies out of four.'

'Any reason why it couldn't be B and D Companies?' I asked.

'Can't think of any,' Hunt smiled wryly. 'Not my call, of course.'

'Didn't you use to command B Company, sir?' asked Max.

'Sure did. With them on D-Day, so I know some of the men quite well. Lots of casualties in Normandy, of course.'

Though Major Hunt is hardly ten years older than us, he belongs to another generation altogether. He's fought a war. Legend has it that, despite the heavy losses suffered by B Company of the Normandy beaches, he's never left behind a dead or wounded man. Utterly reliable.

'Anyway, why are you chaps so fed up with this place?' Hunt asked, the faint shadow of an ironic smile slightly twisting his moustache. 'The whole of the British and Canadian Armies would sell their mothers to come on leave to Brussels.'

Max picked up his empty glass, stood up, stepped sideways to get a better look at the cleavage of the giggling brunette voluptuously smoking a Lucky Strike between two Guards officers at the next table and declaimed in his deepest bass: 'Au revoir, Brussels! Your treasures are nothing compared to those T Force is about to extract from Germany!'

'Steady on, old chap,' Major Hunt growled. 'Need I remind you that T Force is so secret, it hardly exists?'

Two weeks later, we were on the move. A minor miracle.

2

Another War Couple

STANDING IN the sun-baked Chancellery garden on this warm day in late May 1945, Captain Elizaveta Terisova of the NKGB suddenly felt a primal terror course through her veins. Indeed, not an hour passed without her realising how improbably lucky she was to be alive.

Born on the very day – 19th October 1918 – when her mother's country, the Autonomous Socialistic Soviet Republic of the Volga Germans, was created by the Bolshevik government, twenty-six-year-old Elizaveta Terisova had already outlived it by four years: Stalin had abolished the German Volga Republic in August 1941, only weeks after Hitler unleashed Operation Barbarossa and its three million men against the USSR.

She had endured the long campaign which pushed the Nazi beast all the way back to its lair, on top of which she now stood trembling; she'd survived the epic fight that culminated a few days ago in the Red Banner No. 5 being hoisted above the Reichstag by two sergeants of the Special Banner Party, who'd immediately been made

Heroes of the Soviet Union. Admittedly, NKGB units were rarely found fighting at the front; nevertheless, they were close enough to it, when not ahead of it, to sustain significant losses.

War had confirmed the knowledge Elizaveta Terisova absorbed with her mother's milk, namely that, despite the constant horror of it all, nothing matters but life itself. And how unutterably sad it was that her mother's family and her people – the Volga Germans, or *Russdeutschen* – had been persecuted for no other reason than their ethnic origin. For decades on end the German peasants who, at the invitation of Catherine II of Russia, had settled the empty, fertile banks of the Volga river in 1763, had seen the rights granted them by the Empress steadily eroded by her successors. But nothing could have prepared them for the wrath of Joseph Stalin, who four years ago had branded them all Fifth Columnists, to be deported to the vast Siberian emptiness or interned in NKGB-run labour camps.

All of them – including Uncle Gottfried and Aunt Margaretha, on whose farm in the village of Shcherbatovka Elizaveta had spent many a happy summer as a child. And her beloved older cousin Jakob, who'd taught her, a little Muscovite, to love the Volga's black earth and infinite sky, and explained the differences between ox and cow, wheat and barley, as well as the names and habits of myriad migratory birds. Jakob from whom, hardly fifteen, she'd stolen the kiss that, after some twelve years, still burnt her lips and heart. Jakob, the only man she'd ever voluntarily kissed, and whose life – if indeed he was still alive – was now in her hands. Or rather, in those of the craggy-faced NKGB colonel who stood next to her, observing her strange behaviour with professional attention. Colonel Ivan Klimenko, her war-husband.

'Anything the matter?' he asked in his deep voice.

With a smile, she shook her head.

'Who'd have thought?' she mused, encompassing the surrounding devastation with a vague circular gesture.

'What?'

'That we'd make it this far.'

'I did.'

'Yes. You did, Comrade Colonel.'

'What's the first survival rule in the Soviet Union, the Red Army and the NKGB, Comrade?'

She looked at him, trying to assess his mood, and met his pale lavender eyes which still frightened her. He stood still, feet wide apart, long-legged but not excessively tall, broad-shouldered, emanating authority, self-assurance and menacing unpredictability. The raised right eyebrow was the only sign of tension below his scarred forehead.

'Never question the Party or your superiors, and do what you're told,' she recited automatically, looking at his smallish mouth. On his sensuous red lips, the habitual trace of an ironic smile seemed to grow more marked. Though he'd lost several teeth under torture – without confessing – during Stalin's 1937 Great Purge, his jaw line was still squarely symmetrical. On both sides, a deep crease revealed that he was in his mid-forties and capable of boisterous laughter, particularly when the vodka had been flowing. But Elizaveta knew that people who mistook his detached look for anything other than what it was, namely the reflection of an ever-alert, calculating mind, intent on self-preservation and self-gratification, did so at their peril.

'Wrong!' he guffawed, pushing back the rebellious black quiff which, always longer than permissible, needed constant disciplining. 'The first rule is: follow Ivan Klimenko. You ought to know that by now, my beauty. Now, where do you think the entrance to this bunker might be?'

He turned away from her and started walking towards a small concrete tower, carefully picking his way among the debris and unexploded ordnance with the effortless dancing steps of a boxer. Not for the first time, and to her dismay, she couldn't help noticing that he was an improbably good-looking bastard. NKGB operatives typically weren't recruited on account of their looks or athleticism; loyalty to the Party, administrative efficiency and utter ruthlessness were more essential qualities. As a result, even in the fighting units, many intelligence officers, unlike Colonel Ivan Klimenko, tended to exhibit a certain bureaucratic, intellectual look. Think, for example, of the diminutive Captain Kozlov, whose image suddenly emerged from a distant past, and to whom her entanglement with the murderous NKVD – or rather the OGPU, as it was called in those days – could be traced back.

Not only did Elizaveta share her birthday with the Autonomous Soviet Socialist Republic of the Volga Germans, but the Soviet Youth Organisation, or *Komsomol*, had also been born in the same week. Perhaps it was no coincidence that she was equally at ease in both, despite her father's insistence that she never talk to her Moscow friends about her German maternal family.

Her parents had met in a military field hospital in 1917, during the Civil War. Captain Nikolei Fedorovich Terisov was a medical officer in the Red Army; Anna was a nurse of Volga German origin. Between the dashing young doctor and the tall, beautiful nurse, it had been the usual story: love at first sight, the classic coup de foudre. Despite the opposition of both families, they'd married a few months later, in January 1918, just as Comrade Lenin, in his generosity, was not only ending the persecution of ethnic minorities, but also granting autonomy to the Volga Germans. However, some innate prudence, magnified perhaps by the undercurrents he picked up from his conversations with army colleagues, reinforced Captain Terisov's natural discretion, and strengthened his reluctance to reveal himself or his family as in any way different from the Russian masses. The memories of the two chaotic wars he'd fought in quick succession were too fresh for Terisov to forget about the fragility of alliances and the deep roots of Slavonic prejudice. Irrespective of political fashions, some deep instinct told him that the Russian Germans would never be totally safe, and that he could best protect his wife and daughter if they distanced themselves from their origins. Yet his wife Anna, attending medical school in Engels, the new capital city of the Autonomous Republic of the Volga Germans, was doing exactly the opposite; moreover, he never found it in his heart to forbid Elizaveta to spend all summer holidays with her German family, close to her mother, rather than alone in Moscow.

In mitigation of the risk, he demanded that, during the school year, his daughter became an exemplary member of the *Komsomol*. Elizaveta found it no hardship; as an only child living in Moscow with her father and his sister in the years that followed Anna's departure, she was delighted to engage in sports activities with neighbouring children. Together with her peers, she soon learnt that Marxism-Leninism was synonymous with progress, that all bourgeois were reactionaries, and that to doubt the universal wisdom of the Communist Party would be tantamount to sabotaging the Revolution. Trained and hardened by her summers of physical work on her maternal family's farm, she excelled at most sports, could outrun even the older boys, and often volunteered for chores. She had a strong, clear mezzo-soprano voice and a good ear. When the hierarchy realised that her birthday coincided with that of the organisation (Captain Terisov made sure they did), she was ritually selected every year to sing in front of the authorities. She performed as a soloist at the concert organised in October 1928 to celebrate the tenth anniversary of the *Komsomol*, in front of Iosif Vissarionovich Dzhugashvili, the head of the Communist Party, and again fifteen months later, at his fiftieth birthday celebration. Indeed, a picture of Iosif Vissarionovich – or Stalin, as he liked to be called – patting Elizaveta's head with a benign smile had been published on the front page of *Komsomolskaya Pravda*, and many more photographs had been stashed away in her father's safe; he knew their value. Little did Elizaveta know that the benevolent leader and inspired guide whose big moustache had twice tickled her cheek had just introduced agricultural policies that would condemn millions of peasants to death, including Uncle Gottfried and Aunt Margaretha.

So Elizaveta had developed into an icon of the modern, healthy and forward-looking Communist youth intent on playing an active part in the creation of the workers' paradise promised by the Party. She'd never challenged her father's prohibition of any mention of her Volga German relatives to friends or teachers; when asked why she never took part in her brigade's summer camp, she was coached from the earliest age to reply that she was spending the school holidays in Moscow.

Only in her teens did Elizaveta begin to feel slightly troubled by her dual identity. Until then, marching in front of the Kremlin with her brigade, she was a proud and happy Communist maiden full of gratitude for the Party's enlightened solicitude; wielding a scythe in Uncle Gottfried's wheat fields, she was a German farm hand through and through, happy as a lark. She knew that the *Russdeutschen* felt indebted to Comrade Lenin for their recovered freedom, and was reassured by the obviously harmonious relationship between her two universes, which was hardly marred by her father's eccentric ideas about segregation.

In 1929, as Anna was getting to the end of her medical studies, Stalin ordered the collectivisation of Soviet farming. Since most peasants were viscerally averse to being dispossessed of their fields, a new class war had to be waged, for which a new class enemy had to be invented: the kulak. Chosen from the most experienced, energetic and competent farmers, kulaks were to be expropriated from their landholdings, robbed of all their belongings and, together with their families, deported as enemies of the people to far away corners of Siberia, where those who survived the week-long journey in cattle trucks were left to fend for themselves in the wilderness. Uncle Gottfried and Aunt Margaretha, being hard-working and reasonably successful, were eminently eligible as kulaks.

In the summer of 1932, the situation on the farms had become so dire that Anna and Elizaveta, against all regulations and oblivious to Nikolei Fedorovich's warnings, decided to bring from Moscow as much food as they could cram into their luggage. Promoted to the rank of Major in 1928, Nikolei Fedorovich Terisov recognised an ill wind when he smelt one; his political antennae were attuned to the dangers presented by any association with the new class enemies, and he believed that his wife and daughter should lie low in Moscow until the storm blew over. The trouble was, they would have none of it.

'Listen to me, Anna, please,' he pleaded. 'Do you remember internal passports from the old times? Well, I heard on the grapevine that Stalin is going to reintroduce them. Some believe he wants to keep the peasants starving in the country to teach them a lesson, and the town people in the cities, away from it all. You probably won't get permission to travel anyway.'

'Nikolei Fedorovich, how can I deny my own family?' Anna protested. 'For the last five years they supported me when I was studying alone in Engels, far from you. Every summer they've welcomed our daughter so she could be near me, and treated her as their own. They gave her food to bring back to Moscow when the cities were going hungry. Should I disown them in their hour of need?'

'Nobody's asking you to disown your family, Anna dear,' he sighed. 'But they live in an autonomous Republic, and are more than capable of looking after themselves. I'm simply asking you not to place our daughter in harm's way. Right now the least dangerous place for both of you is Moscow.'

Anna had turned to Elizaveta. 'Your father is right, my darling. You should stay with him. I'll make a quick return trip to Shcherbatovka on my own and be back within a fortnight.'

Despite the tantrum Elizaveta threw at the prospect of staying behind, her parents held their ground. Only after she'd refused to eat for several days did they relent.

'Look at you, my baby!' Anna hugged her tightly. 'Skinny as a stray cat. Where did you get this stubbornness from? Why can't you trust me to look after my family on my own this time? Things will be better next year, and you will be able to go and see Uncle Gottfried and Aunt Margaretha and Jakob as usual. Why can't you wait?'

At the mention of Jakob's name, silent tears welled up in the girl's eyes. Anna sensed her daughter's body tense up and whispered: 'Oh my God – is that it? But, my baby, you're hardly fourteen! Jakob will be all right, don't you worry. He's a strong and smart boy. If anybody can find food off the land, it's Jakob. Don't you worry, my lovely, sweet daughter. Have you forgotten Uncle Gottfried's favourite proverb?'

She waited a few seconds and then went on in Volga-German dialect: 'Even a blind hen can find a corn sometimes. Remember?'

As the tears streamed down Elizaveta's cheeks, she burrowed her face against her mother's breast, and felt an odd sense of relief. Yes, in her mind she could hear Uncle Gottfried declaiming the pearls of wisdom he'd received from his forefathers – 'Work with pleasure, for no roasted chicken will fly into your mouth' was another favourite of his – as well as all the crude ones which made her blush once she became sufficiently fluent in his farmyard vernacular. For the first time that night, she was spared the nightmares that had previously haunted so many hours of darkness: visions of Jakob withering, his blue eyes turning glassy as he shrank into the stubble.

Major Terisov was right. Internal passports, the abolition of which had been a key demand of the leaders of the

October Revolution, would eventually be re-introduced to control and restrict the movement of the people, but not until after the final summer Elizaveta spent on the Volga with her mother. Even so, near the end of their long journey down to Engels, disaster beckoned when their train had screeched to a halt in a tiny settlement near the border with the Volga German Republic. Soldiers boarded their carriage and proceeded roughly to inspect all travel documents and luggage. Since 7th August 1932 a decree handwritten by Stalin himself prescribed death by shooting for stealing collective-farm property, and prohibited amnesty in all such cases. Furthermore, anybody trying to smuggle bread across the border from Russia was liable to be arrested and their supplies confiscated.

Inevitably, Anna's and Elizaveta's suitcases contained almost nothing but bread and the other basic foodstuffs which they'd squirreled away over the months – greyish flour and sugar, thin oil, walnuts, some dry pulses, even a piece of lard – hidden under a layer of lingerie.

Within minutes their luggage and papers had been confiscated, they'd been thrown off the train, frogmarched with dozens of fellow passengers into what seemed to be the village school, and locked up in an airless, unfurnished, overcrowded room guarded by an OGPU boy. Nobody in the room dared move or speak; people kept their eyes down and their thoughts to themselves. Only the sweat running down their faces, their fidgety fingers, and the furtive glances they darted at the door every time it opened and a secret service official appeared to call and take away some of the prisoners betrayed their fear. And the smell; indeed it was in this very classroom that Elizaveta had been exposed, for the first time in her life, to the stench of terror. When, after an hour or so, they heard their train pull away in the distance, mother and daughter exchanged a glance, and Elizaveta felt tremendous love as she saw the corners of her mother's mouth tremble and how pale she was. Afraid that she might collapse, she put her arm around her waist and tried to comfort her:

'It's going to be all right, Mama. We're together. And Papa has friends...' But Anna had just fixed her wide-eyed, shaking her head in disbelief at her own recklessness, wondering why on earth she'd led her daughter into such a trap. Again and again, Nikolei Fedorovich's plea rang in her ears: *I am simply asking you not to place our daughter in harm's way... Our daughter in harm's way... In harm's way...*

Not before dusk were they finally called. By then, they had been kept standing in the packed, stifling room for several hours without food or water; several older women lay crumpled on the floor; toddlers were wailing weakly, and Elizaveta had learnt that the smell of urine was an essential component of the odour of fear. They were taken by two unshaven soldiers to another classroom, this one equipped with two dozen basic tables, stools and a framed photograph of Stalin hanging on the wall at a cockeyed angle. Behind the teacher's desk, under Stalin, sat a diminutive man wearing a pale tan Red Army summer uniform with a greenish khaki canvas belt and a brass buckle. The glaring absence of any insignia on the stand-up collar or the shoulder boards of his tunic was enough to identify him as a secret service man, while the piping around the collar and cuffs suggested that, albeit only in his late thirties, he was a commander of some seniority. Scrutinising papers, he ignored his prisoners for a while before suddenly pointing at the jumbled suit-cases that lay next to his desk and asking in a tired voice:

'So, ladies. On our way to a picnic, are we?'

'Please let me explain, Comrade Commissar,' Anna blurted. 'I'm a medical doctor – a Party member since 1920 – on my way to Engels. You must have seen that in my papers.'

She paused expectantly but the man had returned his gaze to his files and seemed not be listening. 'Obviously, I cannot cure starving patients,' Anna went on shakily. 'Nobody can. These few items of food really are essential medicines.'

'Starving? Who's starving?' the officer asked sharply.

'But, Comrade…'

'Comrade Terisova,' he asked with quiet deliberation, 'can you read?'

Taken aback, Anna nodded silently.

'You are coming from Moscow, I believe?'

Again she nodded.

'I believe there are newspapers in the Soviet capital?'

'Indeed, Comrade Colonel,' Anna stuttered. 'We read *Komsomolskaya Pravda* every day. My husband…'

'Were you in Moscow last Friday?'

'No. Yes. We were. We left on Sunday.'

'Then you will have read this copy?' he asked, picking up a newspaper on his desk.

'Yes,' Anna whispered. She remembered it well. Under the headline '*Down With Traitors!*' an article on the front page explained how foreign imperialist powers were trying to spread lies about a famine in the Soviet Union, and even impertinently offered to mount an international relief operation. Several resolutions by collective farmers from the Ukraine and the Volga, rejecting such impudent and unwarranted offers of help, were printed next to it. In conclusion, the paper reported the decree promulgated by the Party, according to which anyone referring to a famine would henceforth be subject to arrest for anti-Soviet propaganda and five years in a labour camp. When Nikolei Fedorovich and Anna, in hushed voices, had discussed this development the following day, he'd referred to 'the inhuman power of the lie'; now Anna was beginning to understand what he meant.

'Comrade Doctor Terisova,' the OGPU man said quietly, 'I believe you have just referred to starving people – indeed I've written down your exact words on the file. You will understand, no doubt, that this leaves me no choice. The law is clear.'

Anna was now shaking violently from head to toe.

'Comrade Colonel – please – you don't understand. I fought for Communism in the Civil War – and so did my husband, Major Terisov.'

'The alternative, of course, unless you can prove the origin of the forbidden items in your luggage, is for me to assume they have been stolen at source, namely from a kolkhoz,' the man interjected. 'Such theft is punishable by death – as no doubt you know.'

Speechless and wild-eyed, Anna stared at him. The man had closed her file, pushed it aside and was wearily opening another one.

'Transit camp,' he said to the guards.

They grabbed Anna by the arms and dragged her to the door. Suddenly she broke loose with a shriek and ran back to the desk in front of which Elizaveta was still standing.

'My daughter!' she screamed. 'She's just a child – can't you see? What are you going to do with her?'

'Clearly, she's old enough to have been infected by your anti-Soviet propaganda,' the officer replied, pointing at the suitcases. 'She was attempting to smuggle illegal articles across the border.'

Anna fell to her knees.

'Please, Comrade, *please*,' she sobbed. 'In the name of God... of your children...'

'Mother, please get up,' Elizaveta said crisply, helping Anna to her feet. To her own surprise, she felt no fear, only icy rage that her mother should be reduced to begging by a colourless functionary. 'The officer is only doing his job. Of course he's right. Nobody is above the law. Isn't that right, officer?'

The OGPU man looked up in surprise.

'That's correct,' he said. 'Nobody.'

'And all citizens have a duty to know the law – isn't that correct too, officer?'

'Of course it is,' the man confirmed with a hint of impatience.

'And the way to keep abreast of the law is for all citizens to read each and every copy of *Komsomolskaya Pravda*, and remember and treasure its contents forever, isn't it, officer?'

'It certainly is one way,' the man replied, slightly unsteadied. 'What is your point, child – assuming you have one?'

'What is your name, Comrade?' Elizaveta asked in a neutral way, looking him in the eye. Anna gasped and clasped her hands in silent despair.

'What?' he blurted.

'I'm sure Uncle Iosif would love to hear about you,' Elizaveta said. 'What's your name?'

'My name is none of your business, and your uncle Iosif none of mine,' he replied brusquely, turning his gaze back towards the door. 'Corporal! Take them away.'

Elizaveta stepped forward and stood tall over the desk. There was nothing childlike in her demeanour. Watching her daughter with a dreamlike mixture of dread and wonder, Anna feared that, though she did not appear in the least hysterical, she'd in fact become unhinged and was about to make matters even worse.

'Can you read, Comrade?' Elizaveta asked in a steady voice, retrieving papers from a pocket she had sewn at the front of her skirt. The man looked bemused as she unfolded half a dozen pages of various issues of *Komsomolskaya Pravda*, the most recent of which was only a few months old, and carefully placed them the right way up on top of the files that cluttered the desk.

'Dear Uncle Iosif,' she mused, fondly caressing the full-page pictures of Stalin with her long fingers. 'Such a bristly moustache!'

The OGPU man stared in disbelief at this collection of cuttings from the Communist Party's main organ, plastered all over with photographs of Stalin kissing Elizaveta on the cheek or patting her on the head. He started reading the articles which listed Elizaveta's achievements as a model *Komsomol* maiden, Stalin's favourite, the one he always wanted to see perform at big official celebrations.

'For God's sake... what the hell...' he stammered.

'Now, Officer, Uncle Iosif wouldn't like this language,' Elizaveta remonstrated mildly. 'He told me that God is dead – didn't you know? Even the dumbest among my *Komsomol* friends know that! Surely you must have read in *Pravda* that his priests are enemies of the people?'

The man took off his round wire glasses and stood up uncertainly. He looked up to Elizaveta who was towering above him across the desk.

'There seems to have been some misunderstanding,' he said.

'Indeed,' she replied, her grey-green eyes flashing through long eyelashes.

For the first time, Anna realised how beautiful her teenage daughter had become. 'Not to worry, Comrade,' she interjected. 'These things happen.'

'Of course they do,' Elizaveta confirmed. 'But they have to be put right, don't they?'

The officer pointed to the first row of children's desks.

'Please, Comrade doctor, won't you sit down?' he asked Anna. 'It will only take a few minutes to put all your luggage back together and prepare your papers. I will personally make sure that you have decent accommodation for the night and good seats on tomorrow's train.'

'May I... may I go and refresh myself?' Anna asked.

'Certainly, Comrade doctor,' the officer answered, gesturing at the soldiers to open the door and show her the way.

Elizaveta watched her leave the room and turned back to the officer.

'Now, officer,' she said with a friendly smile that showed her sharp teeth glittering under her high cheekbones. 'You mentioned papers.'

He looked at her with raised eyebrows.

'Well,' she went on, 'what sort of papers did you have in mind?'

'I will return all the documents we seized from you, naturally.'

'Thank you. I wonder though whether I might trouble you with a request?'

'Of course.'

'You will no doubt agree that such incidents are embarrassing for all parties, and shouldn't be allowed to happen again. Accordingly, wouldn't it be helpful for us to carry a letter from you confirming that we are not to be randomly molested?'

Since Elizaveta had first spoken, the OGPU man had hardly taken his eyes off her, and now the shadow of a smile passed across his face. He nodded slowly, sat down at his desk, pulled out a sheet of paper, picked up a pen and started writing. He quickly filled half a page, signed it with a flourish and affixed a star-like stamp in red ink. Then he rose, walked around the desk, and handed the document to Elizaveta with a formal bow.

'I trust this will be satisfactory,' he said.

TO ALL UNITS OF THE INTERNAL AND FRONTIER OGPU

Please assist in any possible way the Komsomol heroin, Comrade Elizaveta Terisova (born on 19 October 1918 in Moscow) and her companion(s) who is/are travelling in the Volga region at the behest of the General Secretary of the Communist Party of the Soviet Union, Comrade Stalin. The undersigned takes pleasure in confirming that Comrade Elizaveta Terisova is uniquely gifted for challenging field work.

Captain Mikhail Kozlov
OGPU, Main Directorate for State Security, Section 1

'Thank you, Captain Kozlov. I'm sure it'll be fine,' she replied, looking at the signature.

She noticed the document wasn't dated, opened her mouth, thought better of it, folded the sheet of paper carefully, collected all the newspaper cuttings and inserted the whole lot into her special pocket. Then she walked around the desk and pointed at the wall. 'If you don't mind, Captain Kozlov, now we've straightened things between ourselves, we might as well put Uncle Iosif straight, don't you think?' As she talked she pushed Stalin's portrait some twenty degrees to the right so that it hung vertically.

'We will of course replace your baggage,' said Kozlov, pointing apologetically at the dismembered cases on the floor. He asked an orderly to help them carry their load to the village inn and bade them good night. When the door of their tiny bedroom was shut behind them, Elizaveta embraced her mother and burst into tears like the little girl she still was.

IT HAD BEEN thirteen long years since her first encounter with the Secret Service. She was a little girl no more. She knew how to handle NKGB thugs. Yet she still jumped when Colonel Ivan Klimenko, the Berlin sun catching the Red Star on his hat, turned around and shouted impatiently: 'For fuck's sake, woman, are you coming or not?'

3

T for Tanks and Travel

THE STEEL PLATES of the Bailey bridge rattled thunderously as our column crossed the Rhine. I knew that Class 40 bridges were designed to bear the weight of a forty-tonne tank; yet I felt relieved when our Humber armoured car finally started climbing the eastern bank of the great river, with no sign of enemy aircraft.

'Did you see that, sir?'

My driver, Rifleman Richardson, was pointing at a sign on the side of the road. About nine feet high and eighteen feet wide, it clamoured in huge capital letters:

'ENTERING GERMANY.
BE ON YOUR GUARD.
DO NOT FRATERNISE WITH GERMANS'.

'Hard to miss it,' I replied.

'Indeed, sir.'

'Well, at least we now know where we are. I dare say this kind of navigational aid might be useful to those of our Allies who have no idea which side of the Rhine Germany might be.'

Smiling, Richardson changed down a gear to negotiate the badly-repaired remnants of a bomb crater.

'By the way, Richardson,' I took advantage of the momentary drop in the sound level, 'have you read this?'

Richardson glanced at the little red book I was holding, *Instructions for British Servicemen in Germany, 1944*.

'The bit about fratricide, sir?' he asked. 'Yes, of course. Compulsory, isn't it? Besides, it's taught me plenty about the Germans – you know, their history, and how Hitler came to power, and how they all supported him. Evil lot, if you ask me.'

'Fraternisation, Richardson. Not fratricide.'

Our advance from Brussels to the German border had been swift, if only because T Force, by special dispensation, did not have to wait for convoy numbers, tea halts, petrol refilling points, speeds, densities, or report to control posts en route. The only conditions imposed by Q (Movement) had been that we move in small columns of no more than five vehicles at a time, with fifteen-minute intervals between columns. This suited us admirably. Though Major Hunt had been doubtful at first, he'd let me affix wooden signs on all our vehicles which read 'T Force – 30 Corps – Absolute Priority' and this worked wonders on the numerous occasions when we were challenged by Q controllers or irate tank commanders who wanted the road to themselves.

From Brussels our first move had been to Maasbreek

on 30th March, and now we were on our way to Gescher, a small town near Bocholt on the east side of the Rhine. We made slow progress on damaged roads, across the most fought-over country in the world, where the ubiquitous wreckage was still smouldering. As the far as the eye could see, hundreds of gliders were strewn higgledy-piggledy across fields, some smashed against trees, buildings or pylons, silent witnesses to our ferocious airborne attack. One of them had disintegrated on impact when landing atop a massive chestnut tree by the roadside, and a couple of dislocated bodies were still hanging from the branches. I wondered whether anyone would ever bother to recover them, or whether they'd be left to the birds. Almost every bridge had been destroyed by the retreating Germans and replaced by a Bailey bridge. Despite our self-granted right of way, T Force vehicles were often held up as the armies of vehicles pouring into Germany queued at bottlenecks. The constant drone of RAF and USAAF planes overhead was reassuring, the Luftwaffe nowhere to be seen.

Now and then, over the clatter of our own vehicles, we heard volcanic explosions in the distance, and cheered as some German ammunition dump or factory blew up in apocalyptic fireworks, set off either by Allied bombers or SS rearguard units. Around six in the evening, our weary column finally drew into Gescher, where the detachment paused for a few days. We were joined by No. 19 Bomb Disposal Company, placed under our command for our first big operation: Hanover.

On the 6th of April we were ordered to move to Greven, some twenty-five miles to the east. Since most main roads in the region ran along a north-south axis, the east-bound Allied columns had to crawl along secondary roads in terrible condition, obstructed more effectively by our own overheating and broken-down vehicles than by the odd German shell. Once, I heard a loud ping as something hit our armour plating – a sniper's bullet, shrapnel or flying debris.

To complicate things further, as we got deeper into Germany the small bands of cadaverous individuals in filthy rags walking westwards, often bare-footed, always singing and waving makeshift flags representing their nationality, grew ever larger. These were the slave workers on whom the war effort of Nazi Germany had largely depended, former concentration camp inmates and prisoners of war, mostly Belgian, French and Polish, liberated by the forward units of the British Army; the vanguard of millions of Displaced Persons, or 'DPs' as they were now called, that were rampaging throughout the German countryside, foraging for food, women and revenge. As the British column passed, they waved; when I spotted a French flag and shouted '*Vive la France!*' they broke into an enthusiastic, if approximate, rendition of 'God Save the King'.

It was on that road that I had my first dealings with the local population. As dusk fell, we heard a loud hissing noise; for a couple of seconds, Richardson and I looked at each other, wondering whether a shell was just about to hit. Then we realised that the noise was coming from the engine, and that steam was gushing from the bonnet. Richardson pulled over and stopped the engine.

'Sorry, sir. Looks like we're stuck.'

'Let's take a look.'

We got out and lifted the hot bonnet. I stretched my legs and stamped the ground to get rid of the pins and needles in my calves. 'I needed a break anyway. This Humber's no Rolls Royce, is it?'

'I wouldn't know, sir.'

'No, I don't suppose you would. Nor I, really. Anyway, that looks like the radiator filler cap, doesn't it? Why don't you let it cool for a while and have a look inside?'

It turned out that the header tank was empty of water, though no obvious leak was visible. I looked around. Farm buildings were just about distinguishable a quarter of a mile away.

'See that farmhouse?' I pointed. 'Go up there and get a bucket of water. With a bit of luck that should do the trick.'

'Up there?' Richardson repeated nervously. 'But I don't speak a word of German, sir.'

He was breaking out into a sweat. Christ, the man has saved my life, I thought, and here I am, casually sending him on his own deep into hostile territory! For all I knew there could be a whole SS Panzer division lurking up there.

'All right. I could do with a walk anyway. You stay here and guard the vehicle.'

'Yes, sir. Thank you.'

I cocked my pistol and proceeded cautiously up an unpaved country lane. As I approached the house, I spotted white flags hanging out of three top-floor windows, and others affixed to a barn and various outbuildings. We all knew, however, that German rearguard units had no compunction about using white flags to deceive and mow down naïve Allied soldiers. Running from tree to tree, watching for any sign of movement near the windows, I felt dozens of eyes observing my approach, but could locate none of them. I must be the first Allied soldier here, I thought. What are they all thinking? Do they see a heroic conqueror, a scared mouse, a liberator or a brutal invader? What did the inhabitants of French towns and villages think as the first Wehrmacht motorcyclists appeared on their main square?

On the spur of the moment, I decided to walk round the house and look for a back door. I found one, but my first rap on it was so feeble it could hardly be heard. Fuck! What's wrong with me? I banged the door with my gun. An elderly woman opened it, grey hair partially covered by a headscarf, slowly drying her calloused hands on an apron. She stood looking at me. I waved her out of the way and entered a large tiled kitchen. An old man was seated at a wooden table; opposite him an attractive young woman was protectively holding a toddler in her lap, her finger on its mouth, rocking gently back and forth. I wondered whether she was a widow. They just sat and watched me.

'*Ich brauche einen Wassereimer, bitte,*' I said firmly.

They kept staring.

'*Ich meine, einen Eimer voll Wasser,*' I added hesitantly, wondering whether I'd expressed myself clearly enough.

The old woman pointed at a bucket on the floor. I grabbed it, spotted the water tap and headed for it. Water trickled out of it so agonisingly slowly I wondered whether it was about to run out. During the long minutes it took to fill the bucket, I felt their gaze on my nape. Then I turned around, gave a stiff little bow in no particular direction and said: '*Ich bedanke mich.*'

The old woman nodded gravely. With a last glance at the young mother, I walked out, trying not to splash water everywhere, and carefully closed the door behind me.

The water did the trick, and soon the Humber's engine was running again.

'Shall we go, sir?' Richardson asked.

'Just a second.'

I now felt as elated as if I'd won a decisive victory for the Allied cause all by myself. I picked up my roadmap and studied it.

'Tell you what, Richardson. I think if we go up this lane, past the farmhouse, after about three miles we'll get onto this small road here that will save us at least six or seven miles. We might even rejoin the main road ahead of our convoy. Shall we try it?'

'Can't see why not, sir.'

As we drove past the house, there was no sign of life.

'Were there any Krauts, sir?' Richardson asked.

I told him what happened. 'In hindsight, I'm only sorry I didn't think of giving the child the chocolate I had in my pocket,' I concluded.

'Not sure that would have been good, sir. Chargeable offence, if I remember correctly.'

'Damn you, Richardson,' I laughed, 'you seem to know these non-frat regulations better than me!'

The thought that I might have returned the bucket fleetingly crossed my mind; then I forgot about it. For a couple of miles, the country lane meandered between fields that seemed to have escaped the brunt of the fighting. Spring shoots covered the ground in undulating green swards, interspersed with stark hedges from which flocks of birds rose in alarm at the approach of our Humber.

We entered a wood and the peaceful rural idyll was immediately shattered. The scene couldn't have been more different. On both sides of the track, over half a mile, the burnt hulks of half a dozen German tanks were smouldering, and charred bodies were hanging from turrets or scattered on the ground. The metallic smell of mechanised death – cordite, oil, diesel fuel and burnt flesh – hung low under the maimed and silent trees.

'Blimey. Bandits got a bit of a pasting, didn't they? I wonder who gave it to them,' Richardson exclaimed.

'They certainly did. I say – can you go a bit faster?' I asked. There was no point in hanging about where German units had clearly been active a short while ago.

The whine of the six-cylinder petrol engine moved to a

higher pitch as Richardson hurled the three-and-a-half ton vehicle down the dirt lane. I felt every bone in my body rattle as the hard semi-elliptic springs collided with the solid axles. Suddenly we emerged from the covert and the road forked. Right in front of us another tank was ablaze: a British Sherman.

'Stop!' I ordered. 'I need to look at the map.'

Richardson managed to bring the vehicle to a halt just before the fork, some twenty yards out of the woods.

'Hmm…' I hesitated. 'I think we're here – that must be the farmhouse we left behind, and the woodland? But for the life of me I can't see any bloody fork on the map. Anyway, Greven is east of us, so I guess we just go right.'

'Sir!' Richardson pointed at something. 'There!'

Just as I made out the outline of tanks partly dug in about half a mile away, I saw a flash. The first shell hissed over our heads and exploded in the woods behind.

'Reverse!' I shouted. 'Back into the woods, quick!'

Time seemed to slow down as Richardson, with no rear visibility whatsoever, hurriedly reversed the car, aided only by its two small rectangular wing mirrors. We both knew that neither its 14 mm armour nor its .303 Bren light machine gun were a match for tanks.

I trained my binoculars on the tank column. The second and third tanks were turning their turrets and taking aim. They were British. The second shell landed just short and threw up a geyser of soil and rocks that cascaded down on the Humber, affording us momentary camouflage behind a thick cloud of dust. Instead of taking advantage of the cover, Richardson inadvertently drove the car off the road; after heeling over to a dangerous angle, it hit something, so that we had no option but to move forward again to get back on the track. This probably saved our lives as a third shell landed just behind us, rocking the Humber with a giant fist and peppering it with shrapnel.

'Keep going!' I shouted. 'This is only friendly fire. They don't really mean it. Just keep reversing until we're well inside those woods. Then make a U-turn wherever possible. Maybe the shortcut wasn't such a good idea.'

Frantically backing and filling, Richardson was sweating profusely. I reached the No. 19 radio set, turned it on at maximum power and bellowed on channel 3:

'British tank unit located two miles north of Billerbeck, cease firing! I say again, cease firing! You're shelling a British T Force vehicle!'

I waited for thirty seconds. No reaction. There was no reason to suppose, of course, that a tank unit would keep watch on this particular channel. I repeated the message on channel 6. Just as Richardson was attempting to turn the vehicle around in a clearing, a crisp voice crackled over the radio:

'T Force unit, what are your exact coordinates? Over.'

I looked at the map and answered.

'T Force unit, what is your vehicle? Over,' the voice asked.

'Humber Scout Car Mark II. The one you've just been taking pot-shots at. Over.'

'How many of you? Over.'

'Two. Over.'

'Do you mean two cars? Over.'

'Negative. One car, two men. Over.'

There was a lull.

'T Force unit, I'm not sure what the hell you're up to, but those woods are still full of Jerries. We've got them surrounded, and nobody is coming out alive. Now listen: I want you to drive your vehicle very slowly to the edge of the trees, leave it there in full view and get out of it. Then walk towards us with your hands up and no weapons. Bear in mind I cannot guarantee your safety. Understood?'

'Roger. On our way.'

Richardson, now totally drenched with perspiration, worked on another blind U-turn and charged back towards the edge of the thicket.

Walking in the no-man's-land between the German-occupied woodland and the British unit, I felt hugely vulnerable and somewhat foolish. Then anger suddenly welled up inside me. Who were the smug bastards playing these stupid games? What the hell did they think they were doing? As we got nearer, with our hands up, I could see machine guns trained on us, but hardly any men. Only in the last fifty yards did I catch sight of the rest of the unit, eight battle-weary Sherman tanks hidden behind a slight rise in the land. Two of them were re-fuelling from a road tanker. A couple of officers were talking on a radio-telephone next to a jeep. A bit further down, four ragged German prisoners were sitting on the ground, hands on their heads, guarded by a soldier with a sub-machine gun.

I dropped my hands and marched to the jeep.

'Who's the commanding officer here?' I shouted from a distance of ten yards.

One of the officers looked up and barked: 'I am. Captain Belfont. Who the hell are you, and what the fuck are you doing here?' He was short and stocky, with a dirty babyish face and black eyes. I saluted.

'Second Lieutenant Birkett, 1st Bucks, T Force. Did you order your tanks to fire at me?'

'I certainly did.'

'What the hell for?'

'As it happens, lieutenant, there is a war on.'

'A civil war?'

'Have you any identification?'

I produced my papers, which seemed to satisfy the captain.

'Why exactly were you firing at a British Humber car?' I insisted.

'Don't try and be clever with me, Birkett. Whatever T Force might be, only a complete arsehole would have strolled into the middle of a tank battle for the fun of it.'

'Why did you make me leave my vehicle and walk unarmed, right in the middle of your battle – sir?'

'Why? I'll tell you why. See these fellows there?' He pointed to the small group of bedraggled Germans, one of whom met my gaze, a lad in his teens, bleeding profusely from an unattended head wound. 'I've lost two tanks plus crews to their white flag antics. Bloody cheats. They're like cornered wolves, ready to pounce out of their lair any second, but they won't surrender. I wasn't expecting one of our vehicles to emerge out of their den unannounced. Looked like another special from their box of tricks to me. What were you doing there anyway?'

'Had mechanical problems, then took a shortcut on our way to Greven, sir. Trying to catch up with our unit.'

'Shortcut? Hasn't Q given you an itinerary and timings?' Belfont sounded suspicious.

'No sir. We have absolute priority and autonomy for our movements.'

'You do? What's that T Force of yours? Never heard of it.'

Before I could explain, the captain was called to the radio and had an exchange with his superiors; then he turned to his little group of NCOs.

'All right, chaps. We've been ordered to go and wipe out the vermin in that woodland once and for all,' he said. 'We've got support coming in from the other side. Classic pincer movement – but watch out for blue on blue.'

He turned back to me: 'You have ten minutes to get out of the way. Don't even think of going back through the woods.'

'Thank you, sir. Good luck.' I saluted and turned around. 'Wait here, Richardson. I'll get the car down.'

'Actually, I'd prefer to go with you, sir,' Richardson answered.

Belfont looked up with an ironic half smile. 'We'll cover you,' he said. 'But against sniper fire from the covert there is nothing we can do.'

Spewing black clouds of diesel fumes, all of the tanks' engines started rumbling loudly as the men prepared to move back into action.

'Thank you, sir,' I replied.

Before we'd taken ten steps Belfont shouted: 'Wait a second!'

We stopped in our tracks.

'Do me a favour,' said Belfont. 'I need you to look after these Jerries here for a short while. Obviously we can't take them with us. But if we leave them here I guarantee that within half an hour they will have picked up weapons somewhere and start shooting at our backsides.'

'That won't be easy, sir. At a push we could bundle one in our Humber' – I glanced at the bleeding youth – 'but certainly no more.'

'Are you sure? What about your man? Could he guard them for a couple of hours?'

'I doubt it, sir. We need to rejoin our unit.'

'All right then. No shortcuts this time, eh?'

Nervously eyeing the edge of the woods, Richardson and I returned to the Humber at the double. We were about halfway when a long burst of gunfire sent us tumbling to the ground, our hearts in our mouths. In the silence that followed, we realised it had come not from the covert ahead, but from behind us. We looked at each other – first in puzzlement, then in disbelief.

When we drove past them, the corpses of the four German prisoners were lying in a ditch, eyes wide open, and the tank company was fanning out in an encirclement.

GREVEN WAS a seething mass of Displaced Persons of all nationalities, most of them drunk, all of them hungry and in need of shelter, the pitiful, vermin-infested flotsam of the biggest shipwreck in history. As night fell, we eventually found our company in the process of evicting at point of bayonet large numbers of vociferous Italians from a silk spinning factory that seemed large enough to accommodate the whole company. The men were pleasantly surprised to discover that, interspersed among miles of delicate machinery and bales of silk, dozens of cosy little alcoves had been created, most of them equipped with mattresses and silk cushions. Only later, as the ladies of the night, whose working place this had been for some weeks, timidly returned, did the men comprehend the full extent of their good fortune.

In the morning, a bashful Rifleman Richardson brought to me a good-looking German woman in her mid-thirties. As though fascinated by them, she kept looking at her feet, where she sported an unusual combination of black woollen stockings and red high-heeled shoes.

'Sorry, sir – I think she wants to speak to an officer. Not sure what she's about.'

'*Guten Morgen,*' I said.

The woman looked up and started to speak in very fast

German, repeatedly pointing at the floor. With some difficulty, I understood she wanted to show us something in the basement. I ordered Bob Wagg, my platoon sergeant, to organise a party of four men with Sten guns. Following the woman, we all trooped down several flights of stairs and stopped in front of a large steel double door at the lowest level, some two floors underground. The door was unlocked.

On each side of it, an empty chair and a table littered with coffee mugs, registers, pens and telephones stood guard. Behind it, complicated machinery was running over acres of floor space; technicians in dust suits, rubber gloves and boots and facial masks, perhaps two dozen of them, were sitting at scattered desks, tending machines or whispering in small groups. As the T Force team cautiously walked in, all fell silent. I made for a glazed office area on the left where three men in white coats and a secretary were sitting. One of them, a distinguished-looking middle-aged man with wavy white hair rose as we entered.

'Ah! At last. Welcome, gentlemen,' he said in perfect English. ' We've been expecting you – though I was beginning to wonder whether you'd get here before the Russians. I hear they're in Berlin. May I introduce myself? Professor Wilhelm Groth.' He bowed. 'You've just missed my good friend Heisenberg, I'm afraid.'

That name rang a bell. 'Werner Heisenberg? Recipient of the Nobel Prize for physics in – when was it – 1932?' I asked.

'Indeed. I'm afraid Werner dislikes disorder, so he went to his country retreat.'

'When did he leave?'

The professor chuckled.

'You know about Werner's Uncertainty Principle?'

'Not really.'

'Very good answer. People who think they understand it fool themselves. Including myself. Werner would be the first to say that. And it is open to many interpretations.'

'Is it? That doesn't sound very scientific, does it?'

'Does it not?' Groth turned the palms of his hands up in a gesture of mock impotence. 'Well, compared to the attempts of our anthropologists to map out the racial differences between *Herrenrasse* and *Untermenschen*, I'd argue that theoretical physics is reasonably scientific, even if its interpretation is difficult.'

'What the heck is he talking about?' Richardson asked Sergeant Wagg sotto voce.

'Where is Mr Heisenberg to be found?' I asked.

'Nowhere you would know, lieutenant, I'm afraid.'

'Try me.'

'Uncertainty, lieutenant! Impossible to know both the velocity and the location of a particle. Before the war, it used to apply only at the sub-atomic level, you see. But now, it's all changed. On this blighted territory – as in hell – it applies to everything human.'

'What do you mean?'

'You will soon understand. Good and evil, life and

death, friends and foes... No certainty will be left. As for right and wrong...'

'What's going on here?' I interrupted, aware of the many shapeless masked figures gathering by the door. My little squad was getting restive.

'Here? Do you happen to have an interest in nuclear physics? No, I didn't expect you would. In simple terms, we're enriching uranium. The machines you see are centrifuges. Or, more precisely, ultracentrifuges for the enrichment of uranium-235. Pretty much state-of-the-art, I should hope. Admittedly, we've had a few teething problems, particularly with regard to mass production – including a few unfortunate incidents of spontaneous combustion and explosions. Nevertheless we have achieved more than twenty percent enrichment already.'

'Meaning?' I asked.

'Meaning, lieutenant, that Mr Churchill would not want the Soviets to get close to us. Or *vice versa.*'

'Thank you, Professor. You and your colleagues are under arrest. Do you need assistance to collect any personal belongings?'

'No – thank you for asking. As you can see, my luggage is ready.' With a happy smile, he pointed to a large holdall by his desk.

No SOONER had we reported our find than, like a swarm of bees, teams of assessors and investigators, many flown in specially from London, poured in and began buzzing about in ever smaller circles. The next few days were busy providing logistical support for them including accommodation and a mess. With regard to transport, great initiative was shown by assessors and platoons alike, who felt no compunction about waving down any German car they fancied and liberating it from the heinous Nazi yoke. The process involved nothing more onerous than evicting the driver and replacing him or her at the wheel, though a few indignant locals managed to wangle some kind of meaningless handwritten receipt from the conquistadors.

Such was the importance of our discovery that even Lieutenant Colonel Guy Wreford-Brown, commander of the 5th Battalion of the King's Regiment, made an appearance. He turned up in a 1.4 litre Mercedes saloon and parked it next to Max Harrison's recently acquired vehicle, a far superior exemplar of German automotive engineering. On the way to Greven, Max had noticed this splendid motorcar dawdling in front of him as if the war were on another continent. In a characteristic display of fast reflex and tactical opportunism, he'd instructed the platoon sergeant driving his Humber scout car to overtake the prey and stop it. Never in the history of mankind has such a beautiful machine so spontaneously joined the fight for freedom. A shiny phaeton powered by a straight twelve-cylinder under an enormously long bonnet, it was like nothing Max had ever seen before. A strikingly elegant blonde woman who spoke only a few words of English reluctantly got out. With the merest twinge of regret, Max explained that, sadly, it was necessary for T Force to commandeer her car. The woman listened disdainfully, and indicated her desire to have sight of some written authority. Since the requisitioning of civilian cars did have to be authorised, Max had no option but to give her a receipt; as he handed it over, he inhaled whiffs of expensive Parisian perfume. She frowned for a long time at the mystifying foreign scribble which read: 'This beautiful Rhine Maiden somehow had acquired a damned fine car, which she has today willingly donated to the British Army in atonement.' On conclusion of her lengthy inspection, the lady asked him to sign and date the receipt, and the platoon sergeant to witness it; then she carefully folded it in four and put it in her handbag. She opened the passenger door and took out a small leather pouch, a poodle and a fur coat. As she put her hat on, Max couldn't help noticing her high, pointed breasts.

'Can we offer you a lift?' he asked.

'*Bitte?*'

Max pointed at the passenger seat with an inviting gesture.

'*Nein, danke,*' she turned her back on them.

'Sure?' By now Max was painfully aware of the full hips swinging elegantly atop long, black-stockinged legs, and he was wondering how to retrieve what seemed a wasted opportunity. As he recounted to me later with a wry grin, the thought crossed his mind that he'd just been cheated, and maybe should gallantly trade in the automobile in exchange for a smile – to no avail.

Upon his arrival Lieutenant Colonel Wreford-Brown and his entourage were taken by Major Hunt on a tour of the lab. When we reconvened for dinner in the mess the colonel was in expansive mood.

'Here's how,' he raised his glass.

'Here's how,' Major Hunt returned the toast.

'I say, Hunt. Quite a feather in our cap, you know. All the BIOS boffins in London got frightfully excited when they heard about it.'

'Thank you sir. I do know. We've had to play nursemaid to dozens of them over the last few days,' Major Hunt replied.

'How's the evacuation going?'

'All scientists safely delivered to Inkpot, sir. The centrifuges have been crated and will be shipped to the UK as soon as the Pioneers' trucks catch up with us.'

'If I may enquire, sir, what exactly is Inkpot?' I asked.

'I say, Birkett. I hear we owe our fame to your brilliant intelligence work. Good show,' Wreford-Brown interjected.

'Inkpot is a centre in Wimbledon run by our ultimate masters, BIOS – the British Intelligence Objectives Sub-Committee,' said Major Hunt. 'The former Beltane School, in fact.'

'That's right,' confirmed Wreford-Brown. 'It's where all German "personalities" – believe it or not, that's what they call Nazi scientists – are taken and interviewed. Our friend Professor Groth is there as we speak.'

'My sister had a friend who went to the Beltane school,'

Max reminisced. 'Loved its heady mix of progressive education, Druidic ritual and Celtic gods. Splendid girl.'

'Afraid the boarding regime's got a bit harsher in the last four years,' Wreford-Brown smiled. 'Quite a secure place now. Never seen so much barbed wire in London before.'

'Is that for the detainees' protection, or to enforce their incarceration?' I asked.

'Good question,' Wreford-Brown answered. 'A bit of both, I suppose. I should imagine that the good burghers of Wimbledon aren't quite ready yet to share a pint at the King's Arms with the designers of the V-1s and V-2s.'

'So BIOS selects our targets and sends us the investigators?' Max asked.

'Correct,' the colonel answered. 'Except they're called assessors nowadays.' He took a sip of Moselle, swirled it round his tongue and carefully wiped his lips. 'Nice and fruity, if a little bit spritzig. Talking of targets,' he went on, 'rather an impressive automobile you have parked down there, Hunt. What exactly is it?'

There was a pause. 'Actually, it isn't mine, sir,' Hunt said.

'We don't quite know, sir,' Max mumbled. 'Seems to incorporate lots of Mercedes parts, but obviously not a production car.'

'One of our interpreters told me only three were built,' I said. 'Specially made for the top three state officials.'

'I see,' the colonel said reflectively. 'Hitler, Göring... and who else?'

'Possibly Himmler?' I suggested.

'Indeed. I don't suppose it's been donated to T Force by any one of these individuals?'

'No, sir, it hasn't exactly,' Max said.

'What do you mean, "not exactly", Harrison?'

'As Major Hunt mentioned, our requirements for transport shot up with the arrival of dozens of BIOS assessors, some of whom had inflated expectations of the level of service we could offer, sir.'

'Let me guess – loads of bloody civilians disguised as colonels?' Wreford-Brown grumbled.

'Precisely, sir. Some of them objected to being transported in jeeps or Humber scout cars.'

'I see. Did they like Himmler's limousine better?'

'It is proving quite popular, sir.'

'I can well imagine. How did you acquire it?'

'It was donated to us, sir.'

'Donated,' Wreford-Brown repeated with raised eyebrows. 'Who'd have thought so many Germans would fall over themselves to offer motorcars to their liberators? Yet is seems to be happening all over the place. Jolly sporting of them, really.'

'Very much our experience, sir,' Max said with palpable relief.

Lieutenant Colonel Wreford-Brown turned to Hunt. 'Nevertheless, it is incumbent on us to avoid creating the wrong impression, as no doubt you understand, major.'

Hunt nodded.

'By which I mean,' the colonel continued, 'that we cannot be seen to behave like bloody Cossacks.'

'The man is an infernal nuisance,' Max whispered in my ear. 'Can you think of a diversion?'

'Couldn't agree more, sir,' said Major Hunt.

'In particular, we must ensure that our requisitions are proportionate to our legitimate needs, and never amount to looting.'

'Goes without saying, sir.'

'Which means that all transport must be appropriate to the rank and function of users.'

'Absolutely, sir. As mentioned, most of the BIOS assessors seem to be temporary colonels, which is why...'

'Of course. I understand. But there are too many of them, and they come and go. Tell you what, Hunt: I think Brigadier Pennycook would quite like that vehicle. And it would be in keeping with the image that the General Officer Commanding T Force should project. Don't you agree?'

'Excellent idea, sir,' Hunt replied.

'Would you like me to take care of it?'

'I'd be most awfully grateful, sir.'

Second Lieutenant Max Harrison made a small choking sound, but managed to keep his own counsel until the end of dinner. Trying to suppress a fit of giggles, I concentrated on my plateful of *boeuf bourguignon* until the conversation had moved on to safer ground. Later that evening, when we both left the building, Max was quite drunk. He stopped by the sleek monster and wistfully caressed its elongated jaw and curvaceous flanks.

'Won't you do the honours?' I asked.

Max fumbled for his key and ceremoniously opened the door.

'Can you smell her?' he asked when we were both seated.

'Nice. What is it?'

'Chanel Number 5.'

'What was she like?'

'I say, Peter, are you trying to rub salt into my wound?'

'No. Just wondering. Obviously she must have been a lady of some means.'

Max tried to gather his thoughts. 'She made Rita Hayworth look plain.'

'She must be connected to a big fish,' I mused. 'Possibly one of Göring's mistresses? Did you investigate?'

'No. She just walked away.'

'You let her walk away?'

Max slumped in the driver's seat and nodded sheepishly.

'As I told you, I did consider returning the car to her. But it was too late. And the whole platoon was looking. And now I've got no fucking car either.'

I started laughing uncontrollably.

'Terribly sorry,' I panted. 'Come on now, old chap. I'll walk you to your cold and lonely bed.'

Half an hour later, with Max already snoring in his billet, I unfolded the letter from my father that the quartermaster had delivered at lunchtime. It read:

Challens Greens
2.iv.1945

My dear Peter

Thank you for your marvellous dispatch of 25th March. I assume that you have now left Brussels. God knows whether, where or when this letter will find you.

Since you kindly asked, I must first reassure you about my health. The virus that brought me low last winter now seems under control. I'm not sure though whether I owe it the fatigue that still seems to plague me; perhaps it is simply caused by age and the absence of your mother. Ten years already…

But enough about me. How are you?

Though not a soldier myself, I understand your frustration about garrison life. Hopefully, you're now engaged in more worthwhile pursuits, which no doubt the military censor will prevent you from describing to me. Should you already be on German soil, I know you will remember that not all Germans were Nazis. Indeed, as you know, the Austrian psychopath was abhorrent to your mother and her family.

I mentioned in my last missive that the Prime Minister had asked me to be the British Judge at the trial of German war criminals which is due to start in Nuremberg in the autumn, and that I had immediately accepted. Sadly, the Foreign Office, in their unfathomable snobbishness, have since decided that only a Law Lord would do – or perhaps somebody remembered that your dear mother was German by birth. Be that as it may, the Prime Minis-

ter found himself in the unenviable position of having to withdraw the offer I had accepted, and invited me instead to be an Alternate Judge. This means I shall attend all the sessions and replace the principal British Judge in case of illness or other incapacity. All in all, a poor show. Nevertheless, I feel that my duty is to accept, since I believe it supremely important that this trial, born out of political expediency, should be a model of fairness. Not only do I owe it to justice and to the law, but your late mother would have expected no less of me. And since both of us might by then be on German soil, I hope to see you more of you after my arrival in Nuremberg.

Since my elevation to the Bench, I've been eager to win a reputation as a wise, humane judge. I suspect I shall soon find out whether wisdom and humaneness can co-exist with justice in a courtroom. As a judge, my weakness is to understand how compassion is sometimes stronger than vengeance or punishment. For you, a soldier, such understanding will be a strength. Sometimes it requires great fortitude to be gentle and merciful in the fulfilment of public duty, while ensuring that cold justice is meted out to criminals.

Still no news from Hamburg. I fear you should not expect to see your grandparents ever again. That such splendid people should have perished by the sword epitomises the scandal of our time. That they should have been incinerated by British bombs makes me almost thankful for the cancer that spared your mother sufferings that neither flesh nor blood can stand.

The dilemmas you will face in occupied Germany will be no less acute. But fear not: from wherever she is, Sophie continues to love and guide you, just as she did during the first ten years of your life.

God bless.

In contrast to the neat handwriting above it, the signature was an illegible scribble. It could have been 'Papa', or 'Norman'. Or 'Father'. I wiped my tears, blew my nose, snuffed out the candle and fell asleep.

ON 11TH APRIL, T Force reached Hanover. Many buildings were still ablaze, scores more smouldering, the air acrid and dusty. Though most roads were passable, piled-up debris and broken timber encroached on them and slowed down all traffic. As my Humber snaked its way through the eerie desolation, I spotted a lonely figure some twenty-five metres to the left: a woman in her early twenties, immaculately clad in a pretty new dress, seemingly waiting to go to a party. Around her, only ruins. As she stood watching the detachment crawl forward in clouds of dust, immobile and statuesque, the flowers on her frock the only colour in the grey landscape, I couldn't take my eyes off her. What thoughts could possibly be going through her mind?

From the Hanomag truck factory, designs of half-tracked vehicles and radar components were soon seized, as were the telescopes, lamps and night-fighting infrared technology at the Maschinenfabrik Niedersachsen.

More than all these trophies, it was the contents of a medical research facility that were to remain most vividly engraved on my memory. A big, bright room with floor-to-ceiling shelving. On the shelves, glass jars in three different sizes, filled with a clear liquid. In each one was a human foetus. Some, in the smaller jars, were hardly bigger than a grain of rice; others as big as a tangerine. In the medium-sized jars were foetuses the size of an avocado. In the biggest ones, babies were still attached to their umbilical cords, some sucking a thumb with eyes wide open. Two shelves were allocated to twins, and one to triplets. The place was deserted; indeed, with its empty desks and dustbins, clinical cleanliness and deathly formaldehyde smell, it showed no evidence of having recently been occupied. Followed by my men, I walked slowly along the walls; then, in awed silence, we left and softly closed the door. The lab was not on our list of targets.

By the third week of April, the hordes of assessors that had been crawling all over the Hanover targets were beginning to exhaust their interest in them, and the time had come for the detachment to catch up with the advancing Allied formations for the biggest prize of all: Kiel.

4

A Kiss and a Rat

WHEN, AFTER THEIR ESCAPE from the clutches of OGPU, Anna and Elizaveta finally arrived in Shcherbatovka, they found the village changed almost beyond recognition.

First, Uncle Gottfried and his family – having been designated heinous kulaks – had lost their house, the single-level wooden dwelling that their ancestors had built with their bare hands. Their furniture had also been seized, so the home they were now trying to create under the provisional shelter of a neighbour's barn was rudimentary; yet, with typical resourcefulness, the men had already made it almost air- and watertight, and built rustic bunk beds at the back.

Following an atrocious spring, a failed harvest and aggressive grain raids by the authorities conspired to deprive the Volga farmers of food. There was obviously no point in Elizaveta staying in Shcherbatovka only to consume the provisions she'd brought at such risk to herself; after a week, in tears, she'd boarded the train back to Moscow. As the carriage rattled noisily, eyes closed, sobbing as discreetly as she could, she'd relived the events of the previous night.

She had attended the wedding of her friend Yelena, their hosts' daughter – a muted affair by the normal standards of the Volga Germans, sandwiched between two funerals. On the way back from the cemetery, Jakob and Elizaveta had overheard a conversation between the two oldest men in the village.

'Exactly how old are you?' one asked the other.

'You should know I am seventy-four. And you?'

'Eighty-one.'

'Well, it's hardly worth your while walking back to the village, is it?'

At first, Elizaveta had been horrified; then, as the old men guffawed, she joined in the laughter.

A pastor who'd been hiding near Saratov came to celebrate the wedding, and a pig was somehow reclaimed from the collective farm despite the fact that its kidnappers and executioners, the very farmers who had reared it at their own expense, thus rendered themselves liable to the death penalty.

How beautiful Yelena had looked in her long white dress, bridal wreath and veil! After the ceremony in her parents' house, instead of the traditional buckets of wheat, rye and barley that should have been showered upon the newly-wed couple to guarantee their fertility, only a few grains were carefully dropped on top of their heads and immediately picked up from the floor.

'*Viel Kinder – viel Segen,*' the guests had chanted, rhythmically stamping the floor as the accordions and violins came out: many children, great blessing. Much to the delight of all, the bride's shoe had been duly stolen and auctioned. After the ritual exchange of wreath and boutonniere, the blindfolded couple had been lifted by Jakob and three muscular friends onto two chairs tightly bound together; they had groped and kissed, while the onlookers cheered rowdily. Normally, the same thing would have happened to any engaged couples present too, but this time there were none.

'Jakob,' Elizaveta asked after waiting for more than an hour, 'won't you ask me to dance?'

Every summer, they used to wait for these post-harvest weddings with mounting impatience; it was their only opportunity to hold and touch each other, a practice they had grown increasingly fond of in recent years. With an apologetic half-smile he immediately got up and led her into a spirited polka. Looking at him, she felt her throat constrict. How he'd changed in one year! Belying his twenty years, vertical lines had appeared on each side of his mouth, furrows on his forehead, and he'd lost so much weight that his nose seemed bigger. Only his blue eyes and firm chin seemed impervious to the untold pressure and worries he'd been labouring under since his parents had lost their home, livelihood and social status. His grip was as firm as ever.

'Little cousin, I will gladly dance with you the whole night,' he said. 'But that may not be such a good idea.

As the son of kulaks, I am a kulak, an enemy of the people. Apparently there are spies and snitches everywhere: people are hungry.'

Suddenly Elizaveta felt that the time for dancing had passed.

'Come, Jakob,' she whispered, dragging him away from the barn into the warm night.

They didn't stop until they reached the big oak at the edge of the village, in which remnants of the tree house Jakob had built for her many years ago were just visible in the moonlight.

'Do you remember?' she asked softly. 'How we used to spend hours up there, and you would attract the birds and explain their names and habits to me?'

'Those days are gone, little cousin. I kill all the birds I catch nowadays.'

'Big cousin, I wish you'd stop calling me "little cousin",' she said.

'As you wish, little cousin.'

She put her arms around his neck.

'Kiss me – please,' she asked.

'But...'

'Kiss me, or I'll never talk to you again, big cousin.'

Thirteen years later, Elizaveta remembered her first kiss as if it had just happened: his warm, dry but soft lips, the steely hardness of his body pressing ever harder against hers, his hand cradling the back of her neck, hers in his tousled hair, the joyous intoxication of their shared asphyxia, the desire for more...

'It seems you are no child any more, Elizaveta,' he whispered. 'Indeed your mother keeps telling everybody how you handled the secret service thugs like a grown-up woman.'

She tried to pull his head towards hers. 'I had no choice,' she shrugged. 'Unlike now.'

Their second kiss was tender and gentle.

'Jakob, I don't want to go back to Moscow,' she said.

'You must. We can offer neither shelter nor food to anybody. You must survive, and help us from Moscow.'

'I want to stay with you.'

'I love you,' he whispered.

Their next kiss tasted of salty tears.

'What will happen to all of you?' she sobbed. 'Why don't you come to Moscow with me?'

Jakob remained silent.

'I'll come back,' she promised, holding him tightly. 'As soon as I can get enough supplies. I'll never let you down. I swear.'

Jakob took a step back and put his hands on her hips, sending tremors up and down her spine.

'I shall wait for you, Elizaveta Terisova,' he said gravely.

Is HE STILL WAITING, or long dead? As she stands in the garden of the Reich Chancellery in the warm Berlin spring of 1945, that question continues to torment NKGB Captain Elizaveta Terisova, as excruciating as ever. Of course, if Colonel Ivan Klimenko is to be believed, Jakob has been sent to an NKGB-run labour camp long ago, during the mass deportation of the Volga Germans ordered by the Kremlin in August 1941. According to him, not only is Jakob alive, but his survival depends on Elizaveta's continued compliance with all of Klimenko's wishes.

SHE REMEMBERS HOW, the morning after Yelena's wedding, Jakob had accompanied her in the old droshky to the train station in Engels, how he and Anna had waved interminable goodbyes from the platform, dwindling, shrinking, vanishing as in her nightmares, the train slowly accelerating, screened by clouds of hissing steam and billowing black smoke, until she wasn't sure whether the tiny specks she was waving back to were her loved ones, coal dust or just figments of her imagination.

Moving away from the window, she'd eventually found a seat, dried her face and tried to repulse the bleak premonitions which made her shudder. Little did she know that reality would turn out to be more calamitous than her worst fears, and that she would never see her mother again.

Anna had been so shocked by the disastrous decline in public health brought about by general malnourishment that she'd decided to stay behind and help, at least for a few weeks. She'd given her daughter two letters, one addressed to her husband, the other to the Moscow Faculty of Medicine. In the first, she described the outbreaks of typhus, tuberculosis and other infectious diseases that, if left unchecked, threatened to wreak havoc with the weakened population, and asked Nikolei Fedorovich to use his influence to support her application for temporary secondment to the Volga region. In her letter to the Faculty, she quoted the policy statement of Commissar Kaminskii himself:

'Our doctor should have high socialist morals. If he comes to a family on a collective farm, he becomes part of it. It is a question of the new moral fibre of our doctor. Comrade,' she'd concluded, 'I have gone to a collective farm, and it is now my family. I have the privilege of volunteering for a post in the village of Shcherbatovka, which is currently devoid of any medical facilities, and where, if no action is taken, serious epidemics will inevitably break out (at great expense to the fulfilment of grain production targets).'

The People's Commissariat for Public Health, duly alerted by Major Terisov about the wonderful act of selfless socialist heroism performed by his wife, and hardly encumbered by any other candidate, decided to turn Anna into a Hero of the Soviet Union. Her face appeared on posters, inviting young doctors to put aside their egocentric bourgeois tendencies, in order to bring the benefits of modern socialist medical sciences to the Moslem or nomadic tribes that populated the Soviet Asian Republics, as well as to the sixty percent of the population forcibly working on the newly collectivised farms.

When the government re-introduced internal passports, without which travelling was not only illegal but effectively impossible, they made sure Anna did not get one: there was no question of a Hero of the Soviet Union changing her mind and embarrassing the authorities by running away from fieldwork and turning up in Moscow.

It was the autumn of 1932, and Anna was trapped. That winter, her brother Gottfried and his wife Margaretha were deported to Central Asia. After the terrible spring of that year came the even worse spring of 1933. And then Anna's letters stopped.

In answer to her questions many years later, Vasily Grossman, the Soviet war reporter whom Elizaveta was to meet at the front, had replied:

'Do you really want to know, child? All right then. Yes, I was there, as a journalist. The true starvation began when the snow melted in the spring of 1933. People had swollen faces, legs, stomachs. They ate anything at all, from old shoes to ground-up bones. They caught mice, rats, sparrows, ants, earthworms. When the grass came up, they began to dig up the roots and ate the blades and shoots. By then they couldn't even contain their urine...'

Elizaveta had put her hand on his mouth and begged him to stop.

Grossman was a decent man. He did not tell her how the fertile Volga soil was covered with human corpses, and how special brigades gathered these bodies from the fields, streets and houses and threw them into ravines. Nor did he tell her about the growing commerce in human meat, or that people all over the countryside were killing and eating their own children. Neither did he show her his old photographs of the signs and posters put up by the authorities that read:

'EATING DEAD CHILDREN
IS BARBARISM'

In Moscow, Major Terisov and his daughter were going mad with worry. Visions of her emaciated mother stumbling head first into a mass grave awoke Elizaveta several times a night, and she bitterly regretted not having stayed with her and Jakob. Several times she announced she was going back to Shcherbatovka; several times, when she was desperate and impervious to argument, her father had to restrain her. Then she fell critically ill. As a doctor, Nikolei Fedorovich knew better than to belittle the risks; with infinite patience, through the spring months, he spoon-fed his daughter, talked and even sang to her, explained about the censorship, listened to her, and kept her hope alive.

It was at this time that Elizaveta truly discovered her father. During the years her mother had spent away at medical school, she'd been mainly looked after by his spinster elder sister; Nikolei Fedorovich been no more than a distant, if benevolent, figure, whose short daily appearances did little to alleviate her need for warmth. Now, in her fifteenth year, as he spent night after night on a camp bed at the foot of her sick-bed, tirelessly mopping her brow and soothing her whenever she woke up in spasms of terror, patiently coaxing water into her mouth, washing the vomit off her face or combing her hair, Elizaveta understood that her father was also capable of unconditional love. She understood he suffered from Anna's absence – if not from Jakob's – as acutely as she did, and took pity on his exhausted face and greying hair. In the cold darkness that had engulfed her, he was a fragile tower of strength, the only glimmer of light, a flicker, some deep instinct told her, that could all too easily be snuffed out by the simultaneous losses of a wife and a daughter. She decided to get better.

The summer of 1933 came and went without any news from the Volga. Travel to the region was impossible, and any inquiry into the developments in that republic perilous. All of a sudden, a wall had sprung up in the middle of the Soviet Union, beyond which land and people seemed to have dematerialised. Nevertheless, despite the government's threats, rumours of a cataclysmic combination of famine and disease continued to circulate. Elizaveta and her father tried to protect each other from these reports, or, when that proved impossible, to reassure each other that Anna, as a doctor and a Hero of the Soviet Union, was too valuable to the Party not to be looked after properly. Though dated September, the letter from Jakob that, in neutral and guarded terms, informed them of Anna's death did not arrive until November. He also mentioned that his parents had gone away the previous winter, and that he'd not heard from them since.

On receipt of this news, Nikolei Fedorovich crumpled

onto a chair, face hidden behind his hands, shoulders shaking. Never before had Elizaveta seen her father cry; she stood behind his chair and wept with him.

'I'm so proud of her,' she whispered when the first sobbing fit had run its course. 'She knew it would happen, didn't she?'

Unable to speak, her father nodded without looking up. Elizaveta picked up Jakob's tear-stained letter and finished reading it aloud, her voice faltering so often that her father could hardly follow.

'Do not worry about me. Things cannot get worse,' – Elizaveta's hands were trembling so much she had to sit down and place the letter on the table – 'and I have survived so far – though I'd rather be with my parents. What can be done for them? Please try everything you can to find out where they may be. But don't put yourself at risk. Please. Do not even think about coming down here. If ever I get an internal passport, I'll come and see you.'

The rest of the letter she did not read aloud. Both Elizaveta and her father perfectly understood Jakob's code. Though the very existence of the OGPU was unmentionable, and any investigation into the vast reaches of its archipelago of forced labour camps likely to swallow the enquirer, the fact that millions of so-called kulaks had been spirited into its harsh parallel universe wasn't unknown to them.

Nikolei Fedorovich hugged his daughter tightly.

'Your mother was a remarkable woman, Elizaveta,' he said. 'I knew it the minute I set eyes on her. I soon realised that she wasn't to be tamed. Like you, I did try to protect her. And now we have only each other. In these terrible times we cannot be too careful. This letter will have been seen by the censor; maybe they only delivered it as a bait. What happened to poor Uncle Gottfried and Aunt Margaretha is diabolical, but nothing can be done about it. We need to be very, very careful, Elizaveta – please.'

She pressed her cheek against his chest and remained silent.

IN THE FOLLOWING MONTHS, in full agreement with her father, Elizaveta Terisova made two decisions. First, she would study medicine and become a doctor. Her mother's work would be continued. Second, she would try and join the OGPU. This was where real power lay: the power to arrest and deport people arbitrarily, to try them on fabricated charges, to convict them on the exclusive basis of confessions extracted by psychological and physical torture. The power to shoot them. The power to deport entire populations to the wilderness of the Northern Territories or Siberia, and turn them into slaves working in the mining industry, forestry and construction.

The power to help them.

As far as Major Terisov was concerned, the secret service was as safe a place as could be wished for his daughter; he was experienced and pragmatic enough to recognise a case of 'If you can't beat them, join them' when he saw it. Elizaveta had different aspirations. The OGPU needed and trained doctors. Only by joining up could she eventually be of use to the gulag archipelago's inmates. Then somebody would have to tell Uncle Iosif of the injustices and atrocities committed in his name, so that he could put them right. The alternative was to join the vast conspiracy of silence in which most of the population colluded in uneasy fear, aware of what happened to their neighbours and might also befall them if they attracted attention or suspicion. She saw no point in that.

In the following year, the OGPU became the NKVD – the People's Commissariat of Internal Affairs – and launched a major recruitment offensive. In 1937, thanks to a written recommendation provided by their own Captain Mikhail Kozlov to the head of the NKVD, Mikhail Yezhov, the organisation recruited its dream agent, a beautiful eighteen-year-old woman with nerves of steel, just out of school, daughter of a Hero of the Soviet Union, mascot of the *Komsomol*, viewed by some as Stalin's favourite maiden.

Initially, Elizaveta was sent to medical school in Moscow. Some twenty percent of the inmates of the NKVD's two hundred forced labour camps, such as the Kolyma gold and uranium mine, were dying every year. It was difficult to achieve production targets, and the authorities hoped that more doctors would keep the workforce alive a bit longer, despite the atrocious cold and malnutrition.

Just as Elizaveta was nearing the end of her medical studies, war broke out. She was re-assigned to an NKVD

Rifle Division. Out of necessity, she became the 'war wife' of Colonel Klimenko and quickly rose through the ranks. And now, in May 1945, a weary, battle-hardened war veteran, she's received a crucial mission – from NKVD Chairman Merkulov himself. A mission that so far has defeated hundreds of Merkulov's agents. Yet failure isn't an option: Stalin has made that clear. Merkulov doesn't want to end up shot for treason, like his predecessors, Yagoda and Yezhov.

It's a mission crucial to Stalin's imperialistic agenda: find the German uranium stocks. No Soviet atomic bomb can be built without them. Unfortunately, their location appears known to one man only: Adolf Hitler. All other sources seem to have been methodically eliminated by the SS. And the Führer may well have taken his secret to the grave.

COLONEL IVAN KLIMENKO slid his fingers down the edge of the sharp tail-fin of an unexploded bomb protruding from a crater in the Reich Chancellery garden, before carefully circling around it.

'That's where Military Intelligence found the bodies,' he pointed at a blackened ditch surrounded by petrol cans. 'Or their charred remains, rather. Hitler and a blonde woman. And two dogs.'

'How could they identify them?'

'The bunker's chief engineer was still here. Hentschel. He witnessed everything.'

'And they believed him?'

'Not at the beginning. Nobody could believe that Hitler would have been so dumb as to wait for us in Berlin. Stalin still can't. But Hentschel stuck to his story and led them to two dental technicians who confirmed that the corpse's jaws were Hitler's. Apparently, they both recognised some very special molar bridge they'd made themselves for the Führer.'

'Well, that would be proof, I suppose.' She pointed at a dark mixture of mud, ashes and grease at the bottom of the trench. 'Does that mean that some of this muck belongs to the great leader himself?'

'So it appears.'

Intrigued by his tone, she looked up.

'You don't seem convinced, Comrade Colonel?'

'When our own NKGB people arrived, they looked for fingerprints. Not only were the hands burnt like crisp bacon, which was to be expected, but most of the man's fingers appeared to have been deliberately chopped off, as opposed to incinerated.'

'Why would anybody cut Hitler's fingers off?'

'You tell me.'

She frowns. 'No fingers, no fingerprints – fair enough. I can understand why Hitler may not have wanted his body to be recognisable. But if they were going to burn it, why bother?'

'Exactly. And, since the teeth were more likely to survive the fire than the hands, it's even more curious.'

'Does any of this matter? I mean, with positive identification of the jaws by forensic dentists, there can't be any doubt.'

Colonel Klimenko gave his war wife a quizzical look and gestured towards a rectangular, brownish cement block, some twenty-five feet high, with a narrow opening.

'Ready?' he asked.

The Russian Private first class who, proudly wearing his Stalingrad medal, was guarding the entrance, saluted and handed Elizaveta his yellow kerosene lantern.

'Tell me, Comrade,' she asked, 'what exactly is down there?'

'Stinking rubbish,' he sniggered. 'All the good stuff's been liberated a few days ago. If you're looking for stockings and fancy dresses, Captain – too late. We had a whole platoon of female medics in here yesterday. Believe you me: our Soviet doctors and nurses, they were fighting over the frilly bits like bears. Ah! Waving black satin brassieres and pink knickers over their heads – what a sight!'

At the bottom of the stairs they met a corporal who'd set up his quarters in a room with charred walls and ceilings, its floor covered in soot. He was sitting next to his submachine gun, playing with a long-barrelled German pistol, and had no idea that he was in Hitler's study.

The stench was unbearable. The ventilation system had stopped working ages ago, and death had repeatedly struck humans and animals in this deep, dank hellhole. Though the corpses of the former had been removed for identification, nobody had bothered to look for dead rats or unclog the latrines, which were still in use.

A pipe had burst, flooding the long corridor, so that the NKGB officers had to slosh through several inches of muck and slime. Elizaveta stopped and retched. Klimenko spotted half a dozen German gas masks hanging from a wall; he handed her one and donned another. They made the air slightly less poisonous.

It was obvious that units of the victorious Red Army had looted the place in their usual fashion. Among the heaps of detritus, not a single object of value was left; no watches, cameras, dress daggers, radios, clothes, alcohol or weapons. Only broken bottles and glass shards, empty weapon magazines, dented helmets, damaged tin cans, bloodied bandages, scattered playing cards, condoms.

But, despite the poor lighting, something immediately caught the NKVD-trained eyes of Colonel Klimenko and Captain Terisova. Most of the thirty-odd cubicles of the *Führerbunker* were stuffed with papers and printed material: files and dossiers, diaries and journals, military and police manuals, telephone books and radio codes, typed and handwritten letters.

This was doubly extraordinary. First, because until a couple of weeks ago the bunker had been a command post, and the Germans were traditionally fastidious about destroying all equipment and evidence before retreating from any headquarters. Second, because Red Army Intelligence didn't seem to have taken the slightest interest in this material.

When Klimenko held his lamp to the first notebook he picked up, he found himself looking in disbelief at Martin Bormann's personal diary. As he beckoned Elizaveta to come closer and take a look, a shot rang out. They both jumped as its echo reverberated through the concrete catacomb.

Adding to the *Führerbunker*'s body count with his 7.65mm calibre German pistol, the corporal has just shot a rat.

5

A Safe and Clean World

Lieutenant Colonel Wreford-Brown stood up and addressed his assembled officers: 'Gentlemen, the port of Kiel is the headquarters of the German Navy, and home to their most advanced research facilities. If the Red Army gets there before us, they will control the Baltic. Today, 4th May 1945, only we few hundred men of T Force stand between the full might of the Soviet Union and a potentially Communist Scandinavia. We know our duty. Let's be thankful that, at this late stage of the war, such a splendid place in history is offered to us. Good luck.'

As David Hunt, Max Harrison and I filed out of the briefing room, our detachment was ready to leave Lübeck for Kiel. But that very afternoon the German delegation that had been in talks with Field Marshal Montgomery surrendered all German forces in Holland, Northwest Germany and Denmark, with effect from 08:00 hours on 5th May.

Within ten minutes of the signing of the surrender order, General Miles Dempsey of the British Second Army ordered the four corps under his command to desist from any offensive and stay exactly where they were. There was no ambiguity in his words: 'No advance beyond this line to take place without orders from me.'

This was precisely the scenario the Allied Supreme Commander had wanted to avoid: Kiel was still under German control, within reach of Stalin's Red Army, while the Allied armies had to stand still. It presented T Force with a quandary.

Major Hunt had visited T Force HQ in Bremen on 1st May. According to him, he'd received a clear written order from staff officer Major Brian Urquhart: he was to race across sixty miles of German-held territory as soon as possible and grab all the Kiel targets listed in the black book he'd been given – some one hundred and fifty of them. Not only was Hunt supposed to accomplish this with only our two companies and a handful of assessors, engineers and pioneers, but Urquhart, lowering his voice to a conspiratorial whisper, had given him another brief:

'Now listen, David. We expect the Russians to launch their amphibious assault any time. You must grab Kiel before they do.'

'With a few hundred men?' Hunt had asked incredulously.

'If we let the Russians occupy Kiel, they'll control the entrance to the Baltic. And the Kiel canal. It will also deliver to them a year-round, ice-free port from which to threaten the North Sea. I have it on reliable authority that this prospect is so unpalatable to Churchill that he's chomping right through his cigars.'

So, at 18:00 on 4th May, just as the German delegation entered Monty's tent on Luneburg Heath to sign the surrender instrument, five hundred men of T Force Kiel were assembling at Lübeck. In order to move forward, we needed permission to pass through the positions of 8 Corps. At 21:00 I was sent to 8 Corps HQ in Hamburg to seek from its commander, Lieutenant General Evelyn Barker, authorisation to advance across his lines. However, much to my consternation, when I reported to the Duty Officer, I was told that 'Bubbles' Barker had gone to bed early and left categorical orders that no-one – not even a mouse – be allowed through the lines. The staff captain on duty was sorry, but there was nothing he could do.

'With respect, sir, we understand two SS divisions are converging on Neumünster,' I pleaded. 'By the time they get there, the only route from Hamburg to Kiel will be closed. Our orders are to move before 3 a.m. I'm afraid we can't wait until General Barker wakes up.'

'There is nothing I can do. My instructions are clear. Not even a fly is to get through our lines. We have a ceasefire scheduled for 8 a.m. General Barker isn't going to trigger any fighting before then. I'm afraid you'll just have to wait.'

At my insistence, the duty officer telephoned Lieutenant Colonel Bloomfield at T Force headquarters, who duly confirmed that T Force's orders were to advance on Kiel. Next, I asked him to call Brigadier Pennycook, who also confirmed the validity of the order and asked why the hell he should be woken in the middle of the night to reiterate his instructions. Still the captain refused to sign the movement order. Nothing doing. The duty officer apologised, but stood his ground. When I tried to explain to him the incalculable damage the free world would suffer if the Soviets were permitted to occupy Kiel, it proved counterproductive. Reaching for his little red book – *Instructions for British Servicemen in Germany, 1944* – the captain waved it impatiently and asked:

'Are you by any chance familiar with this, Lieutenant?' Before I could think of an answer, he read aloud: 'DON'T go looking for trouble. DON'T fall for attempts to create ill-feeling between us and our Allies, and in particular to stir-up anti Russian feelings.' He yawned and put the book down. 'The war is over, Lieutenant. No need to restart it. Why can't you relax, for God's sake?'

It was nearly midnight. Precious time was passing. Soon the road might be closed by the roaming SS divisions. Some fast thinking was required.

'I suppose you're right, sir,' I replied. 'At least I've tried. Looks like we'll have to wait for General Barker to wake up. May I sit down?'

'My dear chap – make yourself at home. Drink?'

The captain was visibly relieved that not only was the incident over, but he would have company through the long and lonely hours of his night watch. He'd been on duty for some thirty-six hours already and exhaustion was setting in.

'To be honest, I could do with one, sir – thank you. We might as well waste our time together profitably.'

The captain pulled a half-full bottle of Chivas Regal 25 Year-Old out of a drawer and poured two generous glasses. I'd never smelt anything like it.

'Down the hatch.'

Twenty minutes later the bottle was empty. The captain's mood had substantially improved.

'I say, Peacock, we did nail Jerry, didn't we?' he asked jovially.

'We certainly did, sir. Would you excuse me a minute?' I got up and walked to my jeep. On the way, I emptied my overflowing glass. I came back with a bottle of Heidsieck champagne. The captain, who'd fallen asleep at his desk, started as the cork popped with a loud bang.

'Christ all bloody mighty – where did you get that from, Pennycroft?' he asked with a hand on his pistol.

'My mother gave it to me, sir,' I lied. 'To celebrate victory.'

'Here's how,' the captain lifted his glass and drained it. 'To victory. We did lick the buggers, didn't we? Game, set and match.'

'Gave then a damn good hiding, sir,' I confirmed, refilling his glass.

'Capital woman,' the captain mumbled.

'I beg your pardon?'

'Your mother, Cookie. Utterly capital lady.'

'Thank you, sir. I'll be sure to tell her. By the way, sir, do you remember that order I showed you?'

'What about it?'

'Well, you said you would sign it for me, sir. Here it is.'

'Right you are. There! Anything else?'

BEFORE DAWN, I delivered the signed movement order to Major Hunt. T Force was ready to go. At the final briefing, Hunt summarised the situation.

'The first thing is to get there. Kiel is sixty miles away. We'll be leaving all Allied units behind us and penetrating deep into enemy territory. On no account get delayed on the road. On arrival, quickly deploy platoons towards the first ten targets as listed in your black books.'

'What's the position in Kiel itself, sir?' asked Max Harrison.

'As far as we know, some fifty thousand German military personnel. We can only hope they've heard about the cease-fire. Worse: half a million DPs on the rampage.' Hunt smiled wryly. 'Nothing we can't handle, gentlemen. After all, there are nearly five hundred of us. And a few buccaneers from 30 Advance Unit of the Royal Navy, doing their own thing as usual.'

Over the previous weeks, we'd grown used to small raiding parties of Royal Marine Commandos appearing out of nowhere to provision and refuel, then vanishing again in search of targets of particular naval interest. Much to the frustration of T Force staff officers and quartermasters, their interest in coordination and procedure seemed inversely proportional to their great piratical zeal. SAS and SBS teams were also operating behind enemy lines.

'If I may ask, sir – I heard on the radio the Germans surrendered yesterday, and there is to be no forward movement,' Max observed.

'Did you indeed?' Major Hunt replied. 'Well, gentlemen, my orders are to make it to Kiel in time for lunch. Unless I hear otherwise from the commander, that's where I'm heading. With all of you.'

At 07:00 on the wet, miserable morning of 5th May, the detachment left Lübeck for Kiel. First we went through the British lines, then through the German lines, leaving them equally astonished. Before we got to Bad Segeberg, the most forward Allied position, we were overtaken by a convoy of 30 Advance Unit driving at breakneck speed, White Ensign flying on the leading jeep, clearly in pursuit of the last opportunity for glory in the War in Europe that awaited the conquerors of Kiel. However, much to my satisfaction, we caught up with them in Neumünster, where, held up by a badly cratered road, they were busy changing tyres. Three convoys – T Force, SAS and 30 Advance Unit – left Neumünster together around 09:00 for the final 25-kilometre dash to Kiel.

From Bad Segeberg onwards the drive became quite eerie. No traffic either way, no roadsigns, none of the paraphernalia or wreckage of battle, no slit trenches and, ominously, no white flags. Now and then a couple of German soldiers in full kit, stragglers or wounded, were walking on the road; the convoys passed them at such speed that it was impossible to ascertain their reaction.

As we were driving past some woods, Rifleman Richardson noticed several soldiers darting into the cover of the trees, and thought he detected the matte silhouette of tanks. I was engrossed in map-reading and memorising target instructions. Only when we suddenly found ourselves driving past German barracks did I look up and catch the eye of two flabbergasted young sentries who hesitantly raised their guns. I waved cheerily as Richardson accelerated away. They didn't fire. Not on us, anyway.

Over the last five or ten kilometres the density of pedestrian traffic steadily increased. In ever larger groups, more and more fully-armed German soldiers were loitering on the road; some threw their weapons down, others bolted over fences and hedges, most froze on the spot and put their hands up as the convoy passed. Under constant drizzle, the quiet rural landscape, flat and muddy, smelt of earth and spring blossom. Scattered farmhouses and agricultural buildings seemed totally untouched by war, their front gardens coloured by bright tulips; yet I was keenly aware of the fact that the many coverts interspersed between the fields could be expected to hide any number of tank formations or die-hard Waffen-SS units, the smallest of which could easily wipe out British marauders. The words of the duty officer at Corps HQ were still ringing in my ears: 'Not even a fly is to pass through our lines'; I felt uneasy about the shabby way in which I'd treated the captain, and wondered whether I'd inadvertently blighted the man's career, and also whether this particular fly was just about to be swatted by a vengeful German fist.

Suddenly, White Ensign taut in its slipstream, its engine straining to overtake again, the leading jeep of Marines commandos which had fallen behind at Neumünster reappeared at the side of my Humber armoured car.

'What the hell do these chaps think they are doing?' I shook my head in disbelief. 'They never give up, do they?'

Richardson smiled and stood his ground for a while as both cars roared down the road neck and neck. Weighing nearly four tons, our armoured scout car was no sprinter however, and it was an unequal contest.

I saw it first. Hardly had time to shout. Just after a long bend, the wreck of an 88 mm gun was burning on the road, surrounded by plumes of oily smoke. Richardson had to move over to the left. That left no space for the commando jeep. Sideswiped by the much heavier Humber, it ran off the road, smack into an oak tree. Richardson slammed on his brakes and skidded to a halt, throwing me into the windscreen.

'Fuck me!' Richardson exclaimed. 'Pardon my French, sir. What the fuck do we do now?'

Dazed, I slowly turned around. Cautiously, I felt my neck and rubbed my forehead, noticing blood on my fingers. I looked out of the rear slit window. The jeep was missing its two front wheels. Limp and lifeless, two bodies were hanging over its sides; another precariously balanced on its shrivelled bonnet. The fourth one was splayed on the low branches of the tree; like a grotesque scarecrow swinging in the breeze, every five or ten seconds it jerked and slipped lower as twigs broke under its weight. Vapour was slowly rising from the ground where the shattered radiator had discharged. Bags, jerry cans and weapons were scattered about. The flock of indignant crows that had been dislodged by the impact were returning to the crown of the tree, whence the more enterprising among them were already launching cautious reconnaissance raids towards the carrion. Of the White Ensign there was no trace.

'On no account are we to get delayed on the road,' I mumbled, mopping the blood on my face with a handkerchief. 'Drive on.'

Richardson darted a bewildered look at me; then, with trembling sweaty hands, he restarted the stalled engine.

'Poor bastards,' he said. 'Imagine that. Not only dying after the war's ended – but killed by us.'

'For God's sake, Richardson – they were killed by a tree,' I corrected him. 'A German tree at that. Nothing to do with us. And nothing we can do about it.'

'Yes, sir. Quite right. Bloody German tree. Still – poor buggers.'

For a few kilometres, while I was radioing to report the accident and summon help, my heart still pounding wildly, we made such good progress that I was expecting to catch up with the rearguard of T Force any time. Bemused German farmers, no doubt alerted by the recent passage of the convoy, were leading their cattle to safety or silently staring at the solitary British vehicle speeding past them. Partly concealed behind their windows, their womenfolk surreptitiously watched the arrival of the new masters; some were busy putting out white flags. No children were to be seen.

'Put your foot down, Richardson,' I said. 'Our boys will have woken up the whole of the German army by now. We stragglers might get punished.'

No sooner had I finished speaking than we heard the sound of sporadic gunfire ahead. Richardson looked at me. I shrugged and threw my hands up with a thin smile. Rarely had being proved right felt more unpleasant.

All of a sudden, the road was blocked by throngs of DPs who had just broken out of their camps, walking skeletons on a westward pilgrimage. As they waved and screamed frenziedly, Richardson had to slow down to a crawl.

'For Christ's sake, keep going!' I shouted over the din. I knew that if our vehicle came to a standstill we'd probably never be able to move again. As the Humber steadfastly inched forward, it looked more and more likely that in the general commotion some of the emaciated bodies that were begging for food in every European language were going to be pushed under the wheels. Beads of sweat were rolling down Richardson's forehead and more than once he closed his eyes when some slight shudder in the steering column suggested a foot or leg had just been trampled.

'Don't stop. Keep moving – at all costs!' I urged. I slid

the top hatch open and stood up behind the Bren machine gun, gesticulating wildly to demand free passage. In supplicating or threatening gestures, dozens of scrawny hands tried to grab me. Out of the enlarged eye sockets of many of these desiccated creatures tears were freely pouring. Joy, despair, frustration, hunger? Their rags were so scant and tattered that through them I could see bones and joints jutting.

'No food!' I shouted. '*Rien à manger! Keine Nährung! Nichts zu essen!* Move back! *Zurück! Zurück!*'

The clamour from the piteous mob just grew stronger. Amid much jostling, three vociferous men and a skinny girl managed to climb onto the vehicle, one on each of the horizontal front mudguards and two on the flat bonnet. The girl was so close that I clearly saw the pustules and blisters festering all over the parched and dirty skin of her arms and sagging breasts. I couldn't understand a word they were saying, and guessed they must be Slavs – Poles, or possibly Russians.

'*Keine Lebensmittel!* Off! Off with you, dammit!' I shouted furiously, waving them away.

To no avail. We were ensnared. There was nothing for it but to scare them off. I quickly retrieved my Sten gun and fired a burst in the air. The wailing missed a beat, then instantly rose to a mad crescendo. Only at the last second, with half an inch to spare, would the crazed pilgrims stumble out of the way of the front wheels of the Humber. It dawned on me that we would have to fight our way to Kiel. To carry out our orders, we had to kill nationals of friendly countries, starving victims of the Nazis, the skinny girl who was now singing 'God Save the King' and blowing kisses at me. In despair, I brought the barrel of the gun down and fired another volley inches above their heads. With a howl, the hordes closed in from all sides, bony hands frantically extended in gestures of denial, friendship or wretchedness, grabbing my battledress, trying to disarm me. I took aim at the man on the nearside front wing. 'Hop off!' I yelled, shaking with fear and frustration. 'This is your last bloody chance. Off you jump – on the count of three. One!'

Four feet away, the former slave labourer held my gaze, smiling out of oversized blue eyes.

'Two!'

With one hand the man was holding on to the car's wing mirror; he extended the other palm up towards me, as though trying to block off the barrel of the submachine gun or intercept the bullets. Shaking my head in anguished disbelief, I clenched my teeth. I felt the car was about to come to a final stop. On no account get delayed on the road. I had to do it. Now. I only had sight of the man's head and trunk. I decided that it was more humane to put a bullet through his head.

'Here you are, sir!' Richardson called from inside the Humber.

I glanced down the hatch. Richardson was flourishing half a dozen two-ounce bars of Cadbury's *Dairy Milk* chocolate. Without letting go of the Sten gun, I grabbed the chocolate, held it high and slowly showed it to the mob, left and right, right and left. The consecrated Host in a gold monstrance shown to these Poles by the Holy Father himself couldn't have been more effective. Awed by the prospect of divine nourishment, dozens of wild eyes moved left and right, right and left, focusing on this heavenly manna. The racket died down to an awed murmur. With perhaps a split second to go before the former-slaves lunged at me in a rabid assault, I threw the chocolate as far as I could, half to the right, half to the left. With a growl that seemed to emanate from hollow bones more than diseased lungs, they jumped off in a chaotic stampede and started fighting like hyenas. The road was free; but only after we'd weaved our way around the bodies of the DPs who'd been run over or shot by the main convoy could the Humber again reach its maximum fifty miles an hour.

Before eleven, our convoy was climbing up the arched, steel bridge leading into the heart of Kiel. Or what was left of it. Since its first raid on the Baltic port on 2nd July 1940, the RAF had returned many times, unleashing massive firestorms throughout the city. The last of ninety bombing raids had taken place only a couple of nights ago. Once again the town hall had been eviscerated by a bomb that, this time, had penetrated right to its cellars; yet, as we looked down on the devastated city from the high bridge, its medieval belfry, one of very few recognisable landmarks, still jutted out of the ocean of rubble, an explanatory finger pointing towards the sky. All around, millions of tons, millions of cubic metres of smouldering debris and mangled metal, eighty percent of all houses damaged or destroyed, titanic warships – the heavy cruisers *Admiral Hipper* and *Admiral Scheer*, the light cruiser *Emden* – humbled, capsized, or lying on the bottom of the harbour, scuppered by their crews. Where ammunition dumps and all manner of ordnance and heavy weaponry, including artillery and anti-aircraft guns, had been blown up by German units, fires were still raging; without any water supply, there was little the exhausted firemen could do, and plumes of black smoke, dust and ashes combined with the low cloud to bathe Kiel in a funereal half-light. At the first crossroads after the bridge, the convoy dispersed. One company turned right, in search of its first five targets. My platoon went straight ahead with the other company. Our first target was the most valuable of all: the Walterwerke; hopefully, complete with the legendary Herr Walter, the world's leading expert on marine propulsion and designer of the closed-cycle turbine and torpedo.

As we reached the docks, we came under rifle fire from the crew of the *Admiral Hipper*, which was sitting on the bottom alongside the quay where she'd been scuttled. Fortunately, our trucks were too close for the mighty cruiser to engage us with its eight-inch guns or anti-aircraft batteries, any one of which would have wiped us out in seconds. Major Hunt had the company quickly dismount and return fire, bullets ricocheting all over the massive, glittering steel infrastructure overhanging the quay. Soon a white flag appeared on the deck, and Hunt sent me and my platoon to take the surrender of the battleship. Fortunately, as we scrambled up the gangway, I had no time to take in the magnitude of the task.

The ship's captain, Kapitän zur See Hans Henigst, returned my salute. A stocky man in immaculate uniform, he was surrounded by half a dozen officers and a squad of fully-armed ratings, all pointing rifles at our five-strong T Force detachment.

'What do you want?' he asked.

'I've come to accept your surrender, sir,' I replied.

'I'm afraid I cannot give it to you.'

Not a good start. Had we just fallen into the usual trap?

'As you've put out white flags, sir, I don't quite understand,' I said with all the firmness I could muster.

'I can only surrender to an officer of a rank equivalent or higher to mine, lieutenant. You should know that.'

Clearly my recent, automatic promotion to the rank of full lieutenant, while a source of some satisfaction to me, failed to impress the old stickler. I wondered whether to disclose that the highest ranking officer leading T Force Kiel was a simple Army major, definitely junior to a naval captain, and thought better of it.

'I'm very sorry, sir, but that may not be possible,' I said. 'I'm afraid that all our senior commanders are currently busy taking the surrender of the Admiralty.'

'Then I think you should leave my ship now, lieutenant.'

'As you wish, sir. May I point out what the consequences will be if I leave without your surrender?'

Kapitän Henigst raised his eyebrows.

'I will immediately call air support. Your ship will be bombed within half an hour and you and your crew blasted into oblivion. With respect, since the war is over, I'm not sure that will serve any useful purpose – sir.'

The German commander looked at the sailors whose eyes were fixed on his face. With these men, the few survivors of the original crew of sixteen hundred, he'd forced the entrance of the Trondheimsfjord and conquered Norway in 1940, sunk the destroyer *Glowworm* and fought the Royal Navy for five long years, attacked scores of Allied convoys in the icy waters and appalling storms of the North Atlantic. With them, here in Kiel's dry dock, he'd recently endured the venomous RAF raid of 9th/10th April. He looked towards the other side of the harbour, where the elephantine hull of the capsized *Admiral Scheer*, sister ship to the *Hipper*, sunk that same night by the RAF, was obscenely exhibiting her underbelly complete with lifeless propellers and redundant rudder. He saluted his men and said:

'*Danke, Männer.* It's been a privilege. Drop your guns. God bless Germany.'

Then he took his side-arm out of its holster and handed it over to me. Barely an hour later, we found the Royal Navy commandos from 30AU at the entrance of the extensive Walterwerke, where thousands of engineers had been conceiving, designing, building and testing some of the most advanced weapons systems in the world. Preventing this technology from leaking to Japan or falling into Soviet hands was paramount.

The complex was vast; the directors' offices alone occupied a four-storey building, where the storage areas
were noticeably empty of records and documents. Only
the massive submarine pens, covered by yards of concrete, seemed undamaged by bombs. Navy commandos
searched the huge workshops, looking for the fast submarines whose miraculous engines did not need oxygen
to work and could therefore remain concealed underwater indefinitely, unlike our diesel-electric submarines, and
for the guided or zig-zagging torpedoes that could have
changed the course of naval warfare. I stayed in the office block, repeatedly asking the astounded staff the same
question: 'Where is Doktor Walter?'

Eventually we were taken to an oak-panelled board-
room on the top floor where Germany's most famous engineer, a thickset man in his mid-forties with raven black
hair, seemed to have been waiting. Though he appeared
perfectly civil and ostensibly prepared to collaborate with
the Allies, it soon became clear that he wasn't playing
ball. I put a simple question to him.

'Herr Walter, clearly all your archives have been moved.
Where are they?'

'Ah. I'm afraid we were ordered by our High Command to burn all our documents,' he answered. 'Tragic.
My lifetime's work gone up in smoke.'

'What have you been working on?'

'Don't you know?'

The podgy engineer sounded miffed.

'Hydrogen-peroxide closed-cycle engines for underwater propulsion, jet engines for fighter planes, rocket motors…'

'And you've lost all the documentation related to this work?'

'Most of it, certainly. I'm told fifty thousand files, technical charts and drawings have been incinerated over the last five days.'

'Where?'

'Right here. We have our own incinerator.'

'By whom?'

'Our office staff, of course.'

'How many of them?'

Walter looked up in surprise.

'I'm not sure… Perhaps fifty?'

'Would I be right in assuming that the average weight of a paper file, chart or drawing would be less than one hundred grams?' I asked.

Walter shifted his weight from one foot to the other, scrutinising my face. 'It depends,' he said uneasily.

'Let's assume I'm right,' I went on. 'This means you had fifty people spend five days burning five tons of paper. In other words, each employee had to deal with one hundred kilos. They could have done so in one day: that's only ten trips to the incinerator for each one of them, carrying ten kilos. In fact they could have finished by lunchtime. What happened to the famed German productivity, Herr Walter?'

The scientist sat down at the long, waxed board table and nodded slowly.

'Impressive mental calculation, lieutenant. But it is not entirely clear to me what you're driving at.'

'I'm willing to believe you had five tons of documents in this building: I can see the empty shelves. But you haven't spent the last five days burning them, Doktor Walter. I suspect your lifetime's work is still around. But it would be a lot safer under our protection. Do you realise how much the Russians want it?'

Walter got up again and slowly paced the length of the room. I waited.

'Perhaps you're right, lieutenant. And perhaps you're wrong. The fifty thousand documents were incinerated.'

'Doktor Walter, I regret I must place you under arrest,' I replied.

'However, we may be able to help each other,' the engineer continued. 'But first you must get me a written order from Admiral Dönitz's HQ in Flensburg confirming that all my research secrets are to be handed over to the British.'

I immediately reported my conversation to the commanding officer of 30AU, who promptly left for Flensburg. When he returned two days later, carrying the order signed by Dönitz, Doktor Walter finally elected to cooperate with us. It emerged that the files had indeed been burnt, but only after microfilm copies of each had been made, which explained why the process had taken so long.

Under the personal supervision of Doktor Walter, six tin drums full of microfilm copies had been buried at six different beach locations. Technical devices, instruments and prototypes had been sunk into lakes and ponds in the countryside. Having immediately recovered the drums, Major Hunt deployed platoons to guard the other targets until technicians as well as diving and lifting equipment were provided by the Royal Navy. On that day Colonel Wreford-Brown came to visit his company commanders in Kiel.

'Well done, gentlemen,' he said at dinner. 'You seem to have captured the headquarters of the Kriegsmarine complete with a garrison of tens of thousands. Not bad for a couple of hundred men.'

'Thank you, sir' Major Hunt replied. 'To be honest, it was a doddle.'

'Good. There is a small difficulty, though.'

'A difficulty?'

Colonel Wreford-Brown drained his glass of claret and put it down on the table thoughtfully.

'The fact is, David, you're in a spot of bother. The commander of the British Second Army himself is after you.'

'General Dempsey? What on earth for?'

'Somehow, General Dempsey was under the impression that 8 Corps disobeyed his standstill order of 4th May, thus jeopardising the armistice.'

'And did they?'

'As it happens, the commander of 8 Corps, Lieutenant General Evelyn Barker – though a Rifleman himself – has taken grave exception to the charge. He had no difficulty in proving that he had in fact relayed the standstill order to all his units in good time and in the most precise terms.'

'I see.' Major Hunt put down the fork he'd just loaded with a chunk of pork stew.

'According to General Evelyn Barker, one of his staff officers was despicably tricked by one of your junior officers into signing an invalid movement order. In summary, you've deliberately defied the clear orders of a corps commander and wilfully advanced beyond the line fixed by the commander of the British Second Army. Even in normal circumstances this would call for a major rocket. But the circumstances are far from normal. General Dempsey believes that in crossing the agreed line you have given the Germans an excuse to ignore the terms of the surrender and to fight on in Norway and elsewhere. We're talking court martial here.'

A long pause ensued. Only at the end of it did I notice I'd stopped chewing.

'Well, maybe not such a doddle after all,' Major Hunt said.

'If I may, sir,' I interjected, 'when trying to get this movement order, I did call Lieutenant Colonel Bloomfield at T Force headquarters – and he confirmed it directly to 8 Corps.'

'Did you, Birkett? Good move. Let's hope he remembers the call,' Wreford-Brown answered.

'That's not all, sir. I also got Brigadier Pennycook on the line. Most upset at being woken up. He too confirmed the order.'

'I'm afraid Brigadier Pennycook isn't exactly flavour of the month at Second Army HQ. But it might help your case. No doubt you realise, Birkett, that you'll be up against it. Barker is livid. Definitely after your scalp.'

'But isn't it the case that T Force has effectively taken the surrender of the whole of the Kiel garrison and German Admiralty and Navy, all forty thousand of them, practically without firing a shot?' Max Harrison asked. 'I mean to say, sir, we haven't exactly started World War Three, have we?'

'That's probably what annoys Barker most,' Wreford-Brown replied with a wink. 'I understand that when the men of 8 Corps, led by the tanks of the Guards, all spick and span, arrived in parade formation to liberate Kiel this afternoon, they were more than a little miffed to see T Force signs at all junctions, and T Force washing hanging out to dry everywhere.'

'Poor lads. I suppose they'd have preferred being fired on,' Max said.

'Where does that leave us, sir?' Major Hunt asked.

'Unfortunately, David, I have no option but to put you and Birkett under arrest. Since you are the senior major here, you'll have to guard yourself. I've brought you a bottle of champagne in case you get bored – and also to celebrate a brilliant operation.'

'Under arrest?' Hunt repeated. 'I say – that's a bit of a shock. And to think I fought the Boche all the way from the Normandy beaches only to be arrested in Kiel.'

'Don't take it personally, David,' said Wreford-Brown.

'Hopefully it will blow over. Brigadier Pennycook is working his contacts. By the way, he was incredibly chuffed by that twelve-cylinder Mercedes you gave him. Thrilled to bits, in fact.'

'I always knew it was a brilliant idea,' Max Harrison whispered into my ear. 'Might even save your bacon, old boy.'

So it was that, next day, as we sat around a wireless set to listen to the Prime Minister's victory speech, both Major Hunt and I were technically under arrest. Much to our surprise, Churchill's mood, far from being triumphant, was almost as sombre as our own.

'I wish,' the familiar voice crackled over the airwaves, 'I could tell you tonight that our toils and troubles were over. But, on the contrary, I must warn you that there is still a lot to do, and that you must be prepared for further efforts and further sacrifices to great causes.

'On the continent of Europe, we have yet to make sure that the words "freedom", "democracy" and "liberation" are not distorted from their true meaning. There would be little use in punishing the Hitlerites for their crimes if law and justice did not rule, and if totalitarian or police governments were to take the place of the German invaders.'

'I'm wondering, sir – do you see any sign of law and justice around?' I asked.

'Why don't you call me David?' Hunt replied. I nodded.

'Hasn't Stalin already grabbed half of Europe?' Max wondered.

'He certainly has. The question is whether we'll let him keep it,' Hunt answered.

'So are we going to be at war with the Russians as well as the Japanese?' I asked.

'Shh,' Hunt hissed.

We fell silent again as the distant voice roared through its final exhortation: 'I told you hard things at the beginning of these last five years; you did not shrink, and I should be unworthy of your confidence and generosity if I did not still cry: forward, unflinching, unswerving, indomitable, till the whole task is done and the whole world is safe and clean.'

Hunt turned off the radio.

'There you have it, gentlemen. We have officially won the second World War. The BLA has done its job.'

'BLA?' Max asked.

'British Liberation Army, you charlie,' I laughed.

'Actually, I have it from the highest authority that it means Burma Looms Ahead,' retorted Max.

'You may well be right about that,' said Hunt.

'Rather sounds as if old Winston is terrified at the prospect of peace,' I mused. 'Maybe he can't cope with it.'

'What's the matter with you, Peter?' Max asked. 'Why can't you just look forward to the prospect of making the whole world safe and clean – like the rest of us?'

'Because I'm under bloody arrest, and just about to be bloody court-martialled for making Kiel safe.'

'Ah yes, but you forgot to clean it up, didn't you?' Max giggled.

'I'm glad you find it funny.' I kicked him playfully.

'All right. Let me make a practical suggestion to get you out of your pickle. Why don't you invite your friend, the staff captain at 8 Corps, for another victory drink and get him to sign your release order?'

Hunt couldn't repress a smile.

'Oh, very droll,' I groaned. 'I wonder what my father will say when he hears about this.'

'The lawyer? Norman Birkett?' Hunt enquired. 'We might need a good barrister.'

'Unfortunately my father was called to the Bench three or four years ago, sir – David, I mean.'

'Oh well. I suppose the country needs good judges. Wasn't he on some kind of Home Office committee at the beginning of the war?'

'He was. In fact he chaired the Committee on Appeals from internment orders made by ministers under the Emergency Powers Act.'

'What was that?'

'Well, apparently ministers have the power to detain anybody without charge or trial in the interest of national security. Enemy aliens as well as persons suspected of Fascist sympathies.'

'I thought only the Nazis gave themselves powers like that,' Max said.

'Oh no. We did too. The Americans rounded up all their Japs. The Russians deported all their Germans. But the difference may be that in our country there is an appeal mechanism. My hapless father had to sit through some fifteen hundred such cases. And he wasn't even paid to do it.'

'Did he release many?'

'Of course. He once told me that, though MI5 and the Secret Services want everybody interned, he simply couldn't condone the indefinite detention of some simple German *au-pair* girl who's posing no threat whatsoever to anybody. He said he wanted to keep some small element of justice alive in a world in which we are supposed to be fighting for it.'

'Good for him,' said Max. 'But I wouldn't bet on leopards changing their spots. Spooks typically don't care for the rule of law, do they? Your father is a marked man, old chap. As are you, since their curse will be visited down the generations.'

Many a word spoken in jest... What would MI5 make of the fact that my mother was German, née Sophie von Morhof? How would my comrades react, were they ever to find out my secret? Curiously, nobody had enquired yet about my knowledge of the language. How long would that last?

Major Hunt stood up, stretched and grabbed the bottle of champagne.

'Care to join me, gentlemen?'

He poured three glasses.

'To victory.'

'To victory.'

'And to a safe and clean world,' I added.

BERLIN WAS SURPRISINGLY warm as Major David Hunt and I arrived in late May. We'd been summoned by the American General Ray Barker, Deputy Chief of Staff, Supreme Headquarters Allied Expeditionary Force, currently in town to negotiate with his counterpart, Marshall Zhukov, the return of Allied prisoners of war under Soviet control. God knows we'd seen appalling destruction over the last few weeks – yet we were dumbstruck by the surreal cityscape.

The Reichstag was still standing, a colossal hulk so indestructible that even the untrammelled fury of hell could not bring it down; but its cupola was shredded, the square towers at both ends of the façade truncated, its ponderous Neoclassical elevation rendered almost lace-like by myriad direct hits. In a feat of heroic horsemanship, the riders on the equestrian statues atop the peristyle remained in the saddle. From their vantage point, the view in all directions was of a battlefield. Everywhere, all manner of burnt vehicles, Russian T-34 tanks and SU122 tank-destroyers, trams, cars, self-propelled guns, bullet-riddled Volkswagen, German four-barrelled 20mm flak guns, upturned trucks and lorries lay interspersed with thousands of empty shell-cases. All around, the gutted apartment blocks stood gaunt and transparent, empty, roofless husks into which the bright sunlight fell unhindered. The scenery around the Brandenburg Gate was hardly different; here again, the Quadriga, that Napoleon had taken to Paris only to lose it after Waterloo, remained in full gallop above the massive arch, whose columns emerged from a waist-high layer of debris and carcasses. Below the steeds that pull Victory's chariot, a huge Russian banner proclaimed:

'LONG LIVE THE SOVIET ARMIES!'

At its foot, a pretty Russian auxiliary was directing almost nonexistent traffic with the help of two red flags; she didn't bat an eyelid when our English jeep crawled slowly by.

Early for the meeting, we spent half an hour leisurely exploring the centre, where every single tree bore witness to the cataclysm that had befallen the capital of the Thousand-Year Reich. The maimed sycamore trees on Schinkelplatz exhibited more bullet marks than leaves. Out of the fields of rubble behind the main building of the Humboldt University on Unter Den Linden, amputated trunks emerged like malformed poles. Adding insult to injury, and oblivious to the damage suffered by its noble hosts, the ivy that parasitically clinged to them was thriving as never before, its lusciously green garland sheathing and strangling the contorted trees.

For the first time since we'd entered Germany, we observed children at play in the streets. Here, three little girls, dirty hair neatly combed back or held in short plaits, one barefoot, another in sandals and the third in white socks and shiny black Sunday shoes, extracted from a two-storey-high mound of ruins the shiniest pieces of debris and lined them up neatly on the kerb;

then, with the chalkiest bits, they drew on the tarmac realistic pictures of gallows, complete with dangling bodies. There, little boys were re-enacting the Battle of Berlin with improvised swords, lunging at debonair Kazakh soldiers who parried the attack with dustbin lids and gave them a piece of bread for each successful hit, while anxious mothers looked on from makeshift shelters. Squatting among the ruins, women were attempting to cook for their families, pans precariously balanced on bricks above a meagre wood fire. The front of a large apartment block had been sheared off, leaving six storeys of rooms exposed to view; incredibly, despite the scant shelter and obvious risk, some families still resided up there, as though on rickety balconies with no railings. Moving slowly, old women clad in black were foraging for fuel among the wrecked houses. A pale youth found a left shoe in reasonable condition and put it into his rucksack. Soviet troops were omnipresent, both arms covered up to the elbow with stolen watches, washing themselves or their linen in the middle of the streets wherever water was available, resting, looking for alcohol, or going about their various duties. Watched by a silent group of a dozen civilians, a Russian infantryman attempted to wrest a bicycle out of the hands of an unyielding middle-aged woman. She lost both the bicycle and the bag hanging from the handlebar. As it was midday, she wasn't raped.

Twice, our T Force jeep was challenged by Soviet Military Police surprised to see a British vehicle in a city that officially only the Red Army occupied; but each time the combination of a pack of Lucky Strikes and the pass provided by General Barker and countersigned by some Soviet authority or other restored hearty comradeship between victorious Allies.

'One thing I don't understand,' Major Hunt said as we progressed towards our destination. 'Look at all these collapsed buildings. Mountains of rubble everywhere. Yet, over the last few weeks, we always found the roads passable, didn't we? In Hanover, in Kiel, even here, most roads have been cleared. Look: millions of tons of debris, ruins, wreckage, everywhere. Yet we are driving through the city on reasonably tidy roads. Who did the clearing?'

'Good question. Can't have been our side, since we usually moved forward ahead of them. Do you think the women might have been press-ganged to do it with their bare hands?'

'Well, I wouldn't expect much machinery or fuel to have been available to them, would you?'

'I suppose not. The alternative is that perhaps these buildings imploded, so that most of the masonry would have collapsed on the spot, on both sides of the streets.'

Major Hunt reflected for a moment.

'I suppose it depends what we dropped on them,' he concluded. 'High explosive would definitely have blown a few bits and pieces apart. On the other hand incendiaries wouldn't. After the fire you'd get empty shells like these.' His eyes darted right and left. 'Of course, the residents would have been buried alive in their cellars as their buildings collapsed on top of them.'

Suddenly, forbidden thoughts almost breached my defences. I mustn't think of them. Not now. It wasn't only my mother who was dead: all her family – half my family – too. Dead and buried. Or cremated? Hamburg was the worst.

We both knew that for General Ray Barker to have become involved in our case was serious. Despite Brigadier Pennycook's efforts, the matter must have escalated considerably for General Eisenhower's deputy to take an interest. Better not to think about the imminent meeting. To my dismay, we continued speculating about the physics of Armageddon until that dead horse couldn't take any more flogging.

When we arrived, General Barker was in a bad mood. The matter of the return of Allied POWs liberated by the Red Army should have been straightforward. As usual, it was not.

The Russians were playing games, invoking administrative and logistical difficulties to delay releasing the Allied soldiers under their control. They insisted that all the Russian and East European POWs liberated by the Allies be handed over to them first; the problem was that the majority of them had no wish whatsoever to surrender themselves to Comrade Stalin, whose intentions they rightly distrusted. Nevertheless, much to General Barker's dismay, if the Allied POWs were to be recovered promptly, these poor East European souls, freshly released in their millions from Nazi factories and death camps, would have to be shipped to the Gulag – dead or alive. He did not get up as we entered his office and saluted him.

'Ah, the rebel soldiers,' General Barker said without a hint of humour as we stood to attention. He was a clean-shaven man whose crew-cut black hair was just beginning to turn silver at the temples. His eyes were brown and tired, his brows the shape of a circumflex accent.

'With respect, sir, Lieutenant Birkett did nothing but follow my orders,' Hunt replied.

General Barker pointed at the Military Cross on Hunt's chest.

'You have a distinguished service record, Major. Second to none. How could you destroy it in such reckless fashion? What on earth did you think you were doing, disobeying clear and categorical orders?'

'Sorry – I don't believe I have done any such thing, sir.'

'Were you not aware of the standstill order given by General Dempsey?'

'Not directly, sir. On the other hand I had personally received orders from my HQ to proceed to Kiel immediately.'

'From whom?'

'Major Brian Urquhart.'

'On whose authority?'

'With respect, sir, that's a question for Major Urquhart. For what it's worth, I heard on the grapevine the order came from General Eisenhower himself. However it was confirmed by both Lieutenant Colonel Bloomfield and Brigadier Pennycook. I had no reason to defy my superiors, and did not do so – despite the extremely risky nature of the operation.'

'Complete madness, if you ask me. What's the matter with you Brits? Why can't you behave sensibly?'

'That particular question might be best addressed to our Prime Minister, sir. I understand Mr Churchill was quite keen not to let the Russians take Kiel.'

'Your Prime Minister is certainly not keen on our Russian allies – that's no secret. And frankly they are a pain in the butt, no doubt about that either. Just as well they didn't get Kiel, I'll grant you that. But that's not the point, Major – and the risks were enormous.'

'So they were, sir.'

General Barker stood up, the red, blue, white and mauve of his Distinguished Service Medal, Legion of Merit and Bronze Stars ribbons aligned in a surprisingly harmonious array of colour on the flap of his left breast pocket. He walked around his desk.

'What about you, Lieutenant? I have here a report from my British namesake, General Evelyn Barker' – he pointed at a pink folder on his desk – 'that accuses you of wilful deception in order to circumvent clear orders. Disgraceful. Have you got anything to say for yourself? Any reason why you shouldn't be court-martialled?'

'I only tried to execute my orders to the best of my ability, sir. I'm sorry if it's caused embarrassment or confusion.'

'I wish I could believe that.'

'I can confirm it, sir,' Major Hunt said.

'All right then. I will seek confirmation of your asser-tions about the orders you received. If I get it, you're off the hook. If I don't, you'll face a court martial. Insubor-dination is no small thing. I must say however the whole thing sounds more and more like a regular cock-up.'

'Thank you, sir.'

General Barker stepped forward and lowered his voice, so that the two aides who were standing by his desk couldn't hear.

'By the way – congratulations, Major. By all accounts this was a remarkable operation. I couldn't have handled the situation in Kiel better myself. Having the Russians in such a strategic port would be a disaster. Having them anywhere is a goddamn disaster, believe you me.'

'Thank you, sir.'

We saluted smartly and made for the door. As we reached it General Barker suddenly called:

'One more thing! No more misunderstandings, gentle-men. I have not, repeat not, ordered you to mount any kind of raid on Moscow. Is that clear?'

'Crystal-clear, sir.'

As the door closed behind us, we heard sonorous guf-faws. Hunt looked at me, eyebrows arched in puzzlement.

'Crikey! What do you make of that?' I asked.

'I think it got off to a bad start, but in the end he be-lieved us.'

'Anyway, David, thanks for exculpating me. Jolly big of you.'

'We all obeyed orders, Peter. No reason why junior officers should be hassled for that. In fact it would be the end of the bloody Army if one tried to second-guess orders.'

'So you think one should always blindly obey orders?'

'Basically, yes. The alternative is chaos.' He stopped to light a cigarette and winked. 'Mind you, if truth be told, we did generate a certain amount of chaos, didn't we?'

We both began to laugh.

'Shall we go for a quick walk?' Hunt asked 'I've never been in Berlin before. Have you?'

'No. I'd love to see Hitler's lair. Why do you think his body hasn't been found yet?'

'Perhaps Stalin had him stuffed and hung on a Kremlin wall.'

I tried to visualise the image, then shook my head. 'Could he be down in Bavaria, organising resistance with his Werewolves, or whatever they call themselves?'

'That would be pretty pointless, wouldn't it?'

'Who can tell? That's what they used to say about the French and Dutch resistance.'

Ambling toward the Reich Chancellery, we passed a group of barefoot little boys in ragged shorts playing with the remnants of a tank tread, huffing and puffing in their efforts to drag segments of the huge metal caterpillar incongruously stranded on the street cobbles. In the Wilhelmstrasse, adults had turned the area in front of the devastated hulk of the Chancellery into an improvised playground; six of them were see-sawing at opposite ends of a long telegraph pole balancing on a pile of broken timber, three young men in formal hats at one end and three merry young women in long dresses at the other.

Children were looking on, patiently waiting their turn. A one-legged war veteran war sitting on a low wall, attempting to earn money by playing a violin; he was overjoyed when we gave him a cigarette. We moved unchallenged through the ruins of the Reich Chancellery, the former seat of Nazi executive power, the headquarters of a short-lived empire that only a couple of years ago extended from the Atlantic to the Urals. A Russian infantryman was posing in front of Hitler's monumental desk while his comrades took pictures with liberated Leica cameras; another group was standing on the balcony, where the railing was missing.

'Isn't it unbelievable how these Nazi bastards were still fighting on multiple fronts a couple of weeks ago?' Major Hunt asked. 'I mean, look at this. This was the heart and brain of Nazi Germany: totally unserviceable. Its nerve centre: utterly destroyed. And yet somehow they were going on and on.'

'I suppose as long as Hitler was alive they were hoping for some miracle.'

'Probably. But how did they know he was alive, since apparently he hadn't been seen or heard for months?'

I shrugged. 'I suppose they just assumed he was immortal.'

'And now his body is nowhere to be found.'

'The stuff of legend.'

'Come to think of it – how did the Germans learn of their Führer's death?' Hunt wondered

'Same as us, I suppose. Don't you remember? I think it was on May 1st. Dönitz announced on the radio that Hitler had fallen "at the head of his troops", and that he was now in charge.'

'Scant evidence, really.'

'Shall we go and look for the body?'

Hunt chuckled. 'Definitely. After all, we haven't created any major international incident for at least two weeks, have we?'

Emerging into the garden a few minutes later, we stopped and surveyed the mess. Maimed trees, bomb craters, tons of fallen masonry, long beams and short planks, unexploded shells, the soil upturned as though by the blades of some giant, out-of-control plough. Uninviting, to say the least.

'Careful,' said Hunt. 'Lots of ordnance here. Anyway, I wouldn't think there is much to see, given the thorough pasting the place obviously received.'

'What do you think this is?' I pointed at a small concrete block next to an unfinished conical cement tower.

Treading carefully, we got nearer and almost stumbled on the dozing Red Army sentry guarding the entrance to the *Führerbunker*. He jumped to his feet and cocked his gun while shouting torrents of incomprehensible Russian.

'Okay, okay,' Major Hunt said soothingly. '*Da, da*. Peter – what's he saying?'

'No idea. But if I had to guess, I'd think he's not inviting us to proceed.'

'I wouldn't disagree.'

I turned to the Private first class and pointed at the
Stalingrad medal on his chest.

'Medal: very good. We British. English. Allies.'

The man glared at me but piped down. Encouraged, I
again pointed at the medal and clapped my hands with a
friendly grin: 'Medal: bravo, very good. Cigarette?'

I offered a cigarette to the soldier. He grabbed the pack
and prodded his sub-machine gun into my ribs with such
force that I was almost winded.

'All right,' Hunt said, throwing his hands up in a placating gesture. 'Let's go. Somewhat lacking in social graces,
these Mongols.'

'Cheerio, old boy,' I waved the Russian goodbye. 'It's
been a pleasure meeting you. Please give Comrade Stalin
my regards.'

We turned around and walked away. Within twenty
yards of the bunker's entrance, protected from the sentry's sight by a ventilation tower, we stopped to light a
cigarette and look at a shallow ditch. On both sides, several empty jerry cans were lying on the ground. The smell
of a recent fire emanated from the petrol-soaked ground.

'What were they burning so recently?' I wondered
aloud, my T Force instincts on the alert.

'Compromising papers, I suppose.'

'Hmm… not sure. Look. There isn't a single stray scrap
of paper in this garden. Not a cinder.'

As we crouched to have a closer look at the bottom of the trench, a muffled explosion reverberated through the bunker's openings. The Russian sentry rushed inside and started shouting.

'What the hell was that?' Hunt asked.

'Maybe they've found Hitler. After all, he's got to be somewhere. Perhaps nobody's dared tell him the war's been over for a couple of weeks.'

Suddenly two alien-looking shapes emerged at great speed from the bunker. Only when they removed and threw away their gas masks did I identify them as a man and a woman, both Soviet officers. Blinking in the sunlight, they were carrying sheaves of papers and panting heavily.

'Look,' I whispered. 'That settles it. Not only have the papers not been burnt, but these characters are busy recovering them. I wonder what they've found.'

'Remember what General Barker said?' Major Hunt replied. 'No raid on Moscow. Whatever they found, good luck to them. Let's go.'

The tall female Soviet officer took her hat off and walked a few steps towards us, still trying to catch her breath. She danced around the debris, shells and clumps of earth, making straight for a cluster of lustrous red and yellow tulips. She knelt down, but made no attempt to smell or touch them. As though to warm her hands on a campfire, she extended them towards the radiant petals. Her face and hands were catching the sun, flowers around her were shimmering. She seemed unconnected with our sooty, grey surroundings. In tight formation, mallards flew overhead, their shadows racing over the ground. She looked up and her grey-green eyes absorbed the sky. Over high cheekbones she had long blond hair the colour of straw, tied up in a loose bun. Suddenly she became aware of our presence and stared at us, confused. Her eyes conjured up immense, icy steppes into which I wanted to disappear. Waiting for her to raise the alarm, to my dismay I felt an idiotic, uncontrollable grin spread over my face. Through long eyelashes, she held my gaze for a couple of seconds. Under the slightly upturned nose, however, her full lips remained silent and impassive.

'Shall we go, Comrade Terisova?' her companion called impatiently.

Silently, almost reluctantly, she got up and walked back.

I started breathing again. 'Gosh!' I exclaimed as we slunk away. 'What was it you were saying, David? A raid on Moscow? Count me in!'

PART TWO

'This trial can be a very great landmark in the history
of International Law... Aggressor nations great and
small will embark on war with the certain knowledge
that, if they fail, they will be called to grim account.'
*Sir Norman Birkett, Alternate British Judge
of the International Military Tribunal,
Letter to Mrs Cruesmann, Nuremberg,
20 January 1946, quoted by H Montgomery Hyde,
*"Norman Birkett: The life of Lord Birkett of
Ulverston", *first published by Hamish Hamilton Ltd, 1964*

1

Lost in Translation

GESTURING TOWARDS two metal chairs in front of his desk, Vsevelod Nikolayevich Merkulov, chairman of the NKGB, as the NKVD was now called, produced a thin smile that left his round face unruffled and his deeply sunken eyes in the dark. Only the permanent black rings under those eyes betrayed the fact that he was the wrong side of fifty. A ray of October sunshine, reflected on the wall of his office on the seventh floor of the Lubyanka building, made the brass buttons of his tunic glitter. Noticing the rows of medals on his left breast neatly aligned with the second button from the top, Captain Elizaveta Terisova idly wondered how he'd earned them. She sat down next to Colonel Ivan Klimenko and waited.

'It's been four months,' Merkulov said. 'Nearly five, in fact.'

He looked at both NKGB officers with a raised eyebrow. They remained silent.

'What am I to tell the First Secretary?' Merkulov sighed. 'That, with all the resources at our disposal, we've failed to get a couple of simple answers from two Nazi officials?'

He paused.

'I really don't think Comrade Stalin will be impressed. Do you?'

'Please bear in mind we've never been given a free hand,' Klimenko said. 'We'll break them. It's only a question of time. You know that, Comrade Chairman.'

'Indeed, I can't recall many cases where we failed to obtain full confessions from our prisoners. Including, needless to say, thousands of our own underperforming agents.' Merkulov fell silent.

Elizaveta felt he was looking at her, but couldn't be sure. She knew only too well how many of her colleagues had been framed, tortured and killed under the reigns of the present NKGB chairman and his predecessor Beria in order to satisfy Stalin's insatiable appetite for purges.

'The problem,' said Merkulov, slowly and so softly that Elizaveta had to lean forward, 'is that... you've already run out of time.'

Elizaveta's heart skipped a beat. So, that was it – was it? Half a dozen casual words. Sudden. Unexpected. Arbitrary. Final. All it took to obliterate whole families.

'Why?' Klimenko asked. 'We've never been given a deadline. If you give us one we'll meet it.'

'Too late. We need to get Messrs Fritzsche and Raeder back in shape as soon as possible.'

Colonel Klimenko and Captain Terisova exchanged a mystified look.

'An International Military Tribunal is convening in Nuremberg as we speak. It will judge the major Nazi war criminals. Unfortunately, all the accused so far are in American or British custody. Comrade Stalin has decided that our only two captives of any significance should be added to the list and tried. Accordingly, you'll be delivering Hans Fritzsche and Grand Admiral Erich Raeder to Nuremberg before the end of the month. The trial starts on 20th November.'

'Do you mean we are surrendering our two highest-value Germans to the Americans?' asked Elizaveta incredulously.

'Precisely.'

'But they still haven't come clean,' Klimenko protested. 'To be sure, we got a fair amount of trivia from them. But nothing on Hitler's fate. Zero on the location of the uranium stocks.'

'I don't need to be reminded of that,' the NKGB chairman replied quietly.

'Of course, they may have no knowledge of these things,' Elizaveta pleaded. 'After all, Fritzsche was only a third-level official at the Propaganda Ministry, and more than two years have elapsed since Dönitz replaced Raeder as Commander-in-Chief of the Navy.'

Vsevelod Nikolayevich Merkulov was shaking his head. 'Haven't you learnt yet, Comrade Terisova, that the true extent of a suspect's knowledge depends on his interrogators' skill? We've provided you with everything you need: intelligence reports, witnesses, and all our in-house psychologists and psychiatrists. All state-of-the-art, if I may say so. Yet, here you are, five months later…'

'I was only translating, Comrade Chairman,' she whispered.

'Ha! "Only translating…"' he mimicked. 'Perhaps you should have tried to do a bit more, in the interest of the Soviet Union? And for your own sake?'

'But, Comrade Chairman,' Klimenko interjected, 'you will no doubt recall that normal interrogation methods were never open to us? Of course, I now understand why it was necessary that these men remained presentable. But our hands were tied. Now we understand the full picture. Give us a bit more time and we'll get results, without damaging them unduly.'

Ignoring Klimenko, the NKGB Chairman was staring at Captain Terisova. 'The Nazi swine will remain in your custody until Nuremberg,' he said with the shadow of a smile. 'Use that time. Few people get such a second chance. Goodbye.'

Elizaveta hadn't survived years of internal purges and total war without learning to recognise that sort of leer. She knew a protection offer when she heard one, and also the price inevitably attached to it. Not that Klimenko himself had ever been particularly subtle about it: the minute he'd found out about Elizaveta's German-Russian relatives, he'd made it clear that the choice was between her remaining his war-wife, or Jakob being liquidated. He hadn't even bothered to threaten Elizaveta or her father with deportation to Siberia, either because it was obvious, or because somehow he knew her feelings for Jakob afforded him sufficient leverage. She'd had to submit, though Klimenko, despite repeated promises, had never produced any proof that Jakob was still alive – only verbal assurances and vague reports.

Elizaveta instinctively realised that this was another life-and-death moment. She was sitting in a room with two men who both had the power to have her killed on a whim. Both wanted her. Neither could be deceived easily.

Nuremberg. If there was a way out, it had to be Nuremberg. In the American Zone. But Jakob? How could she leave him behind, a shivering skeleton forever shackled to the Gulag universe?

'Thank you, Comrade Chairman,' she held his gaze with a warm smile. 'Colonel Klimenko and I are in your debt.'

Merkulov nodded slowly. '*Bis bald*,' he said, pushing aside the two bulky files that were sitting on his desk and picking up one of his telephones.

Walking out of the room, Elizaveta tried to control mounting panic. Why the German farewell? Was he trying to convey that he, too, knew about her German ties? In that case, Klimenko's protection was not only unnecessary, but a liability. Or was he just trying to impress a beautiful interpreter?

Halfway along the long, empty corridor, Klimenko suddenly caught her hand and stopped in his tracks.

'The names on those files didn't look German, did they?' he whispered.

'No. They were yours and mine.'

'Well spotted. Don't worry. This is par for the course. He just needs to ensure we get everything possible out of the Germans before we deliver them to the Americans. Which we will.'

His hand was steady and not in the least sweaty. Not for the first time, she admired his nerve.

'How?'

'Since Fritzsche is right here,' he pointed to the floor, 'I suggest we start with him. We can go and see Raeder tomorrow.'

'But we still can't touch them, can we?'

'There is touching and touching, my girl. You should know that.'

Half a dozen noisy guards appeared at the end of the corridor. Both officers resumed their walk towards the main staircase and coolly received their salute. Five floors lower, they entered Colonel Klimenko's office where they spent the next two hours planning and rehearsing the interrogation session.

Albeit only seven floors high, the massive NKGB headquarters on Dzerzhinsky Square was known to Muscovites, because of the depths of its cellars, as the tallest building in the world. As the detail led by Colonel Klimenko once more descended underground, Elizaveta shivered.

The man brought to Interrogation Room No. 28

seemed unable to support himself. Two guards dumped Hans Fritzsche on the chair facing the blinding lamp. For reasons that were now clear he'd never actively been tortured, but for several months he'd been on a starvation diet and kept in solitary confinement in a freezing cell with only a few rags. According to standard procedure, he'd also been deprived of sleep and relentlessly interrogated by skilled inquisitors. His tall frame was all bone, and even his nose and ears now seemed grotesquely oversized. Only forty-five, he looked like a frail old man.

Klimenko nodded, and Elizaveta began talking in German.

'*Guten Tag,* Herr Fritzsche. How are you today?'

Blinking, the prisoner mumbled something unintelligible.

'I have news for you, Herr Fritzsche,' she continued. 'Today will be the last day of our interrogations. This means you'll soon be leaving this building. There are two ways out. One is beneath us. The other upstairs. We are going to show you both. Then we'll ask you to choose one. Do you understand?'

'I've already told you everything I know several times,' the man whispered. 'Why can't you believe me?'

'No memory is infallible, Herr Fritzsche. It's our job to jog yours.'

Suddenly the German's head seemed too heavy for him. Klimenko looked at his watch. On his signal, the guards lifted the prisoner to his feet and dragged him out of the room. The gaggle of interrogators, translators and security officers followed. Together they went down another two levels. The absolute bottom.

Pyotr Maggo, the Employee for Special Assignments, had been told to delay all procedures until the arrival of this group. He resented this kind of interference with his work; bunching up executions in this way meant he had time to clean neither himself nor the execution space between shootings. And some of them could be quite messy. Additionally, he'd be late home and his supper would be cold.

With everybody in place, the first enemy of the people was delivered by two young soldiers into the dank, low-ceilinged execution space. They gave Pyotr Maggo a short document that he folded and put in his pocket without so much as a glance. The prisoner turned around.

'Look. The widow of General Pavlov!' Klimenko whispered in Elizaveta's ear. 'He was in command of the Tenth Army when Hitler invaded. Wiped out to the last man. Yet Stalin had him shot for cowardice in 1941.'

Hands tied behind her back, the woman was made to kneel down. 'My children!' she cried. Pyotr Maggo lifted his trusty French-designed Nagan revolver and shot her once in the back of the neck. Brain matter spattered the wall and floor but, thankfully, without bouncing back onto his clothes. Echoes of the shot reverberated off the stone floor and ceiling, drowning the soft thud of the collapsing body.

When they died down, only the noise of Pyotr Maggo's shuffling feet could be heard, as he turned round and went back to his cubicle to finish reading the day's *Pravda*.

Colonel Klimenko looked at Captain Terisova. With a deep breath, she tried to steady her voice and turned to Fritzsche. 'Pick her up,' she ordered.

He raised two shaking, helpless hands.

'Pick her up – or kneel down next to her,' she said.

Galvanised, Fritzsche lifted one of the woman's legs and pulled – to no avail. Klimenko ordered a guard to grab the other leg and led the way towards the crematorium, conveniently located in the same basement. The furnace doors were wide open. After the body had been thrown in, Fritzsche was made to shut them.

It wasn't a busy day: there were only five special assignments on Pyotr Maggo's list. They were over in less than ninety minutes. Fritzsche was then given a mop and two pails of water and ordered to clean the mess. Retching and sobbing, he somehow found the strength to comply. Then he was taken up to the ground floor and shown Dzerzhinsky Square through a window. This was his first glimpse of the outside world, complete with cars, trees and people, in several months.

When he arrived back in Interrogation Room No. 28, he found the bright lamp illuminating a tray on the table. On it were a bowl of steaming hot soup, a loaf of bread and a pack of German cigarettes – Klimenko, always fastidious, had checked the file and procured the correct brand, *Jubiläumsmischung*. Next to them was a neatly-folded khaki woollen blanket.

'So, which is it to be, Herr Fritzsche? The basement exit, or the front door?' Elizaveta asked.

Ogling the loaf of bread, Fritzsche didn't react. His rags were thoroughly soaked, and he was shivering with cold. Klimenko took the bread and slowly passed it back and forth under the German's nose.

'Answer a couple of simple questions and this whole tray is yours, Herr Fritzsche,' Elizaveta resumed. 'First, can you confirm that you worked at Doktor Goebbels's Propaganda Ministry?'

'Yes. You know I've never denied it.'

'Do you accept Nazi propaganda was an integral part of the Nazi conspiracy to wage wars of aggression and commit war crimes against the USSR?'

'If you say so.'

'Do you accept you were part of this conspiracy?'

For the first time Fritzsche's eyes moved away from the food tray to his interrogator. 'I told you I've never spoken to Hitler in my life. Not once. This can be verified. I didn't even work for Doktor Goebbels. I worked for the Reich Press Chief, Otto Dietrich. I was a radio announcer. I know nothing of any conspiracy. Why can't you believe me? Or at least check the facts?'

'Where is Adolf Hitler?'

'For God's sake – how should I know? Is he not dead?'

Captain Terisova moved the light away from the food tray, aiming it at the prisoner. His stench was so unbearable that she had to take a couple of quick steps back.

'So, it's the basement exit then, Herr Fritzsche?'

She watched for a while as the German, with closed eyes, kept rhythmically shaking his head. Bobbing up and down continuously, his Adam's apple seemed to have monopolised whatever little energy was left in his body.

'In early May, you identified the corpses of the Goebbels family, did you not?

Hans Fritzsche didn't open his eyes. 'We've been through that a hundred times.'

'But you want us to believe that when you went to the *Führerbunker*, you saw no trace of Hitler?'

'None.'

'And that you were not privy to the plans Doktor Goebbels and Martin Bormann had made to spirit Hitler out of Berlin?'

'Even if such plans existed, I would have been the last person to know.'

'Where are the German uranium stocks?'

'I was a radio announcer... I don't even know what uranium looks like. I'd tell you if I knew.' He blinked into the glare of the lamp. 'Believe me, I'd be delighted to tell you. Really.'

Elizaveta picked up the food tray and gave it to one of the guards who took it away.

'Well, Herr Fritzsche, we aren't making much progress, are we? It doesn't look like you'll need this food, does it?'

Tears were rolling down Fritzsche's hollow cheeks.

'Shall we make our way back to the basement, then?' she asked softly.

As the guards pulled him up the German suddenly

started screaming. 'Manchuria! That's where they all are. The uranium. And Hitler. I remember – he had special long-range planes. Junkers 390 or something.'

'Have you ever seen them?'

'Yes. No. But I've heard about them. They were based at Rechlin.'

'What quantity of uranium was flown out of Germany?'

'Oh… a few hundred kilos, I suppose?'

'How was it packed?'

'Packed? I told you I'm not a specialist. I wouldn't know.'

Colonel Klimenko got up and left the room. Captain Terisova had the prisoner returned to his cell. All experienced NKGB officers knew when a suspect became so desperate that he started making up stories in order to please his interrogators.

NEXT MORNING they were picked up early by one of the Fourth Directorate's pre-war ZIS-101 limousines.

'Good sign, Comrade,' Klimenko said.

Elizaveta started. They hadn't exchanged a word for the first twenty minutes of the drive.

'What is?'

'They haven't withdrawn our access to the car pool.'

Aware of the fact their teenaged driver was eavesdropping, she just nodded. There was hardly any traffic in the wide avenues of central Moscow, mainly lorries and dirty buses whose drivers had long since learnt to give right of way to any official-looking black limo.

'We should be at the dacha in half an hour,' Klimenko looked at his watch.

'Do you think Fritzsche was playing games?' she asked after a while.

'Unfortunately not. Not only did he wet himself yesterday, he soiled himself too.'

'Well, that leaves only Raeder.'

'Okay. There is only one way to get at Raeder. Let's get ready.'

For the rest of the short drive, they concentrated on role-playing.

In line with NKGB versatility, Grand Admiral Raeder's incarceration conditions couldn't have been more different from those of the hapless Fritzsche. Raeder was detained in one of the Secret Service's dachas, in wooded country some thirty kilometres west of Moscow. He'd been allowed to keep his uniform (though not his medals) and was treated well.

It had been Chairman Merkulov's judgment that German military top brass was unlikely to be broken through physical means. Besides, after his surrender at Stalingrad, General von Paulus had started cooperating with his captors soon enough; there was no reason to believe that an old-school sailor of Raeder's ilk held the Nazi thugs in any particular esteem, or would remain faithful to Hitler. The only problem – as Chairman Merkulov had pithily pointed out – was that so far Raeder had provided only mundane intelligence on naval matters, and none about the two key questions.

The ZIS-101 stopped in front of stone pillars marked: 'Property of the USSR – DO NOT ENTER.' Recognising familiar faces, the sentries waved them through and shut the gates behind them. On both sides of the track, as far as Elizaveta could see, the straight, whitish trunks of thousands of silver birches, only a few russet leaves still attached to them, contrasted with the thick yellow carpet woven at their feet by the bulk of their rotting foliage.

Soon the log cabin came into view, and the two-and-a-half ton limousine, like an ocean liner entering a small provincial port, majestically docked in front of it. Elizaveta got out. She filled her lungs with the wooded aroma, an earthy smell of decaying vegetation, fat mushrooms and smoke. Closing her eyes for a second, she was transported to the forest around Shcherbatovka, and her heart began to palpitate. Jakob, Jakob – where on earth are you? Are you too smelling the scent of autumn?

When Captain Terisova and her boss entered the room, Grand Admiral Erich Raeder was sitting by an open log fire. The guard locked the door behind them. Both NKGB officers saluted. Raeder got up with some difficulty and returned the salute – a stocky man of medium height, broad-shouldered, clearly not in the best of health, but still imposing despite his sixty-nine years of age. Beneath small, piercing eyes, he had a virile face dominated by a strong nose and a firm jaw.

'So, you're back,' Raeder sat down as though standing a minute longer in front of Russian officers were utterly inappropriate.

'I'm glad to see you look much better, Admiral,' Eliza-veta replied. 'Are you happy with your new heart treatment?'

Before Raeder had been captured, he'd run out of pills for his heart condition, and was in a sorry state.

'It's better than nothing.'

'Good. I'll transmit your heartfelt thanks to the cardiologist,' Elizaveta smiled. 'In the meantime we have news for you. You're soon going back to Germany.'

Raeder remained impassive.

'No questions?' Elizaveta asked.

'When?'

'Within a couple of weeks.'

'Good. I'm glad you've finally realised my incarceration is illegal. The war is over. Am I going back home?'

'In a manner of speaking, yes.'

Raeder's eyes narrowed. 'What do you mean?'

'We're taking you to Nuremberg.'

'Why?'

'To be tried by the International Military Tribunal.'

'What for?'

'War crimes and conspiracy to wage wars of aggression, amongst others things.'

'Do you realise how preposterous this is?' Raeder was up on his feet, his face reddening. 'I've served my country honourably since 1896! First the Kaiser. Then the Weimar Republic. Then the Third Reich. My record is unblemished. And now I should stand trial? Why? Because we lost the war?'

'That will be for the prosecution to decide, Admiral.'

For the first time Grand Admiral Raeder looked Captain Terisova in the eye. 'What sort of game are you playing anyway?' Shrugging, he turned away. 'I guess you yourself have no idea – why should you?'

'No games, Admiral. Our orders are to take you very soon to join two dozen high-ranking Nazi criminals in the dock.'

'Will Göring be there?'

'Do you think he should be tried?'

'No. If the fat buffoon is still alive, he should be shot.'

'Why?'

'For wasting untold resources on his pathetic Luftwaffe, which let us down. He lost the war for us. First over Britain in 1940. Then again in Russia. As for me to sit next to him, in a dock or elsewhere, forget it.'

'You're not asking about Hitler, Admiral. Why not?'

'There is no point, is there?'

'Why not?'

'Because Grand Admiral Dönitz told us that the Führer had died a heroic death, fighting to his last breath against Bolshevism. Dönitz may not always be sound in matters of naval strategy, but he's an honourable officer. He wouldn't make it up.'

'You still want us to believe that your only source of information about Hitler's fate was Dönitz's broadcast to the German nation on 1st May?'

'It's the truth. You know perfectly well that since I resigned in 1943 I've been living in retirement with my wife Erika at Babelsberg. That's where your own Colonel Pimenov illegally arrested us on 25th June.'

Elizaveta and Klimenko exchanged a quick glance. This was familiar, unproductive ground.

'I take it my wife will be travelling with me?' Raeder sat down again.

'Ah!' Elizaveta seized the opening. 'There is a difficulty, I'm afraid.'

'You never had any ground to arrest her. This was no more than kidnapping. Disgraceful. Where is she?'

'You see, Admiral, Nuremberg is under American control. We need to make sure that you will come back to us. That's why we'll have to keep your wife. Unless, of course, you answer our two simple questions before you leave. Where is Hitler? Where are the German uranium stocks?'

'This is blackmail!' He was back on his feet. 'Hostage-taking. Scandalous! From now on I won't answer any question unless and until I've received evidence that my wife has safely been returned to the care of my son and daughter. *Verstanden?*'

'With great respect, I think you're misreading the situation, Admiral. You're just about to make your wife's circumstances immeasurably worse.'

Erich Raeder was turning apoplectic. Elizaveta realised that, once more, Colonel Klimenko had unerringly found the crucial weakness; but she started to worry the German might suffer another heart attack.

'You're nothing but... a bunch of reprehensible delinquents,' Raeder sputtered. 'No better than the Gestapo. Leave my wife alone, or…'

Elizaveta waited a few seconds before asking: 'Or… what?'

Raeder turned his back and slumped onto his chair. For a while, breathing heavily, he contemplated the dying fire.

'The uranium was moved west, of course, to escape the advancing Red Army.'

'Where to?'

'A coal mine, now in the British Zone. Out of your reach, thank God. Imagine – you and your lot sitting on a nuclear bomb!'

'Where exactly?'

Raeder looked up. 'That, Captain, is classified information. And you're the last person I would entrust it to.'

'Even to get your wife released from prison? Or, more likely, labour camp?'

'Bring me proof of her release first.'

'We cannot do that, I'm afraid. Not before we verify your information. But if you tell me the exact location now, you'll be re-united with your wife this afternoon.'

Grand Admiral Raeder hesitated. He hadn't seen his seventy-year-old wife since their arrest, more than three months ago.

'If I see Erika in good health this afternoon, and you give me a written promise from the highest authority, I'll tell you what I've heard about our uranium stocks.'

'It's important for you to understand we need more than hearsay, Admiral. Much more. Not to put too fine a point on it, should the information prove incorrect, your wife will be on the next cattle wagon to Siberia.'

'I have no reason to suspect my sources weren't accurate. But I can't guarantee it. Damn you!'

On the way back to Moscow that evening, Elizaveta felt a mixture of shame and elation.

'Well done,' Klimenko patted her on the knee after checking the driver couldn't see his hand in the rear-view mirror.

'Bergkamen. Ever heard of it?'

Klimenko shook his head. 'No. Somewhere in the Ruhr, I suppose. The good news is we have a lot of support among the miners. They always liked Communism.'

'How do we proceed?'

'Simple. As instructed, we deliver these two German bastards to Nuremberg. I'll make sure we are part of the official Soviet Delegation to the Tribunal. Obviously, you'll get cover as an interpreter. I'll be a legal adviser.' He laughed. 'Did you know I actually read law?'

'Yes.'

'Good girl. Anyway, that gets us into the US Zone. Close to the Nazi elite. If needs be, we can also roam with our war reparations teams. That will give us access to any German industrial or military asset we wish to investigate – or claim. In all Occupation Zones.'

'Brilliant,' she said.

Seemingly impervious to the potholes and tramway

tracks thrown in the way of its shiny black and white tyres, the ponderous limousine pitched back and forth as though rocked by an invisible swell. Her head on her war-husband's shoulder, Elizaveta fell asleep.

2

Nibelungen

Martin Bormann threw his tin plate onto the black, beaten earth with a bang that failed to stir his companions. Mopping his brow, he sighed loudly.

'Death by potatoes,' he said. 'That's what's awaiting us.'

'Please do not joke, Herr Reichsleiter. People kill for a potato these days,' Oberleutnant Kurt Welter replied. Nothing in his civilian attire betrayed that he was one the Luftwaffe's greatest flying aces – apart, that is, from the Knight's Cross of the Iron Cross with Oak Leaves on his chest, attesting to his forty-eight aerial victories. A tall, good-looking man in his early thirties, he somehow managed to shave every morning and remain presentable despite the inescapable coal dust.

Bormann, on the other hand, looked distinctly scruffy. While Germany starved, the Reichsleiter had somehow contrived to grow podgier than ever. Constantly out of breath, he seemed much older than his forty-five years. His short torso had inflated so much that any remnant of neck seemed to have been sucked into it. Combed back and greased by sweat and grime, his thinning black hair was receding by the week.

'Why is it so damn hot?' he asked for the hundredth time. 'Welter, you can fly jet fighters. Can't you fix this bloody ventilation?'

'Not without major works, Herr Reichsleiter. This shaft has been disused for years. We would be bound to attract attention.'

'Why don't we all move up to ground level then?'

'It's actually quite cold up there. Let the Werewolves shiver instead. We need them awake, as our first line of defence.'

'Damn you, Welter!' Bormann exploded. 'Can't you ever come up with anything vaguely positive? How long do you think we can wait in this shithole – for God knows what?'

Welter suffered from the stench, lack of ventilation and insufficient exercise as much as Bormann, but he knew better than get into an argument. He cast a look at the far corner, whence indistinct mutterings could be heard. Lying on a bunk, lit only by a flickering candle, an old man with truncated fingers was having difficulty turning the page of a dog-eared book. Having finally succeeded, he read aloud:

'"The history of what man has accomplished in this world is at bottom the History of the Great Men who have worked here."'

Bormann recognised one of Hitler's favourite quotes from Carlyle's biography of Frederick the Great.

'"Democracy never yet, that we heard of, was able to accomplish much work, beyond that of cancelling itself,"' the reader went on.

'"One comfort is that Great Men are profitable company,"' Bormann intoned, reciting by heart.

The old man dropped the book on his lap. 'Thank you, faithful Bormann,' he said.

Bormann decided to grasp the opportunity.

'Thank you, my Führer. May I ask what our next move is?'

'Apart from my godson Adolf, you have another eight children, Bormann, yes?'

'Yes, my Führer.'

'We must set an example of heroic resilience for future generations.'

'Indeed. But…'

'In times of future national emergency, they will be able to look back on us as we look at Frederick the Great today. Do you understand?'

'I do understand why, against my humble advice, you decided to stay in Germany, my Führer. But surely we cannot stay in this hole forever. What's the point of guarding our uranium unless we use it?'

The old man picked up his book. 'Preach revenge against the East and hatred against the West, Bormann. Then the whole nation will rise against the invaders.'

'I agree entirely, my Führer. What about auctioning the uranium to the highest bidder? Stalin cannot build a nuclear bomb without it, and the Western Allies are desperate to stop him. We should be able to name our price.'

'It's never too late to divide the enemy.'

'Will you permit me to make exploratory approaches?'

Much to Bormann's frustration, the old man went back to his reading. Bormann fleetingly wondered whether, as a result of some ghastly mistake, the dull, passive individual on the bunk might in fact be Gustav Weber.

'Listen carefully, Herr Oberleutnant,' he turned to Welter. 'According to our reports, the town of Kamen is occupied by an unusual British unit, whose mission seems to consist in looting our technology. Visit them, and offer them some. After all, you're the world expert on the Messerschmitt 262. The Brits are nowhere with regard to jet propulsion. Insist on talking only to their highest level of command. Make it clear that you will co-operate only with sufficient safeguards and guarantees. Then report to me about the possibility of a uranium deal. Clear?'

Oberleutnant Kurt Welter rose and stretched his legs.

'*Alles klar, Herr Reichsleiter.*'

'We'll also use our infiltrators in the local Communist cells to test Moscow's appetite,' Bormann went on. 'In the meantime, it might be better for you to move on, my Führer. Just in case.'

3

Roses and Cabbages

MOTIONLESS, EYES CLOSED, breasts and toes pointing skywards, Susette was floating on her back. The paddling pool, which the family of Doktor Anton Gräbe called the *Planschbecken*, was only five metres long and one metre deep: too short and shallow for swimming, but a pleasant place to cool off. Next to it, roses and clematis were clambering over a hardwood pergola, their delicate scents tantalisingly swirling around my nostrils.

Between the road and the garden, the family's house, all twelve rooms of it, stood guard over the magic garden.

'*Danke,* my love,' Susette mouthed without opening her eyes or turning her head.

Waves of grateful relief swept through my body. How lucky I was that the whole family didn't hate me! After all, I, Lieutenant Peter Birkett, was literally the occupying power, billeted in their house while they'd had to take refuge in a single room at the local hospital. Admittedly, it was thanks to my intervention that the doctor's two consulting rooms on the ground floor of the big house had been returned to him, much to the relief of his many devoted patients.

In the full glory of her nineteen springs, Susette leapt out of the water and stretched lusciously in the sun. I was surprised and mildly disappointed to see that her swimming costume was dry and perfectly adjusted, revealing not even the slightest shadow over her nipples.

Just as I was getting up to kiss her, her mother Frau Gräbe appeared at a window, ringing a bronze cow bell the size of a cannon. Curiously, the sound didn't appear synchronised with her wild gestures; on the contrary, it had a regular rhythm, which I immediately recognised for what it was: a secret German code, which I effortlessly broke: N-O-F-R-A-T-E-R-N-I-S-A-T-I-O-N-N-O-F-R-A-T-E-R-N-I-S-A-T-I-O-N…

With a rueful smile, Susette dived head first into the *Planschbecken* so elegantly that neither sound nor ripple disturbed its glassy surface.

'Susette!' I tried to scream, but whatever feeble sound was coming out of my constricted throat was drowned by the racket of the cow bell. With feet of lead, filled with dread, I walked towards the pool slowly, so slowly I didn't get there before a nightingale started singing. Everybody knew the pool wasn't deep enough for diving, but only I, as Intelligence Officer, knew that the bottom was made of the top-secret armour-plating T Force had taken from Krupps. The swimming bath was full of scented violets. Susette's costume was floating on the surface. Of the girl there was no trace.

The cow bell finally woke me up. I picked up the telephone. It was Sergeant Wagg. A German woman was begging for help. Her husband was running amok; he'd savaged her and several others. Apparently the German police had refused to intervene. I instructed Wagg to meet me with two armed men at the address the caller – a Frau Schwarz – had given and hurriedly dressed. I checked the time: almost two in the morning. First, I picked up my standard issue 0.38 Smith & Wesson revolver, then thought better of it. As an officer of T Force, I was also entitled to carry a personal weapon of enemy manufacture, such as the 9mm Luger automatic I now strapped on. Somehow, in emergencies, I always felt that the protective power of the old Luger, which used to belong to my father, was more reliable.

So deeply distrusted was the German police after twelve years of Nazi repression that the local population – at least in the British Zone – often turned to the Occupation forces when in trouble. That seemed to suit the native policemen, who saw no merit in getting up in the middle of the night.

It was pitch-dark and bitterly cold when I stepped out into the silent streets. Once or twice, I thought I could hear footsteps scurrying away but, even after my night vision improved, I could hardly see three yards ahead. Everybody knew that there was more going on under cover of darkness than met the eye. Black marketeers, homeless German refugees and DPs, hungry girls selling themselves for chocolate bars, petty thieves and, according to some, members of Hitler's Werewolves, all plying their trade in the small hours. At dawn, it wasn't unusual to find bodies in the streets. Turning right into the deserted Burgstrasse, I wished I'd checked the distance to my destination before setting out. Or, even better, instructed Wagg to pick me up. Just as I started jogging, right on top of the wall I was hugging there was a violent commotion, accompanied by a strident screech. Grabbing the Luger, I jumped to the middle of the road, nearly losing my footing on the uneven paving. Shouting *'Halt! Wer da?'* I caught a fleeting glimpse of two hissing tomcats flying off the wall in a murderous tangle. They landed at my feet and chased each other down the street. The bang of a shot was reverberating. Initially baffled, I realised that I must have fired it myself – God knows where. Lucky not to have injured myself. I put the safety catch back on and pressed on.

I found Sergeant Wagg and his two men waiting in front of a tall tenement building. There was pandemonium on one of the top floors, whence screams could intermittently be heard.

'Third floor, sir.' Wagg pointed at a window behind which dim light was visible.

'How long has it been going on?'

'Half an hour, maybe more, would be my guess. Since I got the call, I mean.'

'German police?'

'According to the woman, they flatly refused to intervene, sir.'

'All right. Let's have a look.'

As we ran up the stairs, the fracas grew louder. A man's voice bellowing, knocks and thuds – it seemed a whole demolition gang was at work up there. Reaching the second floor, we picked up the sound of a woman or children whimpering or crying. On one side of the third-floor landing, above a homemade child's tricycle, several pairs of shoes of various sizes, toys and a beach ball were neatly stacked on shelves. Half a dozen mud-coloured coats hung from rows of improvised hooks. On the other side, inadequately washed laundry had been put to dry on long strings.

No need to knock on the door. It was wide open.

In contrast to the rest of the building, the inside of the flat was a noisy wreck. Among heaps of rubble, a muscular, stocky man was hacking away at a partition with a three-legged stool. He'd already smashed a hole the size of a bear in it. As he swung his improvised ram to devastating effect, plaster and masonry were crumbling on and around him. His hair, moustache and clothes were covered with a thick layer of white powder. Through the opening, despite the swirling dust, I just about distinguished three bodies lying on the floor, two men and an elderly woman. By the entrance door, a young woman in a torn nightgown crouched, shivering with cold, her face battered, trying to muffle the cries of the toddler she held in her lap with one arm. Her other arm was hanging limply by her side at an odd angle. She saw us first, but didn't move.

'*Schnell!*' she whispered through her tears, quickly flicking her gaze to the swarthy madman.

Dealing with violent drunks was something that Sergeant Wagg and his men were used to. In no time they'd restrained and handcuffed the lunatic, who was now sitting on the ground, panting, eyes rolling wildly. He stank of sweat and alcohol. Though unconscious and suffering from broken limbs and head wounds, all three people behind the partition were still breathing. In addition to fresh injuries, they exhibited severe scarring of the face and hands, including mutilated fingers, noses and ears, seemingly due to severe burns. Frau Schwarz haltingly explained that they were her parents and younger brother, who'd turned up in 1943, refugees from the Hamburg firestorm. Her husband, a miner by trade, had never got on with his in-laws, and soon the tensions within their overcrowded flat had exploded. After a few months, he'd built a partition across their sitting room, allocated the cramped space behind it to his guests, and instructed them to remain out of sight at all times. Punctuated by drunken outbursts, an uneasy truce had prevailed to this day, when, in the middle of a drinking session, he'd felt hungry. Unable to find the piece of sausage he was looking for, he'd come to the (not entirely unwarranted) conclusion that his wife had, yet again, given it to her family, and he had gone berserk.

It was nearly four in the morning before the evacuation of all casualties to the local hospital and the transfer of the miner to a police cell were complete. As she was getting into the ambulance, one arm in a sling and the other holding her child, the woman had turned to me.

'You've saved our lives. Thank you. Please don't be too hard on him. My husband is a good man. He was one of the few Communist leaders to resist the Nazi thugs till the end. But… it's just… too much. Do you see?'

'*Bitte schön, Frau Schwarz. Das war nur meine Pflicht,*' I replied. 'Good luck.'

'Your duty? Why is our own police incapable of protecting us? And how is it that you speak such good German, Herr Leutnant?' she asked from inside the vehicle.

Ignoring her questions, I closed the door.

'Thank you, Sergeant Wagg,' I turned to the men. 'Well done, chaps.'

'May I release the men, sir?' Wagg asked.

'Not quite yet. We need to teach the German police a lesson. Sergeant Wagg, I want you to order the entire Kamen force to turn out. Immediately. I want to see every single one of them in the market square in thirty minutes.'

Only as we were preparing to leave the premises did I recognise the typical smell of defeated Germany. Always, everywhere the same, emanating from all the towns and cities of the Ruhr, from their buildings and their drab population, whether they congregated in shops, churches, tenement houses or concert halls. Among its main component strains were the red-tinged briquettes of low-grade brown coal burnt in their stoves and the rancid odour of the overcooked cabbage invariably simmering on top. A distinctive note was added by their home-made cigarettes, manufactured from inadequately cured tobacco grown in courtyards and on balconies. Last but not least, the aroma of human sweat could always be relied on to bind together all the ingredients of this stale cocktail.

At four-thirty in the morning, the bewildered Chief of Police and a dozen constables were forming a compact square on Am Markt.

'*Guten Morgen,* Lieutenant Birkett!' the Chief of Police saluted. 'Anything we can do for you? Any emergency?' He was a benevolent, rubicund man in his early sixties.

I was so angry that my normally fluent German almost let me down.

'Yes!' I shouted back. 'Quite a lot, in fact. Four of your own people have practically been murdered, and none of you saw fit to get out of bed? Has it ever crossed your mind that your duty is to protect the men, women and children of this town?'

'But... with respect, Lieutenant, I understand it was only a domestic incident?' The man sounded mystified.

Alternating between German and English, I harangued them for a quarter of an hour, trying to impress on them that if ever a man with murderous intent was on the rampage, it was an essential part of their duty to attend the scene, protect third parties and take the culprit into custody.

'Now, listen carefully, gentlemen,' I concluded. 'Please take this as my first and last official warning. Never again should the Occupation forces have to do your job. You fucking get out of bed and do it yourselves. Is that clear? Now go to work. Dismiss!'

Hurt and befuddled, the policemen drifted across the square towards the police station. They were harmless enough fellows, doing their best to keep an eye on any activities that might threaten the safety or operations of T Force, the occupying power in Kamen. After so many years of totalitarian rule, the idea of a police force being at the service of their townsfolk was evidently still novel to them. Indeed, when interrogating any individual suspected of Nazi sympathies, their methods were sometimes disturbingly reminiscent of the Gestapo.

NORMALLY, THE constant flow of pedestrians, trams, cycles and horse-drawn carts criss-crossing Am Markt, the central place of the market town of Kamen, HQ of No. 1 T Force Intelligence section for the last few weeks, never ceased to fascinate me. But it had been a tough night; I was now feeling so drowsy that even that spectacle failed to revive me.

To make matters worse, not only did the little scene lack any urban bustle, but it increasingly resembled a slow motion ballet in which, on a grey-green set, gaunt, grey-green actors were grimly battling the excessive force of gravity. As a chilly autumn tightened its grip over the Rhine-Ruhr conurbation, its cold, malnourished and largely homeless population was visibly slowing down.

In the afternoon gloom of this bleak November day, my eyes were hurting. Since eight in the morning, I'd been fighting my way through dozens of requisition orders and applications for crating materials, checking that all necessary clearances to proceed with their evacuation – the all-powerful Forms 80G – had been received, duly signed by the Military Government in Düsseldorf. As usual, I'd had to supervise all the messing and security arrangements for the dozens of assessors sent by BIOS in London, all demanding priority to dismantle and ship to the UK this or that Krupp, IG Farben, Thyssen or Siemens factory, before the Russians could lodge any claim to them. Thankfully, the half dozen men of the Intelligence Section, ably led by the indefatigable Sergeant Wagg, had proved up to the task.

Yet the disturbances of the night, which I was still upset about, had left me only a few hours' sleep, and I'd struggled through the day.

Behind an apathetic donkey, a hearse slowly emerged from Weisse Strasse, headed either to the Evangelische Kirche on the left, or the Katholische Kirche opposite. Unlike most houses in their vicinity, both edifices had somehow escaped any serious bomb damage. My office, located on the ground floor at the corner of the building previously known as Hotel Biermann, afforded panoramic views through two huge panes of plate glass over the cobbled expanse of the square. Because, for some unknown reason, green had been the cheapest paint colour in Nazi Germany, our HQ was green and shabby, as was the Rathaus or town hall opposite, two tall storeys of greenish sandstone above portentous arcades. Nowadays, only in front of T Force HQ were a flagpole and a sentry to be found, the latter's job consisting mainly of saluting Colonel Wreford-Brown. In the far left corner, the Siegessäule partly obscured my view of the police station, and I often wondered what irony had preserved both this Victory Column and the ex-Gestapo quarters from Allied retribution.

The tramlines ran diagonally across the square before disappearing up the road to the north, Am Geist. Sometimes, the tracks were used for passenger or coal trains, whose crawl through the city's heart brought it to a momentary stop. I assumed this was the result of the disruption caused to the rail network by years of Allied bombing. The passenger trains were always dangerously overcrowded, and no amount of security ever succeeded in stopping swarms of ragged children from raiding the freight trains and pilfering lumps of coal by the bucket load. Kamen, after all, was a mining town. Most of its fourteen thousand inhabitants somehow depended for their employment on the huge Bergkamen colliery, located so close to the centre that, when the wind was from the north, its sour emanations easily overran the graveyard before engulfing the residential areas. Often, the deep rumble of its winding gear, visible above the roofline, could be felt in the market square, punctuated by dull thuds.

Unlike most of my fellow officers, I understood why

the freezing locals, deprived of any heating fuel, and often living in accommodation open to the winds, felt compelled to recover some of the coal their men had risked life and limb to extract from their own ground. More than once, when on police patrol with my men, I'd shooed away skinny children without making any serious attempt to recover their piteous loot.

Something was going on in the opposite corner of the square, behind the Siegessäule. Yawning, I got up to get a better view, and stretched my legs. Half a dozen German policemen were coming out of the police station, on their way to the bar opposite. I checked my watch: not yet 4 p.m. Far too early. Had they learnt nothing last night?

A tram rattled by, momentarily blocking my view. No sooner had it passed than an exceptionally tall man appeared. In contrast to the energy-saving ambling of those around him, he was striding with unusual purpose, making straight for the door of the Intelligence Section. I saw the guard stop him. A couple of minutes later Sergeant Wagg brought in a youngish man of distinguished appearance. Under a greatcoat, he was wearing a well-cut dark suit and a clean shirt.

'Hello. What can I do for you?' I asked.

'I've come to offer you my services, Lieutenant.' Hardly a trace of German accent behind the perfect English.

I ignored the extended hand and waved at the chair across the desk. 'What services?'

'I'm a pilot.'

'So?'

'A test pilot. I was in charge of the development of the Messerschmitt 262.'

'The jet fighter?'

'Indeed. As you may know, it was our most advanced aircraft. Vastly superior to anything the Allies had. Or rather, have.'

I tried to sound blasé. 'I'm sure we've already secured the plans and blueprints for the ME 262, and probably several intact planes as well. But thank you for your offer.'

'You don't understand. I flew this machine in combat missions. There are only a handful of qualified pilots with combat experience left. You're going to need me.'

'What exactly are we going to need you for?'

'To fight the Russians, of course.'

I slowly shook my head. I knew that the local population was aware of the increasingly hostile nature of the relationship between the Allies and their one-time Soviet partners. Indeed, I too had formed the view that the Russians were the main threat.

But on my desk, as on every other in the Intelligence Section, lay a copy of the red booklet entitled *Instructions for British Servicemen in Germany*. I opened it at the last page and read aloud:

'Don't believe tales against our Allies or the Dominions. They are aimed at sowing ill will between us.' I stood up. 'Thanks, but no thanks. Goodbye.'

'Let me at least give you my name and address,' the German pilot protested.

This would have been an implicit admission that his

services against the Russians might be needed, so I had no choice but to order Sergeant Wagg to throw him out.

'*Herrgott!*' the man called from the hall. 'Don't you people realise that the Russians are already all over the place? When are you going to wake up?'

I sat down, picked up the little red book and thumbed through the depressingly familiar pages:

'Your Supreme Commander has issued an order forbidding fraternisation with Germans.

'You will see much suffering in Germany and much to awake your pity. You may also find that many Germans will even try to welcome you as friends.

'They have much to atone for. Never has murder been organised on so vast a scale as by the German Government and Army in this war. The German people as a whole cannot escape a large share of responsibility.

'You may see many pitiful sights. Hard luck stories may somehow reach you. Most will be hypocritical attempts to win sympathy. For, taken as a whole, the German is brutal when he is winning, and is sorry for himself and whines for sympathy when he's beaten.

'So, be on your guard. Don't be soft.

'German soldiers have been known to play with Polish or Russian children, prior to these same children being shot or burnt or starved to death. The Germans are not good at controlling their feelings. You may find they have a streak of hysteria. You will find that they may often fly into a passion if some little thing goes wrong.

'Remember many Germans will pretend to have been

anti-Nazis simply because they want to be on the winning side.

'When you deal with the Germans you must be on your guard. There are signs that the German leaders are already preparing for a Third World War.

'Remember that German women will be willing, if they get the chance, to make themselves cheap for what they can get out of you. Be on your guard. Most of them will be infected.

'Marriages between members of British Forces and Germans are, as you know, forbidden.

'Germans must still be regarded as dangerous enemies until the Final Peace Settlement has been concluded and after the occupation of Germany has ended.'

I put the booklet down, rubbed my eyes and wearily picked up another Form 80G.

4

The Cage

MAJOR AIREY NEAVE DSO MC stopped in front of the heavily-guarded gates and drew a deep breath. Ostensibly fumbling for his pass, he stood on the pavement and lit a cigarette. Having repeatedly risked life and limb to escape from German jails, he never found it easy to step into the forbidding Nuremberg prison. Because he held the rank and medals of an older soldier, most people took him for a man of forty, and would have refused to believe he was more than a decade younger. Admittedly, he'd done rather more in his twenty-nine years than most of his contemporaries. He'd learnt to speak German as a teenager, a fact that stood him in good stead in May 1940 after he'd been captured by the Wehrmacht at Calais. After each of his failed escape attempts he'd been grilled by the Gestapo, and finally imprisoned in the high-security fortress of Colditz, whence nobody had ever broken out. Undeterred, he'd started in January 1942 the first successful home-run back to England, already the stuff of legend.

Before the war, during his time at Oxford, he'd been more interested in reading the complete works of Clausewitz than in learning jurisprudence. Accordingly, he'd ended up with an inglorious third class degree in law, as well as an impressive knowledge of the ways in which the war he considered inevitable would be waged. Today, armed with this modicum of legal learning and a couple of years' experience at the Bar, he felt more apprehensive than ever before. He knew he could handle lowly Gestapo bully boys. This time, however, he was about to be thrown to the lions.

As he inhaled thick tobacco smoke, trying to steady his hand, a shabby, overcrowded tram stopped on the opposite side of the Fürtherstrasse on its way to the Old Town. Most passengers, mainly gaunt, emaciated women clad in all shades of black and grey, were either dozing or staring blankly out of its grimy windows. None of them seemed aware of the fact that the top Nazi dignitaries were jailed behind the high walls they were looking at. Two skinny girls, whose shoes had clearly let in more than one autumn shower, got off and began queuing at the gate of the Palace of Justice – probably cooks or cleaners. From their drab appearance, haggard look and smell of antiseptic, Major Neave deduced that they belonged to the thousands of thin, ragged people he saw every day at the foot of the eviscerated shells of their tenement blocks, cooking in the open, dwarfed by mounds of rubble. The luckier ones lived in dank cellars and mildewed basements, the majority under makeshift shelters exposed to the elements. Despite the disinfectant liberally sprinkled by the US Army Medical Service Corps, the stench of the six thousand unburied corpses decaying under the ruins of Nuremberg always re-asserted itself, reminding the survivors of the fact they were but squatters in a huge untended graveyard.

After a last puff, Major Neave threw away his cigarette stub. Both girls instantly dived and fought for it on all fours. After a short but ferocious scuffle, the smaller one gave up. As she got up, a scratch mark on her cheek, he caught her eye. Her face was hostile.

'For God's sake, woman! It's Hitler who did this to you – don't you understand?' he shouted in German.

The girl turned away, while the others seemed not to hear.

With a shrug, Neave jumped the queue and waved his pass at the American GIs manning the gate. While they always affected not to recognise him – or anybody else, for that matter – he was now familiar with most of them, and knew that they would take an inordinately long time to check every detail of his papers. His anger was slowly subsiding. Naturally, he was well aware of the scandalous wastefulness of aerial bombardments aimed at destroying whole cities. Like everybody, he sometimes wondered why so much effort had been expended – as late as January 1945, when the outcome of the war was in no doubt – to obliterate the medieval, residential Old Town of Nuremberg, whereas the newer suburbs, complete with their factories and offices, had been left intact.

But deep down he blamed the Hitlerites for this wanton carnage. And the people who'd voted them into power and done their bidding for twelve iniquitous years. These people, after all, could hardly avoid responsibility for the fact that he, Airey Neave, and so many fine men of his generation, had to risk – and in many cases lose – their lives in order to rescue them.

Making his way across the grim courtyard of the Palace of Justice between the Fürtherstrasse and the prison, he crunched some of the innumerable empty machine-gun cartridges left by the two SS divisions who'd made their last stand here only a few months ago. He checked the progress of the works inside the courtroom. It was being enlarged; a new gallery was being built by teams of German prisoners, most of them former SS. Despite the reassuring presence of many American servicemen crouching behind sandbags, in the courtyard and even in the corridors of the Palace of Justice, fingers on the triggers of their machine-guns, Neave always remained tense. The hardened, fanatical SS prisoners, still in their field-grey uniforms, outnumbered the guards by fifty to one, and some desperate attempt to free their revered leaders could never be ruled out. Surely, many of them would prefer to use their shovels, spades and pick-axes to rescue the jailed paladins of the Thousand-Year Reich, rather than build the courtroom that would present their public humiliation, or indeed the gallows where their grand project, careers, and lives were likely to come to an ignominious end.

Neave found both British judges and Colonel Burton C. Andrus, the American prison commandant, in the Palace of Justice café, the only heated room in the building. A tall man with round spectacles and a beakish nose, his reddish hair a little awry, pointed at an empty chair and smiled.

'You must be Major Neave. Do sit down. We've heard a lot about your exploits. I'm Norman Birkett, the alternate British judge. And this is Lord Justice Lawrence, President of the Tribunal. I believe you know Colonel Andrus.'

Neave sat down and reciprocated the courteous nods of his companions.

'So, Major, are you ready?' Lord Justice Lawrence asked. He was a balding man sporting a wing-collar and a bowler hat; his quiet strength came through his pleasant manner.

'Ready for what?' Neave asked.

'To serve the indictments, of course.'

'I… Well… The first I heard about it was this morning, when I bumped into Judge Biddle, your American colleague, in the foyer of the Grand Hotel. He told me I should report to you.'

'Under Article 16 of the Charter of the International Military Tribunal, the defendants have a right to a fair trial and a counsel of their choice,' Judge Birkett intoned. 'We have appointed you to serve the indictments on them, advise them of their rights, and help select German defence lawyers for them. Any questions?'

Colonel Andrus made a strange snorting noise. Neave felt sweat trickling from his armpits. Two thoughts were competing for space in his mind. The first was that he'd been safer in Colditz than he would be in the cage of beasts such as Göring, founder of the Gestapo and of the concentration camps. Or Ernst Kaltenbrunner, the most senior SS boss now that Himmler had committed suicide. Or the rabidly anti-Semitic sex-maniac, Julius Streicher, dubbed by Hitler the Bull of Franconia, and by others the Beast of Nuremberg. As for Field Marshal Keitel...

'I'm not sure I'm qualified,' he said. 'As you may know, I've hardly practised the law. But, given enough time...'

'I'm afraid there is no time,' Lawrence interrupted. 'The trial is set to begin on November 20th. It seems only fair to give the defendants at least a month to prepare their defence. The indictments should be served on them tomorrow at the latest.'

Again Andrus seemed to have difficulty swallowing.

'What do they consist of?' Neave asked.

'Each bundle includes the actual indictment, a copy of the Charter of the Tribunal and a list of German lawyers. Perhaps a hundred pages or so.'

'To be served tomorrow on twenty-three prisoners?'

'Actually, only twenty. The Russians still hold Raeder and Fritzsche, and have already indicted them. They should arrive today or tomorrow, to stand trial with the others. As for Martin Bormann, we'll have to try him *in absentia*.'

'And Hitler?' With a slight shrug, Lord Justice Lawrence glanced at Judge Birkett who threw his hands up
in a gesture of mystification.

Neave was confused. Was this not billed as the greatest
trial in history? Yet, so far, it seemed marked by improvi-
sation and arbitrariness. The selection of the accused had
been noticeably random: a couple of Army generals, a
pair of Navy admirals, a brace of diplomats, some Nazi
dignitaries, a handful of SS bosses, a few financiers and
industrialists. Now it was to include Stalin's two prisoners. Perhaps Churchill had been right all along, doggedly
insisting that the top fifty Nazis be summarily shot without trial. Or the top hundred – what difference would
it make? But Roosevelt had prevailed. No Nazi martyrs
were to be created. The rule of law would be re-estab-
lished in Europe.

'If I understand correctly, Judge, in the name of due
process, despite my lack of procedural experience, you
want me to serve tomorrow hundreds – no, thousands
– of pages of indictments, written in German on twenty
defendants?'

'Your understanding is correct, Major,' Lord Justice
Lawrence confirmed. 'This is the best we can do.'

'You will, of course, have the help of an interpreter,'
Judge Birkett added with a benevolent smile. 'In fact,
any assistance you may require. Additionally, you'll be
accompanied by Colonel Andrus, as well as a team of
psychologists. You know how keen our American friends
are on this new-fangled… psycho-thing.'

'Not all Americans,' Andrus drawled, his black eyes gleaming through steel-rimmed spectacles. 'Baffles me, if truth be told.' A thickset man in a smart uniform with rows of medals pinned to his puffed-up chest, he carried under his left arm a short baton, while his shiny dark green helmet was sitting on his lap.

'Will you give me a couple of hours to look at the papers, and think about it?' asked Neave. 'I'm really not sure I'm up to it. What if I cock it up? Surely, any subsequent conviction would be unsafe if the indictments haven't been properly served?'

'As Lord Justice Lawrence said, this is the best we can do,' Birkett repeated. 'By the way, just have a look at this document. It's an excerpt from Field Marshal Keitel's indictment. Somehow, we thought you might like to read it to him personally.'

Neave took the proffered sheet, and saw his name on it. After his second escape, General Wilhelm Keitel, Chief of the High Command of the German Armed Forces, had been so enraged that he'd issued and personally signed orders that Neave be taken and shot. He'd even put a price on the head of the British fugitive. As a result, Keitel now risked prosecution for breaching the Geneva Convention and for war crimes. Indeed, all it now needed for the starchy German commander to be charged formally was for his nemesis, Major Airey Neave, to pay him a short visit.

Nodding pensively, Neave returned the paper. 'Well, I hope I shan't make a balls-up of it.'

'You won't,' Judge Birkett beamed. 'After all, you're a member of the Bar, are you not?'

NEAVE SPENT the rest of the day furiously reading through article 16 of the Tribunal Charter, entitled 'Fair Trial for the Defendants', and the key points of each individual indictment.

Just as he was leaving the building that evening, a military lorry with strange markings hesitantly trundled along the Fürtherstrasse from the direction of the city centre. It drove past the massive pillars and heavily adorned facade of the Palace of Justice, stopped and reversed slowly, eventually coming to a halt between the sandbags which protected the main entrance arcade. Closer inspection revealed that the inscription on its plate was written in the Cyrillic alphabet. Out of the corner of his eye, Major Neave noticed that two of the five Sherman tanks that guarded the courthouse had trained their 76mm guns on the new arrival. His first reaction was to move away, but curiosity got the better of him.

Two Soviet officers jumped out of the truck, looked around, exchanged a few words and entered the building. One of them, a middle-aged colonel, addressed the American guards in Russian, only to find a sub-machine gun pointed at him. The other stepped forward and addressed the sentry in what seemed to Neave immaculate German. She was a tall, strikingly handsome woman wearing the four stars of a captain. Her discourse impressed the four GIs on duty no more than that of the colonel; it was clear that they hadn't even noticed the change of language.

'Perhaps I can help,' Major Neave said to the US sergeant.

'Thanks, Major. Maybe you could explain to these characters that they are not getting in without a valid pass. Anyway, I'm calling Colonel Andrus.'

'*Darf ich helfen?*' Neave turned to the girl.

'*Danke,*' she replied without returning his smile. 'We have instructions to deliver two prisoners to Herr Lawrence.'

'Lord Justice Lawrence has left for the day. He doesn't live here. Who are your prisoners?'

'Two Nazi war criminals. I understand they are to be tried by the International Military Tribunal and hanged.'

'I see. What are their names?'

'Propaganda Chief Fritzsche and Grand Admiral Raeder.'

'Ah yes. We've been expecting them. I suggest...' Before he could complete his sentence, Colonel Andrus appeared at a brisk pace, stick under left arm, bristling moustache squarely centred under his steel helmet, accompanied by four Military Policemen.

'What's going on here?' he demanded.

Neave did the honours. 'This is Colonel Burton C. Andrus of the US Cavalry, the prison governor. He'll take charge of your detainees.'

'I'm Captain Terisova, and this is Colonel Klimenko.'

'Does anybody here speak English?' Andrus snapped.

'I believe you're expecting two prisoners, Colonel. These Red Army officers are delivering them.'

'Good . Where are they?'

'Presumably in there.' Neave pointed through the open door at the truck.

'What are they waiting for?'

Major Neave turned to the Russians. 'Colonel Andrus is ready to receive the prisoners.'

'Excellent,' the girl replied. ' We just need him to sign this receipt and we'll be on our way.' She handed Neave a document, which he passed on to Andrus. The US colonel adjusted his steel-rimmed spectacles and glanced at it.

'What kind of a joke is this?' he asked, handing the sheet back to Neave. It was written in Russian.

'What does it say?' Neave asked.

'Only that both men are in good condition, and that you henceforth accept full responsibility for their health and well-being,' Captain Terisova explained.

'Let's have a look at them first,' Andrus countered.

A couple of minutes later two handcuffed, bedraggled Germans and a large detachment of Russian guards stood nervously in the entrance hall. Andrus ordered his sentries to take the prisoners to their cells. He waited until they had disappeared round the corner and nodded towards the document in Major Neave's hands. 'Did they really expect me to fall for that one?' he asked scornfully.

'What do you mean, Colonel?'

'How could I vouch for the condition of these prisoners? For all I know, they might be terminally ill. They could even have been injected with some delayed-action poison.'

'So you won't sign their receipt?'

'No way – not even if I could understand it. You'd better tell them.'

Despite Neave's diplomatic skills, the Russian officers seemed shocked. Colonel Klimenko took his aide aside and animatedly conferred with her. When they came back, Neave noticed that the Soviet colonel's jaw muscles were twitching.

'We understand your position,' Captain Terisova conveyed. 'Unfortunately, it leaves us no option but to take our prisoners back and wait for new instructions. We shall stay at the billet of the Soviet trial delegation.'

'Out of the question!' Andrus interjected before Neave had even finished translating. 'Raeder and Fritzsche are now in my prison – and that's where they are staying until they have been tried. End of story.'

On hearing the news Colonel Klimenko went red and started shouting. The men in his detachment quietly fanned out, close to the walls, fingers on the triggers of their sub-machine guns.

Watching them, Neave was in no doubt that this platoon had seen a lot of street-fighting. And there was a dozen of them, out-numbering the American guards and Military Policemen. Without waiting for any translation, Colonel Andrus stepped forward and confronted

Klimenko. Barking at the tall Russian who was towering over him, the stocky American reminded Neave of a fearless terrier harassing a greyhound.

'Come back in two days, and if our doctors have confirmed the prisoners are healthy, I shall sign your receipt. You have my word of honour. Now, I'd like you to leave these premises before your truck is blown up.' He pointed at the Sherman tanks whose turrets had throughout remained trained on the Soviet transport.

After Major Neave had translated into German and Captain Terisova into Russian, there was a pregnant pause. Then, stony-faced, Colonel Ivan Klimenko saluted, turned round and retreated.

'*Bis übermorgen.* We'll be back,' Captain Terisova said, her grey-green eyes flashing through long eyelashes.

Neave heaved a sigh of relief as the detachment trooped out. Glancing at the American guards, he was amused to find all eyes – even those of Colonel Burton C. Andrus of the US Cavalry – glued to Captain Terisova's high hips.

AT TEN O'CLOCK the next day, the eleven-man indictment party set off. Colonel Andrus and Major Neave led the charge, followed by the American psychologist, Doctor Gilbert (the only German-speaking American officer in the whole complex) and his young British colleague, Doctor George. Two court officials laden with bundles of papers, four GIs and a Jewish-American interpreter, a small man with yellow hair and blue eyes, formed the rear.

Soon their progress along the main corridor of the courthouse was blocked by a bulkhead marked: 'Off Limits – Knock'. A peep-hole slid open. Colonel Andrus showed his pass, and had a word. A door opened. On the other side two armed guards carefully checked all prison passes before letting them through. From that point onward, the oppressive silence was dented only by their own footsteps. They came to the covered walkway, just erected to protect the detainees from public scrutiny or assault whenever they commuted between their cells and the courthouse. Again, they were challenged to show their passes, before having to negotiate, through another peep-hole, a steel door behind which further identification checks were meticulously conducted. At last, through an unguarded door, they broke into fresh air. They were in the prison exercise yard. Unusually for this time of day, it was empty. Normally, prisoners in single file, each one followed by a guard eight paces behind – enough to avoid being surprised by a sudden attack – could be seen pacing the barren ground, but not on this grey October morning. They had all been confined to their cells.

Suddenly, fresh memories of German prisons overwhelmed Major Airey Neave. A powerful spasm wrenching his guts, he feared he was going to be sick. Quickly glancing at the sky, as he used to do in order to allow his thoughts to soar away from Gestapo jails, he saw yet more sentries on the roofs and towers, more rifles, more machine guns. Every muscle, every sinew in his body was itching to turn and run.

Following Colonel Andrus, the party headed for the cell block. Another steel door. Neave was asked to sign their time of entry in a register. Twenty-eight minutes to eleven. Led by the prison governor himself, it had taken them a full half hour to worm their way into the core of the Nuremberg Prison – the putrescent nerve centre of the defeated Third Reich. The door clanged behind them, causing Neave's heart to palpitate uncomfortably. Even the air felt imprisoned here. The deathly silence that followed reminded him of the solitary confinement cell of the Gestapo prison in Plotsk.

'Are you all right?' Doctor George whispered.

Elliott George had been added to the British War Crimes Executive as an afterthought. It had soon become clear that, in terms of access to the accused, Doctor Gustave Gilbert and his US colleagues had priority over all Tribunal officials, interrogators and even defence lawyers. Soon, a German-speaking British psychologist had been flown in from London to redress the balance. He was a pleasant young man with blond hair, freckles and owlish eyes behind improbably thick round glasses. He and Neave had soon struck up a friendship.

'I'll be fine – thank you,' Neave gratefully acknowledged the hand on his arm.

'You will,' Doctor George nodded with an encouraging smile.

On the threshold of the long ground-floor corridor,

Colonel Andrus stopped and turned round. By Neave's reckoning, there were fifteen to twenty cell doors on each side, each manned by a US sentry armed with a revolver and a blackjack who watched his prisoner twenty-four hours a day through a small hatch. At the far end, a steel spiral staircase led to the upper levels. Overhead, acres of wire netting had been installed to prevent detainees from jumping to their death from the platforms.

'Well, Major, shall we kick off with your old friend Keitel?' Andrus pointed at the nearest cell.

'It will be my pleasure, Colonel,' Neave smiled. Suddenly, he felt better – as always, when in action.

The Military Policeman opened the door. The prisoner was sitting, reading the Bible that he'd carried with him through two world wars. His thirteen-by-nine foot cell was furnished with only a collapsible table and chair, both designed to foil any attempt at suicide by hanging. Fresh plaster patches were visible where hooks, bars and shelves had been removed from the walls for the same reason.

The chair was removed at night, and the steel bed was fastened to the floor. In the corner next to the door were a toilet seat and a washbasin with running water. Only by sitting on the toilet could the inmate escape the constant gaze of the warden at his door, though his feet remained visible.

As Colonel Andrus, followed by Major Neave, two MPs, the interpreter and both psychologists, entered his cell, the sixty-three-year old German wearily rose. He was wearing his field marshal's tunic, without badges or decorations.

'Are you Wilhelm Bodewin Keitel, Chief of Staff of the High Command of the German Armed Forces between 1938 and 1945?' Andrus asked formally.

'*Ja, ich bin es.*' Keitel made a hopeless attempt to click his heels. Because no prisoner was allowed shoe laces, he wore drab felt slippers. Next to them, Colonel Andrus's leather boots gleamed triumphantly. Even Keitel's moustache seemed limp and unsoldierly next to Andrus's bristle.

'Listen carefully,' Andrus said. 'This officer – an old acquaintance of yours, I believe – has important news for you.'

Stepping forward, Neave noticed the fear in Keitel's eyes. He took a deep breath.

'I am Major Neave, the officer appointed by the International Military Tribunal to serve upon you a copy of the indictment in which you are named as a defendant.'

Keitel opened his mouth, but no sound came out. Blood drained from his face. One of the sentinels dropped a thick bundle of papers on the table.

'Major Neave,' he said at last. 'I wasn't expecting ever to meet you.'

'I imagine not, General.'

'What am I accused of?'

'Conspiracy to wage wars of aggression. Crimes against peace. Crimes against humanity. War crimes. Read the papers. Then select a defence lawyer. If you have any questions, put them to me tomorrow,' recited Neave.

'All my life, I've served my country honourably. I've never been cowardly or faithless. All I did was to obey the Führer's orders.'

'As you'll see, the defence of superior orders will not be allowed, General.'

'Who says so?'

'The Charter of the Tribunal is included in your bundle. I suggest you read it.'

'I presume it would be inconvenient to recognise that the obligation of soldiers is to obey orders, would it?'

'Be that as it may, General, you appear to be forgetting some of the orders you yourself issued – one of which concerned me personally. And the one you signed on 16th December 1942 instructing your commanders in Russia to shoot fifty so-called Communists for every German soldier killed. That might take some explaining.'

The stiff German commander bowed his head.

The air in the corridor felt almost refreshing as Neave left the cell, wondering whether Hitler, who notoriously claimed that Keitel had no more brains than a cinema usher, had perhaps been right to treat the man with such contempt. On the other hand, both the soldier and the lawyer in Neave felt troubled by the Tribunal's unprecedented decision to rule out any defence of superior orders. He understood its necessity clearly enough: since all policies and actions of the Nazi dignitaries could probably be shown to have originated with the Führer, no conviction would be possible if passing responsibility up the chain of command were permitted. As for Hitler himself, his absence only compounded the difficulty. Yet – did it make sense to put the Nazi regime on trial without its founders, leaders and prophets, namely Hitler, Goebbels, Himmler, Bormann?

'Good,' Neave said crisply. 'One down, nineteen to go. Let's go and indict Göring.'

The man in a grey, oversized Luftwaffe tunic, who didn't even look up as his cell door was noisily unlocked, was very different from the obese drug addict who'd been arrested in Bavaria four months earlier. Back then, when he'd first appeared in front of Colonel Burton C. Andrus of the US Cavalry, complete with sixteen monogrammed suitcases, a red hatbox and a valet, Göring weighed one hundred and thirty kilograms, sported glossy red varnish on all twenty toe- and fingernails, and ingested daily forty of his twenty thousand Paracodin pills. During their painstaking search of his myriad personal effects, Andrus's soldiers had retrieved a potassium cyanide vial from the bottom of a sealed Nescafé tin, and another from the lining of one of his uniforms. Each contained enough poison to kill half a dozen men. Since then, thanks to the ministrations of the "Fire Brigade Colonel" (as Göring scornfully referred to Colonel Andrus), he'd lost more than thirty kilos and been ruthlessly weaned off morphine.

'Up! Get your fat hands down by your side and stand to attention!' Colonel Andrus barked.

The prisoner sighed audibly, rose and limply stood to

attention at a forty-five degree angle to the invading party.

'Are you Reichsmarschall Hermann Wilhelm Göring, born on 12th January 1893?' Andrus asked.

Göring pretended not to understand the question. All waited for the blond interpreter to translate. Captain Gustave Gilbert, the American psychologist, scribbled in his notebook.

'Who else?' the prisoner replied. 'Also Commander-in-Chief of the Luftwaffe for the last ten years. Prime Minister of Prussia. Deputy and successor of the Führer in all his offices.'

Gilbert kept writing.

Andrus moved aside, nearly knocking over the framed photograph of Göring's second wife and eight-year-old daughter Edda. Though fair, the pretty little girl looked touchingly like her father in his heyday. The small cell was crowded and Neave felt shut in with its inmate.

'I am Major Neave, the officer appointed by the International Military Tribunal to serve upon you a copy of the indictment in which you are named as a defendant,' he recited.

With theatrical politeness, but without granting Neave a glance, Göring bowed. He took the copy of the indictment and threw it on the table.

'So it has come,' he said quietly.

'You have the right to conduct your own defence or to be assisted by counsel. I recommend the latter.'

'So it has come,' Göring repeated sombrely.

Doctor Gilbert kept scrawling furiously in his note-book. Neave assumed he found the repetition of this underwhelming epitaph to the Third Reich of great psychological import. Even without nail varnish, jewels or Roman toga, there was something vaguely feminine about the fallen Reichsmarschall. Nothing soft or cuddly, and no trace of homosexuality; rather, the sort of danger-ous femininity exhibited by a tigress.

'You can select your own counsel, or the tribunal can appoint one for you. Here is a list of potentially available German lawyers.'

'Lawyers? I never had anything to do with lawyers, Herr Major. I used to make laws, you see.'

'So you did. You will find your responsibility in promul-gating the anti-Semitic Nuremberg Laws of September 1935 is duly mentioned in your indictment. As is your role in creating concentration camps and the Gestapo.'

'Well then, you'll have to select a lawyer for me, Herr Major. Anyway, I doubt that any German advocate would dare appear in front of your monkey tribunal. Let me have a decent interpreter, and I'll defend myself.' For the first time Göring turned to face the British officer, revealing narrow menacing eyes and wide lips. Despite unusually short legs and a less than imposing stature, his magnetism was palpable. Within touching distance of this fount of Nazi evil, Airey Neave realised with some surprise that he was no longer afraid. But the Tribunal was concerned that no defendant should be without de-fence counsel: the trial had to be seen to be fair.

'I think you'd be well advised to be represented,' he replied.

'Really? Surely, Herr Major, you realise this is all a farce?'

'I suggest you read the indictment.'

'Oh, I shall, Herr Major. Bound to be fascinating. But I cannot see how it could possibly have a basis in law, can you?' He shook his mane, baring his teeth in a mirthless smile. His voice was soft and mellow, yet threatening. This wounded tigress was ready to fight.

'I'm not prepared to discuss the basis of the indictment,' Neave said curtly. 'If you have any questions, put them in writing.'

An ironic smile on his lips, Göring turned away as if to signify the audience was at an end.

'Excuse me, Herr Reichsmarschall,' Doctor Gilbert stepped forward, extending his pad and pen to the prisoner. 'Would you mind writing down a few words summarising your present state of mind?'

Göring didn't hesitate. The American psychologist had never revealed to his captive patients that he was Jewish and worked as an intelligence officer. With his open face, friendly manners, quiet voice, round spectacles and unassuming behaviour, he'd already become the confidant of many of them.

'It will be my pleasure.' Göring took the pad, scribbled briefly and returned it to Doctor Gilbert.

The air in the small overcrowded cell had become unbreathable. His steel helmet glinting in a ray of sun,

Colonel Andrus was impatiently playing with his stick. Major Neave nodded to Göring, who again bowed ostentatiously. After the door of the cell had been slammed and bolted, Neave felt as relieved as after his escape from Colditz.

'What did he write?' he asked Gilbert.

'Der Sieger wird immer der Richter und der Besiegte stets der Angeklagte sein.'

'What the hell does that mean?' Colonel Andrus asked.

'"The victor will always be the judge and the vanquished the accused."'

There was a pause.

'Eighteen to go,' Andrus said. 'Who's next?'

5

Alpha Blue Fox

DOKTOR GRÄBE AND HIS WIFE were justifiably protective of their daughters Sybille and Susette, but not to the point of paranoia. The fact that the family had been illegally evicted from their large house by their American liberators still rankled, but, I liked to think, they were thankful to me for having returned to them the use of the two large consulting rooms on the ground floor, as well as the kitchen garden. Frau Doktor Gräbe – I was never to discover her first name – was a keen gardener; soon she'd resumed working beyond the confines of the vegetable patch, and tidied up the lawns, flowerbeds and even the *Planschbecken*.

Because the whole family now lived in a single, cramped room at the hospital, Susette found it easier to do her homework in her father's surgery. I discovered she was therefore likely to appear in the late afternoon, carrying her books in a battered satchel, and often had to wait for the last patients to go, leaving behind lumps of coal, a couple of potatoes or a courgette by way of payment.

I soon formed the habit of watching her arrival from my window and rushing down to intercept her in the entrance hall. Controlling my breathing, I would affect surprise and nonchalance, and offer to carry her books. She would blush slightly and refuse. Initially she'd been bashful, avoiding my gaze and answering my questions with tense monosyllables. Sometimes, she would be accompanied by her elder sister. At twenty-three, Sybille was only four years older; yet she belonged to another generation, if only because she was mother to an adorable four-year-old girl named Lilli. Many of the younger T Force officers fantasised about the beautiful and mysteriously-adult Sybille; however, her inaccessibility was axiomatic. Sybille's husband was believed to be in a Russian POW camp; her distress at the absence of news was so palpable that it afforded her more solemn protection even than widowhood. Thank God for Lilli, who soon broke the ice.

'What's your name?' she asked, adding, without waiting for an answer: 'What are you doing in granddad's house?' Sybille apologised. Laughing, I crouched in front of the toddler and explained that I'd come to help her family and all the people of Kamen to have a better life.

'But you've taken our house, and we have no food,' Lilli retorted.

'Lilli!' Sybille exclaimed.

'And you sound funny,' Lilli continued.

'Shush, Lilli. Let's go and see whether Granddad is waiting for us.'

Sybille dragged her daughter towards the surgery. I looked at Susette, half expecting another apology. It was hard to tell whether the smile on her lips was ironic or friendly.

'It's perfectly all right,' I said.

'Is it? Do you mean she's right?'

'Well… yes, in a way. But the fact there is not enough food and housing is hardly my fault.'

'That's the problem, isn't it? The blame game. We Germans are not going to win it, are we? Even people who fought Nazism in peril of their life, like my father, they have to be punished – don't they?'

'How did your father fight the Nazis?'

'Don't you know? He kept treating all his Jewish patients – as long as they were still around. Free of charge. And on several occasions he looked after Allied airmen who'd been shot down. He can give you their names – if you're interested.'

'Gosh, I'd no idea. That must have been pretty risky.'

She remained silent. Under her steady gaze, it was my turn to blush.

During the early weeks of autumn, our corridor encounters had become almost daily occurrences, and lasted longer. Susette was less strikingly tall than her sister, pretty rather than classically beautiful, and her teeth were by no means perfect. Nevertheless, I found her liveliness, her mixture of shyness and defiance, her feisty wit and intelligence, quite enchanting. Her high forehead, marked eyebrows and straight nose soon figured in my dreams, as did her well-developed chest. As I manoeuvred ever closer to her, I became quite addicted to her smell. Incredibly, Susette did not carry the cabbage-like odour of defeated Germany; on the contrary, fresh emanations of roses, lavender and soap delicately combined with a more spicy, intensely personal, mysteriously exciting note to form the headiest fragrance.

As for her full lips, several weeks elapsed before I dared place mine on them, and several more before she willingly parted them.

ONE NIGHT, exactly a week after I'd been promoted to the rank of captain, one of my two bedside telephones rang in the small hours of the morning.

'Alpha Blue Fox is moving to Code Red,' a voice whispered conspiratorially. 'Please confirm identification and Code Red credentials.'

'Who's that? Do you know what time it is?'

'I repeat: confirm identification and Code Red credentials.' There was a hint of impatience in the caller's voice, which now sounded more familiar.

I finally found the switch and turned on the lamp.

'If I may ask… who are you, and what the hell are you rabbiting on about?'

'For God's sake, Peter, this is an emergency. I'd be grateful if you could observe the correct procedures. Can't talk in clear, I'm afraid.'

'Oh, hello David.'

'So much for code. Would you mind terribly waking bloody up?'

'I am awake. What's up? Are you calling from HQ?'

After the end of the war, Major Hunt had been posted to T Force HQ in Bad Oeynhausen, succeeding Major Brian Urquhart as GSO II.

'Yes. Any chance of your remembering the emergency code?'

'Unlikely. Nobody ever mentioned it to me.'

'Really? We'll just have to assume this line isn't bugged, then. Now listen carefully. The Russians are just about to hit your area big time.'

'What?'

'Under the Potsdam Treaty they have the right to claim a share of any German military and industrial assets in the Allied Occupation Zones.'

'In addition to their exclusive right to loot their own Occupation Zone?'

'Correct. Well, they are suddenly stepping up their activities in the British Zone. Your area of the British Zone. I have just received three Quadripartite Team inspection requests. All in your area, all ultra-sensitive.'

'Can you give me some details?'

'Yes. But don't write them down in clear. Ready?'

'Go ahead.'

'Number one: Krupps Widia works in Essen. They'll be visiting the plant in forty-eight hours.'

'The place where they used to make carbide steel?'

'Correct. Do you know what's in their cellars?'

'Haven't the foggiest.'

'Eleven tons of yellowcake uranium. We believe it's been hidden there on the way to some central cache. Your job is simple. Make it disappear before the Soviets turn up. Otherwise they will be entitled to make a bid for it.'

'How radio-active is it?' I wasn't feeling sleepy any more.

'No idea. Don't worry about it: just have it shipped to England before the Reds get their paws on it.'

'Consider it done. Anything else?'

'The Russians have also asked to inspect the gun shed at the Krupps factory.'

'Damn. Are they aware of the three monster cannons still left in there?'

'We must assume so. Apparently, your area has been crawling with NKGB for the last month. These guns must be spirited away before the inspection.'

'Bloody hell! I daresay we should have done it long ago. But we're talking big toys here, David. Dozens, maybe hundreds of tons. With sixty-foot-long barrels. They're going to take some spiriting.'

'Do it.'

'Yes, sir. Will that be all?'

Major Hunt chuckled.

'Not quite. Number three: the Vereinigte Aluminium Werke at Lünen.'

'What about it?'

'Do you know the plant?'

'I've driven past it. It's a few miles west of Kamen, on the autobahn.'

'That's the one. The inspection team wants to go there after they've finished with Krupps. They'll draw up an inventory as a prelude to a bid by the Russians.'

'Is that a problem? Don't tell me they have pocket submarines or atomic bombs in their bloody cellars?'

'That will be for you to check before the inspectors get there. No, the problem is simpler. And bigger. About half the machinery has been requested by the British Aluminium Company. Apparently, it's light years ahead of their own stuff.'

I raked my hair back, wondering whether I was, after all, still dreaming, or the target of an elaborate hoax.

'David – you are joking, aren't you?'

'No.'

'Are you asking me to spirit away a whole aluminium complex within a couple of days? Hundreds of tons, maybe thousands?'

'That's the general idea.'

'For God's sake! Just dismantling it would take weeks. Let alone crating and shipping it.'

'I know.'

'So?'

'Please confirm identification.'

'What?'

'Please confirm identification.'

'Captain Peter Birkett, Intelligence Officer, No. 1 T Force.'

'Indeed. Use your wit, Intelligence Officer. Our mission is to make sure the Soviets never see the stuff, or at least can never make a valid claim for it. Understood?'

'Understood.'

'Good luck, Peter. Code Red activated. Alpha Blue Fox out.'

The line went dead.

With a mixture of schoolboy expletives and military obscenities, I got up, put my greatcoat on top of my pyjamas and started pacing furiously. At two in the morning, with only the sketchiest outline of a plan, I called Max Harrison, Intelligence Officer of B Company, and explained the task. No. 1 T Force was currently spread across four locations over a fifty-mile stretch of German industrial heartland. Its headquarters and A company were in Kamen. B Company was in Heisingen, a small town less than five miles from the Krupps factory at Essen. They would have to deal with the uranium and the guns.

As for the Lünen aluminium plant, only ten miles from Kamen, this clearly would have to be handled by A Company. But, since I had no idea how to move a vast aluminium smelter within two months, let alone two days, I decided to concentrate first on marginally less daunting challenges.

At the crack of dawn, Max and I were gloomily surveying the three huge pieces of ordnance that resided in the Krupps gun shed. The smallest was a Howitzer with a bore of fourteen inches; the biggest had a seventy-foot long barrel. Max pointed at the hundred yards of rubble which stretched between the shed and the main road.

'Sorry, old chap,' he said. 'Even if we could find any kind of transport suitable for these monsters, we couldn't get to them. Not in two days.'

'Listen carefully,' I turned to him. 'We haven't got two days. I'll be back tomorrow with transport. In the meantime, you need to bulldoze a path between the shed and the road by midnight.'

'Peter! I haven't got any bulldozers. Nor the labour force.'

'Find them. Get HQ to help. Remember T Force has priority over all other operational requirements in Germany. Get on to it.'

Shaking his blond head, Max lit a cigarette.

'One other thing, Max. These guns are in no condition to be towed. You need to fix up jury axles and wheels.'

'I'll see what we can do. Obviously, even if axles and wheels suddenly grew on trees, it will have to wait until tomorrow. Don't forget I'm supposed to bulldoze a few thousand tons of rubbish with my bare hands today.'

'Negative. I'll be here at ten o'clock tomorrow to start the evacuation.'

'Have you completely taken leave of your senses?' Max exploded. 'Or has your third pip gone to your head already? Don't you fucking realise that each and every task you've assigned me is impossible? How the hell can I execute all of them simultaneously?'

'Sorry, old boy,' I managed a thin smile. 'Not my idea. But think of the alternative.'

'What about it?'

'The alternative, Max, is that in a few months' time we'll be staring at the wrong end of these barrels, as the Russians turn them against us.'

Max drew on his cigarette, inhaled deeply and slowly exhaled a cloud of blue smoke which hung still in the cold morning air.

'Would you please go away?' he said, dropping a generous dollop of ash onto his crumpled trousers. 'I've got work to do. Can't stand here all day chatting idly – much as I'd like to.'

'One last thing. I mentioned this uranium cache in the cellars, remember? Have you found it?'

'We found something. Could be dirt. Could be uranium. Who can tell? Come and see for yourself.'

Accompanied by two armed privates, we negotiated our way across the sprawling derelict factory, down two flights of stairs and along narrow underground passages. A pungent odour emanated from the last vault, where Max shone his torch lamp on a mound of greenish-black material.

'Does this look like yellowcake uranium to you?' he asked, pinching his nose with his free hand.

'Not very yellow, is it? On the other hand, what else could it be? How much do you reckon is there?'

'Impossible to say. If it were coal I'd guess ten or fifteen tons?'

'Sounds about right to me. Now, the bad news, Max. This thing has absolute priority. We need to move it. Yesterday.'

'What's the emergency?'

'Apparently Stalin is very keen to get hold of it. He's already stolen the nuclear bomb technology, you see. All he needs is the raw material.'

'Peter, this stuff has been lying here undisturbed since the end of the war nearly six months ago. Can't it wait another week, while we try and deal with the fucking guns?'

'Negative. We suspect that the NKGB have identified this location. If that's true, they'll be here any minute.'

'Good grief,' Max whispered. 'We'd better get out of this stinkpot before they arrive and talk.'

As we re-emerged from the dank cellars, I eagerly breathed in the freezing draught that was sweeping through the factory, unimpeded by roof or windowpanes.

'Look, Max. Logistically, this is no big deal. Just find any kind of boxes or crates, and stuff them with just enough uranium for two men to lift, but no more. Then load them onto a truck. The challenge is security. Have a fully-armed platoon round this place at all times, and take no chances. Act lively, man – and no balls-ups – right?'

'Perfectly all right, old boy. A doddle.'

Walking towards the Mercedes in which Rifleman Richardson was waiting, I was relieved to hear Max's laughter echoing through the ghostly building. Clearly, the idea of playing a few tricks on the Russians was beginning to tickle him.

On the way back to Kamen, I stopped to inspect the

Vereinigte Aluminium Werke in Lünen, where I met the Intelligence Officer of A Company. Lieutenant Julian Wright-Collins, a year older than me, was as tall and gangly as Max Harrison was plump and rotund; he smoked as much but drank less.

Surprisingly, the complex had escaped years of Allied bombardment relatively unscathed, and acres of plant and machinery were still standing in apparent working order. The items required by British Aluminium covered about one third of the total floor area and, much as I had suspected, would weigh in, when dismantled, at several hundred tons. None of this equipment was going to move soon. Another strategy – preferably a miracle – was needed to prevent it from falling into Russian hands.

'Well, Julian. Any bright ideas?' I asked.

'Sorry, Peter – I'm but a simple lieutenant. You're a captain. Surely bright ideas are your responsibility?'

I didn't rise to the bait. I was aware that, seemingly alone among my colleagues, Wright-Collins resented my recent promotion.

'Can you think of any way to move that stuff within two days?' I asked.

'Short of blowing it all up – no.'

'That's a thought...' I paused to consider it. 'It certainly would stop the Russians grabbing it. But it wouldn't help British Aluminium much.'

'We can't all have everything we want all the time, can we?'

'True. But if we blow this place up the day before the

Quadripartite inspection team arrives, even the most asinine Communist will smell a rat, won't he?'

'So what if they do?'

'At best, a massive diplomatic incident. At worst, World War Three. In any case somebody will want our hides. Correction: everybody will want my hide.'

'That would be somewhat unfortunate, I grant you,' Wright-Collins replied, loading an ivory cigarette holder with a Senior Service and inserting it between his teeth.

'Julian – I seem to recall seeing you reading Machiavelli? What would the maestro recommend?'

'Be Machiavellian, I suppose.'

'Anything more specific?'

Wright-Collins lit his Senior Service purposefully.

'Be pragmatic. Remember that the end always justifies the means.'

'Hmm... Why don't we screen off the area where the disputed machinery lies?' I mused aloud.

'How?'

'Any kind of fencing or hoarding would do.'

'Don't you think it would be a red rag to a bull?' Wright-Collins objected. 'Your Russians are sure to make a beeline for that fence.'

'You're probably right. Damn.' I looked around, vainly searching for inspiration. Wright-Collins blew a perfect smoke ring and watched it slowly ascend, twist and dissolve.

'Okay, Julian. We can't move this stuff. We can't blow it up. We can't hide it. Agreed?'

'Yes.'

'Let's at least identify it. Please ensure that every piece of machinery requested by British Aluminium is located and distinctly, but discreetly, marked. Then draw up an inventory and bring it to me this evening. Understood?'

With the merest shadow of an ironic smile on his angular features, Lieutenant Wright-Collins saluted.

During the fifteen minutes it took the Mercedes to get back to Kamen, I speculated on the glee with which Wright-Collins would watch me fall flat on my face – and whether he might even be prepared to give fate a little push. Admittedly, I had been more than a little proud of the fact that my recent promotion, earned through a mixture of diligence and politics (much more of the former than the latter, it goes without saying), had made me the youngest captain of the British Army of the Rhine.

That hadn't escaped the attention of the ever perceptive Susette. 'How does the English proverb run?' she'd asked innocently. 'You know – the one about pride and a fall?' I'd laughed and silenced her with a kiss.

By mid-morning, I was back at headquarters in the market place of Kamen. Returning the sentry's salute, I headed straight for the office of Colonel Wreford-Brown to make him aware of the ongoing, high-level flap.

'Bloody nuisance,' the commander of No. 1 T Force grumbled. 'Can't understand for the life of me why we still allow the Reds to run rings around us. These Mongols should have been sent back to the steppes last May, if you ask me. Anyway, there we are. Everything under control, Birkett?'

'Not quite yet, sir. Working on it. I might have to trouble you with a number of transport requisition orders during the day, if that's all right. We'll need to pull out all the stops.'

'Absolutely. Anything else?'

'No, sir.'

'Keep me posted, will you?'

'Of course, sir.'

'Jolly good.'

Since the end of combat operations, Colonel Wreford-Brown's enthusiasm for T Force operations had noticeably diminished. Though he never voiced them publicly, he seemed to harbour reservations about the competitive wholesale dismantling of German industry. Either he thought that kicking a starving man on the ground wasn't cricket, or he perceived the administrative nature of the task as unworthy of the military. At any rate, he was clearly more inclined to satisfy his hunting instincts by spending whole days rambling in the countryside with his twelve-bore Purdeys than by looking for industrial secrets. Bringing home a hare or wood pigeon undoubtedly gave him more of a thrill than shipping machine-tools back to Blighty. A practical *modus operandi* had therefore emerged whereby Colonel Wreford-Brown dealt with all standard pay-and-rations issues and Army politics, leaving me and the Intelligence Section to get on with what he saw as looting.

Before midday, Sergeant Wagg and his half dozen men had been briefed and were furiously working the telephones. By three o'clock, they'd found three Scammell low-load trailer towing vehicles, normally used to haul tanks, and arranged for them to drive overnight from Oldenburg in the north of the Zone to Essen. Max Harrison called in to report that B Company was making progress. With a nod and a wink, he'd explained the emergency to the Krupp directors, none of whom could be suspected of Communist leanings. Keen to prevent their most advanced artillery technology from falling into Stalin's hands, they'd sprung into action. In no time, a rusty bulldozer had been repaired; re-fuelled by B Company, it was now clearing the access strip between the gun shed and the road at a rate of knots. Suitable wheels had been found; at least a hundred Krupp workers were busy making the axles that would support them.

'Bloody good work, Max,' I said. 'I knew I could rely on you. When do you expect the guns to be ready for their little trip?'

'The Germans are willing to work all night. I would expect the toys to be on wheels by dawn.'

'Excellent. The Scammels will arrive during the night. Please get them hitched to the guns immediately. Report to me as soon as the convoy is roadworthy.'

'I'm not sure it will ever be roadworthy,' Max chuckled. 'But, with a bit of luck, it should be mobile.'

'That will do nicely.'

'Where are we taking them?'

'I'll be down at the Krupp shed at 7 a.m. Be ready for the convoy to leave at that time. Destination will be disclosed on departure.'

'Right-ho, sir.'

'What about the uranium?' I asked.

'Oh, that? Piece of cake. Yellow cake, to be precise.'

'Very droll. What's happening to it?'

'You asked us to move it, didn't you?'

'Will you please stop horsing about, Max?'

'We're moving it.'

'How?'

'We found a shed load of empty three-inch mortar-bomb boxes. Steel, one handle at each end. We're filling each one with about fifty kilos of the stuff.'

'Brilliant. How much have you boxed so far?'

'Me? Nothing.'

'What do you mean?'

'The Krupp labour force are doing that too. Remember this muck is probably highly radio-active. Worse: it stinks like the devil's own shit. I'd say they've moved about half already. Should be finished tonight.'

'Good. Transport?'

'I've got a ten-ton Mack truck on standby.'

'Fuel?'

'Full tank.'

'Perfect. As soon as it's loaded, draw three Sten guns and a dozen magazines. Give them to Lance Corporal Weatherall and two reliable men, and sit the lot on that uranium. Have them deliver the load to the Station

Commander at RAF Bückeburg. If any bastard tries to interfere, let them shoot him. Got that?'

'Loud and clear, Captain.'

'And get a bloody receipt,' I added before hanging up.

AT FIRST LIGHT, I rode a motorcycle down to Essen. It was another dry, frosty morning. I was so cold that I had difficulty dismounting. Unshaven and covered in cigarette ash, Max greeted me with a limp salute and pointed at three gigantic silhouettes parked between the road and the gun shed.

'Where have you been?' he asked with a crooked smile. 'Alarm clock problems? We've been waiting.'

'Let's go. I'll act as outrider. Tell the drivers to follow me. Take a fully-armed Humber scout car and bring up the rear. Make sure nobody follows us.'

Soon the threatening, but motley-looking convoy was on the road. Slowly, very slowly, I led them towards Kamen. I reasoned that, given the extraordinary axle weight and dimensions of the vehicles, staying on the autobahn was the safest bet. Besides, with a bit of luck, nobody would think of looking for them in Kamen, a small Westphalian mining town of no importance. And it would be easy to keep watch on them until they could be moved on. It took us more than five hours to travel some thirty miles, so that we did not hit the Lünener Strasse before midday. Half an hour later the three giant guns towered over the houses of Doktor Anton Gräbe and his neighbours. Surrounded by large gardens, these four imposing properties, all of which had been requisitioned by the Occupation forces, formed a discrete enclave that would provide as safe a parking place as any for over-sized cannons on the run. I left two guards inside each truck and rode my motorcycle straight to headquarters. Sergeant Wagg updated me on the latest developments: a full inventory of the contents of the Lünen aluminium plant had been received from Wright-Collins during the night, and Lance Corporal Weatherall had watched with his own eyes as his uranium boxes took off from RAF Bückeburg en route for a classified UK destination.

As I reported to Colonel Wreford-Brown, it seemed that the Krupp Widia plant in Essen was now ready to receive the Quadripartite inspection team, which was due the next day. The same, though, couldn't be said of the Lünen complex. At my instigation, Wreford-Brown called Brigadier Pennycook at T Force headquarters in Bad Oeynhausen to explain that his mission was impossible: no earthly power could move an aluminium smelter in two days.

'Captain Birkett tells me that, if London really doesn't want the Soviets to have sight of this equipment, you'll have to call the inspection off,' he summarised.

'Not in my power, Guy,' Pennycook replied. 'First, as you know, we don't organise the inspections, we simply facilitate them. Second, the Russians are already on their way. Third, the minute we tell them they can't inspect something, they'll make it their top priority.'

'I understand, George. But we are in a bit of a pickle here, you see.'

'If I remember correctly, Birkett displayed considerable ingenuity last May, when he was hell-bent on capturing Kiel single-handed. He'd better do it again – unless he mistakenly expects me to save his bacon once more.'

'I'll tell him.'

'You're not going to let the side down, are you, Guy?'

'Or course not. Leave it to me,' Wreford-Brown concluded, before hanging up despondently.

'What do we do, sir?' I asked, replacing the earpiece on the colonel's desk.

'Well. The inspectors arrive tomorrow. I suggest they spend the first day at Krupp's. Leaves you one more day to deal with the Lünen factory. You're not going to let the side down, are you, Birkett?'

'One day to make a twenty-acre aluminium complex dematerialise? I'll do my best, sir,' I replied, more hesitantly than I would have liked.

'Good chap. Do let me know if I can help, won't you? See you tonight at the mess.'

After an afternoon of brainstorming with my team and fellow Intelligence Officers, we were no nearer to a solution. The only new idea involved asking one of the Pioneer Smoke companies under command of 1st Bucks to generate sufficient smoke to shroud the whole Lünen factory in thick fog. However, any wind change would have left the Pioneers and their noisy generators exposed to Soviet gaze, with predictable consequences.

When Max suggested erecting giant mirrors in front of the relevant plant and machinery, I called the session to a halt. After two nights on the move, sleep deprivation was taking its toll; my eyes were red and watery, and my brain had turned into mush. I decided to go back to my billet, shower, shave and change into a clean uniform before dinner.

As I parked the motorbike in front of Doktor Gräbe's house, I found myself in the middle of a minor commotion. Some two dozen civilians, attracted by the unusual sight, were gawping at the elephantine guns whose extended trunks overhung the front gardens, and speculating as to their origin and purpose. The T Force guards were trying to keep them at bay but, in the absence of any barriers, and with no command of the German language, they seemed incapable of preventing the peaceful onlookers from regrouping further along the street. Several children were excitedly lobbing dozens of rapid-fire "why" questions at their parents without listening to the ponderous, technical answers.

'*Onkel Peter! Komm! Schnell!*' a little voice suddenly rang.

I looked up and saw Lilli running towards me.

'Look, Onkel Peter. This is the biggest gun in the world,' she pointed at the fourteen-inch bore Howitzer sitting on the nearest trailer. 'Bang!'

I lifted the little girl and kissed her on the forehead.

'I've picked two mushrooms for you, Onkel Peter,' she beamed. 'Will you give me a chocolate bar?'

'Lilli! Come here, baby,' her mother called.

The whole family was there: Sybille and Susette, looking unusually diffident, their parents, and a dark-haired girl I'd caught only a couple of glimpses of before. Clearly, they were embarrassed by Lilli's public display of affection for an Allied soldier. As for Susette, if ever she were suspected of any kind of relationship with the occupier, she would at best be the butt of a vitriolic whispering campaign, and at worst exposed to vicious assault by disaffected German youths who disapproved of their girls selling themselves to the victors for nylon stockings, chocolate, cigarettes or food.

'Good evening, Herr Doktor Gräbe. Good evening, Frau Doktor Gräbe,' I greeted them formally.

'Good evening, Captain Birkett,' the doctor nodded. 'And congratulations.'

'What for?'

'Your personal collection of war memorabilia seems to be growing apace. I'm sorry that my humble garden cannot house all its contents.'

Not sure how to reply, I simply smiled.

'Our neighbours are wondering whether the fact that all three barrels are pointing East is significant,' the doctor continued. 'What should I tell them?'

'Please tell them to go back home. And not to mention what they've seen to anybody. Now, if you'll excuse me…'

'Please, be my guest,' Doktor Gräbe pointed to the front door of his occupied house.

As I came out of the shower, I heard voices in the corridor. I dressed quickly and went downstairs, ostensibly in search of a glass of water. Screaming with excitement, Lilli was chasing the three young women in what seemed to be a German version of the game of "it".

'I'm sorry, Captain Birkett,' Sybille stopped in her tracks. 'We are making far too much noise. Come, Lilli.'

Before I could protest they disappeared toward the doctor's surgery, preceded by the unknown dark-haired girl. Susette smiled and slowly followed them.

'Wait!' I called. 'Who's that girl?'

She turned around. 'Don't worry. She's my cousin Effi.'

'What's she doing here?'

'She's staying with us.'

'At the hospital?'

'Yes.'

'But I thought you had only one room?'

'We do.'

'So Effi is the… sixth resident of that room? For God's sake…' I raised my eyes to the ceiling, visualising in my mind the dozen rooms of the doctor's house. 'Why didn't you tell me, Susette?'

'Tell you what? That we live in intolerably cramped conditions? First, we're the lucky ones. We have a roof over our heads. Second, didn't you know it anyway?'

'How long has Effi been staying with you?'

'Oh, a couple of months, I suppose.'

'How come you've never introduced me?'

Susette blushed. 'She… doesn't like the British.'

'I understand.'

'No, you don't. She used to live in Hamburg.'

My heart missed a beat. 'Hamburg?'

'Yes. You know what happened there.'

'I've heard rumours. But I've never been.'

'Don't bother.'

'Why not?'

'The place doesn't exist any more. Forty-five thousand people burnt alive. Women and children. Old people too. The really unlucky ones were baked in their shelters – like my aunt and uncle. After the firestorm, when Effi came back from the country to the Volksdorfer Strasse, she couldn't find it. Her parents' building had just disappeared. Vanished. As had all the others. The street was no more. Its inhabitants...'

I just had time to sit down on the bottom step of the stairs. Perhaps because of my exhaustion, I was feeling giddy. Hiding my face behind my hands, I still sensed the room slowly spinning along an oval orbit, from bottom left to top right, again and again; but with eyes closed I was feeling less sick. In my mind's eye I saw them again. An elderly couple, staggering barefoot down a narrow street which, as the tarmac caught fire, was turning into a flaming river of molten lava. The distinguished-looking, white-haired gentleman was in his seventies and wore a tired, but immaculately cut Savile Row suit. His bespectacled wife looked confused and seemed to have difficulty walking; her whitish tibias were visible where chunks of burnt flesh had fallen off her legs. Holding her hand, her husband tried to hurry her along, while she struggled to free herself in order to avoid slowing him down. With a roaring conflagration galloping towards them like the second horseman of the Apocalypse on his fiery red mount, a blinding fireball appeared at the end of the street. They stopped and stood facing each other. Bracing themselves against the burning hurricane, holding both hands, they looked into each other's eyes and smiled. As the inferno engulfed them, they'd already sunk knee-deep into the melted road.

'What is it, Peter? Are you all right? Didn't you know? I mean – about Hamburg, and the rest?' Susette sounded concerned. She sat down next to me and tried to prise my hands away from my face.

'Did you say... the Volksdorfer Strasse?' I whispered. 'In Barmbek?'

Susette yanked my hands away from my face.

'You know it? I thought you just said you'd never been to Hamburg? Peter!'

What to say?

Without opening my eyes, I explained – so quietly she couldn't hear.

'*Bitte, Liebling?* Sorry, my darling, I missed that. What did you say?'

'My grandparents used to live there,' I repeated.

'*Gott im Himmel!* I'm so sorry, my love. Why did you never...?' Susette broke down crying. Pulling her close, I wrapped my arm around her shoulders and kissed her eyelids and temples, my tears mixing with hers.

'It's all right. It's not your fault, darling Susette. I'm just tired. I haven't had much sleep lately. Please don't cry, my darling.' But she kept sobbing until she suddenly sprang to her feet and ran to the surgery calling: 'Effi! Effi!'

I waited for several minutes, but she didn't return. Back in my room, I threw myself on the bed. Immediately I fell into an agitated slumber, in which I was flying a Lancaster III towards a volcano.

A voice suddenly filled the sky: 'THIS IS OPERATION GOMORRAH. THE ANGLOPHILE CITY MUST BE ERASED FROM THE FACE OF THE EARTH. LET HELLFIRE RAIN DOWN FROM MY HEAVEN.' As I dutifully released my lethal cargo of fourteen thousand pounds of incendiary bombs over my grandparents, the volcano erupted. Mountainous ash clouds billowed miles high, turning day into night. My squadron leader and wingman were nowhere to be seen. My radio set was hopelessly silent. Turning around, I saw that, out of the original seven crew, I was the only man left in the Lancaster. Alone. Solely, personally responsible for the bombing. I had to jump, fast, and catch the bombs before they hit the ground.

As I prepared to bail out, the cloud separated and my mother's face emerged. I hadn't seen her since she'd deserted me ten years ago, so I decided not to return her smile. She looked more beautiful than ever – fully recovered from her cancer. Mortally afraid she would disappear again, I tried to explain why I couldn't greet her with a smile, but no sound came out of my constricted throat. I mouthed my mute call as conspicuously as possible, articulating silent invocations with exaggerated lip movements; but Susette put her lips on mine, and Mama disintegrated into ash and dust.

When, at dawn and fully dressed, I awoke from more uneasy dreams, I had a plan. A plan to make the Lünen aluminium complex dematerialise.

6

Fireworks

SWIRLING LAZILY around naked light bulbs, billows of bluish cigarette smoke rose above the noisy tables. Dinner had been plentiful, and pale, dry Moselle had flowed liberally. Young German waitresses were busy serving real coffee in Meissen porcelain cups and French cognac in brandy glasses. When the American investigators lit Havana cigars worth more than the monthly wage of a German miner, Captain Elizaveta Terisova drained her cup, excused herself and got up. Having already ascertained there was no ladies' room in Kamen's Red Mess, she went straight to the gents, where her arrival was greeted with a hush. She quickly tightened the bun that held her blonde hair, checked her tie and went down to the front door. It was guarded by a British infantryman. She tried to open it, but it was locked. Keeping her hand on the handle, she looked at the soldier. He shrugged apologetically and started talking in fast, meaningless English. Elizaveta turned round and went back to the dining-room to fetch her interpreter. Five inches shorter than Captain Terisova, and utterly besotted by her, Lieutenant Aleksandr Vasilevich was a narrow-chested man whose boyish appearance was somehow reinforced by inquisitive dark eyes and a black goatee.

'He says all members of the Quadripartite inspection teams must stay indoors at night,' he translated. 'Apparently, it's for our own safety.'

She chuckled. 'Please thank him for his concern and tell him that we've just come through five years of total war. When it comes to looking after ourselves, we're not entirely inexperienced.'

'He says he's got his orders,' came the reply. 'And that there is a nice garden at the back.'

Elizaveta's task was to make contact with the Communist cell at the Zeche Monopol, the coal mine at Bergkamen, a mile away, and retrieve their findings about the possibility of Nazi uranium stocks being hidden in one or other of its many shafts. She wondered whether to raise hell. Probably not a good idea. First, it was late, and she was tired. Second, the next day would be busy. Third, it would be a shame to antagonise the British so early; after all, over the coming days the Quadripartite team of investigators would have to rely on their hosts for everything from accommodation to transport and secretarial assistance. She went out to check the garden and took a quick stroll, pretending to look at the stars. A cigarette was glowing red near the gate at the back. She went to bed. In the small hours she heard Colonel Klimenko stumbling along the corridor. Fortunately, he didn't stop at her door; she assumed he was too drunk for sex, though with him you never knew. In fact, he probably had no idea where to find her. She went back to sleep.

Breakfast was another lavish affair. Amid the stench of stale tobacco, the same mousy German girls who'd waited at their table late into the night were officiating again. Elizaveta greeted them with a smile, and asked in German how much sleep they'd managed to get.

'*Nur einige wenige Stunden, Frau Kapitän,*' the oldest-looking one replied. Tall and skinny, she might have been eighteen.

'What are they saying?' Klimenko asked as she sat down next to him.

'Only that she didn't get a lot of sleep.'

'Neither did I,' he guffawed, attracting looks from the French inspectors who were sharing their table. 'By the way, what's this?' He was staring at the half-grapefruit sitting on a plate in front of him.

'I've no idea. Looks like half a giant lemon. Or maybe some kind of orange?'

'What do we do with it?'

'Eat it, I suppose.' She discreetly nodded towards the next table where the British investigators were tucking in.

No sooner had the NKGB colonel stabbed his grapefruit with a porridge spoon than a powerful jet squirted upwards, decommissioning both eyes in a blink. With a torrent of profanities, he sent crockery crashing to the floor in a desperate attempt to dab his eyes with a napkin.

Elizaveta took him by the hand and led him to the bathroom, where she rinsed his eyes in fresh water.

'Christ Almighty!' he exclaimed as he recovered his vision. 'Do you think this was an MI5 trick? Trying to blind us before the inspection? Motherfuckers!'

'I doubt it. Anyway, you'll live. And you're not blind.'

'I can certainly see you all right, my girl. Give us a kiss.'

She looked at her watch. 'Not now, Ivan. You haven't had breakfast yet, and we're leaving in ten minutes.'

The steely glint in his eyes shining even brighter than usual, he fixed his gaze on her for a few seconds, then grinned.

'Sometimes I wonder whether you even like me, Captain Terisova.'

As they sat down again at the breakfast table, none of the British officers batted an eyelid. The French kept whispering under their breath.

Just before eight o'clock a dashing young British captain appeared in the mess and addressed the members of the Quadripartite inspection team. Elizaveta guessed he was in his early to mid-twenties, though he exuded a natural authority well beyond his years.

'Good morning, gentlemen. I'm Captain Peter Birkett. On behalf of Colonel Wreford-Brown, Commanding Officer of No. 1 T Force, it is my privilege to welcome you to Kamen. My job is to provide you with accommodation, transport, and any logistical assistance you may require to inspect your targets. I hope that you all had a good night and are ready to go.'

He stopped to let the French and Russian interpreters catch up and let his eyes roam over the room. It was packed with three dozen people: four assessors from each occupying power (half of them civilian experts ranking as full colonels), their assistants, translators, T Force personnel and drivers. As the general grunt of approval which had greeted his words died down, he looked Elizaveta directly in the eye, frowned, suppressed a gasp and swept back his slightly frizzy brown hair with his right hand. When he resumed speaking, he seemed to have lost some of his composure.

'It seems we have a least one lady amongst us, so perhaps I should apologise for an inadequate greeting. Ladies and gentlemen, our programme is as follows. Today, we shall be visiting Krupp's Widia works in Essen. Tomorrow, we shall inspect the Lünen aluminium smelter. We should be back in Kamen by 5 p.m. for the inventory signing ceremony, which will take place in our office. As usual, it will be followed by a party to celebrate the fruitful cooperation of the victorious Allies. Any questions?'

A dozen cars were parked in front of Kamen's Red Mess. The Soviet and French teams were assigned a couple of air-cooled Volkswagens each, while the US and British investigators were shepherded towards the roomier Austin 16s. Colonel Klimenko and Captain Terisova stood next to their car while their assistants vainly tried to squeeze several boxes of equipment into its tiny boot. Captain Birkett approached them and said something. Unfortunately Lieutenant Aleksandr Vasilevich, the

Russian interpreter, was already ensconced inside the other Volkswagen.

'*Il y a un problème? Darf ich Ihnen helfen?*' Birkett tried again.

Relieved to hear him speak German, Elizaveta explained that their equipment wouldn't fit into the boot of the Volkswagen. Mouth slightly open, he listened to her perfect German.

'As you see, no other delegation is carrying any gear. Why don't you leave yours behind? Surely, all you need to draw up an inventory is pen and paper?' He sounded concerned.

'On the contrary, I'm afraid it's necessary for us to do our work.'

'Let me see what I can do.'

He walked to the front of the convoy and talked to the occupants of each of the Austin 16s, presumably hoping to convince them to swap their car for a smaller one. As he came back towards the Soviets, Elizaveta guessed that none of the civilian colonels had volunteered for a downgrade.

'What the hell is going on?' Colonel Klimenko growled in her ear. 'Since you seem able to talk to this boy, why don't you remind him that, having won the war single-handed, we Soviets expect some respect?'

'Hold on,' she whispered as the English officer approached.

'All right,' Captain Birkett smiled. 'Here's the solution. We have a spare Volkswagen. I suggest you just dump your stuff in it and we'll be ready to go.' Elizaveta translated to Klimenko.

'No way do we lose sight of our tools,' he said. 'I wouldn't trust these T Force characters further than Lenin could throw them. You go with it.'

When eventually the convoy snaked into the Krupp compound, the men of B Company were assembled and waiting for them.

'This is Lieutenant Max Harrison. He'll show you round,' Captain Birkett introduced the chain-smoking, somewhat dishevelled young man. 'Feel free to roam as you please.'

All four inspection teams got out their cameras and notebooks and started methodically criss-crossing the vast floor of the ghost steel plant. It didn't take them much more than an hour to reach the conclusion that the combination of bomb damage, fire, and exposure to the weather had put most of the machinery beyond use.

'Shall we move to the gun shed?' Lieutenant Harrison asked after the group reconvened near the main entrance.

'Tell him we want to inspect the cellars,' Colonel Klimenko said to Lieutenant Aleksandr Vasilevich.

'Cellars? Are there any cellars here?' Harrison asked innocently as soon as the interpreter finished.

'There are. The entrance is over there,' Elizaveta said, pointing unerringly at the far corner of the building.

'No problem,' Captain Birkett interjected. 'Every square inch of this complex is open to inspection, ladies and gentlemen. Off we go.'

While the gaggle of inspectors waited at the top of the stairs for B Company to fetch lamps, Elizaveta and her colleagues were busy unpacking some of the equipment they'd been carrying. She could see that Birkett was following her every move with interest and whispering into Harrison's ear. No sooner had the Soviets begun to walk down the stairs than their Geiger counters started crackling. By the time they reached the furthest vault they were continuously roaring. Colonel Klimenko knelt down, picked up some dirt, smelt it, and slowly let it run through his fingers.

'Where is it?' he asked.

'Where is what?' Max Harrison retorted.

'The yellowcake.'

'The yellow what?'

Colonel Klimenko got to his feet.

'The uranium,' he said gruffly.

'I don't know anything about any uranium,' Harrison replied. 'This is the first time I've been down here. Shall we go back up?'

Every step of the way back, with the American and French investigators looking on in amazement, the Russian contingent kept testing the ground with their two Geiger counters and noting down the results. They didn't stop at the top of the stairs, but followed the track across the factory floor to the front entrance and then onto the yard, where the machines suddenly fell silent.

'Are you thinking what I'm thinking?' Elizaveta asked Klimenko.

'Yes. But I don't understand it. Only three days ago we had confirmation from our agent at Krupp that the stuff was still here.'

'The bastards moved it – very recently. Not very difficult, was it?'

'I suppose not. Damnation.'

'At least the guns should still be there. There were no wheels on the photos.'

As they rejoined the main group, the huge metal doors of the gun shed were slowly sliding open. No sooner was the opening wide enough for her to glance inside than Elizaveta stopped in her tracks.

'What the devil…!' Klimenko swore under his breath.

Elizaveta noticed how fast blood seemed to be draining from his face. But her gaze was irresistibly drawn back to the obscenely empty vastness of the shed. She took out of her pocket the latest photograph received only days ago from the local Communist cell and vainly tried to reconcile it with the scene. It was the same building all right; she recognised the lattice of beams and steel girders supporting its roof, as well as the rows of square skylights. But where on earth were the hundreds of tons of seemingly immovable ordnance that filled the picture?

'Unbelievable,' she shook her head. 'These Brits really are something, aren't they?'

'Aren't you coming in?' Lieutenant Harrison called gaily from inside.

Exchanging a look, Colonel Klimenko and Captain Terisova, followed by the rest of their team, slowly walked up to the warehouse. They took photographs of the traces freshly left by heavy-duty tyres, clearly visible in the parking area in front of the shed. They took pictures of the space between the building and the road, which had obviously been cleared of rubble and looked as if a street-sweeping competition had just taken place. They knelt down and photographed the hundreds of metal fragments and shiny steel filings that covered the concrete floor. They collected samples of the uncorroded coils, springs, screws, bolts and swarf that littered the floor, evidence of recent machining activity. The French and American inspectors, seeing that the shed was empty, didn't even bother to go in. They stood by the doors, watching their Soviet counterparts crawling around on all fours with the fascinated expression of anthropologists witnessing the hitherto unimaginable mores of some primitive tribe.

It was a sombre-looking Colonel Klimenko who eventually led the Soviet retreat towards the waiting Volkswagens. Walking past a beaming Captain Birkett, he barked: 'You're in trouble, boy!' Elizaveta saw that the Russian words meant nothing to the English officer, whose grin broadened as her eyes met his. She couldn't help wondering, though, who was in the deepest hole. Locating the Krupp artillery pieces and yellowcake uranium had been the culmination of the NKGB's intelligence efforts since the German surrender. Chairman Merkulov himself had been involved in organising at short notice, through Marshal Zhukov's headquarters,

the Quadripartite inspection that was to result in a Soviet claim under the reparations clause of the Potsdam
treaty. Elizaveta understood only too well the frustration
raging in Klimenko's head – a head that was probably at
stake here. As was hers. What would they report back
to Moscow? That the original intelligence had been er-
roneous? But everybody had seen recent photographs of
three gigantic guns crammed in that very shed... That,
within a couple of days, uranium and cannons had grown
wings or vanished into thin air? It was more than suspicious: it was implausible. It smacked of double-crossing,
treason and betrayal. Even if their star had still been in
the ascendant over Dzerzhinsky Square, they would be
marked. This was the sort of fiasco that no NKGB operative ever survived.

Colonel Ivan Klimenko wasted no time in launching
his counter-attack. He ordered his men to spend long
enough re-packing and loading their Geiger counters
and other equipment to ensure that their cars would be
the last to leave the Krupp complex. An hour later, as
instructed and without warning, all the Russians jumped
out of their vehicles near the Kamen ring road. As their
passengers walked away without a word, the T Force
drivers were left bewildered, and with no choice but to
proceed back to headquarters with their empty cars. In
the knowledge that the town would soon be crawling
with British troops and possibly Military Intelligence officers looking for them, the NKGB team set out about
their business at a brisk pace.

When Elizaveta returned to the Kamen Red Mess later that evening, she saw the sentry by the door crossing a name on a list. Colonel Klimenko was already at the bar, double Steinhäger in hand, surrounded by his interpreter and artillery expert. Western officers were drinking beer in hushed little groups, with no trace of the rowdiness normally exhibited at this stage of the proceedings. Because she'd never tasted it before, Elizaveta ordered a glass of sherry, which she found revolting. She put it down on the counter and, noticing Klimenko's raised eyebrows, nodded with a reassuring smile. Her afternoon had gone to plan. She'd found and emptied the primary drop-box where the local Communist cell had deposited its report about the allegations made by Erich Raeder. The envelope was bulging, and she was impatient to find out whether there was any truth in the Admiral's assertion that the main Nazi uranium cache was somewhere in the Bergkamen colliery. After the Soviets sat down for dinner at what seemed to be their appointed tables, Lieutenant Aleksandr Vasilevich confirmed he'd collected material from the secondary drop-box and successfully established contact with the leader of the Communist trade union at the mine. Two 30-watt, medium-range radio transmitters capable of one hundred and fifty words per minute had been delivered, as well as a dozen pistols and ammunition.

Colonel Klimenko listened to all the reports and then, pausing every time a German waitress approached, he spelt out the next steps.

'As you know, Comrades, the Soviet Union has today been cheated out of its legitimate war booty. This was a criminal act, in breach of international treaties. Naturally, we will in due course teach the perpetrators a lesson that will prevent a repetition.'

Elizaveta involuntarily glanced towards the table where the good-looking English captain was sitting and found his gaze fixed on her. She averted her eyes.

'If I may ask, Comrade Colonel, does this not put all of us in a somewhat... invidious position?' Lieutenant Vasilevich whispered, black goatee a-twitter.

'Since you ask – it does. We're fucked. Unless, of course, we turn the tables on these bastards.'

'How do we do that?' Elizaveta asked.

'Simple. Valuable though the Krupp super-guns and yellowcake might be, they're only a sideshow. The ultimate prize may be lying in the ground right beneath us. Hopefully, the intelligence reports collected today will confirm that the Nazi stocks of enriched uranium are somewhere in the local coal mine. Should the fact be confirmed, Comrades, we'll have to act immediately. It is now clear that every hour counts.'

He waited while the tall skinny German waitress cleared the plates.

'I will start analysing the material immediately,' Elizaveta said.

'Very good. Aleksandr Vasilevich will assist you. Wake me up if you find anything startling or urgent. We'll meet tomorrow morning at 06:00 in my room.'

Elizaveta nodded. She wasn't sure whether the interpreter's services had been offered because Klimenko didn't trust her, or for some more positive reason. Not that she minded; there was a lot of information to go through and translate.

Though the intelligence was bitty and somewhat contradictory, by midnight a picture had emerged. The huge colliery at Bergkamen, called the Zeche Monopol, consisted of several deep shafts. During the last two years of the war, various Reich ministries and dignitaries had deposited valuables in its subterranean nooks and crannies, which had been sealed off and protected with SS guards. Soon after the German capitulation, so many of those artefacts had been looted that the local value of Reichsmark banknotes, gold coins and Impressionist paintings, relative to that of meat or cigarettes, had quickly collapsed. As far as the comrade miners were concerned, there was nothing of value left in the operational shafts, namely Grillo 1, 2 and 3.

About the Grimberg shaft, however, there was little hard intelligence. Since the explosion that, on 11th September 1944, had killed all one hundred and seven Russian slave labourers working the morning shift, the pit had been abandoned. It was rumoured that the young German miners who, on four separate occasions, had since gone missing, were in fact treasure hunters attempting to penetrate it. Their baffling disappearance, coupled with the uneasy awareness of the Russian corpses populating the dark depths of its tunnels, had deterred other would-be tomb raiders. One informant mentioned that the wildest rumours had been circulating for some time. Strange nocturnal comings and goings had been reported by a handful of people, none of whom had been sober enough to provide credible details. Various theories competed to explain these allegations. Some thought they were the product of alcohol, others that the ghosts of the abused and unburied Russians were roaming about the coalfield. One way or another, it had become a no-go area. According to the report's conclusion, the possibility that the Grimberg shaft was, either intermittently or permanently, sheltering criminal gangs, black marketeers or even some of Hitler's last Werewolves, couldn't be discounted out of hand.

It was nearly three in the morning when Elizaveta and her assistant finished their abridged translation and report.

Three hours later, the Russian team convened in Colonel Klimenko's room and checked it for microphones. They found none.

'Well?' Klimenko asked.

'Grimberg,' Elizaveta replied with a yawn.

'Who?'

After Elizaveta's summarised her findings, the NKGB officer reflected for a while.

'Promising,' he said. 'Seems that old Raeder may have told us the truth.'

'The problem is extraction,' Elizaveta said. 'We may be dealing with two sets of opponents here. First, a bunch of die-hard Nazis guarding their most valuable treasure, namely enriched uranium. Second, the British. We know what to expect from them.'

'Shouldn't we call for reinforcement?' the artillery expert suggested.

'We may have to – but it won't be easy,' said Klimenko. 'And we'll lose time. Remember the Brits have always been one step ahead of us so far. They'll soon cotton on to this one.'

'I think we should act immediately,' Elizaveta said. 'First, we're on the spot. Second – and crucially – we need to surprise the opposition.'

'Brilliant!' Aleksandr Vasilevich gushed, his black eyes fixed adoringly on Captain Terisova.

'Don't forget we leave to inspect the Lünen aluminium plant in one hour,' said Klimenko. 'Moreover, we have to bag it. Not only does it have uniquely advanced technology, but we can't risk coming back empty-handed a third time.'

'True,' Elizaveta said. 'But, surely, the first thing is to find out what's really going on inside Grimberg. We need our comrade miners to establish the facts. If they confirm it is the right target, then we'll make plans for extraction.'

'Right,' Colonel Klimenko dropped his voice. 'Listen carefully, all of you. Aleksandr Vasilevich, you're sick. You'll have to stay behind. Make radio contact with our local comrades and instruct them to send a reconnaissance party down into Grimberg as soon as possible. Tell them to liquidate any opposition they might encounter

– but discreetly. The last thing we need is any commotion to alert the Brits.'

'Understood,' Lieutenant Vasilevich confirmed. 'Hopefully any fighting will take place a few hundred metres underground.'

'That's the idea. Instruct the comrades to line up sufficient transport to carry whatever uranium they find. Half a dozen mine lorries will probably suffice. Procure forged coal delivery orders from the colliery office. We'll make a dash for Berlin in broad daylight, with coal on top of the uranium. Autobahn all the way. No reason why anybody should worry about a few coal trucks rumbling along – at least not for a few hours – which is all we need.'

Deep in thought, they fell silent. Elizaveta nodded appreciatively. This was vintage Klimenko: bold, opportunistic, and beautifully simple. So simple it might even work.

'What about radiation?' she asked.

'Nothing we can do about that. Hopefully the stuff will be in the right sort of containers.'

'What will happen to the German drivers? Will they be able to return home?'

Klimenko paused for thought. 'Not our problem, and probably not our decision,' he shrugged. 'We'll ask for instructions on the way.'

BEFORE SUNSET, the party was in full swing. Since it was standard practice to mark the inventory-signing ceremony at the end of each Quadripartite inspection with an alcoholic bash, the Soviets had come armed with two crates of vodka which were duly volunteered to the mess sergeant. Although the inspection of the Lünen aluminium complex had proceeded satisfactorily, Colonel Ivan Klimenko, still smarting from the Krupp debacle, was looking forward to seeing his British allies on all fours. He prided himself on his ability to outdrink Westerners, particularly on straight vodka.

However, when Elizaveta arrived at T Force headquarters on Am Markt that evening, she was immediately presented with a half-pint beer mug filled to the brim with a ready-mixed concoction. There were already some two dozen people milling about the office. She smelled her drink, trying to identify its components.

'*Guten Abend,* Captain Terisova.' Captain Birkett suddenly appeared at her side, mug in hand. 'Fear not: this is no poison.'

'What is it?'

'We've mixed the vodka you kindly donated measure for measure with our best German *Edelkornbratwein*. Do you know what that is?'

'Corn brandy?'

'Precisely. Warranted at least thirty days old. You'll love it. Look at Colonel Klimenko.' Birkett raised his mug towards Klimenko, whose own tankard was just being refilled by the mess corporal, and took a long sip.

'Very good,' she said after trying a small mouthful.

'Glad you like it. Don't be shy – there's plenty more.'

'What makes you suppose I'm shy?' she smiled.

Much to her amusement, he blushed.

'Sorry. Nothing, Captain. Cigarette?'

Accidentally touching his hand, she gently repulsed the extended pack of Craven A. 'No, thanks.'

'Did you know this is the only brand of cigarettes scientifically proven to damage your health?' he asked.

'I had no idea.'

He put the cigarettes back in his pocket without taking one and seemed to hesitate. 'Incidentally... you do realise that we've met before, don't you?'

'Before what?'

'Before you arrived in Kamen.'

'Have we?'

'Yes.'

She laughed. 'Don't you think this least original of lines is a little bit implausible, given our respective histories? Have you any idea how many Soviet troopers try it on me every week?'

'You were in Berlin last May. I saw you coming out of Hitler's bunker. With him.'

'You *saw* me with *Hitler*?' she asked with feigned incredulity.

'No. With *him*.'

Peter Birkett nodded towards Colonel Klimenko who, across the noisy, smoke-filled room, was engaged in a strategic discussion with Colonel Wreford-Brown. 'Your hair was in a bun – like now. Catching the sun. I would have recognised you after twenty years. Anywhere.'

As he took another sip, she noticed he was blushing again. Suddenly, she recalled the scene. The red and yellow tulips, radiant after the rank darkness of the bunker. The gliding shadows of mallards flying in tight formation over the Reich Chancellery garden. Two British soldiers – the first she'd ever encountered – one of them a boy, staring at her, dumbfounded. This boy.

'How strange,' she said. 'Who was the other man?'

'Major David Hunt. He's at T Force Headquarters in Bad Oeynhausen.' He bit his lip, and she guessed he regretted having given away operational details.

'So you were right. We've – almost – met before,' she said.

'What sort of papers were you collecting that day?'

'Tut, tut,' she laughed the question off.

'Do you believe in fate?' he asked self-consciously.

'Do you believe in coincidences?' she retorted with a smile that scattered sparks all over her grey-green eyes.

'What's the difference?'

'You tell me. Or may I ask why you speak German like a native?'

Captain Birkett hesitated again. 'I was going to ask you the same question.'

Elizaveta had no intention of revealing her personal history or private life to a member of the British armed forces, but something in his eyes, the directness of his gaze, the look of attentive eagerness on his youthful face, combined to compel her. 'My mother was born to a Volga German family,' she whispered. 'What about you?'

He drank another mouthful of toxic brew. 'Me? As it happens, my mother taught me German.'

'Taught you?'

'She was... German.'

'Was?'

'Yes. She died when I was ten.'

'*Es tut mir wirklich leid*,' she said softly.

'It's all right. That was a long time ago.'

'Was it?' she teased.

'Fourteen years ago,' he lied. 'Are your parents still alive?'

'Only my father. My mother was a doctor. She starved to death during the great famine of 1933. Caught typhus or something, trying to help our people. By the way, I shouldn't have said that. Mentioning that famine is treasonable.'

'Good God! I'm really sorry. How old was she?'

'Thirty-seven.'

'Two years older than my mother. I expect you miss her?'

Elizaveta felt amused by Birkett's oblique attempt to establish her age, but, before she could answer, Lieutenant Wright-Collins and Lieutenant Aleksandr Vasilevich accosted them.

'Hello, old chap. I hope I'm not interrupting anything – sir?' Wright-Collins slapped Peter Birkett on the back.

'Hello, Julian. You know Captain Terisova, I believe.'

'Of course. I had the pleasure of taking her on a guided tour of the Lünen aluminium plant earlier today. Did she enjoy it?'

'Captain Terisova enjoyed the inspection, though she normally prefers non-guided tours,' Aleksandr Vasilevich translated.

'Excellent,' Wright-Collins beamed. 'Now, we've been delegated by the powers that be' – he pointed across the room at both colonels, still exchanging toast upon toast – 'to ask when the inventories will be ready for signature.'

'All documents regarding yesterday's inspection of the Krupp factory are ready. The aluminium plant inventory is almost typed up. Why don't we deal with Krupp first?'

Elizaveta walked across the room to check with Klimenko, and came back to confirm the plan was agreeable. A few minutes later, Sergeant Wagg disposed the papers in four neat piles on a table covered with an army blanket. Members of the Quadripartite inspection team slowly gravitated towards it, and it took some time for the noise level to abate.

'As usual, it's been a great pleasure, gentlemen,' said Colonel Wreford-Brown. 'Please charge your glasses and drink to the historic Allied victory!'

'To victory!' The French, British, American and Soviet officers raised their beer mugs.

'And to peace in our time!'

'Peace in Europe!

'To Chairman Stalin!' Wreford-Brown called.

'President Roosevelt!' Klimenko reciprocated.

'I'm afraid the poor bastard's dead, God bless him. President Truman!' the American colonel countered.

'Winchon Chustill!' Klimenko responded in a slur.

'Winston Churchill! He won the war all right.' Wreford-Brown raised his glass.

Repulsing the mess corporal who was yet again trying to fill her overflowing mug, Elizaveta glanced at Klimenko, worried that his knowledge of current affairs seemed to have evaporated.

'To Prime Minister Attlee!' she interjected.

'A safe and clean world!' Captain Birkett responded, looking her in the eyes.

Having slept only three hours, Elizaveta knew that alcohol would finish her off, leaving the Soviet team ineffective and vulnerable. However, despite her repeated requests for water, none had been offered, and she was thirsty.

After several minutes during which toasts flowed as liberally as the vodka-and-brandy brew, Colonel Wreford-Brown, swaying on his feet, again tapped his glass.

'Pray silence, gentlemen. You have on this table two English originals of both inventories – the Krupp factory and its gun shed – for each delegation. Please satisfy yourselves that they are correct, sign both and take one. Clear?'

Amid much brouhaha, Elizaveta managed to pick up the documents and shepherd the Soviet delegation to the quieter entrance hall.

'There,' she handed the sheaf to Lieutenant Aleksandr Vasilevich. 'Can you translate it?'

Before the interpreter got to the third page, the artillery expert could be heard snoring on his feet. Rivulets of sweat, running from the metallurgist's brow into his owlish eyes, kept him blinking.

'Please – can we all pay attention?' Captain Terisova urged. 'We need to get this right.'

The translator droned on for a few more minutes, after which Colonel Klimenko sat down on a window sill and poured more fire down his gullet.

'This all sounds fine,' he said. 'Anyway, why bother? We all know the bastards double-crossed us. There was nothing of value there. No guns, no uranium. I can't understand how they managed to print eight pages of fucking nothing.'

'Comrade Vasilevich, may I see our manuscript notes of the inspection?' Captain Terisova asked. She counted the sheets of Cyrillic script. 'Our own handwritten inventory extended to ten pages. Is this compatible with an eight-page English typescript?'

'Not really, but quite possibly, in a manner of speaking, depending on your writing and their typing,' the translator answered, his eyes lacking focus.

'Ah! There you all are. Everybody has signed,' Captain Birkett suddenly interjected.

As they trooped back into the main office, the US colonel got up from the table and offered Klimenko his pen, which was inspected and accepted. After Klimenko had autographed with a flourish both copies of the inventory, he tried to return the pen, but the American embraced him, insisting he keep it as a memento and offering a toast to US-Soviet hegemony. By the time the Lünen inventory was finally produced just before midnight, one third of the participants including the Soviet artillery and metals experts, were busy vomiting in the toilets or the back garden; another third, including Lieutenant Aleksandr Vasilevich, were lying comatose. Colonel Klimenko, legs wide apart, was still on his feet, squaring up to Captain Birkett. When Sergeant Wagg cleared a couple of broken glasses and again arranged papers in four tidy piles on the khaki blanket, most British colonels were sleeping on chairs.

Captain Terisova collected the documents and looked for support. She walked to Klimenko, who seemed to be the last man standing.

'Excuse me, Comrade,' she said. 'This is the aluminium plant inventory. We need to check it. Do you know where our experts are?'

'Nowhere you want to be, baby,' he guffawed. 'What's the problem?'

'There may not be any. We just need to make sure that nothing has been left out of this list before we sign it – otherwise we won't be able to make a claim for the assets.'

'Let me have a look,' he tore the bundle from her hand and flicked the pages. 'Damn! I can't understand a word of it. What kind of gibberish is this?'

'We need to find Aleksandr Vasilevich to translate it.'

'The boy's dead,' Klimenko announced gravely. 'Couldn't hold his liquor. Tell you what: this muzhik here is the real article. Thinks he can drink me into the ground. Ha! He's got no idea I'm going to kill him.' He crashed his mug into Birkett's with such force that they both spilled over, showering the Englishman's uniform with a potent anti-bacterial cocktail. 'To your good health, muzhik!'

'God save the King!' Birkett lifted his glass. He nodded towards the table where a crumpled Frenchman was busy signing his copy. 'Shall we wrap things up?' he asked in German.

'What? Is the muzhik capitulating?' Klimenko growled.

'He wants to get on with the signing,' Elizaveta translated.

'Right he is – bless his mother!' Clutching the papers in one hand, his mug in the other, Klimenko lurched toward the table where he nearly collapsed on the knees of the frightened French inspector, who gave a yelp and eventually managed to extract himself, only to find himself sitting on the floor.

'Hold on, Comrade Colonel! We have no idea what this document says,' Elizaveta cried.

His new American pen already on the page, Klimenko froze.

'What?' he asked without turning around.

'We could check it overnight and return it to them tomorrow,' she urged.

Klimenko seemed to be trying to collect his thoughts.

'Think you're fucking smart, don't you?' he asked in a thick voice. 'Smarter than me, yeah? How come you forgot that we're going away tomorrow, then?' He gave a triumphant snort and wrote his name at the bottom of the inventory.

No sooner had the NKGB colonel signed than Captain Birkett picked up the document and quickly handed it to the rotund blond lieutenant who'd shown the inspectors around the Krupp factory. Elizaveta caught the look both young men exchanged, and her heart sank. She took the remaining copy, folded it despondently and put it in her pocket.

The drive back to the Red Mess lasted only a few minutes, during which both Soviet officers remained silent. Captain Terisova left it to the driver to help Colonel Klimenko out of the Volkswagen and up the stairs. It took her half an hour to retrieve the Cyrillic manuscript notes taken by the Soviet team during the inspection of the Lünen aluminium complex – all thirty-four pages of them. Nearly three times longer than the signed English version now lying next to them.

She collected the papers, rushed along the corridor and banged on Klimenko's door. No answer. She tried the handle. The door wasn't locked. His jacket and tie were on the floor, at the foot of the chair on which he was sitting.

'We've been duped, Ivan.' she waved the papers under his nose. 'You've signed an incomplete inventory – it misses half the contents of the Lünen plant!'

He slowly opened his eyes and blinked. She could see his intoxicated brain painfully trying to get back into gear.

'We need to lodge an official complaint, first thing in the morning,' she said. 'We've been conned, Ivan – yet again. That's why they wanted to get you drunk, the bastards.'

Suddenly he was up on his feet, towering above her. 'Don't you dare ever talk to me like this, bitch!' He tore the front of her shirt, fiercely grabbed her breasts and pushed her all the way to the bed. As, lying on top of her, he ripped through her trousers, she turned her lips – the lips that her cousin Jakob had kissed – away from his alcoholic breath. No point in calling for help; not only would it arrive too late, but the British certainly wouldn't want to press charges, arrest a Russian officer or get involved in Red Army disciplinary matters. When he brutally penetrated her, despite the pain, her clenched teeth let out only a muffled squeal.

As he toiled away, not for the first time, she wondered whether to kill him. Of course, he was much stronger, and a trained killer himself; nevertheless, she'd never doubted she could prevail, particularly when he was blind drunk. So far, her hand had been stayed by a mixture of common humanity, gratitude and practical considerations.

How could she forget that, back in January, Klimenko had saved her own life? The third Belorussian Front had just entered East Prussia. For the first time, the Red Army was fighting on German territory and exacting terrible revenge. As her unit overtook the tide of refugees pouring out of Goldap and Insterburg, Elizaveta saw hundreds of women and children made to lie down on both sides of the road, a raucous army of men with their trousers down standing in front of each of them, revolver in hand. Despite the regulations, many of the soldiers had small silver crosses, religious medals or other amulets round their neck. Bleeding or unconscious women were simply shoved into the ditch, and those trying to protect their children shot. Horrified, Elizaveta had driven on.

But when, later that evening, she'd come across a building whence unrelenting screaming could be heard, she'd not been able to restrain herself. An infantry platoon had found a group of women hiding in a barn, and had some fun with them. One by one, the women and girls were being gang-raped and mutilated, an empty wine bottle rammed up their vaginas. As Captain Terisova got off her jeep, the terrified creatures awaiting their turn fell on their knees, crying out towards her. She instructed her driver to radio for help and walked towards the group.

'Comrades! What the hell do you think you're doing? Don't you know that rape and murder are punishable by death on the spot? Who's in charge here?' she challenged them.

His uniform no more than soiled rags, the platoon sergeant made no attempt at saluting. Smirking, he pointed at a poster affixed to the building which read:

'RED ARMY SOLDIER! YOU ARE NOW
ON GERMAN SOIL. THE HOUR
OF REVENGE HAS STRUCK!'

'Enough!' she bellowed. 'Re-join your unit immediately – or I'll have you all court-martialled!'

'Oh – you will, *babushka*?' the sergeant sneered. 'Now – that's not a nice thing to say, is it?'

Elizaveta realised the whole gang was inebriated, and knew only too well that a drunken Russian soldier was wholly different from a sober one. Alcohol turned them into wild animals, covetous, brutal and bloodthirsty. It also made them lecherous. She drew her pistol. Before she could release the safety catch, a burst of sub-machine-gun fire had cut her driver in half, and somebody had knocked her on the head from behind. When she came to, dazed and bewildered, her knickers had been ripped off, a boot was painfully pressing on her abdomen, and half a dozen men with erect penises were standing above her, arguing about precedence. One of the German girls took advantage of the commotion to make a run for her life, somehow managing to escape the hail of bullets that followed. Elizaveta Terisova closed her eyes, strangely happy that her own life wouldn't have been sacrificed in vain. Radiant and beautiful, Anna, the mother she'd missed so much for twelve long years, opened her arms and beckoned her daughter. As the stinking sergeant lowered himself onto her, she offered no resistance. Covering the man's grunts, a loud voice – Jakob's beloved voice – kept intoning: *I'll wait for you, little cousin… I'll wait for you…* But it soon faded away, and Elizaveta knew then that the blood-red Volga had forever claimed him.

When more shots rang out, she'd assumed the remaining German girls were being executed. But the man on top of her had gone into a strange spasm, before rolling over. She opened her eyes. One by one, the confused soldiers were being picked off by precise, sustained fire. With their pants round their ankles, they were sitting ducks. After the shooting died down, Colonel Ivan Klimenko had calmly walked over and put an end to the convulsions of the sergeant. 'Nobody fucks my war-wife without my permission, asshole,' he'd said before firing a bullet between his eyes.

That's how Captain Elizaveta Terisova learnt she'd acquired a war-husband. He'd gently, effortlessly picked her up, and helped her re-arrange her uniform. Sobbing in his arms, she'd felt strangely safe.

The arrangement had worked reasonably satisfactorily, though it soon turned out that, over the years, Colonel Klimenko had collected a number of war-wives, in addition to his real wife back home.

Now SPENT, Klimenko started snoring. His boots were crushing Elizaveta's toes; she managed to move her legs sufficiently for the pain to abate. She wondered how long this would all go on. Most so-called war-couples had dissolved in the weeks that followed the German capitulation, as men had either gone back to their families on long leave or been demobilised. But the NKGB units were as active as ever, and Klimenko had made clear that he was in no hurry to terminate the arrangement. And that Jakob's life continued to depend on her compliance.

Had this ever been true? Was it still true?

The more sonorous and regular Klimenko's breathing became, the more wide awake she felt. What if he was… finished? Not only had he left Moscow under a cloud, but their current mission was ending in three spectacular failures. No uranium, no super-guns – and now much of an aluminium smelter, complete with the world's most advanced technology, had been spirited away from under their noses. What were the chances of Chairman Merkulov proving magnanimous? What was the probability of Comrade Stalin showing mercy?

Without a shadow of a doubt, the man lying on top of her, her protector and oppressor, war-husband and serial rapist, despite his outstanding war record, was doomed. She had to disengage. Cut him loose and hope for some miracle to save herself.

She freed one leg, then the other, and pushed hard. The big, muscular body rolled over. She got up, collected her torn clothes and put them back on as best she could. Then she picked up the papers and turned off the light.

IT WAS MID-MORNING before Captain Elizaveta Terisova arrived back at T Force headquarters at number 11 Am Markt. The sky was overcast and the light north-easterly wind had an icy bite. She stopped to let an overcrowded tram, crawling with humanity, pass diagonally across the square. Then, followed by a bleary-eyed Aleksandr Vasilevich, she resolutely walked past the crates of empty vodka and brandy bottles awaiting collection on the pavement. Ignoring the sentry, she pushed the door. Sergeant Wagg rose from his desk and blocked her way.

'I've come to lodge a formal complaint on behalf of the Soviet government,' she said.

'We'd like to discus some... issues,' Vasilevich translated.

'Please wait here,' Sergeant Wagg answered, before going through a door. He reappeared a few seconds later. 'Captain Birkett will see you now. This way, please.'

The Englishman rose as Elizaveta, marvelling at the unexpected tidiness of the place, entered his office, the locus of last night's orgy.

'*Guten Morgen!*' he exclaimed with a warm smile. 'What a delightful surprise. Already up and about? I hope you all slept well?'

Seeing his services were no longer required, Lieutenant Aleksandr Vasilevich slumped on a chair.

'We've come to lodge an official complaint on behalf of the Soviet delegation,' Elizaveta waved a bundle of papers. 'The inventory you made us sign last night was incomplete. This was no more than a despicable attempt at depriving the Soviet Union of what is rightfully ours.'

'What on earth are you talking about?'

'I'm talking about theft,' she said coldly, throwing the documents onto his desk. 'Here is the correct inventory. And this here is the pathetic joke list you produced last night.'

'Good God. That's rather a serious accusation, don't you think? Quite likely to lead to a major international incident, I should imagine. What evidence of a mistake do you have?'

She pointed to the papers now littering his desk. 'It's easy to see that the English version of the Lünen inventory is hardly half the length of the Russian draft.'

'It may be easy for you, but I'm afraid I don't speak a word of Russian. If you leave it with me I will have our translators look at it.'

'How long will that take?'

'Oh, no more than a few days, I should think. We certainly will get to the bottom of this.'

'Why can't you do it today? Right now?'

'Well, we're rather busy, you see. As you know, we spent the last few days shepherding the Quadripartite team around, which means we're behind on our normal work. But we'll deal with it as soon as possible, I can assure you.'

Elizaveta knew he was playing for time. The inspectors would leave that morning, the inventories would be filed, and the unlisted machinery was probably being dismantled as he spoke. She decided to change tack.

'Forgive me,' she said softly. 'I thought that, perhaps, we were – or could be – on the same side. Was I naïve?'

'Of course we are on the same side.'

'Have you got any idea what you've done?'

'What do you mean?'

'You thought it was just a game, didn't you?'

'What?'

'Moving the Krupp guns and yellowcake, getting us to

sign a fraudulent inventory for Lünen – all a game, where cheating was allowed?'

His jaw muscles twitching ever so slightly, Captain Birkett remained silent.

'What do you think will happen to all of us?' she asked. 'What do you think will happen to me?'

'Why should anything happen to you?'

'If we are lucky, we'll be shot.'

Taking a step forward and looking him in the eye, she saw his pupils widen. 'All of us. Not that you care, do you?'

Turning away, he stared out of the large pane of plate glass at the passenger train slowly inching forward next to the tramway track across the cobbled square, blocking the view towards the Rathaus. As usual, it was so over-crowded that it looked like a swarm more than a convoy, hungry freezing people hanging on to the sides by their fingernails or sitting atop meagre bags on coach roofs. A major scuffle seemed to be developing in the second carriage, where a group of men were throwing luggage out of the door.

Suddenly, as the train shuddered to a halt, three of them fell out, as though ejected by a surge in its internal pressure. Two landed on their feet, but the third one, short, stocky and wearing a dark blue greatcoat, had to be helped back to his. They immediately tried to climb back on board, but the short man, despite his companions' help and encouragement, seemed unable to cling on to the train.

'Sergeant Wagg!' Birkett called. 'Come here! Quick! Do you see these characters?'

'Yes, sir. The normal struggle for *Lebensraum*, I'd say. Brutal business.'

'The tall man on the right. Have we not seen him before?'

'We have, sir. Not long ago, in fact. He's the Messerschmitt test pilot who offered to work for us.'

'Indeed he is. Tell you what, Wagg: take a couple of men and bring back those three trouble-makers, would you?'

Peter Birkett turned to his Soviet visitors and interrupted Lieutenant Aleksandr Vasilevich, who was doing his befuddled best to provide simultaneous translation to Captain Terisova.

'You see what I mean,' he said with an apologetic shrug. 'It never stops. Because the German police are so useless, we have to maintain law and order – in addition to all our other duties. Would you excuse me for a minute?'

He turned back towards the window, through which Sergeant Wagg and two men with Sten guns could be seen walking. As the little steam engine gave signs of wanting to re-start, they started running towards the second carriage. The Messerschmitt pilot spotted them and shouted a warning. All of a sudden, the older, short man fell face first on the cobbles, where he remained, while his two companions sprinted away. The T Force men gave chase, but came back empty-handed. They helped Sergeant Wagg pick up the man in the blue greatcoat, who had cuts on his face and seemed dazed, and almost carried him back towards the T Force building. Soon the party was back in Captain Birkett's office.

'I'm sorry, sir,' Wagg said. 'Afraid our pilot friend took off before we could jump him.'

'I saw. Never mind. See whether this man needs medical help, and then run the usual checks on him. I'll be with you in a minute.'

Irritated by the diversion, Elizaveta wondered whether it had been orchestrated by Birkett for her benefit. She looked at the prisoner, wondering how German civilians felt about being randomly picked off trains and held in custody by Occupation forces. Blood was dripping from his nose which, perhaps already swollen, seemed abnormally large and pulpy. Breathing heavily, both hands in the pockets of his greatcoat, he was silently staring at his feet, as though unconcerned by the proceedings.

'What's your name?' Captain Birkett asked in German.

The man seemed not to hear the question. Birkett moved closer and repeated it loudly.

'*Ich heiße Weber,*' came the answer. 'Gustav Weber.'

'There, Herr Weber – take this,' Birkett extended his handkerchief. 'After you've cleaned your face, Sergeant Wagg will ask you a few routine questions, and you'll be free to go. Do you understand?'

As Weber slowly, almost reluctantly, extracted his right hand from his pocket, Elizaveta realised why he'd had such difficulty clinging on to the train: he was missing half of each finger. He took the handkerchief and awkwardly mopped the blood that was running along deep creases around his mouth and down his chin. Elizaveta caught a brief glimpse of extraordinarily pale eyes, more grey than blue.

'Come on, grandpa, let's go,' said Wagg, taking his arm.

Before they could take a step, a massive explosion rocked the town. Thousands of cracks instantly turned the big plate glass window opaque. Elizaveta felt the floor vibrate as drawers opened, tall piles of files collapsed and the framed map of the Ruhr which had been hanging on the wall crashed down. Sirens started howling.

'What the hell was that?' Birkett asked, vainly trying to look out of the window.

'Something big, sir. Fucking big,' said Wagg.

'Get everybody out with their weapons, and find out what the hell's going on.'

Birkett rushed to the door.

In the confusion Captain Terisova found herself left behind with Aleksandr Vasilevich and the bemused German. On the spur of the moment, she walked to him, grabbed his elbow and yanked his left hand out of his pocket.

It too was missing the last phalanx of each finger.

She recalled the words spoken by Colonel Ivan Klimenko only a few months earlier, as they stood over the blackened ditch where Hitler's charred remains had allegedly been found: *our own NKGB people couldn't find any fingerprints. All the corpse's fingers had been removed surgically.*

'Quick! Aleksandr Vasilevich, wake up!' she yelled, kicking him in the shin.

'What?' the translator sat up with a jolt.

'Run to the car, and start the engine. Now.'

'But...'

'Go! Now!' she ordered fiercely, drawing her pistol.

As the bewildered interpreter ran out, she shoved the weapon into the back of the hunched figure in the blue coat.

'Please come with me, Herr Hitler – or I'll shoot you.'

For the second time he fixed his mesmeric pale blue gaze on her.

'Ich heiße Gustav Weber,' he said.

But, to her amazement and relief, he started walking.

Watching the billowing cloud of black smoke wreathing upward to the north of the square through field glasses, the British sentry ignored them. Of the twin towers that used to house the winding gear of the Zeche Monopol colliery and dominate the skyline, there was no trace.

PART THREE

'Bebop-a-bebop,
'Ba-ba-rebop,
'Hey!'

1

Hades

IN A GRIM AND SILENT procession, overtaken by tired
fire engines and all manner of T Force vehicles, women
in wooden clogs and men of the afternoon shift were
trudging towards the colliery. Since most had been requisitioned during the war, only a couple of rickety ambulances were left in Kamen; either already on site or
unserviceable, they were nowhere to be seen. Although
it was clear to all that a major disaster had befallen the
Zeche Monopol mine, its true scale beggared belief. The
first thing I had to do was to cordon off the perimeter
and stop the distraught wives and mothers from para-
lysing whatever feeble rescue effort could immediately
be mounted, but this proved a major challenge. I sent
Rifleman Richardson back to headquarters to request reinforcement, and within a couple of hours men of the 9th
Battalion Durham Light Infantry from nearby Unna had
been deployed to preserve order.

Incredibly, even in the offices only a handful of witnesses had survived the explosion deep in the Grimberg

shaft. The whole pit had suddenly turned into a volcano, spewing its fireball a thousand feet into the sky. The gigantic subterranean blast, sparked off nearly three thousand feet underground, had erupted all the way to the surface, destroying head structures and equipment, winding gear and buildings. Its cover blown off, the brickwork of the well was now intermittently visible through noxious fumes. A wildly-jumbled collar of matchwood, mangled metal and coal debris gave the mouth of the shaft the appearance of a smoking crater. Its crumpled steel sheets strewn across the area like discarded accordions, the pit-head's cladding had been shattered. From the deepest coal seams to the surface rubble, everything was on fire.

Soon the Rhein-Elbe fire brigade arrived to lend a hand, followed by the rescue teams of a dozen neighbouring collieries. I had no understanding of mining, nor of fire-fighting; yet, it soon became clear to me that co-ordination and expertise were in short supply. Nevertheless, for hours on end, with the Intelligence Section and A company, I did my utmost to re-establish a modicum of order, and to provide the rescue teams with as much food, drink and logistical support as possible. Getting back to my billet late in the evening covered in smelly soot, I felt despondent at the thought of the hundreds of men still trapped underground.

Susette must have been waiting for me; she burst out of her father's surgery.

'Peter! At last! Are you all right? God – you *are* dirty. What on earth happened?' she asked before I could give her a kiss. '*Vati* rushed out after the bang this morning, and we haven't heard from him since. Have you seen him?'

'Only from a distance, my darling. He was busy treating the survivors. Most of them are badly injured.'

'*Ach Gott!* I can't believe we've had yet another accident at the mine – after everything we went through. This place is well and truly cursed, isn't it?' Tears welled up in her eyes.

'I don't know about cursed. But jinxed, definitely. And now it's on fire from top to bottom, and nobody seems to know what to do about it.'

'Are there men still trapped underground?'

'Hundreds. Whether alive or dead…'

'How awful. And to think that Germany's greatest fire-fighting expert is sitting in prison.'

'Who's that?'

'Don't you remember? It was all over the papers last week. Morsbach, I think his name was. Arrested as a Nazi, next door to us, in Dortmund.'

'Are you sure, Susette?'

'Nearly. Why?'

'May I use your father's telephone?' Within minutes I had convinced Colonel Wreford-Brown of the need to have Herr Morsbach released immediately.

'You always think on your feet, don't you?' Susette asked.

'Not exclusively, my darling. Do you know what I'm thinking about right now?' I ensnared her in my sooty arms with a smile.

'Yes, without a shadow of a doubt,' she replied. But, when I sought her lips, she turned her head.

'Do you think it makes sense to free Nazis on a whim, just because they might be useful?' she frowned.

'Don't you?'

'I'm not sure.'

'What if he's the only man capable of saving the miners trapped underground? Even a single one of them? Isn't it better than the alternative? Believe me: very few so-called rescuers seemed to know what they were doing today.'

'Though it feels damn wrong, I suppose you're right,' she said. 'Pragmatic Brit. So why are you all banging on with this so-called denazification process, if we're just going to release all useful or qualified men? That's only driving our people to the Russians.'

Her mention of the Soviets suddenly conjured up the picture of the tall green-eyed woman I'd left in my office earlier that day, and totally forgotten about. I released Susette from my embrace and took a step back.

'I've had a bloody long day, my sweetheart. Request permission to wash.'

WHEN I ARRIVED at the mine early the next morning I found that more rescue teams had appeared overnight, adding to the confusion. Wearing their best Sunday clothes to fight off the cold, many older children had joined the ranks of women, mostly clad in black, tensely waiting for news. Their group was quiet and immobile, as though standing in a cathedral; those few who spoke did so in hushed whispers, their eyes always fixed on the distant comings and goings of the search parties.

Only half a dozen attempts to penetrate the shaft had yet taken place. Breathing apparatus was in short supply, and its autonomy limited to a couple of hours. Since all lifts, machinery and ventilation systems were out of action, long underground detours were necessary in order to connect with the lower levels of the Grimberg shaft, leaving little time for any work to be done. Many of the men from the Durham Light Infantry, miners by profession, volunteered to help; however, because of their lack of local knowledge and the language barrier, it was decided not to use them. Only one German foreman with enough experience of the Grimberg pit to direct the rescue operations had been found; however he was so hesitant as to be almost totally ineffective. It transpired that, only a week earlier, he'd been denounced as a Nazi by his Communist colleagues and arrested by the Field Security Staff. Despite his release, the incident had left him a nervous wreck. Either that, I thought, or he simply had no interest in risking his life for the comrades who'd ratted on him.

Things were further complicated by the discovery of elevated radiation levels and high radon concentration at the lower levels of the pit, indicating the presence of decaying uranium. Since all known natural sources for such emanations – such as radioactive granite intrusions

– were several kilometres down in the thick continental crust, this baffled the geologists.

Fortunately, Colonel Wreford-Brown's request had been accepted. Discharged from Dortmund's jail by late morning, Herr Diplom-Ingenieur Morsbach was driven straight to Bergkamen where he immediately assumed overall operational control. In the following hours, some two hundred and fifty men with breathing equipment braved the smoke-filled underground labyrinth, attempting more than thirty reconnaissance and salvage missions, followed by another forty the next day. In addition, twenty-nine men were sent to look for survivors without oxygen, working their way up from the second level.

The result of these heroic endeavours was meagre. While the rescuers unexpectedly met eight survivors in the Röttgersbank Road, near the bottom of the pit, elsewhere they mostly found mutilated, carbonised or asphyxiated bodies. In many galleries, particularly along the Ida seam, impassable smoke, depriving men of sight and orientation, frustrated all efforts. As the spreading fires reached methane pockets, new detonations were constantly rocking underground roads and tunnels, threatening to block escape routes. Presumably trapped by such a blast, or killed by an after-damp explosion, or poisoned by carbon monoxide, a six-man party from the neighbouring Fürst Hardenberg colliery never made it back to the surface.

On the third day, the cause of the cataclysm still remained a mystery. But its human cost had become clear.

Some four hundred and sixty-six people, the whole of the morning shift, had been at work when the pit blew up. Of those, only sixty-five, most of them grievously injured, could be saved. Three British officials of the North German Coal Control in charge of the mine, the German director and the underground operations manager all died.

Four hundred and one men had lost their lives. Shattered by the worst accident in German mining history, Kamen was a town in mourning. A small town where four hundred families had been deprived of father, husband, breadwinner. Where four hundred distraught, destitute women would now have to fend for themselves and their children in the midst of extreme post-war penury and devastation, easy prey for local pimps, unscrupulous occupiers and jumped-up satraps.

Kept at bay by the Durham infantrymen, these women, many of whom had practically camped around the site since the beginning, offered a pitiful spectacle. Walking dejectedly towards my car at the end of the third day, I averted my eyes from their gaunt, haunted faces. In the absence of any casualty list or official information, all they knew was that their men were still missing. Whenever stretchers were brought back to the surface, they surged forward and craned their necks, desperately willing the shape lying under the brown blanket, however burnt, maimed or crippled, to be their own husband's.

'*Bitte, Herr Kapitän!*' a voice called.

Hand on the handle of the car's door, I turned round.

'*Hier – Ich bin's – Frau Schwarz!*'

Held back by the chain of British soldiers, a toddler by her side, a woman was waving at me. Despite her heavy winter coat and scarf, aided by the sling which held her left arm, I recognised the woman whose husband had gone berserk a few weeks ago.

'*Guten Abend, Frau Schwarz,*' I walked up to her. 'How can I help you?'

'Have you any news about my husband?'

I suddenly remembered the plea she'd made at the time of her husband's arrest, explaining that he was a miner.

'Oh my God. Was he working the morning shift?' I asked.

'Yes. He was released from prison last week.'

'Please let this lady pass,' I ordered the Durham private. 'Would you like to follow me?' I turned back to Frau Schwarz.

I led her to the Volkswagen and opened the door. She sat down with her child on her lap. I walked round the car and sat behind the wheel. I looked at her pale, shallow face, in which the eyes seemed to have sunken deeply since our last encounter. She looked older.

'How's your arm?' I asked.

'Much better, thank you. Please, can you tell me anything?'

'I'm sorry. I know nothing about your husband – or anybody else.'

'Are they still looking for survivors? My husband is very experienced. And strong as an ox – you know that.

He knows this mine like the back of his hand. I'm sure he's still alive.'

'I believe dozens of rescue missions will be mounted overnight.'

'And tomorrow?'

'Probably the same. But obviously… it will be four days since the explosion.'

'I know,' she whispered, looking away, her face disintegrating into tearless sobs.

'Mummy, can we go home?' a small voice asked. Its thumb already back in its mouth, the child was tugging at its mother's scarf with its free hand.

'Boy or girl?' I asked, taking a pack of sweets out of the glovebox. In direct contravention of Marshal Montgomery's non-fraternisation orders, I unwrapped a purple raspberry candy and gave it to the toddler.

'Boy. He's nearly two and a half. Named Hans – after his dad.'

'Rotten luck. I'm sorry.'

'Nothing to do with luck.'

'I beg your pardon?'

'You don't seriously think this was an accident?' Suddenly she sounded angry.

'What else could it be?'

'Is it true that this old Nazi swine, Helmut Morsbach, is in charge of the rescue operations?'

'Yes. Apparently he's uniquely qualified.'

'Uniquely qualified?' She gave a bitter laugh. 'That may well be true – in more ways than one.'

'What do you mean?'

'Only that Helmut Morsbach has long specialised in burying Communist workers. And that my husband's life seems to be in the hands of the same Nazis who tried to kill him for the last twelve years. I told you Hans was one of the last underground Communist leaders left in the Ruhr.'

'Yes, I remember. But I can assure you that all rescue efforts seem to be proceeding with maximum diligence. Men are risking their lives non-stop to save their fellow miners. Some have already died in the process.'

'More will die in vain.' She turned away, staring straight ahead through the layer of coal particles that lined the windscreen. 'After all these years, they finally got him. I'll never see my husband again,' she murmured in a flat voice.

'Mummy, can we go home *now?*' little Hans repeated stridently.

'May I offer you a lift, Frau Schwarz?' I asked.

Lost in her thoughts, she remained silent.

'I want another sweet,' Hans said.

'Listen – I really think you should go home for the night,' I insisted.

Still gazing vaguely ahead, she nodded. By the time the Volkswagen pulled up in front of her tall tenement building, we hadn't exchanged another word. She wearily got out of the car and turned around.

'Once more, I'm in your debt. *Danke, Herr Kapitän.*'

A bitterly cold wind was howling along the dark and

deserted street as, unable to find an appropriate form of farewell, I drove off.

2

Retribution

LATER THAT NIGHT, the girl stirred and, without opening her eyes, asked in a sleepy voice: '*Wie spät ist es?*' Max Harrison carefully withdrew his numb arm from under her shoulders and looked at his watch.

'Coming up to midnight, my beauty.'

She sat up as though bitten by a scorpion. 'You are making fun of me, *Herr Leutnant?*'

'God no – I wish I were. Time flies in your company, Regine. Come here. Why don't you lie down and spend the night with me? It's cold outside.' He rolled over and started nibbling at her hips.

'*Herrgott!* What are my parents going to say?' Regine moaned, attempting to get up. But her legs were now captive under his.

'Never mind your parents. You're a big girl. Here – give me a kiss.'

She complied, drowning him under a waterfall of long dark hair. Regine, previously an art student, was now one of three waitresses at the officers' mess of B Company in Heisingen. A buxom girl in her early twenties, her English was improving fast; her sexual slang in particular was second to none. Despite the all-pervading reek of tobacco in the room, Max noticed how the original sweetness of her breath had been replaced, over the course of the last three hours, by musky, almost sour, but still sexy emanations. He put his hands on her waist and pulled her down.

'*Nein!*' she protested. 'Please let me go – or my parents will lock me up, and you'll never see me again.'

'Come, come, sweet lover. Just one last time.'

He was happily surprised when she stopped wriggling, but soon discovered he was unable to push his advantage.

'Damn!' he cried. 'I still want you so badly. What's wrong with me?'

'Everything's wrong with you, Mister,' Regine smiled wryly. 'You're fat and you smoke like a chimney. Not that it makes any difference: no Englishman can do it four times in a row – not after drinking a bottle of champagne, anyway.'

'How dare you impugn the virility of your conquerors?' Blue eyes twinkling, he gave one of his infectious whinnying chortles. 'On reflection, I think I'll have you court-martialled, my sweetheart.'

'On what count? Fraternisation?'

'Touché.'

'What does "douche" mean?'

'Never mind.'

'Can I go now?'

With a yawn, he released his embrace and stretched.

'I'll give you a lift. Proper young ladies shouldn't be out on bicycles in the middle of the night.'

'Thank you, Max. You *are* sweet.'

The sublime curve of her breasts never failed to move him. Overwhelmed by a sudden rush of gratitude, he spent a couple of minutes watching as, gloriously naked, Regine combed her smooth hair and deftly braided it into plaits which she wound round her head, instantly turning back into a demure German *Mädchen*. When her dark triangle disappeared behind white lace, Max sighed, got up wearily and gathered his ash-covered uniform from the floor. Soon, his crumpled shirt still unbuttoned over his paunch, he paused in order to watch her put on her stockings.

'Stop it!' she ordered, blushing.

'What?'

'You know. I have told you before. It's not polite.'

'I'll stop watching you when you stop being beautiful, my darling.'

'I bet you will. That's why I'll never marry you – ever.'

'Help! My heart! Help!' Hands clutching his chest, he crashed onto his knees at her feet, seemingly in the throes of cardiac arrest.

'Silly boy,' she patted him on the head. 'Serves you right. I did tell you to watch your weight, didn't I? From now on I'll never again serve you any pudding. Or wine.'

'Then I'll go back to bed and never get up.'

'Then you'll be shot as a fat deserter. Anyway, I'm off.'

'Wait, Regine.' He opened his desk drawer. 'Here. The cigarettes are for your father. The chocolate for your mother. As for these stockings... I haven't decided yet who to give them to. Any suggestions? Maybe your sister?'

'You really *are* very kind, Max Harrison,' she put her arms round his neck. 'I hope you do understand none of this is necessary?'

Softly, tenderly, he put his finger on her lips. 'You deserve so much more,' he murmured in her ear. Then, taking a step back, he quickly fastened every other button on his shirt, loosely knotted his tie and put on his jacket. He lit a Senior Service, inhaled deeply, put his Smith & Wesson revolver back into his holster and stood to attention.

'T Force at your service, *Fräulein!*'

Lieutenant Max Harrison was fully cognisant of the fact that he was about to breach yet more regulations. It was strictly forbidden to use War Department vehicles to transport German civilians, and any encounter with a Military Police patrol would also result in the serious charge of misuse of petrol. Accordingly, he kept the Mercedes's headlights dipped and avoided revving up until the car reached the outskirts of Heisingen. Regine lived in a small village some five miles to the north, not far from the banks of the river Ruhr. He knew the road well, and the drive never took long. On this cold and wintry night, there was no traffic whatsoever, not a living soul – except as they came up towards the village. Oblivious to her safety, a lonely figure was standing in the middle of the road, flagging them down. Max slammed on the brakes. With locked wheels and screeching tyres, the car slid crabwise towards the pedestrian, who just had time to jump out of the way and vanished into darkness.

'You crazy drunkard!' Max shouted. 'Can't you pay attention? Do you want to get killed?'

Wearing nothing but a white nightgown and a long woollen scarf, barefoot, dishevelled and obviously distressed, a woman suddenly opened his door, screaming torrents of shrill German and frantically tugging at his sleeve.

'For God's sake, woman, calm down. Regine, what's she saying?'

'She wants help. Says a gang of drunken Polish DPs are ransacking the farm where she lives, shooting the pigs and raping the women.'

'Bloody hell! Just what we need. Where is this farm?'

The woman pointed to a track that forked off the main road to the right.

'Tell her to find a car or a bike, get to the British unit in Heisingen pronto, and bring us reinforcements,' Max ordered. '*Schnell* – very *schnell!*'

Through her sobs, the woman nodded in acknowledgement. Max engaged first gear. Slightly uphill and enclosed on both sides by dense, solemn tree trunks, the track was just about passable for a passenger car despite occasional deep ruts of which the car's headlights failed to give adequate warning.

'Max, what are we going to do?' Regine asked nervously.

Before he could answer, several shots rang out. With an almighty bang, the windscreen shattered, showering her in sharp glass fragments. The car drifted to the left and came to a juddering halt against a tree. The windscreen wipers came on.

'*O Gott!*' Regine prayed. 'Max! Are you all right?'

She swung round and looked at him. In the reflected light of one unbroken headlamp, despite his slumped position, the hole in his head was clearly visible. Hand over mouth, Regine managed not to scream.

Leaning across the body, she took the gun from his holster and turned off the engine, headlights and wipers. Then, smirched by his warm sticky blood, she slid down from her seat without a sound and crouched, frozen, in the footwell among the myriad shards of glass.

3

Breaking Cover

THE WIND ABATED overnight. In the morning, it was hard to tell whether the battleship-grey hue of the leaden Kamen skies was due to low clouds or smoke from the burning coal seams. Judging from the acrid smell, I came to the conclusion it was a mixture of both. Fittingly, the heavens seemed in mourning; together with a steady drizzle, colder than snow, they were dumping black carbon particles on our stricken town. I turned up the collar of my greatcoat and hurried towards Am Markt. As I returned the salute of the sentry in front of the office, the first hearse appeared, followed by a silent gaggle of women in black rags. Pushing rickety perambulators with one hand, many held shivering children and toddlers with the other. Behind them, coughing and stumbling, stooped and white-haired beneath formless wool caps, a handful of men watched their feet, aiming the business end of their hand-carved walking sticks at suitable gaps between the uneven cobbles. There were no flowers. I watched the sorry cortege until the clop of the horse's hooves, heading for the Evangelische Kirche across the square, faded almost to nothing; then I pulled myself together and entered the building.

'Good morning, sir.' As was his wont, Sergeant Wagg, chief clerk of the Intelligence Section, was already at his desk, munching at an apple.

'Good morning, Wagg. Has the colonel arrived?'

'Not yet, sir. But somebody called first thing this morning. I took a message for you.'

'Who was it?'

'A local woman, by the name of Schwarz. I think she might be the lady we rescued from her husband a few weeks ago, sir, when you decided to turn out the local police force in the middle of the night.' Wagg chuckled. He was remarkable not only for the hours he put in but also for his extraordinary ability to remember all operations, down to the minutest details of equipment serial numbers and technical references.

'What did she want?'

'Says she has some information about the explosion at the mine.'

'Such as?'

'I'm afraid she will only talk to you.'

'Has she left a number?'

'No. She said she'll be home between nine and ten this morning, and you know where she lives.'

'Thank you, Wagg. By the way, have the Russians lodged any kind of formal complaint against us?'

'Not as far as I know, sir. Of course, they might have

gone straight over our heads to Brigadier Pennycook – or even higher, to the Deputy Military Governor.'

'Keep your ear to the ground, will you?'

'Of course, sir.'

I sat at my desk and looked at my watch. It was just past eight o'clock, and getting to Frau Schwarz's flat would take less than fifteen minutes. I rifled through the mail that had accumulated in my deep wooden in-tray over the last three days, looking for urgent correspondence, and initialled half a dozen Forms 80G which had just come in from the Military Government in Düsseldorf. Duly signed by Colonel Wreford-Brown, the papers for my forthcoming leave brought a short-lived smile to my face, till I realised their start date was already two days past. Once again, my long overdue break had been postponed at short notice because of the Quadripartite inspection. Not only did I now feel worn out by several months of frantic activity, but I really wanted to visit my father in Nuremberg and show him my third pip; rumour had it I was the youngest captain in the British Army of the Rhine, a state of affairs unlikely to endure. I also wanted to learn about his activities at the International Military Tribunal.

At nine o'clock sharp, I parked in front of Frau Schwarz's tenement building. Running up the stairs, I instantly recognised the emanations of coal fires, overcooked cabbage and stale, home-grown tobacco that were the hallmark of vanquished, prostrate Germany. The vast third floor landing hadn't changed since my last visit: the wooden child's tricycle, the colourless coats hanging limply from rows of improvised hooks, clogs and boots neatly aligned on shelves. I knocked on the door.

'*Herein!*' a female voice answered.

The flat itself looked different. Not only had all traces of demolition disappeared, but it was now quiet and spotless. The hole in the partition was hidden behind a velvety black drapery. The apartment seemed empty, with the exception of a lonely female figure sitting in an armchair in front of the sitting-room window, her back to the door. For some reason, her pink jumper and red headscarf seemed vaguely incongruous.

'*Guten Morgen,* Frau Schwarz,' I said, closing the door behind me.

'*Guten Morgen,* Captain Birkett.'

'You wanted to see me?'

'I did. Thank you for coming.'

As she turned around to face me, I froze on the spot. First, she was pointing a gun at me. Second, the woman whose piercing grey-green eyes were staring at me through elegantly long eyelashes was not Frau Schwarz.

'You look confused, Captain Birkett.'

'Captain Terisova! What are you doing here?'

'Surprised? Did you think I was dead already?'

'No – of course not,' I shook my head, unwilling to admit the thought had indeed crossed my mind.

She took a few quick steps and thrust the Nagan's barrel against my chest. It hurt. 'Allow me,' she said, swiftly relieving me of my belt, holster and Luger. In contrast to the hard steel pushing against my pounding heart, her fingers felt soft and unthreatening on my waist.

'We never got round to finishing our last conversation, did we?' she moved backwards, pointing at a chair. 'Would you by any chance have some time for a chat this morning?'

'It will be my pleasure.'

'May I call you Peter?' she sat down on the low armchair, crossed her legs and took off the red scarf, freeing masses of long hair the colour of sunlight on straw. The grey flannel pleated skirt she was wearing was too short for her. To my surprise, her long runner's legs seemed clad in American nylon stockings.

'May I call you Elizaveta?'

'Of course. We are going to be friends, aren't we? After all, you did say we were on the same side, didn't you? That is, if I don't kill you.'

'Why would you kill me?'

'Because I've been ordered to.'

'But...'

'There is no but. You and your Heisingen colleague have been sentenced to death.'

'Max? Why?'

'Because nobody cheats the Soviet Union with impunity. We know exactly what happened to the yellowcake and the Krupp guns. And Colonel Klimenko is upset about it. Wouldn't you be, in his position?'

'What position?'

'You're not a terribly good listener, are you, Peter? I've

told you. All Soviet officers associated with this disastrous Quadripartite inspection will pay for your dirty tricks with their heads. Including me. So, you and I might indeed end up on the same side, after all. Both rather dead.'

'I'm sorry.'

'That's a start. But it doesn't help.'

'How does killing me help you?' I tried to keep my tone conversational, but sweat was trickling down my sides.

For the first time, beneath her arched eyebrows, a fleeting smile lit up her eyes.

'Ah. Good question, Peter. Can you perhaps think of a different scenario? For example, one that doesn't involve both of us dying prematurely?'

I took a deep breath.

'We have lot in common, Elizaveta. I'm sure we don't need to die to be on the same side.'

'Don't we? Won't you always be on Peter Birkett's side, first and foremost?

'No, I swear to you.'

'On your mother's grave?'

'On my mother's grave.'

'Good. Here you are.'

Much to my amazement, she walked to my chair and handed back my belt, holster and Luger.

'Won't you help me put them back on?' I asked, getting to my feet, a tide a relief surging through my whole body. Even without heels, she was almost as tall as me.

'Don't push your luck, Captain Birkett. So far, you got me a death sentence, and I've saved your life. Not exactly symmetrical, is it?' She turned her back to me and placed her own revolver on the window sill. I noticed she hadn't put the safety catch back on – perhaps she'd never taken it off?

'What do you want, Elizaveta?'

'I want to live.'

I sat down and waited.

'I want to study medicine in England,' she continued. 'My mother was a doctor. I want to continue her work. You have no idea how much women suffered during this war. I want to help them.'

'I'll see what I can do. It won't be easy.'

'I have already spent four years at medical school in Moscow. Before the war. At the time, I hoped to work in the Soviet concentration camps. That's why I enrolled in the OGPU.'

Four years at medical school, five years of war: if she's started at eighteen she'd be twenty-seven. She must think I'm a baby, I thought with dismay.

'Why the camps?' I asked.

'Because that's where millions of our best people are sent to rot,' she said. 'Including the Volga Germans. All of them. My family.'

'I'm so sorry. What a mess.'

Nodding, she turned away and quickly wiped her eyes with the back of her hand. I sensed that offering physical comfort would be a mistake. Suddenly, I felt very angry.

'What a fucking useless mess! What hope is there for us? Tell me, Elizaveta? What bloody hope? Millions of people killed, in your country and in Germany, to stop Hitler. That had to be right, surely? But what have we achieved? Have we saved the Jews, the Gypsies, the Poles? Not likely. Europe destroyed, and your Stalin the big winner! That's the result.'

'*Ich weiss, wo Hitler ist,*' she said quietly.

For the first time ever her German made no sense to me.

'I beg your pardon?'

'I know where Hitler is,' she repeated.

'So do I. Hitler's dead.'

'He is alive, and Uncle Iosif will pay any price to get his hands on him.'

'Uncle Iosif?'

'Iosif Vissarionovich Dzhugashvili. Stalin to you.'

The nightmarish feeling that I urgently needed to re-connect with reality nearly sickened me. Time was running out. I had to wake up from this surreal dream. Alternatively, if this encounter was really taking place, which, out of the beguiling Elizaveta Terisova and me, was the insane one? And, critically – was she wearing anything under the pink jumper?

'Shall I explain?' Her voice made me jump.

Rubbing my eyes, I nodded.

'Did you Brits know where the bulk of the Nazi stocks of enriched uranium were hidden?'

Wondering whether this was a trick question, I silently shook my head.

'Here. Right under your nose. In the Grimberg shaft at

the Kamen coalmine. We got tipped off by Grand Admiral Raeder.'

'How did you know he was telling the truth?'

'We didn't. That's why we asked the local Communist cell to go and check. Next thing we know, the whole mine complex goes up in some cataclysmic, inexplicable explosion.'

'You don't think it was an accident?'

'No. But none of the comrades involved in that mission survived, so we may never know what happened down there.'

'If the uranium was in the Grimberg shaft, it would have been guarded, don't you think?'

'Since it was Hitler's most precious possession – his last bargaining chip – I would expect so.'

'So the Nazis, when discovered by your Red scouts, decided to blow it up?'

'Either that, or they got into a firefight and accidentally ignited the blast.'

'I see.' I passed my hand through my hair, trying to take in the story. 'Any chance of a glass of water?'

'The kitchen's over there. Help yourself.'

'Can I get you something?'

'Water would be nice. Thank you.'

'What are you doing in Frau Schwarz's flat?' I asked a minute later, handing her a full glass.

'Her husband was the Communist leader at the mine. A brave man.'

'I see. Working for you, was he?'

'He gave his life to resist the Nazi beast.'

'Talking of whom, you said you believe Hitler to be alive?'

'I saw him.'

'Where?'

'In your office.'

'Very funny.' Though she didn't protest, her look told me that in fact she was deadly serious.

'Will you explain?' I asked patiently.

'Do you remember the German who fell from a train the morning of the explosion, when I came to your office to lodge my complaint?'

'Of course. I'm afraid he took advantage of the commotion to amble off. Looked pretty innocuous.'

'That was Adolf Hitler.'

I jumped to my feet and ran to the armchair where Elizaveta Terisova was sitting. Standing over her, I could distinguish every strand of blonde hair and smell her unknown, discreet fragrance. The thought crossed my mind that, in my position, Max would have been able to put a name, a price and a vintage on it.

'What are you saying?'

'You heard.' Above her high cheekbones, her brow was smooth and inscrutable. I resisted the temptation to touch it.

'His name was Weber,' I said. 'Wait… Franz – no, Gustav Weber.'

'Do you know who the real Gustav Weber was?'

I shrugged silently.

'Gustav Weber was Hitler's body double.'

'Double?'

'One of the *Doppelgänger* specially recruited and trained by Goebbels to impersonate the Führer.'

'So the fellow in my office used to be Hitler's double?'

She shook her head. 'No, Peter. He was Adolf Hitler. Different times, different manners: instead of Weber impersonating Hitler, now it's Hitler who impersonates Weber.'

'How do you know?'

'I don't *know* – but I've got a strong hunch. Think about it. Who was more likely to be hiding near the Führer's most precious treasure: Hitler or Weber? Who was attempting to leave Kamen accompanied by a small SS escort on the morning when the uranium stocks were discovered, just before the mine was blown up? Hitler or Weber?'

'How should I know? Anyway, there is no need to speculate. We'll put out an arrest warrant for this chap Weber and compare his fingerprints with Hitler's. Then we'll know who's who, won't we?'

Elizaveta rose, forcing me to take half a step back.

'I'm afraid it isn't that simple.'

Engulfed in the immense, icy steppes in her eyes, I tried to focus on her words.

'Why not?'

'Because Herr Weber has no fingerprints.'

Again the uneasy feeling of oscillating helplessly between dream and reality.

'Everybody has fingerprints.'

'Our friend lost his.'

'Lost?'

She took my left hand in hers and, slowly running her forefinger across each one of my fingers, showed me: 'Each and every finger has been surgically severed – here.'

Devoid of any ring, her hand was strong and warm, and I felt bereft when she let go of mine.

'How do you know?' I asked.

'I checked.'

'When?'

'That morning, in your office.'

'What on earth gave you that idea?'

'I remembered that the charred body found in the garden of the Reich Chancellery on 5th May had no fingers.'

'Hardly surprising if they'd been burnt off?'

'The body was only partly carbonised. Not enough to hide the fact that many fingers had been removed prior to death. Obviously, had it been completely incinerated, nobody would have known. But the Nazis knew they couldn't rely on it. So they took the fingers off. Better safe than sorry.'

'But I thought the remains had been identified beyond doubt through dental records?'

'Yes and no. We have no dental records. But my colleague Captain Deryabin drove the body to the SMERSH base at Buch, for forensic examination. He managed to find the assistant of Hitler's dentist. She formally recognised Hitler's highly unusual bridgework.

Additionally, the skull's dentition perfectly matched her recollection of Hitler's mouth.'

'So?'

'That's all I know. Draw your own conclusions.'

Mystified, I turned around, walked to the window and stared out. The street was quiet. On the pavement, dark desiccated leaves were dancing and whirling. Bracing themselves against the cold breeze, a couple of old women, one laden with timber debris and the other with a coal pail, were shuffling along.

'Surely, a corpse with Hitler's head attached to it is likely to be Hitler's corpse, with or without fingers, isn't it?'

'You would think so, wouldn't you?'

Something in her voice made me turn round.

'But Captain Terisova of the NKGB doesn't – does she?'

'Well…' With two quick steps she came closer and lowered her voice. 'Let's assume for one second that Gustav Weber's dentition is identical to Hitler's. Where would that leave us?'

'With an unlikely coincidence.'

'It would leave us with two fingerless individuals, both sporting Hitler's jaws. One dead, one alive.'

'Possibly. But, in reality, we know nothing about Gustav Weber's teeth, do we?'

Smiling quizzically, still so close that I could feel her light breath on my face, she pushed her hair back in a graceful gesture. As the pink fabric stretched across her breasts without revealing anything of her nipples, I decided she must after all be wearing something, albeit probably not a brassiere, under the woollen jumper.

'Why are you not in uniform?' I asked.

'Why are you?' she smiled.

'I'm… working,' I mumbled, feeling stupid.

'So am I. As it happens, Soviet uniforms aren't wildly popular around here – either with the locals or with the occupying power.'

'Do you realise what risks you are taking? If our MPs or Military Intelligence find you, you'll be arrested as a common spy.'

'I know.'

'Do you also know the penalty for that?'

'Death.'

'So why did you call me here?'

'To shoot you.'

'But you didn't.'

'No.'

'Why not?'

'So that you can redeem yourself.'

I waited with lifted eyebrows.

She took my hands.

'I have to defect, Peter. Otherwise Chairman Merkulov will have me killed. Or worse.'

I was, for once, lost for words. Unable to suppress a stupid grin, I felt torn between elation and gloom: overjoyed by the fact we were holding hands, and weighed down by a strong premonition of impending catastrophe. Looking at myself from the ceiling, I could see I was about to fall for the oldest trick in the NKGB book – and yet walking away, back to the rational and efficient world of T Force, simply wasn't an option.

'What are you worried about?' she asked, sensing my hesitation. 'You'll be a hero. You like that, don't you? Youngest captain in the British Army. The man who found Hitler!'

'Where is he?'

'In a safe place,' she smiled.

Using my last reserves of willpower, I managed to wrench my hands free and crossed my arms.

'What's the deal, Elizaveta?'

'I deliver Hitler to you. You get me a British passport.'

'What if Hitler turns out to be Weber?'

'That's a risk you have to take.'

'Why don't you deliver Hitler to Stalin? You'd be the hero.'

'That's exactly what I'll do if you won't help me. But do we want to give Uncle Iosif such a massive propaganda victory? The party would portray him as the sole victor of the war, who crushed the Nazi beast single-handed. He'd be unassailable – forever.'

'What's wrong with that?'

'Believe me – everything,' she whispered.

'If your Johnny really is Hitler, surely he should be sitting in the dock at the Nuremberg tribunal, together with his underlings?'

'People who believe in due process might think so.'

'Why do we need you? What makes you suppose we can't find him within twenty-four hours?'

'The Communist networks have eluded the Gestapo for twelve years, Peter. Trust me: they know a thing or two about hiding.'

'All right. I need a couple of days to sort this out with my superiors. Anyway, I suspect the matter will be immediately taken out of my hands. Can we meet again, say at noon the day after tomorrow?'

'No. That's too late.'

'Why?'

'If I don't report back by the end of today, Klimenko will get suspicious. For the time being, the local comrades still believe that my instructions are authorised by Moscow. The minute Klimenko makes contact with them they'll realise I'm on my own.'

'How will he contact them?'

'They have radio sets.'

'Do you know the frequencies and codes?'

'Maybe.'

'I see. How can I get hold of you?'

'You can't. I'll call you. I know your office telephone number.'

I wrote a number on a scrap of paper.

'There you are. This is my private number, in my quarters. Call me there tonight at 18:00 hours and, if necessary, on the hour thereafter until I answer.'

Having scrutinised the number with a faint smile, as though checking for hidden promise, she looked me in

the eye. '*Ich bedanke mich, Herr Kapitän,*' she murmured.
'You'd better go now. Check the street first.'

'*Bis bald, Fräulein Kapitän.*'

Firmly shaking her extended hand, I concluded that
the heavenly perfume emanating from her, far from being some kind of sophisticated commercial concoction,
was her natural fragrance. As I ran down the three flights
of steps, somehow, among the mass of confusing information and feelings whirling through my head, this simple fact seemed paramount.

BY MID MORNING, having first walked around the block
for half an hour in a vain attempt to clear my head, I was
back in my office. Lieutenant Wright-Collins was sitting
in my chair, cigarette holder in hand, blowing rings of
smoke towards the big window.

'Hello, Julian. What are you doing here?'

'Morning, Peter. Sounds like you've forgotten our appointment. Overworked? Or just no time for lowly lieu-
tenants?' Flourishing an embossed blue and gold diary,
he read aloud:

'*Nine o'clock. Meet PB at IS headquarters to debrief re
Quadripartite inspection and follow-up.*'

'Sorry, Julian. Something came up. Not unconnected
with the inspection, in fact.'

'I'm all ears.'

'Do you mind if I make a quick call first?'

'Of course not. Make yourself at home.' Wright–

Collins got up and offered his seat with an airy gesture.

I walked round the desk, picked up the receiver and dialled the number of the headquarters of B company in Heisingen, asking for Lieutenant Max Harrison. I was told that Harrison hadn't been seen in the office yet, so I left a request for him to call me back urgently.

'What's the emergency?' Wright-Collins asked, nonchalantly sitting down on a chair across the desk.

'According to some intelligence reports, the Russkis are a bit upset with us.'

'So what's new?'

'Apparently they have identified Max and me as the chief villains. They blame us for cheating them out of the uranium, the guns and the aluminium plant.'

'Just doing your job. Like the rest of us. Can't see why our Eastern friends should take it personally.'

'Only because, in their world, failure is treasonable.'

'Meaning?'

'That each and every Soviet inspector in that Quadripartite team is likely to be shot.'

'Does that worry us?'

'Not particularly. But somehow it worries them greatly. And they may retaliate.'

'What can they do? They're back in their own Godforsaken Zone, we're in control of ours. It'll blow over.'

'Let's hope so.'

Wright-Collins leaned forward, his blue eyes more piercing than ever beneath his long, curly blond hair, and lowered his voice. 'You're not afraid?' he asked.

'Not especially. We live in a messy world.'

'Yes. But predictable enough. Remember Stalin knows his Machiavelli.'

'Enlighten me?'

' *"Since love and fear can hardly exist together, if we must choose between them, it is far safer to be feared than loved."* The man is certainly good at inspiring fear in his own people. As for love...' Wright-Collins removed the cigarette butt from his ivory holder, stumped it out in an ashtray, took a pack of Senior Service out of his breast pocket and inserted a fresh one. Lining up holder and cigarette like the sights of a gun, one eye closed, he carefully checked that they were perfectly aligned.

'Talking of love,' both eyes now slanted, he paused to light his cigarette, 'what happened to your Russian girlfriend?'

'I beg your pardon?'

'You know. The Russian totty you were chatting up during the inventory signing party? Captain to captain, as it were. Capital blonde bombshell. Nobody could fault your taste, old chap, though the same may not be true of your judgment, if I may say. Is she also going to be shot?'

'She seems to think so. Unless she defects first.'

'Fascinating. Have you seen her since the inspection?'

With a perfunctory single knock, Sergeant Wagg popped his head through the door.

'Excuse me, sir. B Company on the line, returning your call.'

'Thank you, Wagg. Put it through, would you?'

Hand on receiver, I picked it up as it started ringing, relieved that Max had been found.

'Max? Where have you been, you lazy slob?' I asked.

'Is this Captain Birkett?' a voice replied.

'Yes. Who's that?'

'Sergeant Anderson. We talked earlier this morning. I'm afraid Lieutenant Harrison had a bit of an accident, sir.'

'Did he? How bad?'

'Quite bad, sir. He was found dead half an hour ago. In a car.'

'Good Lord! What happened? Did he hit anything?'

'Not exactly, sir. In fact, rather the other way round.'

'He was hit?'

'Somebody put a bullet through his head, sir.'

4

Betrayals

VERILY, SHE SAVED my life. She truly saved my life.

Drowning Wright-Collins's voice, this thought reverberated in my head. Staring blankly at the big window, I could see nothing, not even my own reflection. Since the mine explosion, an intricate cobweb of thousands of minute hairline cracks had opaqued the plate glass, depriving me not only of my view of the market square, but also of a certain purchase on reality. Only when Julian banged on the desk did I come out of my reverie.

'For God's sake, Peter! What's going on?'

'They killed Max.'

'What?'

'The murderous bastards killed Max.'

'Bloody hell! How?'

'Shot through the head. Driving his girlfriend back home in the middle of the night.'

'Good grief! Was she involved?'

'Probably not. Lucky to have survived, in fact. Poor old Max. I wonder who will tell his parents…'

'Sounds like your intelligence was correct after all. Better watch your back, old chap.'

Greater love hath no woman than this, that she lay down her life for her friend.

'She wants to defect, Julian. We've got to help her.'

'Defect? The girlfriend?'

'No. Captain Terisova.'

Wright-Collins deliberately expelled a jet of blue smoke from the corner of his mouth. 'Tell me more.'

'She was ordered to kill me.'

'How do you know?'

'She told me. With her gun on my bloody heart.'

'Why didn't she?'

'I told you. She wants to defect.'

Wright-Collins frowned.

'Are you sure it isn't your idea?'

'Yes.'

'Was she involved in Max's murder?'

'I don't think so.'

'Can she prove it?'

'Come on, Julian. She warned me about it.'

'Yes. But too late.'

'Sadly, yes. But she risked her life to save mine.'

'Possibly. Let's hope she can convince the chaps up in Bad Nenndorf.'

'What's Bad Nenndorf?'

'No. 74 Detailed Interrogations Centre. Surely you've heard of it?'

'No.'

'Run by MI5. Originally meant to hold former Nazis, but now dealing essentially with suspected Soviet spies. Pretty hard core.'

'In what way?'

'Operating without much supervision, behind barbed wire. The camp is based in the old spa complex; the bathrooms have been converted into cells. They took out the bath tubs, but left all the tiles on the floors and walls. Ideal. By the way – don't repeat any of that. It's classified.'

'How come you know about it?

'My uncle runs the show. Lieutenant Colonel Robin Stephens. No-nonsense fellow, Uncle Robin. As far as he's concerned, most prisoners are degenerates who arrive riddled with VD, and all are pathological liars. His job is to break them. Very few people can withstand being beaten and starved for a few months. And the cold always gets those who can.'

'The cold?'

'There is no heating in the camp. The cell windows are left open at all times. Apparently, the temperature inside can drop to minus ten degrees Celsius. But that's not all.'

I involuntarily closed my eyes.

'They developed a foolproof treatment,' Wright-Collins went on. 'The prisoners are stripped naked, doused with a bucket of ice-cold water and made to scrub their cell on all fours. No doubts the guards will enjoy watching Captain Terisova splashing about in that position. As soon as the water's frozen, another bucketful – start all over again. Day and night.'

'Good God! Are you telling me that British forces are involved in systematic torture?'

'Let's not exaggerate. Enhanced interrogation techniques, at most. Anyway, cells have to be cleaned, don't they? But, if truth be told, frostbite on the feet and legs isn't the worst. Hands are more serious, I'm told, because you lose the use of them so you can't eat any more.'

'Why is this tolerated?'

'National security, of course. Stalin is infiltrating hundreds of agents into the Western Zones. It's crucial for the democratic future of Europe that we identify these spies, find out everything they know about the NKGB networks and, if possible, turn them around.'

'So we're treating innocent people and Communists exactly like the Gestapo used to? Incarcerating suspects on the basis of rumours and denunciations, and torturing them until they confess? Without regard to international law?'

'International law doesn't apply to Bad Nenndorf. It's trumped by national security.'

'Nobody's above the law.'

'You really should brush up on Machiavelli, Peter. *Win through your actions, never through argument.* We've won the war. That makes us the good guys. We've got the guns. We make the laws.'

'Surely, we won the war *because* we're the good guys. As soon as people back home realise what's being perpetrated in their name, there will be outrage. Your uncle will be court-martialled.'

'Will they ever know? Bad Nenndorf is beyond the pale, Peter. It's a black hole. Answerable neither to London nor to the Allied Military Government. As for the folks back home, what if they actually don't want to know?'

I rose, walked around the desk, and stood over Lieutenant Wright-Collins.

'Then we'd have fought yet another world war for nothing. Max's death would be pointless. And the current proceedings in Nuremberg would be a sick farce.'

Wright-Collins threw his hands up in a placating gesture.

'At least we can agree on that.'

'Anyway – there is another reason why Elizaveta can't go to Bad Nenndorf. Apart from the fact she saved my life, I mean.'

'What's that?'

'She says she can lead us to Hitler.'

An incredulous smile slowly spread across Wright-Collins's angular face.

'Peter... Really... You're not going to fall for that one? Seriously? Do you know how many times Hitler is sighted every week, in Bavaria, Brazil, Argentina and Manchuria? Have you any idea how many people offer to sell him to us every month?'

'I know. But this is different.'

'Oh, it is, is it?'

I turned my back on him and shrugged. Before I could sit down at my desk, Colonel Wreford-Brown rushed in.

'Ah! There you both are. Dreadful business. Most unfortunate. Any details?' I quickly summarised the news from Heisingen, leaving out any mention of Elizaveta Terisova. The colonel stood still for a few seconds.

'You were close to Harrison, weren't you, Birkett?'

'Yes, sir.'

'Mighty fine Rifleman. Had a quick tongue – held no fear of rank.'

'Very true, sir.'

'What do you think happened?'

'According to the passenger in his car, he was killed by a rampaging gang of DPs, sir.'

'I see. In that case we must hunt down these bandits.'

'Yes, sir. An alternative theory is that Max and I are on an NKGB hit list.'

'Why would you be?'

'It seems the Russians got wise to the fact we spirited away lots of critical stuff right under their noses, sir.'

'Hmm… I doubt they would risk a major diplomatic incident over a botched inspection. There is enough left in Germany for them to plunder. And we'd have to think jolly carefully before trying to implicate them in the assassination of a British officer, for exactly the same reason.'

'Of course, sir.'

'Having said that, one of my officers has been murdered. Bad precedent. I want his killers' scalps. Why don't you nip down to Heisingen and find out how they're getting on, Birkett?'

'Certainly, sir.'

Having closed the door behind Colonel Wreford-Brown and Lieutenant Wright-Collins, I stood, lost in confusing thoughts. After a while, I sat down at my desk and called a Nuremberg number. I was lucky: the Court had just risen for the lunchtime recess, and Judge Birkett was quickly found in the cafeteria. Our conversation lasted the best part of half an hour.

A few minutes later, a Major Airey Neave rang from Nuremberg and gave me his private address and telephone number.

THERE, BUT FOR *the grace of God…* The reality of Max's death only hit when I stood before his mortal remains. The inert lumps of flabby flesh that used to be Lieutenant Harrison now seemed strangely unconnected with him. The bandages wrapped around the head, trying to constrict whatever brain matter it still contained, reminded me of the Egyptian mummies I'd seen at the British Museum.

In order to hide my tears, I leaned forward and searched Max's pockets. I found his lighter. Made from an old pocket watch case just under two inches wide, it comprised two pieces of brass and copper core assembled to form the fluid cavity. On one face, hovering high above a single-arch stone bridge, some kind of early pre-Zeppelin airship had been engraved, probably before the Great War. On the other, both arms raised above her head as if to hold her hair in place, offering herself in full frontal view, knees close together like Botticelli's *Venus*, a wide-hipped, slim-waisted nude girl was etched across the diameter. Devoid of the tarnish that dulled the rest of the surface, her protruding breasts and mons veneris gleamed as though lit by an inside fire. On her right, a wheat sheaf snaked along the circumference, symmetrically matched on her left by a vine heavy with leaf and grape. Staring at it, I half expected Max to sit up, grab the lighter, unscrew the cap covering the wick in a familiar gesture and, delighted at his practical joke, light a cigarette with an outburst of whinnying laughter.

'I'd like to keep this,' I said quietly to Sergeant Anderson. 'I shouldn't think it's worth very much.'

'Of course, sir. I'm sure Lieutenant Harrison would have liked you to have it. He was such a nice man. To think he was only twenty...'

We fell silent. Could Max really be gone? Would all traces of his existence vanish within a few decades, leaving the universe unaware of the fact he'd ever been born? And yet an inanimate brass lighter can survive its many successive owners and two world wars. Strange. Could an all-powerful, benevolent God have willed the assassination of twenty-year-old Max Harrison? Or was it all random? Max dies. I live. A day? A month? Fifty years? It will make no difference in the end: nobody will remember or care.

Damn. I miss you already, you silly old duffer! But I will get your killers, if it's the last thing I do. Rest in peace, old chap. Perhaps you're the lucky one.

I released Max's cold, inert hand, pocketed the lighter and quickly turned around.

My interview with Regine did not last long. Albeit sedated, the girl was still prone to bouts of hysterical sobbing. It soon became clear that she'd been in love with Max and wasn't a suspect. Unfortunately, she wasn't able to provide any useful description of the woman who'd flagged down their car.

I agreed with the Commanding Officer of B Company that the official report would relate only the heroic death of Lieutenant Max Harrison as he gallantly attempted to protect civilians from the exactions of drunken and murderous DPs, while leaving out any mention of Regine.

The armoured Humber scout car I'd selected for my trip to Heisingen afforded protection from the kind of sniper attack that killed Max, but it was excruciatingly slow. Though I drove it flat-out all the way back to Kamen, it was nearly six-thirty when I parked in front of Doktor Gräbe's house. I was half an hour late for my telephone appointment. I ran up the stairs and rushed into my room. Would Elizaveta call at the next appointed time? Why had she not warned me about Max's imminent killing? Its black Bakelite shell shining like that of an ancient tortoise, the receiver remained lifeless and inscrutable.

Suddenly, I felt the need to hear Father's voice. The calm, measured words, the clipped tones that, while sometimes – often, even – irritating, always conveyed so much wisdom and warm humanity. I dialled the number.

'Major Neave, War Crimes Executive,' a voice answered.

'Oh, hello, Major Neave. This is Captain Birkett – Judge Birkett's son. Is my father around?'

'Afraid not, Captain. All eight judges are in conference. Might go on some time. Can I help?'

'Probably not. Thank you, Major.'

'Any message?'

'No, thanks.'

'Are you still planning to deliver a parcel to Nuremberg tomorrow?'

'Absolutely. I shall be leaving as agreed – first thing in the morning.'

'Safe journey, Captain Birkett. I'll tell your father you called. He'll be glad to see you, I can tell you that.'

I hung up, took off my tie and belt, opened my shirt collar and threw myself on the bed, wishing I could magic a bottle of Johnnie Walker out of thin air. No sooner had I caught my breath than there was a faint knock on the door. I jumped to my feet, heart racing. It was Susette.

'May I come in?' she asked timidly, watching the corridor over her shoulder.

It was twenty to seven. I opened the door wider and made way. Never before – except in my dreams – had Susette entered the room in my presence. However, throughout the summer an invisible hand had placed an egg-cup full of violets on my bedside table and magically contrived to refresh and renew them well into October. That these modest blooms originated in the little copse between the house and the railway line was clear, as was the fact that they hardly travelled thence under their own steam. However, the nature of the assistance they received on the way remained mysterious. Recently, purple asters and white chrysanthemums had followed. Were they deposited by Elli, the shy seventeen-year-old 'washerwoman' who, blushing to her neckline every time I appeared unexpectedly, made my bed and dusted the shelves? Or were they tokens of Susette's love?

'Do you like your room?' she asked. 'It used to be mine.'

Suddenly I felt embarrassed by the collection of tea-stained mugs on the window sill. At least the black and white pornographic photographs Max had given me in Brussels weren't on display. 'I'm sorry,' I said.

'Don't be. I'm glad it's occupied by you. Do you see the big lime tree there?' She pointed at skeletal branches just visible through the window. 'In summer, with your window open, you'll hear the nightingale. All night long. I used to think it was singing for me. Sometimes I joined in.' She gave a little embarrassed laugh.

Suddenly, with absolute clarity, I recalled the vivid nightmare I'd had a few weeks ago. Susette's rueful smile was precisely the same as when she'd dived head first into the violet-filled *Planschbecken*, never to reappear. The nightingale had sung then. It had sung for her, a poignant, tragic aria.

Susette put her hands round my neck and dragged me down to the bed. She looked frightened.

'What's wrong, Peter? Tell me.'

'It's only work, my darling. Sorry.'

'It's not only work, Peter. Tell me! Can't you trust me?'
I kissed her.

'I trust you with my life, my love. But you can't afford to reciprocate.'

'What on earth do you mean?'

'I'm a soldier. My best friend was murdered last night.'

'Max?'

'Yes.'

'Oh, Peter…' Both hands on my nape, she gently pulled me in against her chest and cradled my head. 'I'm so sorry, my love. I liked Max.'

For a while, eyes shut, fear and tension draining out of my body, feeling like a little boy starved of cuddles for too long, I let myself be gently rocked.

'Come,' she whispered, lying down on the bed. 'You do know I love you, don't you? With all my soul. And all my body.'

I let myself fall on top of her. A hill for every valley and a promontory for each cove. I had no inkling that bodies could fit so perfectly. So… exquisitely. When I raised myself on my elbows, searching her eyes, her gaze was direct, unafraid and honest.

'*Ich liebe dich,*' I whispered, overwhelmed by gratitude.

'*Bitte* – I'm not asking you to love me. I'm yours anyway.'

'I do love you,' I repeated; and this time I meant it.

She lifted her head, her lips seeking mine. There was something wild and lost in her dilated hazelnut pupils.

I playfully pecked her forehead, dark brows, eyelids and nose before tantalising her half-parted lips. I felt her breathing quicken and her legs move.

'I'm sorry – it's my first time,' she whispered.

'For what?' I teased.

'You know.'

'Same here,' I smiled. Overwhelmed by thankfulness, I opened the front of her blouse and slid my hand under her brassiere. Her breast felt warm, soft and firm. She gasped and closed her eyes. Time stopped.

We both started when the telephone suddenly shrieked. I jumped to my feet. Susette covered herself. Picking up the receiver, I motioned to her to stay still. It was Elizaveta. She sounded rattled.

'Well?' she asked. 'Have you made any progress? Time is running out.'

'Why didn't you warn me about Max?'

'Max Harrison?'

'Of course – who else?'

'What are you talking about, Peter? I did warn you about him.'

'Yes – but too bloody late.'

'Oh God. Did they kill him?'

'Yes. You don't have to pretend to be surprised.'

'When?'

'Last night.'

'I'm truly sorry. One should never underestimate Ivan Klimenko. That's why we have to make our move now. Tonight. He's closing in on me.'

'What do you mean?'

'He's been contacting the local Communists, asking about my whereabouts. By now he'll have put two and two together. Without the support of our networks, I'm dead. I need a hiding place now – for me and our friend.'

'I'm planning to drive both of you to Nuremberg first thing in the morning, where things are being organised at the highest level.'

'Can't we go tonight?'

'No. The chances of being stopped by the Military Police in the middle of the night are far too high. I can pick you up at seven.'

'My friend and I need shelter for the night, Peter.'

'Hold on a minute, will you?' I covered the microphone with my hand and turned to Susette. 'Is there a basement here?' I whispered urgently.

'Yes, of course.'

'Has it got a lockable door?'

'Several. One for each room.'

I blew her a kiss and, turning my attention back to the telephone, gave Elizaveta the address of the house.

'Can you get here by yourself?' I asked.

'No. I've got no transport, and my friend isn't keen on walking.'

'Are you still at Frau Schwarz's?'

'No. We had to move on.'

She gave me an address in the Querstrasse, a small street off the Münsterstrasse in the vicinity of the cemetery.

'I'll be there in forty-five minutes,' I said before hanging up.

Under Susette's silent gaze, I adjusted my clothes, picked up my belt and holster and buckled them on.

'Who was that?' she asked.

'Work. I'm afraid I have to go out.'

She got up and buttoned up her blouse.

'Promise me you'll be careful. Will you be long?'

'Possibly. Don't wait for me.'

Coming close to me, she smiled. 'Waiting is what we girls do, isn't it?' She offered me her lips and waited. I gave her a quick kiss.

'Can you show me the basement?' I asked.

There were four cavernous areas beneath the house. The first one, replete with huge insulated pipes and all manner of valves, housed the central heating boiler, various pumps and hot water cylinders. Next to it, a vast coal storage area was almost empty. Presumably as a result of the earlier requisitioning of the house by US fighting forces, the depleted wine cellar, still redolent of the sweetness of Gewurztraminer, Riesling and vintage port, was littered with broken bottles and glass shards. At the back was a windowless, low-ceilinged general storage area, half-full with the paraphernalia left by growing children and passing generations: old sleighs and modern skates, dusty prams and broken dolls, musty suitcases and mouldy medical magazines, three-legged chairs and moth-eaten Panamas. Having satisfied myself that the door lock worked, I put the key in my pocket.

'You'd better go home before it gets too late, my darling,' I said as we emerged into the entrance hall.

'What do you need the basement for?'

'Short-term storage. Sorry, Susette – got to run.'

'Remember, Captain Birkett: I love you. No heroics. Right?'

'Right.' Ignoring her open arms, I turned around and opened the front door. She closed it softly behind me. The night was moonless.

At first the Querstrasse seemed empty. However, as I was preparing to park, two figures emerged from some recess and stood on the pavement, dazzled by the headlights. I opened the passenger door of the Volkswagen and waited, but they stood still. After a few seconds I got out.

'What are we waiting for?' I asked.

'He won't move,' Elizaveta answered. The barrel of her gun was burrowed deep in the blue greatcoat of the man standing hunched next to her, whose hands were tied up behind his back. His pepper-and-salt stubble had grown so much that it not only hid any trace of the cuts he'd suffered when falling from the train, but also totally changed his physiognomy.

'Oh yes he will – won't you, Herr Hitler?' I answered, grabbing the man's elbow.

'*Ich heiße Gustav Weber,*' the man said in a low guttural voice – but he walked to the car and soon was sitting at the back, next to Elizaveta. Fifteen minutes later we reached Doktor Gräbe's dark and quiet house. Before long, his fingerless hands and his feet tightly bound, the prisoner was lying quietly behind two locked doors on an old mattress I'd found in the cellar.

'He should be all right for the night,' Elizaveta said as we climbed the stairs back up to the main entrance hall. 'He's the quiet type, and I fed him before leaving. Not that he eats much anyway. How safe is this house?'

'Safe enough for one night. We're the only occupants. Unless your NKGB friends are planning to pay us a visit, of course.'

She shrugged. 'Sadly, I'm not privy to their plans any more.'

'This is the kitchen,' I indicated. 'Not very well stocked, I'm afraid. It's only used for breakfast. I should have some bread and milk – and maybe some Bratwurst.'

'That would be nice, thank you.'

Without taking off her drab grey coat, she watched wordlessly while I rummaged in the cupboards, looking for a jar of the homemade rhubarb-and-apple jam my aunt regularly sent from Kent. I put the sausages into a frying pan which immediately generated thick greasy smoke, then cut two slices of rye bread, heated the milk and self-consciously poured it into two chipped cups. We sat down on wooden stools at a table so small that, every time we moved, our knees touched.

'Sugar?'

'*Bitte.*' She helped herself to two spoonfuls.

'Where do you get it from?' she asked.

'What?'

'The sugar.'

I shrugged. 'So – how have you been getting on with our friend?'

'*Ich heiße Gustav Weber,*' she mimicked with an Austrian accent. 'That's all he ever says. Quite boring.'

'It certainly would be very tedious if it turned out to be true.'

Until that point, I hadn't seriously entertained the thought that her prisoner might be Adolf Hitler, and certainly wasn't going to make a fool of myself shouting from the rooftops that I'd found the Führer or some reincarnated avatar of his. Nevertheless, the intelligence value of a *Doppelgänger* was potentially considerable, as were the possible political ramifications. That's why my father had advised me discreetly to deliver the prisoner to the Nuremberg authorities.

Looking at me with a cryptic half-smile, she drank her milk. We ate our stale, crusty bread and a small piece of overcooked Bratwurst without a word, while I desperately tried to muffle all munching noises and to prevent crumbs from falling all over my clothes. Whenever I stole a glance at her, I met her steady grey-green stare.

After we finished, she washed the cups and unerringly put them back in the right place. I felt tired.

'Shall we go up?' I asked.

She nodded and followed me. I opened the door to my room, turned the light on and, inviting her with a wave of the hand. 'Please excuse the mess.' I looked at the crumpled bedspread with some embarrassment.

She stepped forward. 'Chrysanthemums,' she murmured, touching the flowers lightly. 'At least they're white...'

'Do make yourself comfortable.'

She took off her coat, revealing the same pink jumper and grey flannel skirt she was wearing at our previous encounter. I moved to the window and drew the curtains. At the same instant, hearing light footsteps in the corridor, we both looked up in surprise. I pulled my Luger out of its holster and released the safety catch. Swiftly, I moved to the side of the door, turned off the light and waited. The footsteps seemed to be running away, possibly down the stairs. After a few seconds the front door banged shut. I ran to the window and slightly parted the curtains, but the darkness was thick and impenetrable. As quietly as possible, I opened the window and listened. After a while, leaving the window slightly ajar, I turned round and put my revolver back in his holster.

'Who was it?' Elizaveta asked.

'No idea,' I lied. 'Possibly my "washerwoman" – she's got keys. Or Doktor Gräbe. Sometimes he works late in the surgery downstairs.'

I was expecting her to ask why in that case the house was dark when we'd arrived, but she let the matter rest. Remembering Max's lighter, I fumbled in my pockets till I found it, unscrewed the cap, lit the candle that stood on the bedside table next to the flowers and carefully screwed the cap back on top of the burning wick.

'Probably safer not to put the lights back on,' I said.

'My driver will be here at seven, with an armoured car. We should be in Nuremberg in time for lunch.'

'What will happen there?'

'My father is one of the two British judges of the International Military Tribunal. He has access to the British Prime Minister. We'll get instructions on arrival.'

'Peter – what will happen to me?'

'I'll take care of you.'

She gave a small laugh.

'I've heard this a few times in my lifetime – last from Klimenko.'

'I will take care of you,' I repeated.

'I see. You're different, are you?'

'Yes. Maybe.'

'You'd better be.'

'Let's get some rest,' I suggested. 'The bed is yours. Do you want me to find another room or to sleep on the floor here?'

'Depends how different you are. Anyway, I can sleep on the floor.'

'Certainly not. Even our guest in the cellar is sleeping on a mattress, for Christ's sake.'

'I'll tell you what. You take the mattress, and I'll sleep on the bed base. All right?'

'If you insist.'

A few minutes later, both fully clothed, we lay in the dark, a few feet apart. The thought that she was lying on Susette's bed was disconcerting. I focused my attention on Elizaveta's breathing, wondering whether I'd be able to tell when she fell asleep. But it was I who later woke with a jolt when she touched my shoulder.

'Peter! Can you hear?'

'What?'

'Listen. Is it some kind of signal?'

Now wide awake, I sat up. Sobbing and lamenting, ebbing and flowing with melodious whistles and haunting, repeated phrases, a pure contralto was filling the night.

'It's a bird,' I said.

'I know – a nightingale. But that's impossible.'

'Why?'

'Because nightingales are migratory birds. This one should have crossed the Sahara desert weeks ago.'

'Maybe it's just late?'

'If it overstays its welcome, it will die.'

'How do you know?'

'Jakob knew about birds.'

Unexpectedly, I felt a pang of jealousy. 'Jakob?'

At first hesitantly, then more freely as I kept asking questions, she told me the astounding story of her childhood in Moscow and Shcherbatovka, how her mother had given her life to the starving Volga peasants, and how Stalin had wreaked terrible havoc on their communities. She described the infinite expanse of black soil where tall yellow flowers worshipped the sun, and how her cousin Jakob caught rabbits but never hunted migratory birds. How, as a boy, he'd promised to bring water to the village, and taught her to identify the Tundra Bean geese and the white storks on their way to mythical African wintering grounds. She didn't mention their first kiss – there was no need.

Enthralled, I failed to notice that the nightingale had fallen silent. But when, in the dead of night, drenched in tears, Elizaveta Terisova eventually fell asleep in my arms, I knew there was no point in being jealous of Jakob.

My rival was no more.

5

Trial and Error

Doesn't Hess look totally mad?' Neave whispered.

'Which one is he?' I asked.

'Can't you tell? First row, second from the left.'

'Oh – I see what you mean.'

Unshaven, his deep-set black eyes staring straight ahead under bushy eyebrows, the man to whom Hitler had in 1924 dictated *Mein Kampf* in a shared cell of the Landsberg prison, the companion the Führer made his deputy when grabbing power nine years later, the quixotic leader who'd defected to England in 1941 to negotiate peace terms with the King, only to sit out the war in English jails, gaunt and wild-looking, Rudolf Hess was indeed a pitiful sight.

'So far, he's spent his whole time in court sleeping or reading novels,' Neave explained.

'Perhaps he's not so crazy if he can read?'

'I'm really not sure. During his years in English prisons he suffered from amnesia, and attempted to kill himself twice. Your father thinks he was only indicted to please

Stalin, who suspected all along he was sent to Britain to plot against the USSR.'

'Is that Göring sitting next to him? He seems pretty relaxed.'

'Doesn't he just? He's been trying to re-establish his authority over his colleagues, as the legitimate successor to Hitler. He wants them to present a united front.'

'Has he succeeded?'

'Partially. Some of his co-defendants despise him – the military men, you know, Jodl, Dönitz, Raeder. And Speer hates him.'

'Why does he look so smug then?'

'I suppose he just enjoys being centre-stage again. Once a showman, always a showman. Besides, he thinks he ran rings round the prosecution yesterday.'

'What about?'

'Oh, some arcane details about his role in the invasion of Austria.'

As an officer of the court, Major Airey Neave sat below the judges' bench. On 29th November 1945, the courtroom was packed to the rafters, yet he managed to keep the seat next to his for me. Each of the two hundred seats reserved for the press was occupied, as were the hundred and fifty visitors' places. Supported by the new IBM technology, dozens of interpreters were ready to translate the proceedings simultaneously into four languages.

I was glad my father had taken Neave into his confidence and tasked him with finding a safe place to hold a potentially high-value prisoner for a couple of days, unbeknownst to the Americans and, crucially, the Russians. This hadn't been difficult: Neave had been billeted in a neo-Gothic eight-bedroom villa in Zirndorf, south-west of Nuremberg on the road to Ansbach, which provided ample accommodation for me and my driver, as well as my prisoner and his warden Captain Terisova, now re-christened Lise and deemed German.

Since the beginning of the trial nine days earlier, things had gone fairly well. Neave mentioned his relief that the defence lawyers had mounted no challenge to the valid-ity of the indictments he'd served on the defendants, and updated me on their various antics. Having entered a plea of not guilty, all but one were now sitting in the dock. Much to Colonel Burton C. Andrus's visible dismay, Doktor Robert Ley, former alcoholic leader of *Strength Through Joy*, the Nazi mass tourism organisation, had succeeded a month earlier in strangling himself in the corner of his cell. He'd fastened the zip of his GI jacket to the lever of the toilet's cistern, and twisted the hem of a wet towel into a noose around his neck. Andrus had him buried in an unmarked grave in the prison grounds, and immediately quadrupled the watch on the cells. In-stead of one guard for every four cells, which meant each prisoner was checked every thirty seconds, he placed a man in front of every door, so that the inmates were un-der constant watch. All night long, through a hatch in the door, a spotlight shone on the face of each detainee, whose hands had to remain visible above the blanket at all times. Any verbal exchange between guards and prisoners was prohibited on pain of court martial. This, according to Neave, hadn't stopped the unfortunate GIs assigned to guard duty from initiating, behind Andrus's back, a thriving black market in Nazi dignitaries' autographs.

Much miffed, the prosecutors had to put a wordy motion in front of the Tribunal, declaring that Ley had 'succeeded in accomplishing his exit from the court of judgment and from the world of living men'.

Ernst Kaltenbrunner was in hospital with a brain haemorrhage. Apparently, the tall, tough-looking boyhood friend of Adolf Eichmann and SS extermination camps supremo had become sick with fright. Stripped of power, he'd taken to cringing, whining, and blaming his dead master, Heinrich Himmler, for each and every action and policy of the SS. Doctor Gilbert, the American psychologist, found that his massive frame concealed 'a weak, vacillating will and an emotionally unstable schizoid personality'.

Following the exact order in which they had been indicted, the remaining twenty defendants were seated in two lines, with Göring, Hess, Ribbentrop and Keitel on the front row. Behind them, wearing white Sam Browne belts but no firearms, legs apart and hands behind their backs, half a dozen white-helmeted sentinels stood stiffly at ease, eyes restlessly scanning their part of the room. Only Colonel Andrus wore an easily accessible pistol in a shoulder holster under his tunic; military policemen carried white-enamelled 'billies' made of mop handles, which Andrus, not unreasonably, deemed sufficient for crowd-control purposes. At the back of the courtroom, in the centre of the floor-to-ceiling oak panelling, a built-in clock dominated the proceedings, its long white hands visible to all but the accused whose last days, it was widely assumed, they ticked away.

'All rise!' barked Colonel Andrus of the US Cavalry.

At ten-thirty precisely, a door opposite the dock opened and the judges entered. First came the Americans: the balding, moustachioed Francis Biddle and his burly deputy John Parker, wearing rimless spectacles and a friendly smile. The scholarly little French judge, Professeur Henri Donnedieu de Vabres, was preceded by a huge walrus moustache and followed by his pleasant-faced deputy, Monsieur Robert Falco.

The civilian suits and subfusc dear to Western jurists held no more appeal for the Soviet contingent than the concept of fair trial. Looking awesome in grey uniform adorned with epaulettes and facings of maroon and gold, the stern-faced Major-General of Jurisprudence Iola J. Nikitchenko and his wavy-haired deputy-cum-NKGB minder, Lieutenant Colonel Alexander F. Volchkov, walking in step, made a suitably martial entrance. My father sat down between the President of the Court, Sir Geoffrey Lawrence, whose benign face emerged from an immaculate wing collar, and Nikitchenko. He searched the room and, his eyes briefly stopping on me, gave an imperceptible nod.

The US deputy prosecutor, General William Donovan,

rose and requested permission to show a film revealing the conditions found last spring by British and American liberation forces in certain concentration camps. Amid some agitation in the soundproofed projectionist's room high up in the corner, a large screen unfurled. Göring, who'd hoped to pick up where he'd left off, vainly asked his lawyer to object. With the exception of the overhead fluorescent tubes above the dock, the lights went out.

Few in the Nuremberg courtroom were prepared for the horror. I certainly wasn't.Even Reichsmarschall Hermann Göring had to shield his face.

Watching prisoners being burnt alive in a barn, Hans Fritzsche, facial muscles contracting spasmodically, sat aghast. Tense, Field Marshal Wilhelm Keitel took off his headphones, glaring at the screen out of the corner of his eye. When, pointing at piles of emaciated dead bodies in a slave labour camp, a burly British colonel announced to the camera that he'd already buried seventeen thousand, Rudolf Hess looked more bewildered than ever. Grand Admiral Erich Raeder shuddered and turned away as, first, the charred remnants of human corpses inside the Buchenwald crematorium, and then a lampshade made of human skin filled the screen. Watching scenes from Dachau, Fritzsche recoiled, biting his lip. All skin and bone, wasted male bodies were piled in their hundreds in a high pyramid. Fluttering in the breeze, their rags and loin cloths created a disconcerting illusion of movement among the cadavers, which seemed doomed to eternal stirring and twitching. Pale and visibly upset, Joachim von Ribbentrop, champagne salesman turned foreign minister, alternately looked at the ceiling and at his feet. Only occasionally did he steal a quick look at the screen.

The rest of the film consisted of footage taken by the Germans themselves. One scene showed SS troopers rounding up women and children at bayonet point in the Warsaw ghetto, and then methodically machine-gunning them down. Laughing with glee at their own prowess, healthy young men waved cheerfully at the camera. At this sight, Albert Speer, Hitler's architect, an air of extreme sadness on his face, swallowed hard, his Adam's apple repeatedly bobbing up and down. A pretty female doctor proudly described the ghastly experiments performed on the women inmates of the Belsen concentration camp. Grand Admiral Dönitz hung his head low and closed his eyes. At the mention of a bulldozer clearing up corpses, Ribbentrop looked up. He saw dozens of naked female bodies disintegrating under the brutal onslaught of a rectangular steel blade that swept and shoved them like so many worms towards a gaping pit, scraping so much dirt on the way that human flesh, crunched bone and earth were instantly mixed into compost. Ribbentrop averted his eyes and stared at his feet again. A little boy aged six or seven emerged with his mother out of the smouldering ruins of Warsaw; bewildered and terrified, both up held their hands. In the next scene, the camera closed up on their dead bodies, splayed on the ground, a few feet apart. Grand Admiral Dönitz covered his eyes with clenched fists. Ribbentrop, blinking as though blinded by the projector's light, kept mopping his brow, lips pursed. Leaning forward on the balustrade and looking bored, Göring had long ago stopped watching.

Holding my handkerchief over my mouth in a desperate attempt to silence my retching, I turned my back to the screen.

On the public benches, those with personal experience of the concentration camps had their terrible memories re-awakened. Even among the hardened war correspondents and other hacks, several had to leave the courtroom, dozens were crying quietly, and a handful had fainted. The defence attorneys, who were in the main anti-Nazi, looked distraught. Having only reluctantly accepted the task of defending lawless genocidal renegades, they now seemed utterly dejected.

At long last, the lights came back on.

Heavy silence fell. To say we were all dumbstruck wouldn't begin to describe the funereal thickness of this silence. It was more than the absence of the noises necessarily produced by any significant assembly in a confined space. Rather, it felt like the air in the courtroom had become so poisonous that none present wanted to breathe. The accused remained petrified. When, under the huge wooden cross hanging above the door, the nauseated judges wordlessly filed out, the men in the dock were slow to rise, as if crushed by the weight of their guilt. Only Hess could be heard, muttering loudly: 'I don't believe it.' His own cockiness deflated, Göring shushed him. In the oppressive stillness that followed, with all present still punch-drunk, the court adjourned for the day and the prisoners were taken back to the cell block, where both psychologists, keen to collect their reactions, followed.

Desperate for fresh air, I ran out.

Major Neave found me outside, on the Fürtherstrasse forecourt, between the fortified wrought-iron railings and the stone arcades of the Palace of Justice, smoking a cigarette with awkward little puffs that must have revealed my lack of practice.

'Terribly sorry, Major. Made rather a fool of myself, I'm afraid,' I said with a sheepish smile.

'As it happens, Peter, I don't think you have.'

'Wasn't expecting anything of the kind. And I thought throwing up at the foot of the Bench would be bad form.'

'Entirely to your credit, old chap. Faced with such iniquity, throwing up is the only rational reaction.'

'I don't know about rational. I don't think I had any choice.'

'As you like. The only honourable reaction then.'

'Lily-livered comes to mind.'

Neave put his hands on my shoulders.

'The only reason why some of us were more or less able to control our emotions is that we're familiar with the material, not because we're heroes. That's precisely the trouble, you see. Over time, we'll get used to these pictures. They'll become interesting archive footage. Historians will watch them as evidence of the existence of an extinguished tribe of barbarians. Nobody will throw up any more. And you know what? We'll do it all again.'

'You mean the Germans will do it again?'

'Possibly. Or the Americans. Or the Russians. Or the Brits. People.'

'Now look here, Airey. You know as well as I do that we'd never tolerate such unconscionable crimes – let alone perpetrate them!'

'Do you really think human nature is different on opposite sides of the English Channel?'

'Actually, yes, I do. Of course, I'm not saying we don't have criminals or psychopaths in our midst. But at least they know they're acting illegally, and so conceal their misdeeds. Remember those SS boys smiling at the camera in front of the bodies of the civilians they'd just murdered? That's the difference, you see. They had no fear of punishment. On the contrary, they expected congratulation. Can you imagine any British unit not only torturing civilians, but also recording the scene on camera? What kind of system would they have to be operating in?'

'War. The environment that unfailingly produces the kind of behaviour you've just described is called war.'

'But, Airey – you've been held by the Gestapo, for Christ's sake! You know what they were like. Are you actually saying that we're no better than these Nazi swine?'

Neave took a Senior Service from his breast pocket, lit it with a match, inhaled deeply, exhaled slowly through his nostrils, and drew on it again.

'Have you heard of Katyn?' he asked, smoke now coming out of his mouth.

'Katyn? Where the SS murdered thousands of Polish prisoners in 1940?'

'One of the key charges listed in the indictment I had the pleasure of serving on Göring last month: murdering nine hundred and twenty-five Polish officers in the Katyn forest near Smolensk.'

'Isn't that grist to my mill?'

'The Soviet prosecutor, General Rudenko, is now insisting the indictment be changed.'

'In what way?'

'He wants the number of victims to be increased to eleven thousand.'

'Well – does this not show that the Nazis were uniquely evil?'

'Not entirely. You see, there is overwhelming evidence in front of the Tribunal demonstrating that, in fact, the Soviets did it themselves. On Stalin's express orders. They slaughtered more than four thousand Polish officers at Katyn, as well as another twelve thousand people: priests, writers, musicians, poets and teachers. The plan was to eliminate the whole Polish intelligentsia. Pretty similar to Hitler's initial order to his troops, which, if memory serves, was "ruthlessly to exploit this region as a warzone and booty country, to reduce it to a heap of rubble."'

'I see. What's the court going to do?'

'Better ask your father. My guess is that they will be instructed to kow-tow to Stalin, and the Soviet judges, having righteously sat in judgment on the evil Nazis, will vote to hang the lot.'

My long cigarette butt had been cold for some time. Keen to avoid a civilian stampede, I discreetly dropped it to the ground, stamped on it and slumped wearily onto the plinth of a massive pillar.

'And this?' I asked, encompassing in a sweeping gesture the whole Bavarian Central Courts of Justice complex, its ponderous pinkish-brown stone slabs, carved façade and the four oversized Allied flags competing for attention at the end of tree-like poles.

'What about it?'

'Only a few months ago this very courtroom was bedecked with swastikas. Ranting Nazi judges, sitting under Hitler's portrait, were sentencing dissidents to hang from meat hooks on piano wires. Right?'

'Nazi justice was no less of a parody than Stalin's show trials.'

'But what about our justice? Are you saying it's equally flawed? That the perpetrators of unspeakable atrocities should escape prosecution?'

'Good God! Not only am I saying nothing of the kind, Peter, but I'm proud to be part of the process. You should have heard the fine opening speech of Robert Jackson, the US prosecutor. First, he outlined crimes so calculated, so malignant, so devastating that civilisation could ignore them only at its peril. Then he asked the court to strike a blow for peace by condemning the Nazi war machine and its leaders. Last, he stated that, if the law was to serve any useful purpose, it must condemn aggression by any nation – including those who sit here in judgment.'

'A man after my own heart!'

'And mine. He concluded by saying that the Tribunal's mission was to put the forces of international law, and most of all its sanctions, on the side of peace, so that men and women of goodwill in all countries may live peacefully under the law. Your father congratulated him on what he thought was a very fine speech.'

'Did he? Is that the sort of comment a judge should offer the prosecution?'

'*Touché*. And I thought I was the lawyer here!' Neave laughed. You're not going to cross-examine me, are you?'

'No. But, if truth be told, I was rather surprised that the Members of the Tribunal should be sitting as both judges and jury.'

'Good point. But I can assure you that most of them are trying their best to ensure a fair trial – which is more than the Germans ever got under Nazi rule, notwithstanding Göring's views.'

'What does the fat man think?'

'That the victor will always be the judge, and the vanquished the accused.'

'Typically cynical.'

'Time will tell.'

I looked at my watch.

'Talking of time – we'd better go back in. My father will be waiting.'

We found Papa working alone in the judges' room among towering piles of papers. Until the beginning of the trial, the judges had had to queue up with everybody else in the cafeteria and pay their three Reichsmarks to have a grubby lunch unceremoniously dumped on an aluminium tray. However, a private dining-room in the court building had since been made available to them, whither his colleagues had now repaired.

Rising, my father greeted Major Neave courteously, then, his eyes lingering for a second on the unfamiliar third pip, heartily shook me by the hand.

'Good to see you, Peter,' he said. 'You look well.'

'Good to see you too, sir.'

I felt like hugging him but, embarrassed by Neave's soldierly presence, decided against it.

'Did you manage to get some lunch?'

'Not yet. But, to be honest, I'm not feeling particularly hungry.'

'Nor I, thank you, Judge,' Neave added.

'I quite understand. Well, since my fellow judges kept their appetites, we have the room to ourselves. How was your drive from Kamen yesterday, Peter?'

'Uneventful. Major Neave was waiting for us on arrival. He's provided us with excellent facilities.'

'Good. So, that prisoner of yours – still unidentified?'

'He claims to be Gustav Weber, Hitler's body double.'

'I see. May I suggest that, for security reasons, we refer to him henceforth as Prisoner HW?'

'Prisoner HW,' I repeated.

'So, Peter, what exactly is the story?' my father asked.

Trying my best to be methodical and factual, I recounted the events of the previous weeks, from the Quadripartite inspection to the mine explosion and the approach by an NKGB defector of German origin, complete with a prisoner she alleged to be Adolf Hitler, but whose only utterances had been to assert his name was Gustav Weber. Occasionally interjecting with queries that betrayed a razor-sharp mind, my father scribbled notes in illegible shorthand.

'Clearly, the first requirement is to establish the identity of this individual,' he opined. 'In the most unlikely event that he should be Adolf Hitler, the repercussions would obviously be monumental. And very embarrassing for the Western powers. You'll recall, only a few months ago, Stalin told President Truman in no uncertain terms that Hitler was alive. The inference was that he was in the custody of the duplicitous Western powers, who intended to use him in the coming war against Russia.'

'So Stalin would feel vindicated if it turned out that we are indeed secretly holding Hitler,' Major Neave said. 'And he'd go crackers.'

'Indeed. Conversely, if – as must be more likely – Prisoner HW is an inoffensive old man, the last thing we need, apart from the ridicule that would be heaped on us, is any kind of scandal. I talked to the Prime Minister within minutes of your first call, Peter. Mr Attlee's instructions are straightforward: keep the whole thing under wraps until the identity of Prisoner HW is established. If he's Gustav Weber or Hans Schmidt, release him as quickly and discreetly as possible. If he's Hitler, report back to him immediately.'

'Who else is in the know?' Neave asked.

'Here? Only my colleague, Judge Lawrence.'

'How long do we have?' I asked.

'The Prime Minister obviously understands that the probability that Hitler came back from the dead is negligible. And he knows only too well how many false sightings have already been reported. Anyway, he expects the matter to be cleared up within a few days. Failing which MI5 will take over.'

'I'm sure we won't need the spooks,' I said quickly, fighting off visions of men in raincoats dragging Elizaveta Terisova into the freezing, tiled cells of Bad Nenndorf. 'There is only one difficulty. I forgot to mention: the chap has no fingers. *Ergo,* no fingerprints.'

My father lifted his eyebrows. 'The tops of his fingers have been surgically removed,' I confirmed.

'Really? How odd. And *prima facie* quite suspicious, I must admit. But there are many other ways to identify a man. Look for distinctive signs. Find his family, his friends, his colleagues.'

'I can see two problems with this line. First, the cat will be out of the bag the minute we confront any third party with Prisoner HW. Second, most of his friends and colleagues may well be sitting in this prison.'

'Only true if Prisoner HW actually is the Führer, isn't it?' Major Neave asked.

'Not necessarily,' I answered. 'The only people capable of differentiating between Hitler and his double might be his closest aides and sidekicks.'

'Even then, perhaps only if they saw them side by side...' my father mused. 'Anyway, we're more likely to get a political answer from that lot than a factual one. They'll decide who Prisoner HW is in accordance with their political agenda. They'll want either a dead hero, or the greatest orator of modern times to defend Nazism in this court.'

'We know that Göring feels it would be inconceivable for the sacred person of the Führer to be sitting in the dock,' Major Neave said. 'He holds that there was nothing cowardly in Hitler's presumed suicide. According to him, it was a noble sacrifice that saved Germany from the greatest possible humiliation.'

'So he can be expected to identify Prisoner HW as Gustav Weber,' Judge Birkett concluded. 'And the others will no doubt follow his lead.'

'Anyway, Peter's point about discretion stands,' Neave said. 'It's a bit of a vicious circle: we don't know who Prisoner HW is, but we can't show him to the people who might be able to identify him.'

'On the other hand, it may be that nobody can identify him with absolute certainty,' I said.

'What do you mean?' my father asked.

'Well, presumably the whole idea behind the double was that he became indistinguishable from his model. And the last time anybody saw Hitler was seven months ago, in a badly lit underground bunker, when he was under extreme stress. If he's still alive, he's probably changed significantly.'

'In fact, most of our prisoners haven't seen Hitler for much longer than that,' Neave pointed out.

'I think we can safely conclude that a confrontation between the defendants and Prisoner HW would serve no useful purpose,' my father said.

'And also that whoever thought of chopping off Prisoner HW's fingers was a smart cookie,' I added. 'So, without witnesses or fingerprints, how do we identify our man?'

'First and foremost, through his dental records,' my father answered.

'Is that conclusive?'

'Absolutely.'

'Better get cracking, then.'

'What if we don't find them?' Major Neave asked. 'They might be lost. They might have been destroyed. Or they may be in Soviet hands – after all, they found Hitler's presumed remains. Surely, they would have performed a forensic dental investigation immediately.'

Eyebrows raised above round horn-rimmed spectacles, Papa threw up his hands.

'If I may be so bold, Judge – there might be another avenue,' Neave said.

'What do you have in mind, Major?'

'Precisely that, sir. The mind.'

'The mind?'

'Even if twin bodies are indistinguishable, that's unlikely to apply to their minds. Surely, inside his head, Prisoner HW is either Hitler or Weber.'

'That goes without saying, Major,' Judge Birkett said with a trace of judicial impatience. 'What exactly is your point?'

'My point, sir, is that it might be easier to get into the man's head than to identify what's left of his body.'

Papa turned to me.

'I thought Prisoner HW was playing dumb?'

'That's correct. Whenever addressed, he either doesn't react, or says: *"Ich heiße Gustav Weber."*'

'Does he exhibit any obvious signs of dementia?'

'I wouldn't know.'

'This might well be a case for Doctor George,' Airey Neave suggested.

'Who's he?' I asked.

'Elliott George is the British psychologist attached to the Tribunal. German-speaking. Incredibly knowledgeable about National Socialism, and what makes the Nazi mind tick. Good man.'

'Indeed,' my father said. 'I'll talk to him and swear him to secrecy.'

I cleared my throat.

'Anything else?' Papa asked.

Although I really wanted to talk about Elizaveta, it didn't seem appropriate to do so. Anyway, I wanted even more to see her. As an Intelligence Officer, I felt she had more to offer.

6

Team Sansouci

VILLA SANSOUCI was set back from the quiet road leading south-west from the little town of Zirndorf, protected by dark, ancient chestnuts in the midst of a neglected garden almost large enough to qualify as a park. Elizaveta rarely left the premises, if only because the town was crawling with soldiers of the US 26th Infantry Regiment who occupied the barracks built by Reichsmarschall Göring in 1940 for the Luftwaffe.

A Nuremberg dentist was called in to examine Prisoner HW's teeth. According to his findings, only five of them were free of partial or total prosthetic replacement. The nine-unit bridge he'd found on the prisoner's top jaw was a monstrous contraption which contravened all accepted principles of good practice. In particular, the freely suspended teeth at each end had aroused his professional scorn. Never in his twenty-four-year career had he encountered such a ridiculous device, whose chances of withstanding for any time the relevant functional loads were negligible. His advice was to replace the offending pontics with a denture. However, on hearing the word, Prisoner HW had become agitated. The dentist had concluded his report with a mention of the patient's offensive halitosis, which might be symptomatic of some sort of latent infection.

Prisoner HW's health was assessed by an Army doctor, and found to be poor. His hearing and eyesight appeared defective, and he suffered from elevated and somewhat irregular blood pressure. He ate little, refusing all meat and fish, and suffered chronic digestive problems. Particularly noteworthy was his general atony which, according to Doctor George, bordered on catatonia. Whether it was induced by psychological causes, such as acute clinical depression or schizophrenia, or by his generally deficient metabolism, it was far too early to say. One way or the other, Prisoner HW was as meek as a lamb and gave Elizaveta no trouble.

On the second day, Airey Neave retired to his room after dinner to prepare for the next court hearing and Elliott George drove off to his billet. For the first time, Elizaveta Terisova and Peter Birkett found themselves alone in the dark, formal dining-room.

Over the previous couple of days, their relationship had been purely professional. They understood the magnitude of the challenge, and implicitly accepted that any emotional entanglement, whether real or perceived, would be dangerous. Peter's efforts to negotiate a *laissez-passer* for a Soviet intelligence operative would be fatally undermined by any allegation of personal involvement with Elizaveta. Were his integrity or objectivity to be impugned, his chances of keeping MI5 out of the picture – and Elizaveta out of Bad Nenndorf – would diminish. Both Peter and Elizaveta knew that, if she was going to survive, she had to get to England as soon as possible.

Yet, she often thought about that first night when they had lain side by side, listening to the impossible song of a lost nightingale. She recalled how upset he'd been at her mention of Jakob – how relieved he'd sounded after surmising that Jakob belonged to a bygone past – and her own disloyalty made her shudder. Thankfully, in that quiet room in Kamen, as he gently wiped her tears, her blushes had remained concealed by darkness. And his chest had felt so wonderfully warm and solid under her cheek that she'd almost let her guard down.

'Two days gone already, and not much progress,' Elizaveta sighed.

'I'm flying to Berlin first thing in the morning. We need to find Hitler's dental records.'

'How long will you be gone?'

'Forty-eight hours, at most. In the meantime, you must keep up the pressure on the prisoner. Elliott has a few tricks up his sleeve, for which he'll need your help.'

'I know. Any progress regarding my British passport?'

'These things take time. And we need to lie low.'

He looked away and took a sip of wine. Elizaveta's heart sank. Was she being used – yet again? What right did she have to expect Peter Birkett to be different from all the selfish, predatory males who, over the years, had offered her their protection?

'Don't look at me like that,' he protested. 'My father is working his contacts, through the proper channels. This is the best way. Trust me.'

Trust him?

Until now, despite all the uncertainties, she'd felt almost as safe in the relative cocoon of Villa Sansouci as she had lying in his arms a few nights ago. Naturally, as a high-value defector, she was now prominent on the NKGB's target list; however, the house was discreet and heavily guarded. She regretted having had to relinquish her Nagan revolver, but understood that her current status – or lack thereof – made it unavoidable. Her position, her life and her prospects were all in the hands of Captain Peter Birkett. She had to prove that she'd fulfilled her side of the bargain, and hope he would – and could – reciprocate. The words he'd spoken during their first evening together in Kamen still rang in her ears: 'I'll take care of you.' Strangely, she'd believed him. On the other hand, since when had it been sensible to entrust one's life to any man, let alone a junior British officer still wet behind the ears? What influence could Peter Birkett be expected to wield on anything, let alone matters of state? What if his apparent intelligence, decisiveness and energy were no more than youthful arrogance? His self-confidence no more than immaturity? But she had no choice.

'I trust you,' she smiled.

His face lit up. 'You won't regret it. I swear.'

Into the small hours, they talked of absent mothers and

distant fathers, of the futile horror of war, of their shared dream of a safe and clean world. Of the medical vocation which ran in her family and of his own strange absence of vocation. They talked of many other things too. And when he took her hands, in a low whisper, she told him how she had become Colonel Ivan Klimenko's war-wife.

JUST BEFORE LEAVING for Berlin, Captain Birkett ordered Rifleman Richardson to stop shaving the prisoner's moustache. HW didn't protest, but immediately went on hunger strike. The next morning, Elizaveta decided that, in order to assess his resemblance with the Führer, it was more sensible to use a false moustache than to risk losing him. Accordingly, on the second day, Rifleman Richardson dutifully removed the offending bristle from HW's quivering upper lip, and surreptitiously affixed a dark, square artificial replacement. Before the prisoner could react, Elizaveta had succeeded in taking a photograph. Surprised, HW lifted his droopy eyelids and fixed her with an icy, metallic gaze that made her shiver. He tore off the offending moustache and threw it on the ground, before relapsing into his usual catatonic state.

The photograph was inconclusive. On the one hand, despite the shorter hair, the angry face staring at the camera certainly could have been the Führer's; on the other, how many elderly men, disguised with a Hitler moustache, would look rather like him on a blurry snapshot?

It soon became clear that, due to Prisoner HW's nocturnal insomnia, there was no point in attempting to wake him up at six or seven in the morning. Rifleman Richardson and Major Neave's batman, a taciturn Brummie called Fred Carpenter, shared the unenviable task of getting the captive dressed and clean in time for the ten o'clock daily interrogation. Although neither man had been told anything about the identity of their charge, Rifleman Richardson made a point of always waking him up by whistling 'God Save the King' into his ear at point-blank range.

The interrogations, such as they were, took place in the sitting-room, whose heavy Biedermeier furniture had survived the war without a scratch. They were conducted in German by Major Neave (when his presence wasn't required in court), Captain Birkett or Doctor Elliott George. However, it didn't take them long to realise that Prisoner HW only came to life when addressed by Captain Terisova. Accordingly, not only was Elizaveta – or rather Lise, as she was now known to all – attending the sessions, but she also frequently had to repeat questions that the prisoner otherwise ignored. Whether he could better hear high-pitched sounds, or was simply more responsive to a female voice, was a moot point.

Prisoner HW stuck to his sketchy story. He was Gustav Weber, a truck driver from Bavaria, who'd been kidnapped back in 1933 in order to impersonate the Führer. Over the years, in order to maintain or enhance his likeness to Hitler, he'd been subjected to repeated cosmetic operations at the Zeitfeld clinic in Berlin, which he described as torture. He admitted having succumbed to alcoholism, yet never asked for a beer, let alone wine or liquor. Just before the end of the war, most of his teeth had been brutally extracted and his fingers cut off, for reasons he failed to understand. All he wanted was to find his wife and family, whom he hadn't seen for eight years.

Meagre though they were, even these few details had emerged only over an inordinately long time, and mostly outside the formal interrogation sessions. Elizaveta soon sensed that Prisoner HW liked her company; she sought to exploit the fact. During his daily walk among the tall chestnuts at the back of the house, where they couldn't be seen from the road, she would ask him one single question, such as where he'd grown up, and make clear that, unless it was answered, she would either return him to his room or leave him in Fred Carpenter's sullen care. Three times, Prisoner HW had ignored her, and she'd left him. On the fourth occasion, he mumbled something like: 'Munich. Angelika – have you forgotten?' As he shuffled unsteadily over the blackening leaves, seemingly unaware of the armed sentries surrounding them, Elizaveta suddenly feared that his apparent senility might be more than an act. But on the rare occasions when she caught the flash of his ice-blue eyes, his gaze penetrated her inner core.

To try and breach Prisoner HW's defences, Elliott George came up with a couple of ingenious experiments. First, he somehow procured a three-month-old Alsatian puppy and, without warning, let it loose in the detainee's room. Much to his disappointment, HW exhibited no more interest in the animal than in the noisy crows that nested in the chestnut trees outside his window. Next, the psychologist wired up the prisoner's room, in order to record any soliloquy or dreams in which he might indulge. Unfortunately, HW spent his time alone dozing on his chair or bed and, in spite of all manner of noisy nightmares, never produced any intelligible sounds.

Doctor George also showed HW detailed maps and photographs of the city of Linz, Hitler's birthplace, for which, until the very last days of the Third Reich, he was known to have harboured the most grandiose redevelopment plans. Yet again, no flicker of recognition had been detectable under the captive's sagging eyelids. Pictures of a triumphant Führer beneath the Arc de Triomphe, inspecting the Tomb of the Unknown Soldier, and later viewing Napoleon's sepulchre in Les Invalides, taken in June 1940 on the occasion of his one and only trip to Paris, left HW utterly indifferent. The psychologist, having never before encountered such apathy, concluded that the patient was suffering either from acute depression, or from some form of mental deterioration, or both. He couldn't exclude the type of degenerative dementia first described in 1906 by the German psychiatrist and neuropathologist Alois Alzheimer. Indeed, the fact that HW could only ingest food in smaller pieces, or puréed, was consistent with such a diagnosis, as were his apparent memory loss and disorientation. However, Elliott George thought it less and less likely that the prisoner was Adolf Hitler, or at any rate that he still possessed the mental characteristics which previously defined Adolf Hitler's identity.

Captain Elizaveta Terisova begged to differ. Deep down, she knew that Prisoner HW was the former Führer. She also felt that, though patently diminished, he was putting up a well-rehearsed act. Impassiveness provided him with the safest and most convenient hiding place. She also knew that, at the end of the war, many Nazi chiefs had vainly tried to evade capture under false identities; Himmler himself had shaved his moustache and wandered for several days in the Flensburg region under the name of Heinrich Hitzinger, before his unusually clean and comprehensive set of papers aroused the suspicion of a British Army unit. When an equally moustache-less Robert Ley had been captured by paratroopers of the 101st Airborne Division, he'd told them he was Doktor Ernst Diestelmeyer. In all these cases, identification had been swift and easy: there was no shortage of enemies of top Nazis willing to oblige, particularly among former colleagues.

But, crucially, none of them ever had a body double. And they all had fingerprints.

Though it was never discussed, Elizaveta recognised that her own future depended on her ability to prove that she'd delivered to the British the genuine article, as opposed to a forgery – however impressive. Sometimes she wondered whether, the wish being father to the thought, her predicament coloured her judgment. The fact that a man called Gustav Weber had been painstakingly transformed into Hitler's perfect *Doppelgänger* had been verified. That Prisoner HW seemed emotionally disconnected from the ex-Führer's passions and triumphs was indeed disconcerting. Yet he had seemingly been smoked out of his uranium-filled lair by the Bergkamen mine explosion: surely this was highly suspicious. More fundamentally, Elizaveta felt a quiet certainty in her bones. As far as she was concerned, whoever this decrepit individual might currently be, he doubtless used to answer to the name of Adolf Hitler.

After three days Captain Birkett returned from Berlin. He immediately rang Sergeant Wagg in Kamen to catch up on T Force news.

'Good to hear from you, sir. How's the leave going?' Wagg asked.

'Fine, thank you, Wagg. Anything happening your end?'

'Still swamped by requisition orders, sir. And short of crating material and transport. The usual.'

'I'm sure you're coping admirably.'

'Holding the fort, sir. It'll be good to have you back.'

'Thanks, Wagg. Anything else?'

'No – apart from our two new recruits, sir.'

'What new recruits?'

'Didn't you know?' Wagg dropped his voice. 'Two fellows from Military Intelligence have set up camp here. Tipped off about a Soviet spy ring operating around Kamen. Led by a female, apparently.'

'Keep me posted, Wagg, will you?'

Wondering who'd set the MI5 hounds on Elizaveta's spoor, Peter Birkett slowly replaced the receiver in its cradle.

As soon as Major Neave returned from the Nuremberg courtroom, the Sansouci team convened in the drawing-room around a few bottles of Paulaner Original Münchner Urtyp, the sort of lager that the Germans still managed to produce in small quantities, but had long since been unable to afford themselves.

'Welcome back!' Neave raised his glass. 'Any luck?'

'Thank you. Good to be back,' Peter answered, looking at Elizaveta. 'As a matter of fact, yes. I think we might be in luck.'

'Did you find Hitler's dental records?'

'Almost.'

'Almost?'

'Hitler's dental work was carried out by a certain Professor Blaschke, who had a clinic in the Chancellery. So I went to see him.'

'Was he useful?' asked Elliott George, his freckles the same colour as the beer in his glass.

'He wasn't there. Unfortunately, he's been detained by the Americans since 28th May.'

'Presumably they are after the same information as us,' Neave reflected.

'So I went looking for Professor Blaschke's assistant, Käthe Heusermann.'

'Whom you didn't find either,' Captain Terisova stated.

Peter turned to her. 'How do you know?'

'Because I got to her on 9th May, along with Vasili Ivanovich Gorbushin, deputy Chief of Counter-Intelligence in the 3rd Shock Army. The poor woman has been sitting in an NKGB camp ever since.'

'Well, that certainly explains her disappearance,' Peter said. 'But how did you find her?'

'Back in April, I was assigned the task of finding Hitler, dead or alive. Naturally, I wasn't the only operative with that mission. As usual, Stalin would have made sure that all military and intelligence units were in competition.'

'Is that why you were at Hitler's bunker in May?'

She smiled at the recollection of their first encounter.

'So what did Doktor Heusermann have to say?'

'We showed her an upper jaw bridge and a lower jaw with teeth, extracted from the charred body found in the garden in the Reich Chancellery. She confirmed they belonged to Hitler.'

'Why didn't you mention it before?'

'Because, coming from me, it's at best second-hand hearsay, and at worst disinformation. I wouldn't expect your people to believe a word of it.'

Elliott George raised his hand.

'Peter, did you find any records in Professor Blaschke's office?' he enquired.

'No. His secretary said Hitler's files were collected and sent to Martin Bormann in the *Führerbunker* at the end of April. Nobody's seen them since.'

'Seems we're back to square one,' Neave sounded disappointed. 'I thought you said you'd made progress?'

'Blaschke's secretary sent me to a dental technician by the name of Fritz Echtmann, who prepared all of Hitler's bridges and crowns. He remembered each and every one perfectly, and gave me detailed descriptions and sketches. He says one in particular was a work of art, consisting of no fewer than nine teeth. Unique in the history of dentistry, to quote him.'

'Or maybe not so unique,' Elizaveta interjected. 'The Nuremberg dentist who inspected Prisoner HW's teeth found a similar contraption.'

'Once he's compared these pictures with his own findings, we should know where we stand,' Peter said, waving a sheaf of papers. 'I'll have them delivered to him first thing tomorrow morning.'

'Excellent,' Major Neave concluded. 'I was planning to pop into the Grand for a drink tonight. Anybody care to join me?'

'Sounds good,' Peter replied.

'Count me in,' the blond psychologist chimed in.

'What about you, Lise?' Peter asked. 'We still have a seat.'

'I'm not sure…' Part of her wanted to accompany Peter, but she felt nervous about leaving the shelter of the villa.

'You'll be all right,' he insisted, draining his second bottle of Münchner. 'And it's fun.'

'I'll be ready in five minutes,' she smiled.

Airey Neave marvelled at Peter Birkett's driving skills, which, if anything, seemed enhanced by the couple of beers he'd drunk. Soon, Peter parked the open jeep on the station side of the hotel, among rows of identical jeeps and pick-up trucks representing the victorious nations.

Riven by explosions, the devastated landscape separating the hotel from the Hauptbahnhof had only partially been cleared. Cheap, heady singing could be heard through the cold drizzle. At first sight, the Palast-Hotel Fürstenhof, or Grand, as it was commonly known, had much in common with the Palace of Justice. First, both had improbably survived eleven Allied bombing raids with only minor damage. Second, the massive stone building, its five storeys sandwiched between high arcades and a tall slate roof, looked almost as daunting as the Bavarian Central Courts of Justice; indeed, it seemed the same imperial architect might have been given a free hand to inflict his bombastic vision on both sites. Third, their respective populations largely overlapped. Back in August, the Interrogation Division had been transferred from Paris to Nuremberg and, like the major prosecution teams, housed – often two to a room – in the Grand Hotel. All in all, several hundred staff lived there. Since the city's water was contaminated, they depended for their supply on the huge canvas drums US sappers had installed on wooden tripods in the corridors. Only officers and civilians ranking as such were accommodated at the Grand, but hordes of reporters, in search of sex, booze and gossip, gravitated towards its bars, as did the staff and dignitaries of all delegations.

'Welcome to America,' Neave said as his party entered the low-ceilinged foyer, the vastness of which was partly obscured by hefty marble pillars. He led the way to the long bar adjoining the huge ballroom called the Marble Room. The place was swarming with all manner of military and civilian dress. Evidently in charge, the Americans, with tall, shrill girls in immaculately cut uniforms and nylon stockings, outnumbered all other nationalities. Neave greeted a posse of staid British barristers sitting in a corner of the bar, the black box calf of their bespoke Church's shoes gleaming below grey pinstriped trousers. Hell-bent on oblivion, observers from those nations which had been raped and pillaged by the Waffen-SS but did not form part of the prosecution – mostly Poles, Ukrainians, Czechs, Dutch and Belgians – were getting quietly sozzled. None did so more efficiently than the East Europeans, who mixed beer and vodka in a one-to-one ratio. Dignified and sombre, clearly pining for their Chateau Lafite 1929, the French, most of them survivors from the Resistance, unhappily tried to adjust to American liquor and K-rations. On a small podium, accompanied by a piano, a weary German girl was singing the same folk songs that, only six months ago, she'd been crooning in front of an audience of Nazi bigwigs. Her thin voice was intermittently drowned by the lively chatter of Allied officers, interpreters, hacks and secretaries. Scribbling into a notepad, the United Press correspondent, a good-looking young man called Walter Cronkite who was fast making a name for himself, was respectfully listening to a tirade from Robert Jackson, the chief US prosecutor, whose rubicund face was positively glowing. Heads thrown back, throats palpitating, pretty WRENS laughed stridently at the inaudible jokes of jostling young soldiers.

'Not many Russians around,' Peter Birkett remarked.

'They live with their women in the villas around Nuremberg,' Neave replied. 'Not very popular with their neighbours.'

'Why?' asked Doctor George.

'Let me guess,' Elizaveta smiled. 'Might it be that they get a bit noisy at night? Possibly rowdy?'

'Apparently they sing and dance all night long, drinking to the death of all Nazis,' Neave replied. 'Last week, when a couple of French officers complained at dawn, the Russians opened fire on them. Lucky to escape with their lives.'

'Some of them seem reasonably well-behaved,' Peter pointed to a Soviet officer with a long ashen face, quietly reading a newspaper at the bar.

'Don't you recognise him?' Neave asked. 'That's Lieutenant Colonel Volchkov, the alternate Soviet judge. I've never seen him drunk. But not all Russians are so well behaved, believe you me. Only last week, we heard a shot just outside the hotel. A Red Army general stumbled into the foyer and dropped down dead. Shot by one of his own colleagues. Both blind drunk, of course.'

'So what happened?' Peter asked.

'Oh, we continued dancing in the Marble Room while

the corpse was removed. Mustn't embarrass our Soviet Allies, must we?'

'Can we go?' Elizaveta asked suddenly. She'd gone pale, and Airey Neave noticed she'd turned away from Volchkov.

'Go where?' Peter Birkett asked.

'Anywhere. To the Marble Room.'

'Of course. Is anything the matter?'

'Volchkov. He's my boss's boss. NKGB. No legal training whatsoever. His main role is to watch Judge Nikitchenko. Look – he's not reading his paper, only pretending. Eavesdropping. If he sees me, I'm dead.'

Screening Elizaveta from the Russian's gaze, Birkett quickly walked her over to the ballroom. In an atmosphere verging on hysteria, the vast Art Déco expanse teemed with sweaty bodies undulating to the rhythms of a jazz orchestra. Struggling through the crowd, they beat a group of American lawyers to the last free table only because Peter Birkett, elbowing revellers out his way, spotted it from afar and made a dash for it.

'Would you like to dance?' he asked Elizaveta as the rest of the group caught up with him.

'I think I'd rather go home.'

'You're safer here, with us. Come on, it will do you good.'

She hesitated, then took his extended hand and followed him.

'This is madness,' she murmured.

Major Neave and Doctor George sat down, lit cigarettes and tried to attract the attention of a waiter.

'Good-looking, isn't she?' the psychologist said.

Neave nodded. Elizaveta Terisova was undeniably turning heads. As she abandoned herself to the syncopated rhythm and lascivious harmonic complexities of the newfangled bebop, her long blond hair shone under the chandeliers as though lit by the sun itself. Swollen by perfectly shaped breasts, her pink woollen jumper – one of only two sets of civilian clothes she seemed to possess – clung tightly to her narrow waist. After a few minutes, confused by the unfamiliar beat, she put her hands on Peter Birkett's shoulders and closed her eyes.

'Without a doubt,' said Neave, long after Elliott George had given up waiting for a reply. 'Extraordinarily beautiful. Doesn't that make you suspicious?'

'I suppose it should. Hardly her fault, though. I've got a good feeling about her.'

'I bet you have. You don't really think she's delivered us Hitler, do you?'

'She certainly believes so.'

'That's as may be. But what about you, Elliott?'

'It all depends what you mean by Hitler.'

Airey Neave darted a quizzical glance at the young man sitting next to him.

'Would you care to explain?'

'It depends on your definition of a person.'

'I'm a person. You're a person.'

'One man's person is another man's *Untermensch*. The Nazis didn't consider Jews, Slavs or Gypsies to be persons.'

'That's exactly why the sorry bastards are going to hang!' Neave immediately regretted having raised his voice, and looked around to check whether he might have been overheard. 'Surely that's doesn't mean we too have to get confused?'

'The problem of personal identity goes back a long time,' the psychologist smiled apologetically. 'Given that we undergo constant changes, what makes us the same person today as yesterday? Is an adult the same person as the baby he used to be?'

'What's any of this got to do with Hitler?'

'Quite a lot. Have you ever heard of Locke?'

'What do you think, old boy?'

'Sorry. Well, Locke understood that we need empirical criteria to establish the sameness of a person through time. Otherwise, trying to pin responsibility for past actions onto anybody would be futile. As a lawyer, surely you see the point.'

Neave's ears pricked up.

'What did Locke suggest?'

'He held that personhood resides in the unity of consciousness, and in particular in the presence of memory of past actions. The case of Rudolf Hess comes to mind.'

'Are you suggesting that, because Hess is amnesic, he isn't Hess anymore?'

'That certainly is Locke's view. Would it make sense to hang a man who's either brain dead, or cannot remember his past actions?'

'If that man is Adolf Hitler – absolutely.'

'Ah, but that's exactly the point. Would such a man *be* Adolf Hitler?'

'To hell with you, and all your fellow psychologists!' Neave drained his gin and tonic in one gulp, nearly choking on the lemon slice.

A broad grin on his friendly freckled face, eyes twinkling behind thick round spectacles, the young man cheerfully raised his glass. 'But you see my point, don't you, Major? Insofar as Prisoner HW seems to have impaired mental functions, he's probably neither Gustav Weber nor Adolf Hitler. Or perhaps he's both.'

'You bloody civilian eggheads never give up, do you?' Neave laughed. He spat the last lemon pip into his glass, put it down on the table and looked around. Peter and Elizaveta had been swallowed up by the magma of teeming bodies. Airey Neave felt the intoxicating beat of the drums course through his veins. Under the table, his feet developed a life of their own. Squinting against the haze of cigarette smoke, he scanned the room. A young woman in Soviet uniform hesitantly approached, looking for somewhere to sit. Neave recognised the gorgeous red-headed interpreter who always officiated for the Soviet judges. The drudgery of many a tedious afternoon in court, listening to the repetitive ramblings of long-winded lawyers, had been broken by the frisson of their exchanged glances.

No sooner had Major Neave jumped to his feet and gestured to Elizaveta's empty chair than he regretted it. She wasn't alone. Half a dozen paces behind her, carrying two glasses, a tall Soviet colonel doggedly stumbled forward, bumping into furniture and showering dancers with champagne.

With a grateful nod, the girl sat down and crossed her legs, revealing shapely calves and high heels that were definitely not Red Army issue. Surprised, her escort stopped in his tracks and plonked both glasses on the table so forcefully that he spilled the last drops of champagne. Towering above Neave, his broad chest covered in medals and decorations that made the British officer's Military Cross and Distinguished Service Order look positively inadequate, he let loose a long series of Russian expletives. Only then did Airey Neave recognize the familiar angry bass.

This was Colonel Ivan Klimenko, the man who a few weeks ago had nearly started World War Three when delivering Grand Admiral Raeder and Hans Fritzsche to the Nuremberg Tribunal.

'I'm Svetlana,' the girl said. 'My friends call me Sveta. And this is Colonel Klimenko. He doesn't speak English.'

'How do you do? My name is...'

'Don't be modest,' she interrupted with a smile. 'We all know the legendary Major Airey Neave. The only man ever to escape from Colditz.'

'Colonel Klimenko and I have met before,' Neave pointed at the chair onto which the Russian had slumped. He was breathing heavily and reeked of alcohol.

'Have you?' She turned to her companion and exchanged a few sentences in Russian. 'The colonel thanks you for your invitation to share your table,' she said.

'My pleasure. By the way, this is Doctor Elliott George.'

'Aren't you one of the psychologists?' she asked.

'Guilty as charged,' Doctor George nodded solemnly.

'Perhaps you can explain something to us,' she went on. 'Why is it that you and Doctor Gilbert have unlimited access to the defendants, while our own Soviet prosecutors are severely restricted?'

'Search me,' George shrugged apologetically. 'Maybe because we're a bunch of inoffensive shrinks?'

'You don't look like a shrimp to me,' she frowned.

'"Shrink" is a slang word for psychiatrist,' Neave explained.

She turned to him. 'Is it? Thank you, Major. I *love* learning new words. In fact, I *love* all novelty.'

Neave's mind was racing. It was crucial to prevent Elizaveta and Peter from coming back to the table. However, he had no idea where they were. If he went looking for them in one corner of the huge ballroom, they were bound to reappear from the opposite direction.

'Excuse me a second,' he stood up and peered through layers of swirling blue smoke.

'What do you think of this music?' Elliott George asked.

Svetlana lowered her voice. 'In principle, we do not approve of American art. However, because Negro music was anathema to Hitler, I personally make an exception for jazz.'

429

'Rather catchy, isn't it?'

She threw her head back and laughed delightedly. 'Catchy? What a *lovely* word. *Spasebo*.'

Then things happened incredibly quickly. So quickly, in fact, that when interrogated immediately afterwards, Major Neave had trouble trying to reconstruct their exact sequence.

First, he noticed Klimenko fixing him with an odd expression. Leaning forward, the Russian seemed fascinated by Neave's left shoulder. Or something beyond it.

Neave turned. A pink blot registered at the corner of his eye. Instantly, he moved towards it on an interception course, trying to place himself between the colonel and Elizaveta.

Behind his back, a racket – glasses, a chair, a table, falling to the ground.

The fear in Elizaveta's grey-green eyes. Her mouth, wide open in shock.

Something – a missile? – a body? – flying through the air.

Peter Birkett landing on Elizaveta, throwing her onto the floor, just as the first shot rang out. Svetlana's shriek.

The gun in his hand. Blood.

Klimenko staggering forward, revolver in hand, looking for a line of sight to the bodies on the ground.

A second shot. The recoil: he himself must have fired that shot.

A third shot. Fired by Klimenko as he fell onto his knees.

430

A stampede. People trying to get away or flattening themselves on the floor.

A thud. Klimenko's head hitting the marble slabs. Blood.

Elliott George gaping, more owlish than ever.

At the other end of the vast ballroom, the jazz band still playing. Bebop-a-bebop.

People dancing.

Ba-ba-rebop.

Half a dozen American MP's, sub-machine-guns at the ready. Trying to sort the dead from the living.

A US Army doctor tending the wounded. Calling for ambulances.

Bebop-a-bebop.

Ba-ba-rebop.

Hey!

PART FOUR

'A writer worth his salt at all has an obligation
not only to entertain, but to comment
on the world in which he lives.'
Abby Mann, author of "Judgment in Nuremberg",
after winning his Academy Award, 1961.

1

Jesting Pilate

I CAUGHT ONLY a glimpse of it from the stretcher. Erect atop the Rothenberger Strasse entrance to the US Military Hospital, the hieratic eagle had lost none of its bellicosity. Clutching the world in its talons, sharp beak at the ready, as oblivious today to the wretched human traffic crawling beneath it as it was when thousands of mangled survivors from the Eastern front were being wheeled in, it disdainfully peered over our heads to the far right, beady eyes focussed on the final Nazi victory. Like so many, it had been wounded, part of a stone wing blown away during the American assault; yet somehow this insult affected neither its symmetry nor its balance, and in no way detracted from its aloofness. It clearly was made of stronger stuff than me.

In the closing months of the war, despite the huge red cross painted on its roof, the six-storey central section of the main building had been obliterated by aerial bombing. Indeed, it was the racket of the recently-begun re-building works that awoke me from a restless slumber populated with raptors. At first, I felt utterly disoriented, then gradually remembered that my bed was in the medical wing run by the US 116th General Hospital. I tried to move. Winced. Cautiously trying to feel my left shoulder with my right hand, I was surprised by the huge volume of the dressing.

I dimly recalled what a chubby Californian surgeon had explained about the gas-sealed Nagan M1895, NKGB standard issue revolver: well able to fire its 7.62 mm bullet at thirty yards into a soldier in full battle dress and go right through him.

'Lucky to be alive,' the doctor had concluded. 'The bullet missed the heart by a couple of inches, if that. At least we won't have to extract it, judging from the exit wound. But it hasn't done his shoulder much good.'

'What's going to happen?' a male voice had asked.

'We need to remove the loose bone fragments and re-align the joint. Only then will we be able to form a reasonable prognosis. Worst case is that shoulder mobility will be permanently impaired.'

Try as I may, that's all I could now recollect.

Footsteps. I waved my right hand.

'Anybody there?' I called, surprisingly feebly. 'Hello?'

Smiling hazelnut eyes, an ever so slightly upturned nose, luminous skin – a rosy-cheeked face appeared in my outer field of vision. I blinked.

'Susette?'

'Good morning.'

'What are you doing here?'

435

'I'm Sister Joy, of the US Army Nurse Corps. I've been on the night shift. You slept well.'

Surprised by the Midwestern drawl, I closed my eyes, a sudden spasm of anxiety wrenching my guts. Waves of ominous sensation, spreading from my abdomen, breaking into my consciousness and bouncing back down. I had neglected Susette. Forgotten, rather. No, no, if the abject truth be told – betrayed. Betrayed was the word.

'Captain Birkett?'

Slowly, purposefully, I fought off the ghastly shadows and tried to reconnect with reality. An odd pale-blue headdress, half veil and half cap, was precariously perched on top of wavy auburn hair.

'How are we this morning, Captain Birkett?'

'What's the time?'

'Seven-thirty.'

'How long have I been here?'

'Why, I guess some thirty-six hours since they brought you in.'

'I'm thirsty.'

'That's good. I'll get you some breakfast.'

An hour later, thanks to generous portions of orange juice, cornflakes, toast, two scrambled eggs and sugary tea, I felt my spirits revive. Provided I didn't move, the dull pain in my shoulder was bearable; only when I attempted to change position did it flare up as though a red-hot iron were buried deep under my skin. I soon learned to avoid any unnecessary gesture and to regulate my breathing in order to control the throbbing. Waiting to be shaved, I heard some sort of argument about visiting hours floating down the corridor. It was followed by the beat of heavy, regular footsteps across the wooden floor.

'Good morning, son,' my father boomed with a worried smile. 'Sorry to barge in outside visiting hours, but I had no choice. Must be in Court by ten o'clock.'

Never had I been happier to see him. I extended my right hand which he squeezed harder and longer than usual. He looked tired and old.

'Good to see you, Papa. How is she?'

'Who?'

'Elizaveta.'

'As far as I know, Captain Terisova is well. One might surmise this is not unconnected with the fact that, as I understand, you gallantly volunteered to intercept the bullet which, *prima facie*, was meant for her. May I sit down?'

'Of course, Papa. Just try not to shake the bed, please. How are you?'

'I'm all right. What about you? Are you in pain?'

'Not too bad. Unless I move.'

'Good. Seems you were lucky. Perhaps a good opportunity to slow down and think. Might I ask what you were all doing at the Grand?'

'Just having a drink, really.'

'Didn't you realise you risked running into all manner of Soviet characters?'

'No. I'd never been there before.'

'But Neave knew the place.'

'To be fair, we had a couple of beers before we decided to go to the Grand. Elizaveta didn't want to. I made her.'

'No point in crying over spilt milk. The main thing is for you to get better. Don't forget: I've only one son.'

'How could I? I've only one father.'

Unmentioned, as ever, remained the absence that filled both our lives: that of his wife and of my mother.

Papa got up, looked around and, though the next bay was empty, drew the curtain around the bed.

'I talked to the Prime Minister yesterday,' he lowered his voice. 'The Russians are kicking up one hell of a fuss.'

'Are they?'

'I should say so. Stalin's complained to Attlee *and* Truman. He suggested Major Neave either join the accused in the Nuremberg dock here, or be handed over to stand trial in Moscow for the murder of a Soviet officer.'

'Did Airey kill Klimenko?'

'He most certainly did. Fortunately there are scores of witnesses, all testifying that Klimenko was blind drunk and fired his pistol at you without the slightest provocation. There have already been so many firearms incidents involving inebriated Russians that nobody's particularly surprised. Captain Terisova plays no role in the official version.'

'Is Airey safe then?'

'I should think so. He'll probably get yet another gong for courage in the presence of the enemy or something.'

'Please, Papa, don't make me laugh, under any circumstances,' I pleaded. 'It hurts. What did Mr Attlee say?'

'He reminded me that we have already exceeded the deadline for identification of Prisoner HW. He wants MI5 to take over.'

'We can't let that happen, Papa.'

'Why not?'

'They'll send Elizaveta to Bad Nenndorf.'

'Bad Nenndorf? What on earth for?'

'It's the secret MI5 prison where they torture suspected Communist infiltrators.'

'Stuff and nonsense. Never heard of it. You mustn't believe all the rumours put out by Soviet propaganda, Peter. We British are no torturers. Enhanced interrogation techniques, at most, but no torture. And only in exceptional circumstances. Anyway – forgive my asking – how do we know the beautiful Miss Terisova isn't a Soviet plant?'

'For God's sake, Papa. NKGB hit-men were taking pot-shots at her only two days ago. Isn't that sufficient proof?'

'I suppose so. After all, that Russki could hardly have anticipated that you'd stop his bullet, could he?'

'He wanted her dead.'

'Be that as it may, London feels that, after such a regrettable international incident, Prisoner HW is even more of a hot potato than before. We simply cannot afford to be caught red-handed by Stalin, hiding Hitler.'

'But our Johnny may not be Hitler.'

'Try and explain that to Stalin. Anyway, it's an absurd

situation, which London simply isn't prepared to tolerate any longer.'

'We're making good progress. I brought detailed sketches of Hitler's teeth back from Berlin. Doctor George will find a way to unmask our man. We just need a bit more time.'

'We've got three days. From yesterday morning. I told Neave.'

'But that leaves only today and tomorrow!'

'I know. Nothing I can do about it.'

'Why the deadline?'

'Göring starts his defence tomorrow. The Tribunal needs to know whether to treat him as the heir to Hitler and current leader of the Nazis – or not. The dynamics of the whole trial will be affected. The prosecution certainly couldn't be asked to change course midstream.'

'So they wouldn't like us to deliver Hitler to the Court?'

'Not after tomorrow night, anyway.'

'I see. Then we must immediately get her a British passport.'

'I suppose we're back to the beauteous Miss Terisova?'

'Don't tease, Papa. It's matter of life and death. Whoever gets her first – NKGB or MI5 – she's doomed.'

'Haven't you done enough for her already?'

'She saved my life. Does that count for nothing?'

'I seem to recall that you recently discharged that debt with not a little panache. What more does she expect?'

'I'm sure she does *not* expect to be thrown back to the lions. And I fully intend to honour my commitment.'

'Commitment?'

'When she offered to deliver Hitler to us, I guaranteed to look after her.'

'Yet she may have delivered a lorry driver named Gustav Weber.'

In frustration, I took a deep breath and was instantly rewarded with a sharp pain in my shoulder. 'Please, Papa,' I gasped. 'Her mother was German. Died when she was a child. I swore. On my own mother's grave. Will you please help – for Mama, if not for me?'

Looking away, my father immersed himself in the study of the wall behind the bed, where minute flakes of glossy greenish paint were peeling off in parallel waves, like ridges on a sand dune after a desert storm. Seconds, maybe minutes ticked away. Regretting already what may have sounded like an attempt at emotional blackmail, I opened my mouth to apologise – just as Papa gave his considered answer.

'I'll see what I can do, my boy.'

I MUST HAVE DOZED for a while after my father's departure, since I didn't hear the footsteps of the nurse who'd replaced Sister Joy. I woke up with a painful jolt as the soft-spoken black girl swished through the white linen curtain, making the rings jingle on the curved metal rail.

'Visitors for you, Captain Birkett. Is it all right?'

I nodded.

'*Guten Morgen,*' a voice called.

'Hello, Elliott,' I smiled as the familiar freckles of Doctor George came into focus.

'Let me introduce my assistant, Lise,' George winked.

Elizaveta was standing one step back, lips slightly parted, her expression serious, peering at me with a mixture of shyness and intense concentration. For the first time, noticing the precursors of tiny wrinkles at the corner of her eyes and mouth, I saw the beautiful mature woman she would one day become, and how much I would love her.

'Come nearer,' I indicated the other side of the bed. She stepped forward and took my hand between both of hers, then quickly released it as if surprised by her own gesture – but not before the electric shock had spread throughout my whole body.

'What are you doing here?' I whispered. 'You have no papers. If the Americans challenge you…'

'What did I tell you, Lise?' Doctor George interjected. 'Of course he's right. This is insane.'

'I'm sorry,' she said with a smile that suggested exactly the opposite. 'Anyway, since when do psychologists know anything about insanity?' Reflecting light from the green wall, her eyes had turned into emeralds so brilliant that I wondered if she'd been crying.

'Can't understand how you Russians won the war with no sense of discipline,' Doctor George shrugged. 'More to the point: how are you feeling, dear boy? You gave us a bit of a fright.'

'To be honest, I gave myself a fright too.' I turned to the

girl. 'Perhaps you should select your friends more carefully in future. This chap Klimenko always seemed a bit pushy. None of my business, of course.'

'I'll bear that in mind – if I ever get to choose my friends. That would be a novel experience.'

'Where's Neave?' I asked George.

'He's attending court today.'

'My father popped in this morning. Told me that we're running out of time.'

'Apparently so. We need positive identification of Prisoner HW by tomorrow evening.'

'Any progress?'

'I took your Berlin dental sketches to the local dentist yesterday morning. He confirmed that they match exactly the pontics in HW's mouth.'

'Surely that's conclusive, isn't it?'

'Except Stalin will never buy it,' Elizaveta interjected. 'I told you: he already knows that the teeth of the corpse from the Reich Chancellery garden exactly match Hitler's too.'

'So we have two bodies with exactly the same teeth – one dead, and one alive,' I said. 'How's that possible?'

'In principle, there is no reason why it should be impossible,' George said. 'Given enough time and money – and a mad bastard of a dentist – even you could be fitted with a Hitler mouth. Complete with the stench.'

'I think I'll pass on that tempting offer, thank you. I've got a bit of work to do on my shoulder first.'

'I go back to my original assertion: given two indistinguishable bodies, we must concentrate on the minds.'

'Sounds good, Elliott, but we haven't got a mind-reading machine, have we? And even if we had, it wouldn't be much good if our chap is actually *losing* his mind, would it?'

'He hasn't lost his mind,' Elizaveta chipped in. 'At least, not all of it. And not all the time. He has... ups and downs.'

'How do you know?' the psychologist asked.

'Slavonic genius,' she smiled modestly. 'And feminine intuition.'

'We conducted one slightly rushed experiment yesterday,' Elliott George turned to me. 'We had a Hasidic Jew prepare and serve Prisoner HW's meal. Just picture it: HW watching this Pole, clad in black *rekel* and trousers, black fedora above long curly sideburns, praying while he cooked the most kosher meal ever. Sight to behold.'

'The mind boggles. What happened?'

'Nothing. HW ate his dinner and went to bed.'

'No sign of emotion or agitation?'

'None whatsoever.'

'Damn!' I exclaimed. 'That is amazing.'

'Why?' Elizaveta asked.

'Because, if our chap were Hitler, the very proximity of a Jew would have him convulsed in fear and loathing, wouldn't it?'

'And what would it prove?' she shook her head. 'Think about it. If you exposed most of the Nazis currently in the dock to Jews, they would respond with disgust and hatred. Streicher would be foaming at the mouth. Others too. And so would large segments of the anti-Semitic German, French or Polish populations. Yet, not every rabid anti-Semite is Hitler, is he?'

'An allergy to Jews may not be sufficient proof of Hitler's identity, but it might reasonably be deemed necessary,' the psychologist protested.

I suddenly felt very tired.

'Let's face it. We've lost the game, haven't we? First, nobody wants this man to be Hitler. Second, there is no way out of this conundrum. We can't establish the identity of a man with no fingerprints and somebody else's teeth. Not beyond doubt, and certainly not by tomorrow night.'

Doctor Elliott George and Captain Elizaveta Terisova exchanged a look and bent conspiratorially over the bed.

'I beg to differ. We have just enough time to play our last card,' the psychologist whispered in my ear.

'What card?'

'Our best card.'

We spent the next thirty minutes discussing the details of the plan in hushed tones. As American nurses and cleaners came and went, I was glad we were speaking in German.

2

Family Reunion

IN THE PITCH DARK and heavy stillness, the doors of the 1.4 litre Mercedes seemed to clang unusually loudly. A dog barked. Now frozen, the white dampness that had condensed on the windscreen at dusk had to be noisily scraped off. Since it was impossible to fit all the luggage in the boot, one large bag ended up next to Elizaveta on the back seat. Major Neave was at the wheel, Doctor George next to him. Neither had opened the rear door for her, perhaps because of absent-mindedness, or because they didn't want to look like competing suitors. There wasn't a soul to be seen in the centre of Zirndorf. Soon, having exchanged hardly a word, they were skirting round the southern suburbs of Nuremberg, on their way to the southbound autobahn.

Elizaveta had hardly slept. Whenever exhaustion delivered her to the threshold of slumber, Ivan Klimenko's threatening ghost appeared. While, splayed open under a drunken Red Army sergeant, she begged for help, he stood by impassively, his right arm raised in a stiff salute. Then he burst into demonic laughter, clicked his heels and faded away, only to re-appear as soon as she closed her eyes.

Whenever, in an effort to soothe her mind, she recalled the short carefree moments at the Grand, her headlong surrender to the intoxicating jazz music, the vengeful shadow of her late war-husband burst through her defences. And then there was no escaping the images of her elderly father, confused and emaciated, joining Jakob in some God-forsaken labour camp north of the Arctic circle.

But the worst flashback to haunt her mind was the instant when, still possessed by the bebop rhythms, breathless from dancing so close to Peter Birkett, she'd suddenly found herself looking down the barrel of a gun. None of her training had been any good, nor had her much vaunted reflexes. She'd stood there, paralysed, defenceless, a rabbit in headlights, overwhelmed by the knowledge that Klimenko wouldn't, couldn't miss. Of the myriad thoughts swamping her mind at that instant she could only remember one: 'No! Not yet! Not now!'

Things had happened so quickly. The first shot. She remembered the bang, and thinking that Klimenko hadn't had time to screw the standard issue NKGB silencer to the muzzle of his Nagan. Breach of regulations.

Then she was on the floor, as if struck by the falling roof. Convinced she'd been hit.

Two more shots. And then blood, running on her

face. Not hers. His. Peter's. Peter had taken care of her. Offered his life for her. To her.

God! How relieved she'd felt yesterday, in the hospital, seeing him out of danger! She was bursting with such gratitude that she needed to direct it towards somebody, some kind of benevolent deity or guardian angel. In the end, the words had spontaneously escaped: 'Thank you, darling Mummy. You love me so much!'

By the time they reached the motorway near Feucht, the Mercedes' engine had warmed up enough for the heating system to function properly. Feeling safer in this transient, fast-moving cocoon than she had for weeks, Elizaveta stopped shivering and dozed off.

07:25

'Good morning, Captain Birkett. How are we today?'

Peter opened his eyes, blinked and yawned.

'Good morning, Sister Joy.'

'Are we hungry?'

'Ravenous.'

'Good. Breakfast is here. Shall we sit up?'

07:57

Judge Birkett adjusted his tie, carefully combed the thin hair at the back of his head, and dusted his shoulders. He put on his long navy-blue overcoat, black hat, white scarf and spectacles. Engine running, headlights piercing the darkness, his official black Austin 16 was waiting in front of the house. The elderly German driver jumped out, bowed, took the heavy legal briefcase from the judge's hand and opened the door. Sir Norman Birkett folded his tall body onto the rear seat and extracted a bundle of papers from the bag. He sensed that today might be the critical point in the already long and tedious history of the Nuremberg trial. Today, Reichsmarschall Hermann Göring was to take the stand.

08:12

Just after passing Dachau, they encountered an American checkpoint on the motorway slip road. Though Elizaveta understood none of the exchange, it was clear that Major Neave's papers and demeanour impressed the GIs. Having perfunctorily shone their torch lamp into her face, they saluted and waved the car on. On their left, the overcast sky was beginning to glow with the first signs of an anaemic, wintry dawn. As they reached the dark, silent city, the remains of gutted tenement blocks arose on all sides, their tall elevations almost transparent against the ghostly eastern skies. The city looked so uncannily similar to Nuremberg that, for a few seconds, Elizaveta wondered whether the car might have turned around while she slept; then she remembered that after some time all cadavers look similar, and that there was no reason, after seventy-one bombing raids, to expect Munich to look any different.

'Welcome to Munich, the birthplace and official capital of National Socialism,' said Neave.

'Hard to get used to it, isn't it?' Doctor George asked, as though reading her mind.

She nodded.

'I heard that more than half the buildings have been obliterated,' Neave said. 'Par for the course.'

'Do you think that it can ever be rebuilt?' Elizaveta asked.

'How would they do it?' pondered George. 'They're starving and freezing. Most of their men are dead, crippled or in Soviet labour camps. They have no fuel, plant or machinery.'

'That leaves the women,' she said. 'Don't underestimate the women. When men have finished destroying, we're always called on for the re-building.'

Inching along the Brienner Strasse towards the centre, they reached the Königs-Platz. Leaving behind the monumental gateway of the Propyläen, they found on their left the shell of the Führer-Bau, its vast congress hall and innumerable committee rooms open to the winds, and the wrecked Verwaltungsbau, home to the administrative machinery of the National Socialist party. The famous Braunes Haus, headquarters of the Party, had been severely damaged by aerial bombing and gutted by fire.

'Hats off to the RAF,' Neave said. 'They made quite a thorough job of it, didn't they?'

'Do you really believe that Hitler's apartment is intact?' Elizaveta asked.

'So we're told. We'll soon find out.'

Near Palais Royal, they turned into Prinzregenten-strasse, leaving the Englischer Garten on their left.

'Did you know this park was laid out by our own Earl Rumford, back in 1789?' Elliott George asked.

'I most certainly did not,' Neave replied. 'Are you making it up?'

'I spent a year here before the war, as a student. That's where I learnt German – or Bavarian, rather. It's not only the city that looked different then – the park too.'

'In what way?'

George pointed to the treeless six hundred acres. 'This land was covered with the finest timber you've ever seen,' he said. 'Centuries-old specimens of local and exotic species.'

'Probably cut for firewood,' Elizaveta said. 'And now the place is a big vegetable patch. Or will be in the spring.'

'It doesn't feel like spring will ever come back here,' mused Neave.

As soon as they crossed the river Isar the level of destruction seemed less intense. Whole blocks emerged from the rubble, seemingly intact. The Prinzregententheater, built to Richard Wagner's specifications at the turn of the century, had suffered only minor damage; the four columns supporting its neo-classical peristyle were still standing, its entablature pockmarked with bullet holes.

'There we are: Prinzregentenplatz,' announced Neave, pulling over as they reached a large crossroads. 'Anybody see number sixteen?'

'There.' Elizaveta pointed across the junction.

There it was: an elegant mansion block, five storeys of bourgeois gravitas under an immaculate sloping roof of black slate – Adolf Hitler's home since 1933. On the second, third and fourth floors, large balconies, loggias almost, protected by carved stone guardrails, punctuated the cut corner overlooking Prinzregentenplatz. Abutting on these terraces, coiffed by pointed triangles, tall turrets, pierced on three sides by high rectangular windows, gracefully rose above the roof.

'See that French window with the Roman arch on the second floor balcony?' Neave asked. 'That's Hitler's flat.'

For a while they sat in awe, taking in the scene. Inadequately equipped against the cold, shadowy pedestrians were huddling together at bus stops. Cyclists hurried to work. Carrying schoolbags and shivering in breeches too small for them, three boys walked past the Mercedes and inspected its passengers, eyes lingering on the legs of the blonde woman on the back seat.

'It reminds me of St Paul's cathedral,' Elliott George mused.

'Does it?'

'Don't you remember? For years, after each night's bombing, there stood St Paul's – intact. Surrounded by acres of smoking ruins, but miraculously untouched. It didn't take long for Londoners to conclude it was under divine protection. I guarantee the good Catholics of Munich, faced with similar irrefutable evidence, drew the same conclusion with regard to the Führer's home.'

'Once a shrink, always a shrink,' Neave smiled. 'Okay, team. Shall we get to work?'

He pulled out and drove the Mercedes across the square to the foot of number sixteen, where only two cars were to be seen, an empty US Army jeep and a black Volkswagen. Only after they'd parked did they notice the two men quietly sitting in the Volkswagen, their faces invisible between low hats and upturned collars.

'Aha. Company. We'll need to be as brief as possible. Let's try and carry everything up in one go,' Neave suggested after a quick glance at the men.

Carrying a couple of crates each, they entered the building through the main door and found themselves in a hall smelling of disinfectant. The wooden steps were wide and not steep, fifteen of them leading to the half-landing, and the same again to the first floor. The staircase was well lit by several windows, and its walls protected by green tiles opposite a solid oak handrail. Slightly out of breath, Airey Neave dropped his load on the second floor landing and knocked on a door to his left.

'Is anybody expecting us?' Elizaveta asked.

'The housekeepers should have been briefed.'

He knocked again, louder – but to no avail. As he moved across the landing to the other door, it was opened warily. A stocky middle-aged woman clad in a black dress and flat black shoes stood silently behind it.

'Frau Schissler?' Neave asked. '*Grüss Gott*. I'm Major Neave, of the British War Crimes Executive.'

The woman stepped back without a word. They entered

the spacious hall of Adolf Hitler's apartment and deposited their bags on the well-waxed herringbone parquet floor.

'Would you be so kind as to show us around, Frau Schissler?' Neave asked.

'*Aber natürlich,*' she replied with a thick Bavarian accent. The first door led into Hitler's study. It seemed its owner had only momentarily stepped out of the room. On the wall, a large photograph of the Führer in full rhetorical flight, right arm extended over thousands of frenzied, adoring female faces, hung in a gilded frame next to an amateurish alpine landscape. On the spotless mahogany desk, the lamp was switched on, and the telephone and ink blotter looked as if they'd just been used. Standing at an angle to the desk, the armchair seemed to have just been pushed back in a rush.

'Look, Lise!' Doctor George pointed at a black-and-white photograph in a silver frame. 'There she is. Angelika Raubal.'

Elizaveta stepped forward and peered at the portrait of the smiling young woman who'd committed suicide in this flat, aged twenty-three.

'Who's the other?' she asked.

'No idea,' Elliott George shrugged. '*Bitte, Frau Schissler, wer ist das?*'

'Frau Hitler – our Führer's mother,' the woman answered. 'I've never met her, of course.'

'How long have you worked for Herr Hitler, Frau Schissler?' Neave asked.

'My husband and I have served the Führer since he bought this flat – that would be some fifteen years, I suppose.' She stopped and hesitated. 'If I may ask, *meine Herren* – are you British or American?'

'British.'

'I once had the pleasure of serving coffee to your Prime Minister. A Mr Shamborlain, I believe. Sitting right here.' She nodded towards a green leather chair by the wall. 'A true gentleman. September or October 1938... I've never been very good with dates, I'm afraid. Anyway, he and our Chancellor got on well, that much I remember.'

They all stared at the empty chair facing the empty desk, remembering the empty promise of 'peace in our time'. Like the rest of the apartment, Hitler's bedroom was large and high-ceilinged. The only picture in the room was an oil portrait of Geli Raubal – a full-frontal nude. Her right hand loosely holding a muslin veil low across her shins, she looked straight at the viewer. The perspective was odd. She was squarely facing the painter, but her right breast and nipple were drawn far to the left of the canvas, beyond the contour of her chest. In the bottom right-hand corner, it was signed '*Adolf Hitler*'.

They stood before it silently until Elizaveta felt so disturbed by the deep shadows concealing the sitter's eyes that she moved away and started investigating the bedside drawers. In the second one she found a Walther 6.35 pistol, its oily black barrel gleaming on a white cloth. Doctor George picked it up.

'Perfect,' he said. 'Just what the doctor ordered.'

They sat on the bed gazing at the full wardrobes under the disapproving eye of Frau Schissler, who eventually shooed them off and straightened the bedspread.

'Could we see Fräulein Raubal's room?' Doctor George asked.

'What for?' the woman asked.

'Could we just see it?'

Shaking her head and muttering under her breath, Frau Schissler led the way.

'What was that noise?' Neave stopped in his tracks in front of a closed door in the hallway.

'That will be my husband. In the kitchen.'

Neave opened the door. A man, busy shoving fuel into a kitchen range, looked up. In his late fifties or early sixties, he had the strong calloused hands of a manual worker, short cropped hair and a Hitler moustache below a prominent nose. Pulled almost as high as his armpits by ridiculously short suspenders, his baggy navy-blue trousers could have been mistaken for an oversized boiler suit, lending him a Chaplinesque appearance.

'*Grüss Gott!*' he straightened up and bowed.

Having reciprocated his greeting, Major Neave turned back and followed Frau Schissler to the other end of the hall.

'Thank you, Frau Schissler,' Neave said as they all congregated in Geli Raubal's bedroom. 'We won't need your services any more. I suggest you and your husband take the day off and come back tomorrow.'

Five minutes later they heard the front door open and shut.

'Right,' Major Neave turned to his two acolytes. 'I'll install the sound equipment. Elliott, you work on Lise. We haven't got all day.'

10:01

All eight judges sat down. The President of the Tribunal declared it in session. Judge Birkett noticed that the courtroom was more packed than usual. Clearly, and probably rightly, press and public expected Reichsmarschall Hermann Göring's defence to constitute the high point of the trial. His defence counsel, Doktor Otto Stahmer, sounded confident. Only three days ago, the Tribunal had criticised the Occupation authorities for allowing press attacks on the defence lawyers, and reminded the Allied military command that all advocates were under the protection of the Court, which would not tolerate any further interference with the course of justice. Doktor Stahmer's bold opening statement suggested that this had considerably boosted the defence's morale.

10:05

On his way to the bathroom, Doctor George picked up Geli Raubal's photograph from her uncle's desk. He put it down on the shelf by the basin and walked to the hall to collect his black leather bag. Feeling increasingly apprehensive, Elizaveta looked around. Unlike the other rooms, the windowless bathroom was small and claustrophobic.

Opposite the door, a white bathtub occupied its full width, surrounded by wall-to-wall, floor-to-ceiling square yellow tiles. A photograph of the Führer in his customary grey tunic, hands on hips, swastika on armband, stood on the bathtub ledge. On the left, beneath a plain wall mirror, a circular washbasin of white porcelain protruded almost to the middle of the room. Opposite, on top of a simple dresser made of white painted wood, stood a plaster statue of Geli kneeling, naked, both hands in her hair and pert breasts lifted.

'Well, as you can see, Lise,' Elliott George pointed at Geli's portrait, 'our first challenge is that Angelika had short, wavy auburn hair. And you have long, fair, straight hair. But worry not: I have a bagful of hairdressing paraphernalia.'

'You must be joking,' she retorted.

'My tonsorial skills might be a bit of a joke, I'll grant you that. As for the rest of the plan, I assure you there is no jocular aspect to it.'

'What makes you so sure it will work?'

'The fact that it cannot fail.'

'All plans can fail. I wish Peter were here.'

'You're not going to let the side down, Lise?' A concerned look on his friendly face, he looked intently at her. 'Listen. You're free. Nobody's going to force you. But today you can force Prisoner HW to reveal his identity. And if you do, I understand there will be goodies coming your way. Including a British passport and a place at medical school in London. It's up to you, Lise.'

'What if something goes wrong?'

'What could go wrong? We'll be here at all times, hidden a few feet away.'

'What if he says nothing?'

'Then I'll stuff my hat with all your beautiful hair and eat the lot.'

'That's a promise you may live to regret, Elliott.'

'Listen. According to my research, Hitler truly fell in love with only one woman: his niece, Angelika Raubal. She came to live with him in this apartment in 1929, when he was forty and she was twenty-one. In Nuremberg, I interviewed all the detainees: each one confirmed that he was utterly besotted with her, and madly jealous. However, two years into their sadomasochistic affair, she found in Hitler's pocket a letter from the nineteen-year-old Eva Braun, which confirmed her suspicions: dear Uncle Alf was two-timing her. After an argument with Hitler, she shot herself in the chest – with his pistol. But to me, as a psychologist, what's interesting is Hitler's reaction. He was suicidal – withdrew from public life, refused to see anybody for weeks. He even became a vegetarian, claiming that meat reminded him of Geli's corpse.'

'Shame he didn't actually commit suicide at the time.'

'When he finally emerged from seclusion at Lake Tegern, Hitler's nature had changed for the worse. I believe that's when he took leave of his humanity. After this crisis, his fear of emotional pain prevented him from engaging in any meaningful relationship. He lost the capacity to empathise.'

'We all know Hitler is a monster, Elliott.'

'Indeed. But here's the key fact. Since Geli's death, Hitler has kept a bust or a portrait of her in every single one of his studies and bedrooms: here, in the Reich Chancellery, in Berchtesgaden. Apparently, even in the room in the *Führerbunker* where he married Eva Braun.'

'The old romantic,' Elizaveta shuddered.

'I believe Adolf Hitler never freed himself from the spectre of his dead lover – and never will. Tenuous though it is, his only connection to humanity is through his niece. But here is the crux, Lise. Geli Raubal means nothing to Gustav Weber. Out of a confrontation with the ghost of Geli Raubal the truth is bound to emerge. Do you see?'

'Of course I see,' she said in a flat voice. 'Where do you want me?'

'Why don't you kneel in front of the bathtub?'

'Like her?' She pointed at Geli Raubal's statue.

Elliott George picked up steel scissors.

She did as she was told and, lifting up her hair with both hands, offered her bare neck to him.

It only took a few minutes for most of her silky blonde hair to fall to the bottom of the bathtub. Wordlessly, she collected it and put it into the metal bin under the basin.

When she ran some water to clean the tub, she was surprised to find it pleasantly warm.

Doctor George saw she was shivering. 'Why don't you fill it up?' he suggested gently. 'Not only will it relax you, but it will be much easier for me to do the colour.'

She glanced at him hesitatingly, gave a slight shrug and started undressing. The prospect of her first hot bath in months suddenly seemed irresistible.

'Wait outside,' she said. 'I'll call you.'

The tub was just the right length. Luxuriating in the intensely pleasurable hot water, feeling the muscles of her neck, shoulders and legs gradually loosen, she dozed off. From the deepest recesses of her unconscious, where they had hidden since the blissful summer days in Shcherbatovka when Uncle Gottfried and Aunt Margaretha were telling her biblical stories, shorn lambs and sacrificial scapegoats suddenly broke free. She called Jakob to help corral them; but the broad-shouldered young man who turned to face her, clad in traditional Volga German Sunday best, had Peter Birkett's winning smile. When she re-opened her eyes, she was surprised not to find herself in her parents' Moscow flat.

Then it hit her. *She was in Hitler's bath.*

Like a rocket, she shot out of the tub and stood dripping, shaking, a cramp in her left calf. All around, the square yellow tiles seemed to close in on her. Looking for a towel, she tried to control her breathing. Then she saw Geli's statue impassively looking at her.

'Damn you, Geli,' she muttered through clenched

teeth, clambering back into the bath. 'Calm down, girl. You can do this.'

Still hot, the water immediately cured her cramp. Curiously, there were no fewer than three soap holders on the tiled wall. From the nearest she extracted the dry remnants of a whitish bar, held it to the light and looked at it, fascinated. A couple of grey hairs were stuck on its surface. Without doubt, Adolf Hitler, conqueror of Europe, Führer of the Thousand-Year Reich, mesmeric idol of millions of German women, her uncle-to-be, her fiancé, had held it in his hand. Washed his Aryan cock with it. Closing her eyes, she opened her legs and slowly, deeply, soaped herself.

10:36
Doktor Stahmer concluded his vigorous address to the Court and called Hermann Wilhelm Göring.

The Reichsmarschall rose from his seat in the left corner of the dock. Baggy light-blue trousers tucked into shiny black boots, a thick bundle of papers under his arm, shepherded by a fresh-faced MP, he processed majestically to the witness box. No sooner had he taken the oath than it became clear he was planning to use his examination-in-chief as a platform to defend and justify the National Socialist revolution. Led by his counsel's easy questions, eyes searching the courtroom, sensitive to every shift in the audience's mood, he put in the performance of his life, painting a glittering picture of

Nazi ideals and achievements. Although the prosecutors had for months tried to instil into the Bench their own paranoia about the risk of the proceedings being used for Nazi propaganda, Judge Lawrence let him get away with resounding declarations of selfless patriotism.

'I did not want war, nor did I bring it about. I have done everything to prevent it through negotiations. The only motive which guided me was all-consuming love for my people, its wellbeing, its freedom, its dignity and its life. And for this I call the Almighty and the German people as witnesses!' the Reichsmarschall intoned.

There was much nodding in the dock, even by men like Schacht, who were not his friends.

Göring then related how he'd helped build up the Nazi Party as a force for national renewal, and presented his own version of the bloody purge of SA leaders in 1934. He explained the policy of keeping the church out of politics, and how sad he was that it had proved necessary to send some unruly clerics to concentration camps. Only when he tried to justify the anti-Semitic Nuremberg laws on the basis of the aggression that Jews had perpetrated against the Nazi state did many of his co-defendants hang their heads. But as he recalled how the Party had eliminated unemployment, built motorways and factories, re-armed Germany, and annexed Austria – all feats for which he proudly claimed personal credit – again their enraptured eyes were upon him. Hess got so carried away he started clapping and had to be restrained.

Judge Birkett began to feel distinctly uneasy. He saw

the admiring glances from the press gallery, and heard the murmurs of approval from the public. The Soviet judges on his right were sitting stony-faced; the French judges at the other end were fretting.

'Throughout long centuries of monarchy, Germany always had a leadership principle,' Göring concluded, looking directly at the Bench, then at the prosecutors. He paused for effect, and then, with a mischievous smile, added: 'It is the very principle on which both the Roman Catholic Church and the USSR are governed.'

Sniggers could be heard among the press corps. All Soviet officials in the room seemed petrified. Stealing a quick glance at his neighbour, Judge Birkett noticed little droplets of sweat glistening on the temples of Judge Nikitchenko.

Within a couple of hours, Göring skilfully navigated his way through the thousands of pages of repetitive, confusing infamy inflicted on the court by prosecutors over many tedious weeks. He gave a clear account of the honourable attempt by inspired leaders to rebuild a Germany unjustly crushed by the Versailles Treaty. Contrary to all other defendants who pleaded ignorance and denied any responsibility, he proudly claimed it.

'Though I received orders from the Führer, I, Reichsmarschall Hermann Göring, assume full responsibility for them. They bear my signature. I issued them. Accordingly, I do not propose to hide behind the Führer.'

It was a formidable performance by the old trouper, which guaranteed him the leading role he'd been craving since the opening of the trial, if not since the demise of his beloved Luftwaffe five years ago.

Led by the same angelic military policeman, Göring strutted back to his seat, sat down and mopped the sweat from his face. Impassive, both Soviet judges kept their eyes fixed on the clock high up on the wall opposite.

Judge Lawrence called a recess for lunch.

12:45

Clad in a short fluffy towel, Elizaveta stared. The tall, dark-haired girl stared back, short wavy hair parted low on one side, as was fashionable before the war. 'You look vulgar,' Elizaveta told her. As the wardrobe door swung open, taking the mirror with it, the girl frowned and disappeared.

Elizaveta examined the photograph of Geli's corpse that Doctor George had placed on the bed. A light-coloured blouse, a pleated skirt. Obviously, one couldn't tell the exact hues from a black-and-white picture. The difficulty soon disappeared: most of the tops in Geli's wardrobe were white, and the plain skirts either grey or dark blue. She opened a drawer and selected white silk knickers, which fitted her perfectly. Geli's brassieres, however, were all too big. Elizaveta laid three white blouses on the bed, wondering which one to choose. They all smelt of mothballs, but one appeared less clean than the others. The faded outline of a large stain was clearly visible on its front, where the cleaning process had worn out the cotton fabric. This probably was the very garment in which Geli Raubal had bled to death. This was the one.

12:55

Never had time passed so agonisingly slowly. Peter Birkett found it impossible to concentrate on the copy of the *New York Times* that the nurse had kindly brought him. He wondered how things were going in Munich. Had they got access to the flat? Was Elizaveta safe? What if she'd been right all along, and Prisoner HW turned out to be Hitler? Would he be indicted alongside his accomplices and, if so, would he take the stand? On the one hand, he might be insane or senile; on the other, his old powers of oratory might return. Would the Germans again unite behind him? Would he unleash his Werewolves on the Allied forces?

These questions, and myriad others, kept churning in his mind, leaving him anxious, frustrated and febrile. He paid no attention to the patter of small feet running across the ward until suddenly a little girl cried:

'There, Mummy! Onkel Peter, in the bed!'

Rosy-cheeked and clad in black up to the little ribbons which held her blonde pigtails, it was Lilli.

'Lilli! What are you doing here?' Peter turned his head, expecting to see Susette; but the tall woman standing a few paces back, also dressed in black, was Sybille.

'What happened to you, Onkel Peter?' Lilli asked excitedly, pulling at the bed sheet. 'Why do you have that thing on your shoulder?'

'I had an accident, Lilli. Nothing serious.'

'You're not going to die?'

'No.'

'Are you sure? Everybody dies. Even snails.'

'That's true, Lilli. But only when they are very old.'

'Auntie Susette wasn't old.'

Peter cast a quick look at Sybille, still standing immobile a few feet back, clutching her bag, her face hard as stone.

'What are you talking about, Lilli?' Gasping as pain shot through his shoulder, he sat up and grasped her hand.

'Mummy said not to be sad. Auntie Susette is just going to sleep for a long, long time. But nobody's playing with me any more.'

Aghast, he turned to Sybille. She opened her bag, took out an envelope and, without stepping forward, threw it on the bed.

'I'm only doing it for her,' she said.

'For God's sake – what happened?'

'She drowned herself in the *Planschbecken*.'

'What?'

'You heard.'

'When?'

'What do you care? Three days ago.'

Sheltering his eyes with his good hand, he let out a low wail. 'No... no! Was it an accident? Please, Sybille...'

'Don't be sad, Onkel Peter,' Lilli patted his hand. 'One day, she'll wake up – won't she, Mummy? And she'll play with me again.'

'If you have one ounce of decency, Captain Birkett, never, ever set foot in our house again, or show your face in Kamen,' Sybille said harshly. 'Come, Lilli.'

'*Auf Wiedersehen, Onkel Peter!*' Lilli deposited multiple kisses on Peter's hand before clambering off the bed.

'Wait!' he cried.

But they were gone.

With trembling fingers, he picked up the letter. Black ink on a recycled brown envelope, addressed to Herr Kapitän Birkett in big, perfectly-formed letters.

Mein Liebling *Peter,*

It was the day Max died. You were lost.

That day, when we made love – we did make love, didn't we? – I can still hear your voice whispering 'I love you' in my ear. That day, when we made love, my darling, I asked you for nothing. I held you to nothing. I wanted nothing. Only to be yours.

That day was the happiest day in my life. Thank you for that day, my darling.

It was the saddest day of my life too. The phone call. I could hear you were talking to a woman.

"Work," you told me. "Don't wait for me. Go home."

But I was home.

"Waiting is what we girls do," I replied. Do you remember? I would have waited for you forever.

And I did wait for you that evening in my father's surgery, praying for your safe return.

You did come back. With the old man and the blonde girl. Tall, so tall. Beautiful. Oh, so beautiful.

Work, you said.

The tall blonde girl who slept with you in my room, the day we made love. For we did make love, didn't we?

And now I might be pregnant. Carrying your child. Poor baby – the bastard child of an occupier and a slut.

The shame. Its prospects would be even worse than Lilli's, bless her. At least her dad was a German soldier.

It is my fault. Deep down, I always knew I should have resisted you. Yet I just couldn't. Is it my fault?

And now you have disappeared.

I'm not afraid of dying.

Please, my love, don't ever do it again.

All I ask is that, in memory of your stupid, loving Susette, you remember that conquerors' pleasures can wreck lives.

Please, don't do it to the impossibly beautiful blonde girl – not even to her.

Because of you, I cannot love her. Yet, because of you, I cannot hate her.

Will you grant me a first and last request? If you can bear being reminded of me, please look after Lilli. Don't let her starve. She's innocent. So innocent she too loves you.

Death holds no fear. We've all stared it in the face, day after day, for so many years!

My only regret is not to be able to kiss you goodbye, my love.

Please forgive me – and forgive yourself.

Your loving Susette

13:40

Following Lieutenant Colonel Volchkov's unseemly explosion, in the privacy of their dining-room, the eight judges finished their meal in silence.

'I'm sorry to labour the point,' Judge Nikitchenko resumed over coffee. 'But we simply cannot let Göring get away with this.'

'Please remember the charter of this tribunal. We are committed to providing these men with a fair trial,' Justice Lawrence pleaded yet again. 'Their lives are at stake.'

'With respect, I think you're missing the point. We all know that none of these criminals can possibly escape with his life. Don't we?'

Sometimes Judge Birkett despaired of his Soviet colleagues' capacity even to understand the concept of fair trial.

'I certainly do not know that,' he objected.

'The point is,' Nikitchenko pressed on, 'that the life of two dozen Nazi scoundrels is immaterial. These people have killed forty million Europeans, most of them Soviet citizens. Our mission is to discredit their system and ideology. That's why we're here.'

'Absolutely right!' Volchkov banged the table. 'And

what are we doing? Allowing Göring to deliver an apologia for Nazism! Soon he's going to accuse the Soviet Union of having started the war. Next he will accuse us of having killed the Poles in Katyn. This is outrageous!'

'Calm down, gentlemen,' Judge Biddle interjected. 'There is no cause for such agitation. It is true that Göring made the most of his examination-in-chief. Good for him. But our system is an adversarial one. This afternoon he's going to be cross-examined by the US chief of Counsel, Justice Robert H. Jackson. You've heard Jackson's opening statement, haven't you? Have no fear. He's the best. He'll tear into Göring.'

John Parker, the alternate US judge, took off his rimless spectacles and started polishing them with his napkin 'Will he?' he muttered. 'I'm not sure…'

Judge Birkett, who'd been furiously scribbling, lifted his head.

'I agree that we cannot risk losing control of Göring's cross-examination,' he said. 'That would mean an ignominious end to the trial. My suggestion is that the Court make the following statement when we re-start this afternoon: *"This Tribunal gives clear and firm notice that no irrelevancy in the answering of questions will be tolerated."*'

'Not a bad idea,' said the little French judge, pensively twisting his walrus moustache.

'Better than nothing,' Nikitchenko grumbled.

'Forgive me – on the contrary, I think it will do more harm than good,' Judge Parker objected. 'First, I don't think it would be proper to change the rules of the game halfway through the match. Second, this Tribunal's hard-won independence, and therefore the credibility of its findings, would be fatally undermined if we're seen to rescue the prosecution. Third, Jackson would probably be miffed if we publicise the fact that we don't think him equal to the task.'

'Miffed?' Judge Biddle chortled. 'Jackson is a proud man. He'd be mortally offended.'

'I think we'd better follow the advice of our American colleagues on this one,' concluded Sir Geoffrey Lawrence, President of the International Military Tribunal. 'Jackson's a big boy. He'll be all right.'

15:26

Fred Carpenter, Major Neave's batman, bundled Prisoner HW into the front passenger seat of a Humber armoured car and adjusted the blindfold. Then he sat down behind him, handgun on his knees, and locked the doors from the inside. Rifleman Richardson took the wheel. It was already getting dark. Headlights on, he stopped at the gate of Villa Sansouci, then swung left behind the four motorcyclists on the road towards Munich, followed by both escort cars.

16:30

Within ten minutes of Justice Jackson rising to his feet, alarm bells were ringing so loudly in Judge Birkett's head that he could hardly hear the proceedings. Suave, adroit, fast and calculating, Göring soon proved the superior of the American prosecutor. As one of the most gifted barristers of his generation, Birkett knew that the art of cross-examination consisted in destabilising the witness by way of quick thrust-and-parry in order to lead him to the prepared pitfall. Clearly, Jackson, despite his great charm and legal expertise, had never learnt the basics of cross-examination. Overwhelmed by masses of documents from which he read lengthy quotations, he had no chance of catching Göring off guard. On the contrary, the wily German, who understood English perfectly, waited for the protracted questions to be translated; then, eloquently and with restrained use of gesture, he displayed his immense ability and knowledge of all the documents, as well as his razor-sharp mind.

Pity Andrus didn't keep him on the pills, thought Judge Birkett.

As Göring's long-winded answers droned on, Jackson became more agitated. Unfortunately, it was impossible to rule that Göring's replies were wholly irrelevant. He was far too smart for that. Having been informed, like all the other defendants, that he had the right to answer 'yes' or 'no' to a question and then to add any relevant explanation, he took full advantage, turning every response into a discourse and every retort into a counter-attack.

Up to this point, the absent Hitler had dominated the proceedings, a dreadful, oppressive spectre, unseen but constantly invoked. But not today. Today, as the confidence of the Reichsmarschall grew proportionately to his accuser's discomfiture, magnificent and malevolent, the resonant tones of his baritone louder by the minute, he reigned supreme. In the hushed courtroom, the public and the press, vaguely conscious of witnessing a turning point, listened in awe as he accused the Russians of deporting over a million and a half Poles and Ukrainians to labour camps, and explained how the war had effectively resulted from geo-political forces beyond the control of men. Even the French judges unconsciously nodded when, looking them in the eye, he deplored the murderous bombing raid on the Atlantic resort of Royan, a town obliterated by the US 490th Bombardment Group three weeks before the end of the war in order to test their new napalm bombs.

Judge Birkett knew then that the great battle was being lost. Once again, one man's oratory was turning the tide of history and perverting the course of justice. Yet, where oratory was concerned, compared to his master, this man was but a bumbling amateur. Powerful though it was, his performance was no more than a salutary warning.

Thank God, thank God the Court did not have to contend with Adolf Hitler. If the Tribunal finally got its act together – if it promulgated the necessary ban on irrelevancy in the answering of questions – there might be partial recovery.

The position might be improved, and the damage mitigated.

18:10

'Final rehearsal,' Elliott George announced. 'Do you mind putting this on?'

Elizaveta took the gold swastika pendant and put its chain round her neck.

'Is this what you call a press night?' she asked.

'I'm afraid we forgot to invite the press,' he smiled. 'Anyway, that's the bed where Raubal shot herself. Would you mind lying down?'

Elizaveta did as she was told.

'Where exactly did Geli shoot herself?'

'In the chest, unfortunately. Messy. Can you move closer to the edge of the bed? I'd like your right arm to hang down the side.'

He took a couple of steps back and inspected the scene.

'Good – what do you think, Neave?'

Neave finished concealing the microphone wires under a rug and looked up.

'She doesn't look very dead to me,' he said.

'She will,' Doctor George answered.

He rummaged in one of his bags and took out various boxes, jars and pots. In the first one was a whitish powder with which he made up Elizaveta's face. In the second was red ink.

'Lean back and relax while I kill you,' he said.

She complied.

Figuring a right-handed person could only shoot herself in the left breast, he poured the red ink on her. She gasped as the cold liquid swamped her nipple, then slowly spread across her chest. He then carefully placed the Walther 6.35 on the floor just beneath her limp hand.

'Don't move,' he said, striding to the centre of the room. He turned round.

Speechless at the results of his own handiwork, he gaped in awe. The ashen woman whose glassy eyes were staring into nothingness, the thin fabric of her blouse stuck to her skin, revealing an exquisite, blood-red breast, was the sexiest corpse he was ever likely to see.

19:05

After the Court adjourned for the day, Judges Lawrence and Birkett met in the office of the British prosecutors to take stock. All agreed that Jackson's performance had been humiliating, and could have catastrophic consequences.

'Well, tomorrow it will be your turn,' Birkett told Sir Hartley Shawcross. 'Göring is now rampant. Do you think you'll be able to turn the situation around? This will be your last chance.'

'Of course, Shawcross, the Tribunal must be seen to be impartial. But if you need...' Before Justice Lawrence could finish his sentence, a WREN appeared at the door.

'Telephone call for you, Judge Birkett. Downing Street.'

'May I take it here?' Birkett asked.

Sir Hartley nodded.

'Will you excuse us for a minute, gentlemen?' Lawrence asked.

Shawcross collected his cigarettes and lighter from his desk and walked out of the room, followed by his colleague, Sir David Maxwell Fyfe. Birkett picked up the receiver.

'Sir Norman Birkett?' a woman asked. 'Hold on, please.'

Soon the familiar voice was crackling down a poor line. 'Sir Norman.'

'Good evening, Prime Minister.'

'I hear alarming reports of a poor show in court. Stalin's beside himself. Any substance to them?'

'I'm afraid so, Prime Minister. The Charter of the Tribunal allows defendants to amplify their answers to questions in any way they think relevant. Göring took advantage of it to run rings around Jackson.'

'Was there nothing you could do?'

'Not really, sir. Despite his fine legal mind, Jackson simply proved unequal to the task. He's simply no good at cross-examination.'

'What does Lawrence think?'

'I think Sir Geoffrey is as concerned as the rest of us. Would you like to speak to him?'

'Later. I say, Norman – where have you got to with your mystery prisoner?'

'I believe the team is conducting final identification checks prior to the expiry of the deadline tonight, Prime Minister.'

'Are they? Capital. Can you get them to stop immediately?'

'I can try, but I fear it may be too late, sir.'

477

'Have you already got positive identification?'

'I don't know, sir. I was in court all day, and the testing took place in Munich.'

'You can see what I'm driving at, Norman, can't you? Today, Göring took control of the trial. God knows what the consequences will be. Can you imagine the damage Hitler – a much better orator – would wreak in the same position? Do you honestly think you could control a rampant Führer on the witness stand?'

'It depends on the circumstances, Prime Minister,' Birkett answered cautiously. 'A strategy would need to be agreed in advance between all eight judges.'

'I rest my case,' sighed Clement Attlee. 'Please be sure to have the result of your identification test sent to me overnight by signal. I have convened a Cabinet meeting at seven o'clock tomorrow morning to discuss the issue. Good night.'

19:06

There was a knock on the door. Doctor George swiftly removed the pail of freezing water in which Elizaveta's hands had turned suitably blue. Major Neave turned all lights off, except the kitchen's whose door he left ajar, and a bedside lamp in Geli's bedroom. Prisoner HW, manacled and blindfolded, was standing on the landing between Rifleman Richardson and Private Carpenter. Neave silently pointed to the manacles. Richardson extracted the key from his pocket and unlocked them.

Neave then nodded towards the kitchen door, behind which both men disappeared. He grabbed Prisoner HW's arm and led him into Geli's room. Leaving him standing in the middle of the room, facing away from Geli's deathbed, he swiftly concealed himself behind the curtain, making sure the heavy fabric immediately stopped moving.

Legs apart, even more stooped than usual, slightly swaying back and forth, Prisoner HW stood rooted to the spot for a moment, rubbing his wrists and shaking his head.

'*Hallo?*' he called hesitantly.

He waited a while, then took off his blindfold. Despite the poor light, he kept blinking and rubbing his eyes, seemingly not registering his surroundings. Then he slowly turned around. Faced the bed. Froze. Ran towards it.

With an animal groan, he collapsed on his knees and took the cold hand limply hanging by the bedside.

'*Nein! Nein! Nein!*' he panted. '*Ach, Gott!* Geli! Why? How could you do this to me? Wasn't the Führer's love enough? You ungrateful, silly girl! What's wrong with you? I love you, Geli darling. You are my blood. What right did you have to spill it – you sacrilegious murderer? It is sacred blood, you cunt. You've spilt the Führer's consecrated blood. You have betrayed the Führer's sacred person! What for? Answer me! What for, selfish little cunt? Did you forget I can love only you, my own flesh and blood? Too old – is that it? Is that why you betrayed me? I taught you everything. Eva... Eva means *nothing* to me, Geli. How many times must I tell you? Nothing! We only need the little slut to shelter us from the prying eyes of the Jewish press, that's all. Don't you understand? Do you want the Jews to write filthy stories about us, my love? How you used to delight in crouching over me, showing me everything, raining your warm, holy pee on my face? Do you think the fucking Jews could understand our sacred love, any more than the sacred love of Sigmund and Sieglinde?'

As he raised her cold hand to his quivering lips, Elizaveta felt disgusting tears and dribble burn her skin. She wondered how much more Neave wanted, and whether the tape recorder was working. In an effort not to tense up, she tried to concentrate on feeling something in her toes – a trick she'd learnt at the dentist's.

'What will become of Uncle Alf?' Adolf Hitler moaned. 'It was all for you, Geli. All for you. There is no German woman I cannot have – you know that.'

Adolf Hitler, former Chancellor of Germany, got up and tenderly placed the girl's right hand on her blood-soaked breast. However, as he bent down, his terrible breath in her face, any relief Elizaveta felt was short-lived. Feeling his stubby fingers under her skirt, she nearly jumped with revulsion – yet, in a triumph of the will, she managed not to twitch.

'I chose you, little cunt,' he whispered into her ear. 'I created you. I forgave you everything – even your dalliance with my chauffeur. *Um Gottes Willen!* My fucking *chauffeur*, Geli!'

Suddenly he was shouting, his guttural voice invading her head and her soul, fucking up her mind, his mutilated fingers creeping higher and higher, groping her flesh.

'Have you no faith, Geli? No pity? No love? Were you born to betray me, little cunt? Like the others?'

Inexorably sliding along her thigh, his fingers had now passed the frilly lace of Geli's panties. Still, in a supreme effort, silently shouting for help, she managed to remain lifeless.

'Do you think you can get away with it? Stupid cow! You're mine! Mine alone! Forever! From Sieglinde, only Sigmund can beget Siegfried! Open your legs! I'll show you! In death as in life – you're mine!'

In a paroxysm of rage, he suddenly tore off her panties and pressed himself down on her. As though shot through with a thousand volts, she threw him off with a terrifying scream. Arms hugging knees, shaking uncontrollably, she heard Adolf Hitler's head hit the floor with a thud.

Initially dazed, his face distorted by pain, he got to his knees. Saw the pistol on the floor. Picked it up.

At that precise instant, Major Airey Neave DSO MC of the British War Crimes Executive and Captain Elizaveta Terisova of the NKGB were both struck by the same sudden, shocking realisation. They hadn't emptied the gun's magazine.

Neave pushed the curtain aside and started running. Elizaveta heard the safety catch come off. Still several yards away, Neave launched himself into a flying rugby tackle. Fixing Elizaveta with icy blue eyes, Adolf Hitler lifted the gun with a sardonic smile.

Recoiling, she held his gaze. Stunned. Neave landed short. Utterly winded, he skidded along the waxed floor.

Grey-green eyes. Pale, pale blue eyes – bloodshot. Dilated irises. The colour of steel.

All that's left of the world.

'Till death do us part, my love,' Adolf Hitler sniggered.

She closed her eyes and saw a white stork, mute and majestic, gliding straight and true above the mighty Volga without ever flapping its wings.

Hitler put the barrel of the gun in his mouth and pulled the trigger.

23:48

Pulse racing wildly, Peter Birkett woke up with a start and opened his mouth to scream.

'Sshh!' The woman put her forefinger on his mouth. 'It's me.'

It was her. Except it couldn't be. This woman had short dark hair. And she was covered in blood.

Yet – the grey-green eyes, as deep as the infinite steppe – hers. The heavenly natural fragrance – hers!

'You were sobbing in your sleep,' she murmured, caressing his wet temples.

Softly, he touched her cheek and also felt tears.

'Oh God. What have we done to you, Elizaveta? I'm so sorry. Will you ever forgive me?'

'I'm here, my love. I'm here.'

'*Gott sei Dank!*' he pulled her down.

Taking great care not to hurt his shoulder, she gently lay down next to him. In a low whisper, she recounted the events of the day – how terrified she'd been, and how lucky it was that Hitler's gun turned out not to be loaded. Together, they wept – like the orphans they were, for the children they were no more. Neither knew why the other was sobbing, and perhaps it did not matter. There was so much to cry about.

On her dawn round, Nurse Joy found them chastely asleep, fingers intertwined. Shaking her head, tut-tutting under her breath, she looked at them for a while, wondering how the girl had managed to enter the ward unnoticed. Then she smiled, drew the curtain around the bed and tiptoed away.

3

The Morning After

NEAVE BREEZED IN at eight o'clock on the dot and dropped a suitcase on my bed.

'A very good morning to you, old chap,' he said. 'Enjoying the life of Riley, are we?'

I carefully replaced my cup on the breakfast tray. 'Not particularly. Happy to swap places any time. I heard you had all the excitement yesterday.'

'Did you? Well, that explains where Lise was last night, I suppose. Not that we were worried, of course.'

'She did update me. Still sinking in, to be honest. Seems that we truly, incontrovertibly hold bloody Hitler, doesn't it? Exactly as Elizaveta said all along.'

'Where is she?'

'Negotiating a change of clothes with the nurses. Shouldn't be long.'

'Excellent.' Neave pointed to the suitcase. 'Speaking of which, I brought you a fresh uniform. I can wait half an hour, but no more.'

'Am I being discharged?'

'Your father is coming to Villa Sansouci at ten. If you want to attend, you'll have to discharge yourself.'

'Why?'

'We sent a signal to London overnight, informing them of the positive identification of Adolf Hitler. Attlee convened an emergency Cabinet meeting at seven this morning. Judge Lawrence and your father should hear from them before nine.'

'What are they deliberating about? Surely, the next step is to hand him over to the International Military Tribunal?'

'One would have thought so. We'll soon find out.'

Forty-five minutes later, with Elizaveta's help, freshly shaven, left arm in a neat white sling, I looked almost like a soldier. Greedily filling my lungs in the Rothenberger Strasse, where Rifleman Richardson was waiting at the wheel of a black Volkswagen, I was surprised by the sharpness of the air. As the car started, I noticed tiny icicles hanging like frozen saliva from the beak of the stone eagle perched above the doorway.

The gates of Villa Sansouci were shut. Richardson stopped the car and Neave got out to parley with several sentries who immediately appeared from left and right, sub-machine-guns at the ready.

'What's going on?' I asked as the car restarted, pointing to two Humber armoured cars on the lawn.

'Had to increase the security level, while trying not to alert the Yanks,' Neave replied. 'We also have half a dozen snipers on the roof.'

Getting out of the Volkswagen, I detected shadows behind nearly every big tree in the park.

Elliott George was waiting for us in the sitting room, next to a bottle of Krug champagne and some glasses.

'We've done it!' he exclaimed. 'What did I tell you? All in the mind. What a day for psychology! Welcome back, Peter.'

I winced as he shook my hand effusively.

'Where's Hitler?' Neave asked.

'Locked up in his room. Carpenter's on watch.'

Somehow both question and answer seemed surreal.

'Good. I see you've already opened that bottle.'

'Indeed. My first champagne breakfast ever. Care to join me?'

He filled four glasses, waited for the foam to subside and topped them up.

'To psychology!' Elizaveta raised her glass.

'To Team Sansouci!' I replied. 'And to your British passport, Elizaveta.'

'Can you imagine Colonel Andrus getting his paws on Hitler?' Neave smiled. 'That will be a sight to behold.'

'Can you imagine Hitler in the dock?' Doctor George retorted. 'The press will go crazy. So will the public. Andrus will have his work cut out.'

'I wonder how Göring will react,' said Neave. 'He loves strutting around as the big cheese, successor to the Führer. I'm not sure he'll enjoy being demoted again.'

'Fascinating,' said Elliott George. 'I might write a book on it. *Inside the Nazi Mind*" – rather catchy, don't you think?'

'Can't wait,' I smiled.

'I think it will drive you nuts, Elliott,' Elizaveta objected. 'Believe you me: the Nazi mind is fatally warped. If you want to remain sane, keep your distance.'

'Do you still want to be a doctor, Lise?' George retorted.

'You know I do. Like my parents.'

'How could doctors help patients if they refused to expose themselves to the risk of contagion?'

'Your point is well made – as far as bodies are concerned. But I doubt it applies to minds.'

'Why not?'

'Penicillin.'

'What?'

'It a new drug the Americans have been using for the last couple of years. Kills bacteria. So, not only are infections cured, but the patient is no more contagious. Unfortunately, there is no drug to kill obnoxious ideas. They just go on replicating forever.'

'Ah, but my point is that psychology *can* and *will* change that unsatisfactory state of affairs,' pleaded Doctor George.

'Here they come,' I interjected, watching through the window the silent approach of my father's black Austin 16. It came to a halt opposite the front steps, next to the Volkswagen. My father laboriously unfolded his tall body and retrieved his briefcase. Cap in hand, his German driver opened the rear door on the other side of the car, bowed and stood to attention.

The president of the International Military Tribunal,

Judge Lawrence, got out. Rifleman Richardson led both men into the sitting room. Coats were taken away and greetings exchanged. Papa carefully shook my hand.

'How are you, Peter? I wasn't expecting to see you here.'

'I was discharged this morning, Papa. I was getting seriously bored in that hospital bed.'

'May we offer you something, gentlemen?' Major Neave asked.

Lawrence surveyed the empty champagne bottle and glasses. 'A cup of coffee would be marvellous, thank you, Major.'

'Same for me,' said my father. 'White, one sugar.'

The magistrates sat down side by side on massive Biedermeier armchairs made of pink leather on dark carved wooden frames, whose obscene exuberance they instantly tamed through sheer judicial gravitas. Lord Justice Lawrence was wearing his customary wing collar and fidgeting with the bowler hat on his lap.

'No point in beating about the bush,' he opened proceedings. 'You gentlemen – I beg your pardon, lady and gentlemen – believe you have proof of Prisoner HW's identity. Am I right?'

Elizaveta, sitting demurely on a chair at the back of the room in the incomplete uniform of an American nurse, failed to react to his acknowledgement. With the arrival of the judges the conversation had switched from German to English, leaving her mystified.

'Yes, Judge,' said George.

'What evidence do you have?'

Neave pointed to a flat container on a dresser.

'A film reel?'

'No, Sir Geoffrey. A tape recording.'

'Can you play it?'

Neave extracted the tape from the shiny metal cylinder and carefully slotted it into the tape recorder, connecting its loose end to an empty reel. After a couple of false starts, Hitler's guttural rantings suddenly filled the room.

'I love you, Geli darling. You are my blood. What right did you have to spill it – you sacrilegious murderer? It is sacred blood, you cunt. You've spilt the Führer's consecrated blood. You have betrayed the Führer's sacred person! What for? Answer me! What for, selfish little cunt? Did you forget I can love only you, my own flesh and blood? Too old – is that it? Is that why you betrayed me? I taught you everything. Eva... Eva means nothing to me, Geli – how many times must I tell you? Nothing!'

Elizaveta ran out of the room. Indistinct thuds and screams came out of the speakers; then, only a continuous, low-level hiss, which they listened to for a minute, avoiding each other's eyes.

'Whose voice was that?' Judge Lawrence finally asked. 'And what is he saying?'

'It's Adolf Hitler, Judge. Prisoner HW, as we used to call him,' Neave pointed at the ceiling. 'Professing undying love for his niece Angelika Raubal.'

'Can you prove it?'

Neave, George and I exchanged uncomprehending looks.

'We were there,' Neave said. 'Three of us.'

'Including the Russian agent?'

'Yes.'

The bowler hat on Judge Lawrence's lap started rotating.

'That leaves two of you. In the face of the overwhelming forensic evidence and testimonies showing that Hitler died in the Berlin Bunker last April, your tape may not carry much weight.'

'I beg to differ, Sir Geoffrey,' I interjected. 'Surely...'

'No point in speculating,' my father interrupted. 'The PM has reached a decision.'

We all waited in silence while Rifleman Richardson delivered a tray with coffee and US ration biscuits. Papa added a lump of sugar, drank a mouthful, wiped his mouth with an immaculate white handkerchief and cleared his throat.

'The Cabinet met this morning and decided that Prisoner HW is to be released immediately.'

Neave, George and I looked at one another in disbelief.

'*What?*' I jumped to my feet. 'They want to release *Adolf Hitler* – the greatest criminal of all time? What on earth is your Tribunal for, Papa?'

'Ah, well – I'm afraid it's part of the problem. London is outraged that Göring succeeded in using the trial to indulge in Nazi propaganda. In the knowledge that Hitler is a much better orator than Göring, they decided not to give him the same opportunity.'

My father cast a sideways glance at his colleague who

continued: 'Indeed, there are many other insurmountable issues. Take sanity. We already came a cropper once, trying to indict old Gustav Krupp, who's virtually gaga. As Major Neave knows, the British War Crimes Executive had to make a humiliating U-turn. And amnesic Hess is a constant embarrassment to the court.'

'To conclude, London sees the position as hopeless,' my father added. 'If Hitler is senile, we cannot put him on trial. If he's *compos mentis*, he'll use the trial to defend Nazi achievements and embarrass the Russians.'

'God forbid we embarrass Uncle Joe,' muttered Neave. 'Such a sensitive man.'

'Hitler isn't *legally* insane,' Doctor George protested. 'I can prove it: I'm a psychologist. Surely, the Tribunal can learn from its mistakes and ensure Hitler is kept on a tighter leash than Göring was?'

On Judge Lawrence's knees, the bowler hat was rotating faster than ever. We all sat wordless, watching it with glum fascination.

'There you have it,' my father sighed. 'Nothing would give Sir Geoffrey and myself more pleasure than to sit in judgment on Adolf Hitler. But it's not going to happen. In fact, this whole incident never happened. No mention of it will be permitted. All of you will have to come to the Tribunal tomorrow and sign up to the Official Secrets Act 1939. You will remain bound by it until your last breath.'

'What if it leaks?' I asked, feeling my face burning red.

'I think we may rely on the Secret Service to take any

necessary steps to ensure it doesn't,' my father answered sombrely.

'Is this a warning, Papa?'

'It's my best assessment of the position.' He threw his hands up in a placating gesture.

'So what happens next?' asked Neave.

'Have you still got the prisoner's original papers in the name of Gustav Weber?'

'Of course.'

'Are they in order?'

'Perfectly.'

'Good. Give them back to him and put him on the seven o'clock train to Hanover tonight.'

'Just like that?'

'Just like that.'

'Any escort required?'

'No. It's all being taken care of. Any other question?'

I looked at George and Neave who were both shaking their heads, as much in frustration as to indicate an absence of questions.

'All clear, Judge.'

'We'll see you tomorrow, gentlemen.' Lord Justice Lawrence rose and placed his bowler hat on his head.

While we all waited in silence for coats and scarves to be retrieved, my father took me aside and put his hand on my good arm.

'Don't take this whole debacle personally, Peter,' he whispered. 'We're only small cogs in the machinery of a deranged world. Better to accept it.'

Struggling for words, I noticed, in the hallway's wall mirror, a novel cobweb of blue swollen veins pulsating on my temples.

'By the way,' he continued, 'it's not all bad news. Captain Terisova's new British passport will be available as soon as she signs the Official Secrets Act. I trust that will make a couple of small cogs happy.'

I found my voice at last.

'Thank you, Papa!' I cried, already halfway to the adjoining room.

'THE LORD: Is nothing right
on your terrestrial scene?
'MEPHISTOPHELES: No, sir! The earth
is as bad as it has always been.
I really feel quite sorry for mankind.'
Goethe, "Prologue in Heaven, Faust Part One",
translated by David Luke,
Oxford University Press 1987

Acknowledgements

THE CONCEIT FOR this novel – or a similar one, in which Hitler was actually to be tried in Nuremberg – first emerged in a conversation with my agent, Charlie Viney, more than ten years ago.

I'm also grateful to Julie Ann Godson, not only for helping with the historical research, copy-editing, book design and layout, but also for putting me in touch with Michael Howard, the real-life T Force Intelligence Officer who inspired the fictional character of Peter Birkett. It had been Michael's life-long ambition to see his story properly told; I immediately saw how it might provide the perfect vehicle for my Hitler-in-Nuremberg novel.

Although Michael, eighty years old when we first met, was most generous in sharing with me his memories and records, health and other issues on my side slowed down progress to such an extent that I worried I wouldn't be able to complete the novel in my lifetime, let alone his. I was therefore delighted to be able to help him publish his memoir in a non-fiction form: *Otherwise Occupied: Let-*

ters Home from the Ruins of Nazi Germany was published by Old Street Publishing in 2010.

I am also indebted to my sons Olivier and Philippe Bonavero, my daughter-in law Natasha O'Hear and my friend William Parente for their helpful comments on early drafts of the book.

The locations and events in this novel are the usual mixture of the real and the imaginary, but the characters and their actions are entirely fictitious, with the possible exception of some historical figures.

A Note on the Author

Yves Bonavero was born and educated in Paris, and holds a first-class degree in Philosophy and German from the University of Oxford. He worked in the City of London for fourteen years until, at the age of thirty-seven, he founded Bonaparte Films and the A B Charitable Trust, whose mission is to defend and promote human dignity. In 2015, the trust endowed the Bonavero Institute of Human Rights at the University of Oxford.

Yves's first novel, a psychological thriller in a nautical setting entitled *Something in the Sea*, was published by Bloomsbury in 2006. He lives in London.

16794528R00291

Printed in Great Britain
by Amazon